BEGINNER'S PLUCK

"What do you think you're doing with that stupid pike?"

"I'm guarding the palace!"

Inos snorted before she remembered that snorting was not regal. "From what? Dragons? Sorcerers? Imperial legions?"

Rap was growing angry, she was pleased to see. "I challenge strangers."

Tommyrot! She suppressed another snort— and there, as if sent by the Gods, a stranger came strolling across the yard toward the gate.

"Right!" Inos said. "Challenge this one."

Rap clenched his jaw. "Stand back, then!" He swung his pike to level, advanced a step, and demanded loudly, "Who goes there— fiend or froe?

The stranger stopped, raised his eyebrows. "You're new at this, aren't you?"

MAGIC CASEMENT

Part One of
A MAN OF HIS WORD

Dave Duncan

A Del Rey Book
BALLANTINE BOOKS • NEW YORK

The author gratefully acknowledges receiving a grant from the Alberta Foundation for the Literary Arts to support the writing of this novel.

A Del Rey Book
Published by Ballantine Books

Grateful acknowledgment is made to The Society of Authors as the literary representative of the Estate of John Masefield for permission to reprint two lines from ''Sea-Fever'' from SALT WATER POEMS by John Masefield.

Library of Congress Catalog Card Number: 90-91850

ISBN 0-345-36628-X

Manufactured in the United States of America

First Edition: December 1990

Cover Art by Don Maitz

Again for Janet,
sine qua non

The voice I hear this passing night was heard
In ancient days, by emperor and clown:
Perhaps the self-same song that found a path
Through the sad heart of Ruth, when sick for home,
She stood in tears amid the alien corn;
   The same that oft-times hath
Charmed magic casements, opening on the foam
Of perilous seas, in faery lands forlorn.

KEATS, Ode to a Nightingale

❊ CONTENTS ❊

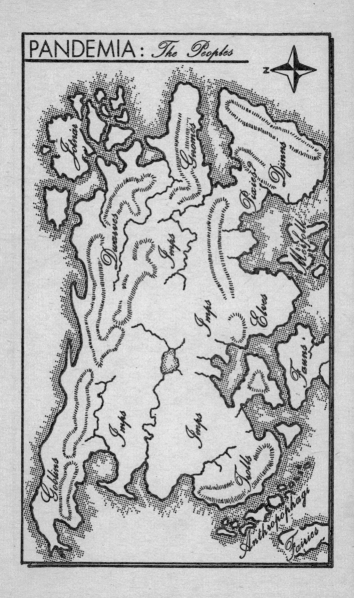

PANDEMIA: *The Peoples*

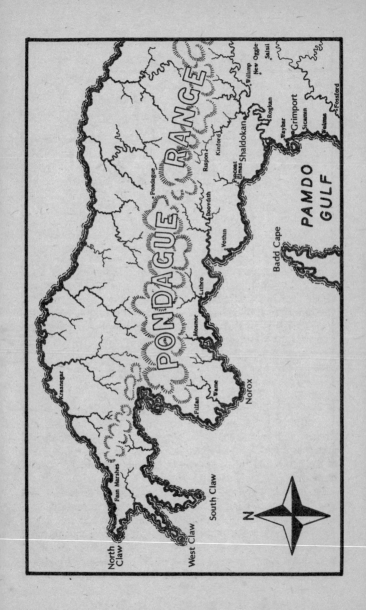

⟪ ONE ⟫

Youth departs

1

Since long before the coming of Gods and mortals, the great rock of Krasnegar had stood amid the storms and ice of the Winter Ocean, resolute and eternal. Throughout long arctic nights it glimmered under the haunted dance of aurora and the rays of the cold, sad moon, while the icepack ground in useless anger around its base. In summer sun its yellow angularity stood on the shining white and blue of the sea like a slice of giants' cheese on fine china. Weather and season came and went and the rock endured unchanging, heeding them no more than it heeded the flitting generations of mankind.

Two sides fell sheer to the surf, pitted with narrow ledges where only the crying seabirds went, but the third face ran down less steeply, and on that long mad slope the little town adhered as grimly as a splatter of swallows' nests. Above the humble clutter of the houses, at the very crest of the rock, the castle pointed black and spikey turrets to the sky.

No mere human hand could have raised those stones in a land so remote or a setting so wild. The castle had been built long centuries before by the great sorcerer Inisso, to serve as palace for himself and for the dynasty he founded. His descendants ruled there still, in direct male line unbroken . . . but the present monarch, good King Holindarn, beloved of his people, had but a single child—his daughter, Inosolan.

* * *

Summer came late to Krasnegar. When inhabitants of milder lands were counting their lambs and chicks, the brutal storms still rolled in from the Winter Ocean. While those lucky southerners gathered hay and berries, the wynds and alleyways of the north lay plugged with drifts. Even when night had been almost banished from the pallid arctic sky, the hills ashore stayed brown and sere. Every year was the same. Every year a stranger might have given up hoping and assumed that summer was not about to happen at all. The locals knew better and in patient resignation they waited for the change.

Always their faith was rewarded at last. With no warning, a cheerful wind would blunder in to sweep the ice floes from the harbor, the hills would throw off their winter plumage almost overnight, and the snowdrifts in the alleyways would shrink rapidly to sullen gray heaps sulking in shadowed corners. A few days' rain and the world was washed green again, fair weather following foul as fast as a blink. Spring in Krasnegar, the inhabitants said, had to be believed in to be seen.

Now it had happened. Sunlight poured through the castle windows. The fishing boats were in the water. The tide was out, the beaches were clear of ice and obviously eager to be ridden on. Inos came early down to breakfast, busily spinning plans for the day.

The great hall was almost deserted. Even before the fine weather had arrived, the king's servants had driven the livestock over the causeway to the mainland. Others would now be outside attending to the wagons and the harbor, cleaning up the winter's leavings, and preparing for the hectic work of summer. Inos's tutor, Master Poraganu, was conveniently indisposed with his customary springtime rheumatics; there would be no objections from him, and she could head for the stables as soon as she had grabbed a quick bite.

Aunt Kade sat at the high table in solitary splendor.

Momentarily Inos debated the wisdom of making a fast retreat and finding something to eat in the kitchens, but she had already been noticed. She continued her approach, therefore, practicing poise and trusting that a regal grace would compensate for shabby attire.

"Good morning, Aunt," she said cheerfully. "Beautiful morning?"

"Good morning, my dear."

"You're earlier than—ooof!" Inos had not intended to make that last remark, but her breeches tried to bite her in half as she sat down. She smiled uneasily, and her sleeves slid quietly up her wrists.

Aunt Kade pursed her lips. Aunts could be expected to disapprove of princesses arriving at meals in dirty old riding habits. "You appear to have outgrown those clothes, my dear."

Kade herself, of course, was dressed as if for a wedding or a state function. Not one silver hair was out of place, and even for breakfast she had sprinkled jewelry around her neck and over her fingers. In honor of the arrival of summer, she had donned her pale-blue linen with the tiny pleats.

Inos restrained an unkind impulse to remark that Kade appeared to have outgrown the pale-blue linen. Kade was short, Kade was plump, and Kade was growing plumper. The wardrobe she had brought back with her two years ago was barely adequate now, and the local seamstresses were all at least two generations out of date in fashioning attire for ladies of quality.

"Oh, they'll do," Inos said airily. "I'm only going along the beach, not leading a parade."

Aunt Kade dabbed at her lips with a snowy napkin. "That will be nice, my dear. Who is going with you?"

"Kel, I hope. Or Ido . . . or Fan . . ." Rap, of course, had long since departed for the mainland. So had many, many others.

"Kel will be helping me." Kade frowned. "Ido? Not the chambermaid?"

Inos's heart sank. It would not help to mention that Ido was an excellent rider and that the two of them had been out six or eight times already recently in much worse weather than this. "There'll be somebody." She smiled thanks at old Nok as he brought her a dish of porridge.

"Yes, but who?" Kade's china-blue eyes assumed the tortured look they always did in these confrontations with her willful niece. "Everyone is very busy just now. I shall need to know who is going with you, my dear."

"I'm a very competent horsewoman, Aunt."

"I'm sure you are, but you must certainly not go out riding without suitable attendants. That would not be ladylike. Or safe. So you will find out who is available and let me know before you leave?"

Restraining her temper, Inos made noncommittal noises to the porridge.

Kade smiled with relief . . . and apparently with complete innocence. "You promise, Inos?"

Trapped! "Of course, Aunt."

Such babying was humiliating! Inos was older than Sila, the cook's daughter, who was already married and almost a mother.

"I am having a small salon this morning. Nothing formal, just some ladies from the town . . . tea and cakes. You would be very welcome to join us."

On a day like this? Tea and cakes and burgesses' fat wives? Inos would rather muck out stables.

Disaster! There was no one. Even the youngest and most inadequate stableboy seemed to have been assigned duties of world-shattering importance that could not be postponed. A frenzy of activity possessed everyone still remaining in the castle, and there were few of those anyway. The boys had gone to the hills or the boats. The girls were busy in the fields or the fish sheds. There was no one.

No one of her rank! That was the real problem. All of Inos's friends were the children of her father's servants, for Krasnegar possessed no nobility below its king, and no minor gentry either, unless one counted the merchants and burgesses. Her father counted them; Aunt Kade did so unwillingly. But servants and gentry alike, the boys were vanishing into trades, the girls into matrimony. There was no one around with leisure to escort a princess, and the prospect of that spirited gallop along the sands began to fade like a mirage.

The stables were almost deserted, by man and beast both. As she went in, Inos passed Ido bearing a bundle of washing on her head.

"Looking for Rap?" Ido inquired.

No, Inos was not looking for Rap. Rap had long since gone landward with the others and would not be back before winter. And why should everyone always assume that it had to be Rap she wanted?

She spent a wistful while agrooming Lightning, although he did not need it. What he needed was more exercise. She had inherited Lightning from her mother, and if her mother had still been alive, then they . . . well, no point in thinking about that.

As Inos left the stable, she passed old Hononin, the hostler, a gnarled and weatherbeaten monument whose face seemed to have been upholstered in the same leather used to make his clothes.

"Morning, miss. Looking for Rap?"

Inos snorted a denial and pranced by him, although snorting was not regal. And probably that way of departing was what the writers of romances called a "flounce," and that would not be regal either. She would not be able to go riding, and Aunt Kade would know she was still around the palace. Would she hunt down her niece to impose the tea-and-cake torture on her? With some relief, Inos decided that Aunt Kade probably wanted her at the affair no more than she wanted to attend. Unfortunately, Kade might decide that duty required her to promote Inos's education in the social graces.

At that point in her misery, Inos found herself out in the bailey, and there was a wagon heading for the gate.

She had promised Kade that she would not go riding alone. No one had said she could not go down to the harbor unaccompanied . . . or at least into the town itself . . . not *recently*, anyway.

The guard was the problem. The token sentry would not likely say anything, but nosy old Sergeant Thosolin liked to sit in the guard room and watch who came and went all day. He might consider that he had authority to question Princess Inosolan. Even if he didn't, he probably would.

She hurried across the cobbles to the wagon, then strolled casually beside it as it clattered and jingled through the archway. There was just room for a slim princess to walk between the high rear wheel and the greasy black stones. The noise reverberated astonishingly in that narrow space. She was shielded from the guard room; she marched past the sentry without a glance; a moment later she was in the outer court, feeling like an escaped ferret.

If a king could safely walk unaccompanied around the town, then his daughter could, yes?

Inos did not ask the question aloud, so no one answered it.

She was in no danger. Her father was a popular monarch and Krasnegar a very law-abiding place. She had heard tell of large cities where what she was doing might be foolish, but she was certain that she would come to no harm in Krasnegar. Aunt Kade might object that being unaccompanied was unladylike, but Inos could see no reason why her father's independent kingdom need be bound by the customs of the Empire.

A single wagon road zigzagged down the hill, but Inos preferred the narrow stairways and alleys. Some of those were open, some roofed over. Some were bright and sunny, some dark, others partly lighted by windows and skylights. They were all steep and winding, and this fine day they bustled. Inos was recognized often. She received smiles and salutes, frowns and surprised glances, all of which she acknowledged with a confident and regal little nod, as her father did. She was growing up—they must expect to see her around often in future. And yet, hurrying down the steep little town, Inos saw no one of any interest, only thick-shouldered porters and wide-hipped matrons, tottering crones and sticky-mouthed toddlers. None but the dull remained in Krasnegar in summer.

From time to time she caught glimpses of slate roofs below her and the harbor below those. Two ships had arrived already, the first of the season, and there she was headed. The early arrivals always made Krasnegar nervous, for in some years they brought sickness that would slash through the town like a scythe—it was less than two years since one such epidemic had carried off the queen. But the harbor was where the excitement would be, where the fishermen and whalers of Krasnegar itself mingled with visitors come to trade, stocky, urbane ships' captains from the Impire and the foreboding flaxen-hair jotnar of Nordland—tall men with ice-blue eyes that could send shivers down Inos's arms. She might even see a few sinister goblins from the forest, each leading a party of his wives, loaded with bundles of furs.

Then Inos stumbled to a halt halfway down an open staircase. It was wide and sunny. It was deserted except for two women standing in conversation, but one of them was Mother Unonini, the palace chaplain. From the way the two were poised to move, they were just about to complete their chat. If Mother Unonini looked up and saw Inos unescorted, she would certainly have questions to ask.

A door opened beside Inos, emitting a woman with a package under her arm. Inos smiled at her, took hold of the door, and went in, closing it firmly in a tinkle of silver bell.

The small room was lined by shelves bearing rolls of fabrics. The large lady in the middle was Mistress Meolorne. She looked up, hesitated, and then curtsied.

Rather flattered by that, Inos bobbed in return. She had come shopping, she decided—a most ladylike occupation to which no one, even Aunt Kade, could possibly object.

"Your Highness is the only lady in Krasnegar who could wear this."

"I am? I mean, why do you say so?"

Mistress Meolorne beamed and bunched rosy cheeks. "Because of the green, your Highness. It exactly matches your eyes. Your eyes are exceptional, remarkable! They are the key to your beauty, you know. I believe you have the only truly green eyes in the kingdom.''

Beauty? Inos peered at the mirror. She was draped in a flowing miracle of green and gold silk. Of course she had green eyes, but now that she thought about it, who else did?

"Imps like myself have dark brown eyes," Meolorne said. "And the jotnar have blue. Everyone but you has either brown eyes or blue."

Rap had gray eyes, but Meolorne could not be expected to know a minor palace flunky. Everyone else was either jotunn or imp, one or the other. Imps were short and dark. Jotnar were tall and fair. In summer, jotnar turned red and peeled disgustingly. Imps tended to sicken in winter.

"I'm neither, am I? Mistress, I don't think I've ever thought of that!'' Inos's father had brown hair and . . . brown eyes. Paler brown than most, she decided.

"You are a diplomatic compromise, your Highness, if I may say so? Your royal father rules both imps and jotnar here in Krasnegar. It would be inappropriate for him to favor either one or the other."

Inos was about to ask if that made her a halfbreed, then thought better of it. Of course the kings of Krasnegar could not be a pure strain. For generations they had played off their predatory neighbors by taking wives from first this side and then that. Normally when imp and jotunn married, the traits did not mingle, and the children took after one parent or the other, but so many royal outcrosses had eventually produced a true mixture in Inos. She must remember to ask her father about it. How curious that she had never noticed before! She was neither tall nor short. Her hair was a rich deep gold, not the flaxen of a jotunn. She did not peel in summer—indeed she took on a splendid tan. And she certainly did not pine in the long nights, as the imps did. She was a true Krasnegarian, and the only one.

"The bronze for your complexion, the gold for your hair, and the green for your eyes," Mistress Meolorne murmured. "It was designed by the Gods especially for you."

Inos looked again at the miraculous fabric that enveloped her. She had never owned anything like this before. She had not known that such material existed. What a gown it would make! Gold dragons on green fields and fall foliage . . . Whenever she moved the dragons shimmered, as if about to fly. Aunt Kade would be ecstatic over it and delighted that Inos was taking an interest in clothes at last. And her father would certainly not object, for she must expect to start playing her part in formal functions soon, as she neared her coming of age. She would ask Kade to advise her on the design.

"It's the most beautiful thing I have ever seen," Inos said firmly. "I absolutely must have it. How much is it?"

2

No one had ever suggested that Mistress Meolorne might be a sorceress, but the thought occurred to Inos as she panted up the last alleyway that led to the castle. Three and a half gold imperials? How had she ever been bewitched into agreeing to pay so much for a mere swatch of silk?

Aunt Kade would have hysterics.

Aunt Kade must not be allowed to find out.

The best strategy was certainly for Inos to go to her father at once and explain that she had saved him the trouble of choosing a birthday gift for her. True, her birthday was still some time off. Also true, he had never given her anything worth three and a half gold imperials—not close, even—but she was growing up and she needed such little luxuries now. Surely he would understand when he saw the silk itself and she explained why she had chosen it and why it was so suitable. He would be pleased that she was beginning to take more of an interest in ladylike matters . . . Wouldn't he?

She had some jewelry of her own that she might be able to sell—if she was able to sneak back into the town again. She might raise a half imperial that way. A straight "three" would sound a much neater, rounder sort of number.

Father would understand, of course, that the only alternative was his dear daughter's tragic suicide from the highest battlements. Possibly she could live without the silk—she had managed so far—but she could certainly not endure the shame of having to return it. So he would congratulate her on her good taste and see that the money was sent as she had promised.

Wouldn't he?

She reached the top of the lane and paused to catch her breath, and also to reconnoiter the courtyard. There was only one gate to the castle and it opened into this cobbled outer court. Now there was no wagon in sight to provide cover, only a few ambling pedestrians. The summer sun was high enough to smile in over the ancient stone walls and brighten the pigeons that strutted around, cleaning up the horse droppings. Relics of winter snow bled quietly to death in corners. A man-at-arms was standing as rigid as his pike beside the gate, with two mangy dogs snuffling aimlessly beside him. Within the big arch of the entrance, nosy old Thosolin would be lurking in his guard room.

It was none of Thosolin's business, she decided firmly. Whether or not he had the right to stop her going out, he certainly could not stop her coming in. She did not recognize the petrified man-at-arms, but he looked as if he were taking his job unusually seriously and so would not interfere. She squared her shoulders, adjusted the silk below her arm, and began to march.

She had every right to go into the town by herself, and if she chose to do so in shabby old jodhpurs and a leather doublet that might have been thrown out by one of Inisso's stablehands, well, that was certainly not Thosolin's business either.

She wondered who the guard on the gate was, he must be somebody new. It was not until she had almost reached the arch that—

"Rap!"

He rolled his eyes in alarm and almost dropped his pike. Then he came even more stiffly to attention, staring straight ahead, not looking at her. Inosolan bristled angrily.

His cone-shaped helmet was too small, sitting like an oversize egg in the nest of his unruly brown hair. His chain mail was rusty and much too large. His very plain face was turning from brown to pink, showing up his freckles.

"What on earth are you doing?" she demanded. "I thought you were off on the mainland."

"I'm just back for a couple of days," he muttered. His eyes rolled warningly toward the guard room door.

"Well, why didn't you tell me?" She put her hands on her hips and inspected him crossly. "You look absurd! Why are you dressed up like that? And what are you doing here? Why aren't you at the stables?"

Pudding, the gang had called Rap when they were all small together. He'd had almost no nose then, and not much more now. His face was all chin and mouth and big gray eyes.

"Please, Inos," he whispered. "I'm on guard duty. I'm not supposed to talk to you."

She tossed her head. "Indeed? I shall speak to Sergeant Thosolin about that."

Rap never suspected a bluff. "No!" He shot another horrified glance toward the guard room.

He had grown, even in the short time he had been gone, unless it was those stupid boots. He was taller than her now by quite a bit, and the armor made him seem broader and deeper. Perhaps he did not look quite so bad as she had thought at first, but she would not tell him so.

"Explain!" She glared at him.

"A couple of the mares had to come back." He was trying not to move his lips, staring straight through Inos. "So I brought them. I'm going back with the wagons. Old Hononin had nothing for me to do, with the other ponies away."

"Ha!" she said triumphantly. "Well, you still aren't doing anything very much. You will take me riding after lunch. I'll speak to the sergeant."

A mixture of fury and stubbornness came over his face, wrinkling his wide nose until she half expected the freckles to start popping off like brown snowflakes. "Don't you dare!"

"Don't you speak to me like that!"

"I won't ever speak to you again!"

They glared at each other for a moment. Rap as a man-at-arms? She remembered now that he had expressed some silly ambition to play with swords. It was an idiotic idea. He was tremendously good with horses. He had a natural gift for them.

"What good do you think you're doing standing here with that stupid pike?"

"I'm guarding the palace!"

Inos snorted before she remembered again that snorting was not regal. "From what? Dragons? Sorcerers? Imperial legions?"

He was growing very angry now, she was pleased to see, but he made a great effort to answer civilly. "I challenge strangers."

Tommyrot! She suppressed another snort; and there, as if sent by the Gods, a stranger came strolling across the yard toward the gate.

"Right!" Inos said. "Challenge this one."

Rap bit his lip. "He doesn't look very dangerous."

"Challenge! I want to see how it's done."

He clenched his big jaw angrily. "Stand back, then!" As the stranger drew near, Rap swung his pike to the level, took one pace with his left foot, and demanded loudly, "Who goes there—fiend or froe?"

The young man stopped, raised his eyebrows, and considered the question. "You're new at this, aren't you?" he asked in a pleasant tenor.

Rap turned very red and said nothing, waiting for an answer.

Inos suppressed a snigger, letting just enough escape that Rap would know it was there.

"Well, I'm not a fiend." The stranger was quite young, slim, and not very tall, but a blond jotunn nonetheless. Anyone less like a fiend Inos could not imagine. He wore a brown wool cloak with the hood back, a leather doublet, and rather baggy brown hose. She decided that his clothes were all too big for him, which made him seem shabbier than he truly was. He was fresh-faced and scrubbed and clean—a point of note in Krasnegar—and the sun blazed on his white-gold hair.

"Definitely I'm not a fiend," he repeated. "I'm a wandering minstrel, so I suppose I'm either a to or a froe. Yes, I must be a froe."

"What's your name, minstrel?" Rap demanded hoarsely.

"My name is Jalon." But the stranger's attention had wandered to Inos. He bowed. "And I know who this is. Your humble servant, Highness."

He had big blue eyes, with a dreamy air that she found quite appealing. On impulse, she held out her hand. He took it in his long minstrel's fingers and kissed it.

"I saw you when you were very small, Highness." He had a charming smile. "I knew then that one day you would amaze the world with your beauty. But I see that I underestimated it."

He was a very nice young man.

"If you're a minstrel, why haven't you got a harp?" Rap was still holding his pike at the challenge position.

"How long did you see me?" Inos asked. He could not be so very many years older than she was. She could not recall any minstrel so young. Perhaps he had been an apprentice accompanying his master.

He smiled vaguely at her and turned to Rap. "Harps are heavy." He pulled a pipe from a pocket in his cloak and played a trill.

"Do you sing, too?" Rap was still suspicious.

"Not at the same time," Jalon said solemnly.

This time the snigger escaped completely, and Rap shot Inos a murderous glare from the corner of his eye.

Jalon did not seem very worried by the pike. "But I do play the harp and there used to be a good one on the mantel in the hall, so I can borrow that again, I'm sure." He did not seem as if he would be very worried by anything at all—and there certainly was a harp on the mantel.

"Wait here!" Rap put his pike over his shoulder rather clumsily and swung around, stamping his boots and apparently headed for the guard room.

That would not do at all! Inos did not want Sergeant Thosolin, and perhaps others, coming out and seeing her wandering unaccompanied, carrying home her own purchases. "Rap? Should you go off and leave me helpless with this dangerous stranger?"

Rap stopped and spun around, almost grinding his teeth.

"And the castle!" she exclaimed. "What if a troll comes, or a griffon? And you're not here to guard us!"

"You come with me, then!" He was quite furious now.

"No!" Inos said. "I think you should take Master Jalon to the guard room with you if you think he is dangerous. You are welcome in my father's house, minstrel." That sounded very gracious and regal.

The stranger smiled and bowed to her again. He strolled toward the guard room with Rap. Inos lingered for a moment, then slipped through the archway, unobserved and very satisfied.

Like the town itself, the castle was all up and down, and she was soon puffing again as she hurried up the endless steps toward her chamber. Halfway there she met old Kondoral, the seneschal, picking his way carefully down an especially dark staircase. He was small and stooped and white-haired, with gray, withered skin and eyes so rheumy that she did not like to look at them . . . but quite a pleasant old relic when he did not talk your ears numb. His memory for recent events was failing. He repeated the same stories endlessly, yet he could remember the remote past quite well.

"Good day to you, Master Kondoral," she said, stopping.

He peered down at her for a moment, clutching the rail. "And to you, Highness." He sounded surprised, as if he had expected someone much younger.

"Do you know a minstrel called Jalon?" Inos was still bothered by her inability to recall that polite young man. Minstrels came but rarely to remote Krasnegar.

"Jalon?" Kondoral frowned and pulled his lip. "Why, yes, my lady! A very fine troubadour." The old man beamed. "Is he come here again?"

"He is," she said crossly. "I don't remember him."

"Oh, no, you wouldn't." The old man shook his head. "Dear me, no. It has been many years! But that is good news. We shall hear some fine singing from Master Jalon if his voice has not lost its thrill. I remember how he brought tears to all our eyes when he sang 'The Maiden and the Dragon'—''

"He doesn't look very old," she said quickly. "Not much older than me." Well, not very much.

Kondoral shook his head again, looking doubtful. "I can recall hearing tell of him when I was young myself, my lady. This must be a son, then, or grandson?"

"Perhaps!" she said, and dodged quickly by, before he could start reminiscing.

Several staircases later she reached her summer chamber, at the top of one of the shorter spires. She had taken it over the previous year and loved it, although it was much too cold to use in winter. It was circular and bright, with walls so low so that the high conical ceiling swooped almost to the floor. There were four pointed dormer windows and from here she could look down on all of Krasnegar. She laid her precious packet of silk on the bed and started pulling off her riding clothes and dropping them on the rug.

To the north lay the Winter Ocean, sparkling blue now and smiling under the caress of summer. The swell broke lazily over the reefs, showing hardly any white at all, and seabirds swooped. To the west stood the castle's towers and yards, roofs and terraces, a thicket of black masonry. Southward she could see the town, falling away steeply to the harbor. Beyond that lay the beach and then the hills, rounded and grassy. Those hills were certainly part of her father's demesne. He also claimed the moors that lay beyond the horizon, although she had seen those only rarely, when she had gone hunting with her parents.

Stripped to her linen, Inos grabbed up the silk and attempted to drape it over herself as Mistress Meolorne had done for her. She did not succeed very well, but the effect was still spectacular.

Never had she seen such a fabric. She had not known that threads could be so fine, so soft, so cunningly woven; nor that it was possible to make such pictures with a loom. Gold and green and bronze—the colors shone even brighter in her room than they had in the dingy little store.

And there was so much of it! She tried arranging a train and almost fell over, making the golden dragons writhe. Originally it must have come from distant Guwush, on the shores of the Spring Sea, Meolorne had said—a great rarity in these parts. She had bought it many years ago from a jotunn sailor, who had probably looted it in a trifling act of piracy. Or perhaps it had come over the great trade routes and been pillaged from some unfortunate city. But it was old and very splendid and obviously destined to display the royal beauty of the Princess Inosolan of Krasnegar.

Three and a half imperials!

Inos sighed to the mirror. Her father must be made to understand. Suicide was the only possible alternative.

But why had she promised that the money would be sent that very day? She should have left herself more time for strategy.

Yet a gown fashioned from this glory would be worn only on special occasions, so it would last for years. She had stopped growing taller, so she would not grow out of it. She still had to grow more in other directions—she certainly hoped she had more to grow in other directions—but that could be handled with a little discreet padding that could be removed when it was no longer required. She wondered how much padding Aunt Kade would allow.

Well, there was nothing to be gained by standing in front of the mirror. She must talk to her father. She began to fold the silk again, while pondering what to wear for the interview. Probably her dowdy brown worsted, too small now and patched. That would do very well.

3

It took Inos some time to locate her father, but she was eventually informed that he was in the royal bedchamber, which was astonishing news at that time of day. It also meant more stairs, but anywhere meant more stairs in Krasnegar.

The royal chamber was located at the top of the great tower, known as Inisso's Tower, and she wound her way up the spiral stairs that ran within the walls. There were far too many levels—throne room, presence chamber, robing room, antechamber . . . Pausing to catch her breath in the withdrawing room, Inos wondered, and not for the first time, why in the names of all the Gods her father did not move his quarters to somewhere more convenient.

The withdrawing room was her favorite, though. When Aunt Kade had returned from Kinvale two years ago, she had brought a whole roomful of furniture—not the heavy, antique, stuffing-falling-out furniture that cluttered most of the palace, but supremely elegant gilt and rosewood, with incredibly slender legs, with roses and butterflies embroidered on the cushions, and the woodwork all glossy. There was no room more gracious in all of Krasnegar. Even the rugs were works of art. While Inos would never be so disloyal to her mother's memory as to admit the fact, she loved the withdrawing room as Aunt Kade had remade it.

Sufficiently recovered to move, she crossed the withdrawing room, went up more stairs, across what they now called the dressing room, but which had been her bedroom until quite recently, and finally—more slowly than when she had started—up the final stair to her father's door.

It was ajar, so she walked in.

With very mixed feelings, she glanced over the clumsy, massive furnishings. She came here rarely now, and for the first time she saw how shabby they all were, the trappings of an aging widower who clung to old familiar things without regard to their state of wear. The crimsons had faded, the golds tarnished, colors and fabrics become dull and sad. The drapes were shabby, the rugs a disgrace. Her mother's portrait still hung over the fireplace, but it was blurred by smoke stain.

Many, many icy mornings Inos had cuddled into that great bed between her parents, under the heaped furs of winter, and yet those memories were overlain now by a last transparent image of her mother, burning away in fever when the great sickness had come on the first ship of spring and stalked all that terrible summer through the town.

Never mind that . . .

No one was there!

Furiously she pouted, glaring around as if the furniture itself were at fault. The drapes on the four-poster were pulled back, so her father was not in bed, and she could not imagine him going to bed in the middle of the day anyway. She eyed the wardrobe, but the chances that King Holindarn of Krasnegar would hide inside a wardrobe did not seem worth crossing a room to investigate. The windows were deeply recessed, but on those, also, the drapes were open. There was nowhere . . .

Uneasily Inos turned to retrace her steps and then hesitated. A vagueness niggled at the back of her mind. She took another quick glance around, shrugged, and moved toward the stair again . . .

And stopped again. Her scalp prickled. There was something wrong, and she could not place it.

Well! Setting her teeth firmly, she faced the room. Forcing oddly reluctant feet to move, she began to walk very slowly all around the chamber, looking suspiciously at everything, in everything, and even under everything. This was her father's bedroom and she was a princess and there could not possibly be anything dangerous to explain this curious apprehension she—

The high dresser at the far side had been pulled forward, away from the wall.

No, that could not be important . . .

WHY?

Why had the dresser been moved? And *why* had she not noticed it at once? With goose bumps crawling over her arms, she forced herself to peer around behind this errant dresser. The door there was ajar. The shivery feeling vanished, leaving a sense of disapproval. Why had Inos never known that there was a door there? She glanced up at the horizontal beams and the planked ceiling. In all the other towers, the top room had a pointed roof, as her own chamber did. So there was another room above this one! She had never realized.

How very curious!

Procrastination was not one of her failings. Carefully holding her precious silk away from the cobwebby back of the dresser, Inos moved to that diabolically tempting door.

She saw steps, of course, as she had expected—another flight curved around inside the wall, just like all the other stairs. These were very dusty. The tiny windows set every few paces were exactly as she would have expected, also, but gray with grime and draped in cobwebs. The musty air was rank with the odor of mold.

A secret room? How very, very interesting! Now she did hesitate, but only for a couple of seconds. Curiosity overcame caution and even the silk was forgotten as she slipped through the narrow gap and started to climb.

Quietly, though.

Probably there was nothing up above here at all, and her father would welcome her just as happily as he would do anywhere else. On the other hand, it was very peculiar that she had never heard anyone ever mention this unknown room. It could not be any of her business. She was trying to be on her best behavior. She was holding a packet of silk that had cost three and half imperials. She . . .

". . . is much too young!" said her father's voice.

Inos froze against the icy stones of the wall. She was almost at the top and obviously the door was open. The voice had echoed as if the unseen chamber were bare and unfurnished.

"She's not as young as all that," another voice replied. "You take a good look at her. She's very nearly a young lady now."

Her father muttered something she did not catch.

"In the Impire they would regard her as old enough already," said the other. Who could that be? She did not recognize the voice, yet it must be someone who knew her, for there could be no doubt who was being discussed.

"But who? There's no one in the kingdom."

"Then Angilki, perhaps?" It was a dry, elderly voice. "Or Kalkor? Those are the obvious choices."

Now Inos could guess what was being discussed. She gasped, and for a moment considered marching straight in through the door and announcing that she had no intention of marrying either Duke Angilki or Thane Kalkor or anyone else for that matter. So there! Only the packet of silk stopped her.

"No, no, no!" her father said loudly, and Inos relaxed a fraction. "Either of those two, and the other would start a war."

Or I shall! she thought.

An infuriating silence followed, one of those pauses when meanings pass without words, in smiles or nods or shrugs, and the speakers are not even aware that they have stopped speaking. But eavesdroppers are. It was not regal—it was not even polite—to eavesdrop. Inos knew that. But she told herself firmly that it was not polite to talk about someone when they were not there, either. So she was perfectly entitled to listen to—

"I never met Kalkor." That was her father again, farther away.

"You can live without the experience, my friend."

Friend? She knew of no one who addressed the king that way. "Bad?"

"Rough!" The stranger chuckled quietly. "Typical jotunn . . . winter-long drinking parties, probably wrestles she-bears for exercise. Sharkskin underwear, I shouldn't wonder."

"That one's out, then!"

Inos certainly agreed with her father on that.

"Angilki's too old for her," he said. "It will have to be a neutral. But you're right about Kinvale. Next year, perhaps."

The stranger spoke quite softly, so that she had to strain to hear. "You may not have that much time, friend."

Then another pause, but not so long.

"I see!" Her father's voice, curiously flat and expressionless.

"I am sorry."

"Hardly your fault!" The king sighed. "It was why I sent for you—your skill and your honesty. Honesty and wisdom. And I knew you would not hold back the truth." Another pause. "Are you sure?"

"Of course not." Inos heard footsteps on bare planks, receding. Then the stranger, from farther away: "Have you tried this?"

"No!" That was her father's monarch voice.

"It might tell you."

"No! It stays shut!"

"I don't know how you can resist."

"Because it causes trouble. My grandfather discovered that. It has not been opened since his time."

"Thinal saw one like it once," the visitor muttered. "It stayed shut, also. For the same reasons, I suppose."

She had no idea what they could be talking about. They seemed to have moved to the far side of the room, near the south window. She strained to hear the voices over the thumping of her own heart.

"Even if I am right . . . about you . . . then there might be hope . . . if we two were to cooperate."

"No, Sagorn, my friend. I have always refused and I always shall, even for that. Don't think I don't trust you."

The stranger—Sagorn?—sighed. "I know whom you do not trust, and you are right. And you have not told your daughter?"

"Heavens, no! She is only a child. She couldn't handle that!"

Handle what? Inos wanted to stamp her foot with frustration, but of course she was hardly daring to breathe, let alone stamp.

"But you will?"

Another pause.

"I don't know," her father said softly. "If . . . if she is older when . . . or maybe not at all."

"You must!" The stranger spoke in a tone that no one used to a king. "You must not let it be lost!" His voice reverberated in the empty room.

"Must?"

Inos could guess at her father's mocking, quizzical expression.

"Yes, must! It is too precious . . . and it is Krasnegar's only hope for survival. You know that."

"It would also be her greatest danger."

"Yes, that is true," the stranger admitted. "But the advantages of having it outweigh the disadvantages, do they not?" His voice became diffident, almost pleading. "You know that! You . . . you could not trust me with it? If I promised that later I would tell her?"

She heard her father's dry chuckle. He had come closer. She must be prepared to run.

"No, Sagorn. For her sake. I trust *you*, friend, but not . . . certain others."

The other man sighed. "No, certainly not Darad. Never trust him. Or Andor."

"You keep them away, both of them!" That was a royal command.

"Yes, I will. And so will Jalon."

The stranger's voice was suddenly very close. Inos wheeled around and started down the stairs as fast as she could safely and silently go. Jalon? The minstrel? She was sure that was the name she had just heard. What had he to do with this? And who was this Sagorn?

Then—

Dust! With horror she saw her own footsteps below her, mingled with those of her father and his visitor, giveaway marks on the deposits of years. Coming up, she had not noticed them, but going down they were obvious, even in the dim glow coming through the grimy panes. Panic! They would know that she, or at least someone, had been listening.

At the bottom she stumbled against the heavy door and the rusted old hinges creaked horribly. She squeezed through the opening, dashed across her father's bedroom, and was plunging down the next stairs when she heard a shout behind her and then a clatter of boots.

It was a race, then. She must escape from the tower and, certainly, she must hide her precious packet of silk until the storm blew itself out.

She reached the dressing room, skidded on a rug in the middle of it, regained her balance, dashed down the next flight, and burst into the withdrawing room, into an astonished collection of six matronly ladies just sitting down to Aunt Kade's midmorning salon.

For a long moment Inos wavered on one foot, with the other still in the air and arms spread like a cormorant. She stared her horror back at their surprise, poised on the verge of sprinting through their midst and out the door on the far side. She was very tempted—at least she would be able to dispose of the silk—but the way was cluttered by all those ladies on the edges of their gilt and rosewood chairs, by Kel the footman with a serving trolley laden with Aunt Kade's finest china and her magnificent, enormous, silver tea urn giving out its usual disgusting odor of burning whale oil . . . And then Aunt Kade had risen, and all the others did so also, and it was too late.

Aunt Kade's plump face was turning pink and assuming that fretted look that Inos so often provoked these days. Whether to welcome or scold . . . She was probably also chewing over problems of protocol and the dowdy brown worsted. Then she made her decision.

She beamed. "Inosolan, my dear! How nice that you can join us! May I present these ladies? Mistress Jiolinsod, Mistress Ofazi . . ."

Feeling as if her head had come off and floated out through a window, Inos forced a smile on a face not there. Tucking the silk behind her in her left hand, she offered her right to each of the simpering matrons. To be invited to one of Princess Kadolan's tea parties in the palace was a screaming social success, and to meet Princess Inosolan as well was probably a stupid honor.

Especially, she realized, when the princess was wearing her dowdy brown worsted, regally emblazoned—at least on the right sleeve—with silver cobwebs. Oh, horrors! There were probably cobwebs on her hair and face, also, while the society ladies were all dressed in their best gowns and bonnets, and loaded with every piece of jewelry they owned or, likely, had been able to borrow.

Boots on the stairs! With a wail, Inos jumped loose from the fourth introduction and started backing away from the door.

Her aunt spluttered at such gaucherie. "Inos!"

And then the door flew wide and a man appeared in the doorway—an elderly man, tall and stooped. He folded his arms and straightened, and his gaze swept the room. Inos had never seen him before, she was certain, yet he had known what she looked like. He had a gaunt face, with a hooked nose like an eagle's beak and fierce blue eyes. Deep clefts ran down at the sides of his mouth, emphasizing the nose and the strong chin. Wisps of white hair showed under the brown hood of his cloak. His gown bore traces of cobwebs.

"Doctor Sagorn!" Aunt Kade exclaimed in delight. "How nice that you are able to join us! May I . . ." Her voice tailed away as she saw how the newcomer was staring ferociously at her niece, as that niece continued to edge backward.

Inos was fighting a spring tide of panic, drowning in rising terror before that deadly glare. Her hips touched the trolley and she could back away no farther. Where was her father? Why had he not come, also?

And how in the world had this sinister old man come down the stairs so quickly? He must have outrun her and her father both, yet he was not even panting. She was.

"Inosolan?" Aunt Kade sounded vexed. "What are you holding behind your back, dear?"

Her mouth opened and nothing came out.

"Silk!" said the terrifying Sagorn. "Silk with yellow dragons on it."

A sorcerer!

Inos screamed in terror and turned to flee.

The trolley crashed over, spilling cakes and wine in all directions.

Aunt Kade's special and enormous silver tea urn seemed to shake the castle as it struck the floor with a deafening boom. Tea exploded over half the ladies.

Staggering, Inos trod a creamy chocolate flan into the rug and almost fell. Then she hurtled out and down the stairs, leaving Aunt Kade's midmorning salon in ruins and confusion.

4

Whimpering in her panic, Inos fled down all the rest of the staircases; raced in turn across antechamber, robing room, presence chamber, and throne room; burst out into the great hall; and there alarmed a group of small children being fed an early lunch. Out on the terrace she ran, not at all sure where she was going. Startled pigeons and seagulls clawed their way skyward, while the yellow cat that had been stalking them flew over a wall. She rounded a corner and saw ahead of her the open doorway of the palace chapel. She dived through it, seeking refuge in religion. Surely she would be safe from a sorcerer in the house of the Gods?

She skidded to a halt in the cool dark interior, panting and deafened by the thunder of her heart, which seemed to be beating inside her head. The chapel was a small building, with room for only twenty or thirty people on its ancient pinewood pews. Its walls were immensely thick and it was said to be even older than the rest of the castle. At one end stood the offering table, before the two sacred windows, one bright, the other black and opaque, and on the table stood the sacred balance, its pans of gold and lead symbolizing the battle between good and evil. The air was clammy and musty.

She hurried forward to the table and was about to drop to her knees when a dry voice spoke behind her.

"Well!" it said. "Do we have a sudden repentance?"

Inos uttered a shrill squeak and jumped.

Arms folded, Mother Unonini was sitting stiffly erect on the front pew. The palace chaplain was a dark, grim woman, who seemed very tall when seated. With swarthy face, black hair, and black robe, she was indistinct in the gloom, except for a clear glint of satisfaction shining in her eyes. "To what do the Gods owe the pleasure of this visit, my dear?"

"There is a sorcerer in the palace!"

"A sorcerer? How unusual!"

"Truly!"

"Come and sit by me, then, and explain," the chaplain said. "We can't have you spouting random prayers in your condition— you might summon all the wrong sort of Gods. Long meditation and right thinking are essential prerequisites for prayer."

Still trembling, the reluctant Inos went and sat beside her. Her head was immediately lower than Mother Unonini's, but at least Inos's feet still touched the floor. The chaplain had never forgiven Inos for imitating her waddling gait during the last Winterfest party, even though the king had made his errant daughter apologize in public afterward. Inos's attendance record at church school was not going to help much, either.

"What is that you have in your hand? Let me see." Unonini took the silk and unfolded some of it and held it down for the light to shine on. "Well! You were bringing this as an offering, perhaps?"

"Er . . . no."

"The table could certainly do with a new cloth. This is very nice. Where did you get it?"

"It's my birthday gift from Father . . ." Inos trailed off weakly.

"Does he know that?"

"Well . . . I mean, not yet." Inos twisted round to make sure that the sorcerer was not standing in the doorway. She felt trapped now, snared in this dark little room with the unfriendly Mother Unonini, and a sorcerer possibly lurking outside.

"Perhaps you had better begin at the beginning."

Inos hung her head and began at the beginning. Her breath was returning and her heart slowing down. Little as she cared for Mother Unonini—who bore a strong smell of fish that day—at least a chaplain ought to know what to do if that terrifying Sorcerer Sagorn came after her. When she had finished, there was a pause.

"I see." Mother Unonini sounded as if she had been impressed in spite of herself. "Well, let us hear your interpretation of these strange events."

"What?"

"Don't say 'what' like that. It is not ladylike. You know what I mean. All things and acts contain both the Good and the Evil, child. We must try to be on the right side in their eternal conflict. It is our duty always to choose the Good, or at least the better. Let us begin with the sorcerer, if that is what he is. Is he evil or is he good?"

"I . . . I don't know. If he is a friend of Father's . . . Perhaps he murdered Father?"

"I hardly think so. Don't jump to conclusions! His Majesty probably stayed behind to close the door again. He certainly would not want unauthorized prowlers up in Inisso's chamber."

"You knew about that room?"

"Certainly!"

"You've seen it?"

"No," Unonini admitted, with a hint of annoyance. "But I could guess that it would be there. Inisso was a great sorcerer—a good one, of course—and so he would have had a place of puissance at the top of his tower. There may be all sorts of arcane things still up there, things that do not concern prying young ladies."

Inos decided that the old witch was probably right. She had not been choosing the Good when she went snooping, nor when she listened to the conversation. So perhaps she had been on the wrong side of the eternal conflict. In that case, the sorcerer might be a good sorcerer, and his anger had been directed against the wickedness in her. It was very upsetting to think that she might be on the side of the Evil, and she suddenly wanted to weep. Preferably on someone's shoulder, but certainly not on Madame Unonini's.

"This silk, now," Mother Unonini remarked. "Let us talk about that. Tell me what good and evil lie in this silk."

Suppressing a snivel, Inos said, "I should not have taken it until I could pay for it."

"That is correct, child. Go on."

"Or at least until Father agreed to buy it for me."

"Very good! So what must you do now?"

"Take it back?" Inos wondered if this was how a breaking heart felt.

"Oh, I think it is too late for that." Mother Unonini sighed a heavy waft of cod. She wiggled her dangling feet. "Mistress Meolorne may have already made arrangements to spend the money you promised her."

Hope flared in Inos like the brightness of the window. "I can keep it?" Then she saw the look in Mother Unonini's eye and the brightness of the Good turned to the darkness of the Evil. "No?"

"We must not seek to profit from malefaction, Inosolan. Is this not correct?"

Inos nodded.

"So, what must you do?"

Inos tried to think of the appropriate text. "Find the greatest good?"

The older woman nodded with satisfaction. "Now, as I said, the offering table could do with a new cover—"

"Don't bully the child!" said a voice with the brazen authority of a trumpet fanfare.

In front of the offering table stood a God, a figure so brilliant as to be unbearable to look on, although it shed no light on the rest of the room.

With simultaneous gasps, Inos and Mother Unonini fell to their knees and bowed their heads to the floor.

Perhaps Sagorn was a sorcerer, Inos thought, or perhaps not; but this was certainly a real God. All her terror came pouring back tenfold and she wished she could melt into the ground.

"Unonini," said that terrible voice—somehow it sounded like thunder and yet it was not loud and it did not echo, *"what do you know about this man Sagorn?"*

Mother Unonini made a sort of croaking noise and then whispered, "His Majesty told me that he was coming. That he is a great scholar . . ." She paused.

"Go on!"

"That he was an old friend of his Majesty's. They traveled together in their youth."

There was a tense silence. That dark and icy chapel should be hot and brilliant from the divine fire, but it was not. The flags were cold and gritty under Inos's knees. They smelled of dust.

"So?" the God asked in a voice that Inos thought would not be heard outside the door and yet could have laid low the hills.

With obvious reluctance, Mother Unonini said, "So I do not think he is evil, or a sorcerer. I . . . I should have told her that, to reassure her."

"Yes, you should!"

Inos had covered her face with her hands. Now she opened her fingers just a tiny bit and peered through them. She could see the God's toes. They blazed so brightly that her eyes hurt, yet the floor beside them was still dark. Greatly daring, she sneaked a glance upward at the glory of the God.

He . . . it . . . she . . . No, *They,* she remembered. Gods were always "They." They were a female figure, or so it seemed. They seemed to be without clothes, but she felt no shock or shame as she would have done if They had been really naked. For one thing, her eyes were watering so much that she could not see Them properly. For another, there was a white rainbow glow about Them, a radiant nimbus that flowed incessantly, a surging tide of iridescence. Within it she seemed to catch glimpses of a female body of incredible beauty and grace, radiating also compassion and affection—

Then suddenly it had a maleness of strength and power, and a terrifying anger that made her very glad she was not Mother Unonini. Inos could feel the chaplain trembling at her side as that divine wrath washed over her.

Her eyes ached so much that she closed them quickly and bent her head again. It had been like trying to see the rocks in a tidal pool when the sun was shining on the ripples, but these ripples were waves of beauty and strength and maleness and femininity and love and splendor—and now anger. Yet in that glimpse of unbearable blazing glory, she had the strange feeling that she had seen familiarity. Her mother, perhaps? Could that have been her mother's face in Their coldly burning radiance? She did not feel quite so fearful, then. Probably the God was well meaning and just could not help looking so awesome.

"Unonini," the voice rumbled, and somehow it was now male, also, although the pitch did not seem to have changed, *"what is wrong with the cloth on this table?"*

The chaplain whimpered. "Nothing, God."

"So where is the Good and where is the Evil in frightening the girl into making an offering of something she does not own and does not want to offer?"

The chaplain wailed louder. "God, I was wrong! It was more an Evil than a Good."

"You are sure? Gods can mislead, also, remember!"

"I am sure, God. I was being spiteful."

"Very well," They said, more gently. *"Repent!"*

The waves of anger faded, to be replaced by something which so wrenched Inos's heart that she wanted to weep and laugh at the same time. After a moment's silence, the cowering Unonini began to make very curious noises that Inos eventually decided were sobs.

Then the God spoke again, and this time the voice had returned to being softer, feminine. *"Inosolan?"*

Now it was her turn and she had been on the side of the Evil. "Yes, God?" she whispered.

"You will have to try a little harder, won't you?"

Inos heard teeth chattering and realized they were hers. "I shall return the silk, God."

"No need for that."

She looked up in astonishment and had to close her eyes at once against the sudden agony. "You mean Father will buy it for me?"

The God laughed. It was simultaneously a quiet chuckle and an awe-inspiring explosion of vast, immortal enjoyment. It should have been deafening and it should have echoed around and around the tiny chapel, but it did neither. *"That and many others. We do not say that you deserve this. We are only making a prophecy. There are hard times ahead for you, Inosolan, but you may find a happy ending if you choose the Good."*

She said, "What must I do, God?" and was astounded to realize that she was questioning Them.

"Seek to find the Good," They said, *"and above all, remember love! If you do not trust in love, then all will be lost."*

And They had gone. Without waiting for a reply or thanks, without demanding praise or prayers, neither worship nor ritual, the God had vanished.

5

Mother Unonini had uttered a great wail and prostrated herself completely.

Inos considered that procedure for a moment and then decided that it was not called for. Nor did the chaplain seem to want to continue their earlier conversation. Come to think of it, old fishy-breath Unonini had been most divinely snubbed and put down. The God had made Their appearance to save Inos from Mother Unonini's spite.

Feeling very calm and pleased now, Inos rose and walked out of the chapel, blinking at bright sunshine that was nothing compared to the brightness of a God. She had seen a God! Most people lived all their lives without such an honor. What a pity she had been wearing her dowdy brown worsted, she thought, and then scolded herself for such improper vanity.

Nevertheless, she decided to go back to her room and change. Once she was looking a little more regal and *princessy* she would see what she could do to patch things up with Aunt Kade and the man who was obviously not a sorcerer. And she must show Father the silk that he was going to buy for her. *That and many others,* the God had said? Most curious!

She had seen a God! It would be a topic of general interest at dinner.

She headed toward her chamber, walking with her head very high, feeling elevated. Yes, elevated! It was as if she weighed nothing at all and had to reach her toes down to touch the ground as she walked. If she passed anyone on the way, she did not notice. She came to the stairs and began to float up them . . .

But by the time she struggled to the top, her mood had changed totally and she seemed to weigh as much as the whole castle. She dragged her reluctant carcass up the last few steps and could hardly find the strength to open the door. She staggered in and the first thing she saw was herself, in the mirror, her hair still all smeared with cobwebs and her face as white as a seagull, with a seagull's round, bright eyes.

And behind her reflection, her father was sitting on her bed, waiting for her. She saw an expression of impatience change instantly to alarm. He jumped up and held out his arms and then he was hugging her tight and holding her head as she buried her face in his soft velvet collar and began to sob.

Still holding her tight, he sat her down beside him on the bed and held her for a long time as she sobbed and sobbed and sobbed.

And sobbed.

At last she was able to find one of her mother's linen handkerchiefs and wipe her aching eyes and blow her nose and even, somehow, manage a small smile. Her father regarded her with a worried frown. He was wearing a deep-blue robe and he looked very regal with his short brown beard—very comforting and reassuring. A little tired, perhaps. His velvet collar was stained with tears and cobwebs, and she dabbed at it with her handkerchief, feeling stupid now, and childish.

"Well!" he said. "You haven't had a good cry like that in a long time, young lady. What provoked all that?"

Where to begin? "I thought he was a sorcerer!"

"Sagorn?" Her father smiled. "No! He's a very learned man, but he's not a sorcerer. I don't think it would be possible to eavesdrop on a sorcerer, my princess." Then the smile faded. "He's also a very private man, Inos. He does not like to be spied on. How much did you hear?"

"You said you would not marry me off to Kalkor. Or Angilki." She paused and thought carefully. "I didn't understand the rest, Father. I'm sorry."

"Sorry?" He laughed ruefully. "You realize that you almost burned down the castle?"

"*No!* How could I . . . Oh, no! The urn?"

"The urn," he agreed. "That disgusting, smelly, *hideous* old thing that your aunt is so absurdly attached to. The oil went everywhere. Luckily young Kel was quick-witted enough to throw a rug over the flames . . . Well, don't do it again! And that's all? All that weeping because you thought you'd met a sorcerer?"

She wiped her eyes again and fought down an insane desire to laugh. "No. Then I met a God."

"What? You're serious?"

She nodded, and told him. He believed her, listening solemnly. Then he stared at the floor and tugged his beard for a while, looking worried.

"Well, I'm not surprised you were upset," he said at last. "Meeting Gods must be a very scary experience. I fear it means trouble. We must discuss it with Sagorn. But I'm not sorry to hear about Mother Unonini, I must say." He glanced sideways at her, his eyes twinkling. "I can't stand the woman, either! But don't tell anyone I said that!"

"You can't?" She was astonished at both his words and his conspiratorial grin—not regal at all!

He shook his head. "It's very hard to find a suitable, well-educated chaplain willing to live in a place like Krasnegar, Inos."

"There's nothing wrong with Krasnegar," she protested.

He sighed. "Well, I agree with you. But many wouldn't. Now, what was all this about silk?"

She jumped up and fetched the silk from where it lay beside the mirror. She shook it loose and draped it over her shoulder for him to see and, before he could speak, she hurriedly explained how the gold matched her hair and the bronze was just right for her skin and the green for her eyes. "I was hoping you would buy it for my birthday?" she finished hopefully.

He shook his head and motioned for her to sit again. She dropped the silk, feeling her spirits drop with it. As she sat, he lifted a small leather box from the bed beside him.

"I am giving you these for your birthday." He opened the lid and she gasped.

"Mother's jewels!"

"Yours, now."

Pearls and rubies and emeralds! Gold and silver!

"They're not a great fortune," he said, "but they are all good pieces. Beauty, not riches. Some of them are very old. This belonged to Olliola, Inisso's wife . . ."

She was overwhelmed, listening with open mouth as he told her the history of some of the jewels. Then she hugged him and wanted to start trying them on, but he closed the box.

"As for the silk . . ."

Trouble! "Yes, Father?"

"Where did you ever find something like that?"

"Mistress Meolorne's."

"I might have guessed!" He smiled. "How much?"

"Well, more than I meant to pay, but—"

"You sound just like your mother," he said. "How much?"

Inos bit her lip and whispered the terrible truth.

"What?" He stared at her. Then he quickly turned away, and after a moment she realized that he was laughing.

"Father!"

He looked around at her, and his laughter exploded aloud. He bellowed with laughter. "Oh, Inos, my pet! Oh, princess!" He laughed some more.

She felt hurt, and almost angry.

"Come!" he said at last, still fighting down amusement that she did not understand. "Come and meet Doctor Sagorn."

Once it had been called the Queen's Room, but now it was His Majesty's Study. Inos had not been in it very much recently, although it was almost the only place in the castle that could ever be classed as cozy in the winter. She preferred now to seek warmth and friendship in the kitchens, mostly. The familiar chairs and sofa had not changed since her mother's time, but they suddenly registered on her as the furniture in her father's bedroom had done—old and shabby, and not regal. She was annoyed to see the long and bony form of Doctor Sagorn stretched out in her mother's favorite chair.

He rose awkwardly and bowed to her, and she curtsied. She had insisted on changing and felt much better in her cypress-green wool. It was too warm for this weather, but it did have a hint of padding and it did make her look older.

Keeping her gaze firmly on the threadbare rug, she apologized.

He bowed again. "And my apologies to you; Highness, for frightening you." She thought he could have put a little more conviction into the words. "Your father and I were perhaps a little too trusting in not locking the bedroom door." The old blue eyes gleamed nastily. "We put too much faith in the aversion spell. It must be wearing thin, I suppose, after so many centuries."

"Spell?" Inos echoed. "Sorcery?"

"Did you not feel it?"

"She thought you were a sorcerer," her father remarked, smiling as if that were a big joke.

"Alas, no! I should hardly go around looking like this if I were a sorcerer, now would I?" Doctor Sagorn attempted to match her father's smile, but his angular face looked even more predatory when he did that.

Inos could not think of a ladylike answer to that question, so she countered with one of her own. "How did you know about the silk and the dragons?"

"I saw you in the road! You were clutching it as if you thought all the Imperial armies would be trying to snatch it from you. You went by me at a tremendous rate."

Her father chuckled and gestured for her to sit. "Like the time you befuddled the customs men in Jal Pusso, Sagorn?"

Sagorn guffawed and folded himself back into the chair. "More like you and the meat pies!"

Her father laughed in turn. Evidently these were old adventures that Inos would not be invited to share. Now he had produced a decanter of dwarfish-cut crystal that she had only seen once or twice before, and three of the precious matching goblets—three! To her astonishment she found herself sitting on the edge of the sofa and holding one of those goblets. Sagorn must have noticed her surprise, and her father had noticed that he had noticed.

"I think Inos has earned this," he said. "Sip, my dear. It's powerful."

Sagorn sipped and sighed. "Superb! I would not have expected this in Krasnegar. Elvish, of course."

The king smiled. "Valdoquiff itself. Kade brought a cask of it from Kinvale. I hoard it like a dwarf."

He was answering a question that had not been asked. Obviously Sagorn and he knew each other well. Inos felt a little reassured, and sipped at her drink. She did not care for the taste— like drinking nettles, and the fumes burned the inside of her nose— but certainly it was an honor—and a sign of forgiveness? She felt very grown-up!

"Now, Inos," her father said, settling back in his chair. "Tell Doctor Sagorn about the God."

"God?" The eagle's eyes flashed to her again.

Inos related her experience once more. When she was done, she thought she had managed to maintain a very matter-of-fact decorum. There was a long silence. Sagorn scratched at his cheek in deep thought. He emptied his goblet. Her father rose and re-filled it.

"Had the God not come, Holindarn, what would you have done?"

She had never heard anyone except her mother and Kade call her father by name like that.

Her father shrugged at the question. "Given my daughter a hard scolding, sent Meo a couple of crowns, and dispatched Unonini out of here on the first boat."

The old man nodded, then smiled mockingly. "The silk would have stayed in the chapel, then?"

"I do not steal from Gods!"

"Quite! The silk seems unimportant. If the Gods did not want this chaplain woman to return to the Impire, They could have found a simpler way to produce the effect, I should think." Sagorn turned his calculating eyes on Inos again. "So the message to you seems to be the important part. But Gods do not meddle in trivial matters . . . Are you in love at the moment, young lady?"

Inos felt herself turn very pink. "No! Of course not!"

"Hardly!" her father protested mildly.

Sagorn sent him an odd glance. "So she is going to fall in love? She will have a choice to make? Highness, has your father ever explained the importance of Krasnegar?"

Inos shook her head dumbly.

"Well, Krasnegar is very unusual. You have jotnar here and you have imps. There are very few places in all Pandemia where that combination exists in peace. Did you ever hear of the Mad Sorcerer?"

She shook her head, surprised at the sudden shift in subject.

"It's a name that was given to Inisso. Does it not seem strange that a man of such vast power would choose to build his tower in a barren, isolated spot like Krasnegar? But he was not so crazy as he seemed, I think. This is a very strategic little town. It has the only good harbor in the north."

Why was he telling her this? He seemed very solemn. Inos glanced at her father, and he frowned as if to tell her to listen carefully.

"Both Nordland and the Impire think they should own Krasnegar. Is that not so, Majesty?"

"It has always been so."

"And it has always had a king, not a queen regnant!" Sagorn said triumphantly. "So you see, Highness, the thanes and the Impire will all take a great deal of interest in whomever you choose as husband. Yet they both need you."

"Need me?" she asked. "Us?"

He nodded. "Need Krasnegar. There is much your father must teach you if you are to rule here after him. Salt, for instance. Even humble things like salt. The jotnar need salt to store their meat over the winter. Salt doesn't sail well, so most of it comes overland from the south in the summer, to Krasnegar. Goblins and jotnar trade furs for it. The Impire wants furs. Things like that.

The imperor would not like to see a jotunn king in Krasnegar. Nordland wouldn't like you to marry an imp.''

"But they'll both accept me as queen?" she protested, looking to her father. She had hardly ever thought about being queen. That would be after he died, and she was *not* going to think about that.

He nodded—a little doubtfully, she thought. "If you are old enough and strong enough, and if they approve of your choice of husband. Most husbands like to give the orders, you know."

She snorted, not caring that snorting was not regal.

"Well, that doesn't have to be for years yet, does it?"

For just a moment . . . then he seemed to change his mind. "I certainly hope not. What I think my learned friend is saying, though, is that you may have to choose a husband quite soon—in a year or two, even. And your decision will be important to very many people. The God was telling you to remember love when you decide—a divine hint. Right, Sagorn?"

Inos spoke first, suddenly seized by a horrible doubt. "You're not going to marry me off to some horrible old duke, are you, Father?"

Her father laughed. "Not unless you want me to. No, Nordland would not stand for it, anyway. That's what I mean—your decision might start a war, Inos!"

She gasped at such a horrible idea, and swallowed the last of whatever it was in her glass. It made her cough. If enjoying this vile stuff was a requirement for adulthood, then she had farther to go than she had thought.

Her father rose. "I'll send for some lunch, Sagorn, unless you'd prefer the hall?"

It was a hint of dismissal for Inos, and Inos had still not settled the terrible matter of the silk.

"No. A snack here would be fine," the old man said, with a strange smile at her father. "As you know, Sire, I am not much of a party man."

"Tonight, perhaps, though? I understand that we have a very fine minstrel visiting us. Kade is organizing something."

Inos was being edged to the door. "Father? The silk?"

He looked surprised, then laughed loudly again. "Three and a half imperials, you said?"

She nodded miserably, and he laid heavy hands on her shoulders. "Inos, darling, that much would buy Meo's whole stock!"

"Meo?"

He smiled and, perhaps, blushed a little. "Meo and I are very old friends. You used to play with the servants' children when you were little; so did I. I've known Meo all my life. I even thought I was in love with her once. Who went with you this morning?'' he added, suddenly suspicious.

She confessed—no one.

He sighed and patted her shoulder. ''This has to stop, Inos! You're growing up. You're not a child anymore. You can't run around by yourself. Nor with stableboys and scullery maids—clambering after bird's eggs, digging clams . . . I've been neglecting you.'' He chuckled. ''Perhaps Meo thinks I have been neglecting her—I haven't seen her in years. Or else she was sending me a message.''

''Message?''

He nodded. ''A message that my beautiful daughter should not be wandering the town by herself. No, Meo doesn't expect three and a half gold imperials!''

That was better. Much better.

Her father chuckled. ''I'm very tempted to send the guard down to arrest her for extortion and then sentence her to stay to dinner, but her neighbors would gossip. Did she have any other quality stuff?''

With sudden excitement, Inos remembered what the God had said. ''Only one other silk, Father. It had flowering trees on it. Apples, she said. Do apples really grow from flowers? But she has a drooly turquoise satin and three soft linens and a roll of silver mohair—''

He laughed. ''I was going to send you out with your aunt this afternoon, but perhaps I'll come as well. If Doctor Sagorn will excuse me for a little while, I shall visit my old friend Meo. She's a widow now. I expect she's lonely. But you can have all of those, and more besides—all the fine dresses and gowns we can make or find for you.''

''Father! You mean it? But—but why?''

He smiled sadly. ''I wasn't going to tell you yet, but I suppose I must. Because you have to leave Krasnegar.''

6

> *I loved a maiden,*
> > *Maiden oh . . .*
> *I loved a maiden,*
> > *Long ago . . .*
> *I left my land, I left my kin,*

I left my all, her heart to win.
Maiden, maiden, maiden oh . . .
Long ago . . .

Jalon's voice floated through the great hall like flower petals. Inos felt shivery listening to it. She thought of the glory of the God she had seen that morning; she thought of moonlight on snow, of the string of pearls she was wearing, and of white gulls against blue sky. Great beauty always made her shivery and she had never known such singing. Any other minstrel she had ever heard was a honking goose compared to this Jalon. The hall was full of people, yet there was no sound except the tremulous throb of the harp and a gloriously clear tenor voice floating under the high rafters.

Flower petals!

Inos was sitting with her father and his guests at the high table, on the dais at one end of the great hall. More townsfolk and the senior castle staff flanked tables along both sides. At the far end the lesser folk sat on the floor in front of the big fireplaces. The stones above them were black with the grease and smoke of centuries, and the high rafters overhead were black, also. Many a winter's day she had shivered at this table, staring wistfully along the length of the hall to the leaping flames hissing and spluttering as grease dripped into them from the creaking spits, a princess envying servants. But today the hearths were dark and bare and the hall was hot, not cold. The sun loved Krasnegar in summer and would not leave it. Men fell down from exhaustion before the sun did, and after an hour or so it came smiling back, ready for another endless day. So the sun was still shining in the windows, laying sparkling bridges of light across the room in the floating dust.

I gave her gold, and rubies, too,
I gave my all, her heart to woo.
Maiden, maiden, maiden oh . . .

It was warm up there at the high table with her father and Aunt Kade and all the distinguished guests who had been rounded up from the town at very short notice to hear this minstrel . . . and perhaps to say good-bye to Princess Inosolan? No, never mind that.

Aunt Kade had dug out her ancient lapis lazuli velvet, which made her seem plumper and shorter than ever and was usually worn only at Winterfest. It was much too hot a garment for this weather and her face was pink and shiny as she smiled contentedly around at the guests. She'd had her hair blue-rinsed. Smiling at the thought of Kinvale? No! No! Think of that tomorrow.

Mistress Meolorne was there, beaming happily, perhaps musing on all the wonderful fabrics she had sold to the court that afternoon—and all of them for less than a single imperial, as the king had predicted. He and she had laughed together like old friends.

Her father did look tired, almost as if he were sitting in shadow when everyone around him was in sunshine.

There were merchants there, with their wives, and a few ship captains, and the bishop and the school teachers; old Kondoral, cupping his ear, tears running in his wrinkles; Chancellor Yaltauri; and Master Poraganu. There were few of the castle staff, for so many were away in the hills, and especially not many young folk, but she could see Lin, who had broken his arm cutting peat of all things—how could he have managed that?—and Kel and Ido and Fan . . .

And Rap of course.

They were all sitting on the floor at the far end, near the great fireplace—small, wide-eyed children at the front, cross-legged or hugging knees, entranced by the music; the junior staff like Rap gathered behind him. As always, the palace dogs had clustered as close to Rap as they could get.

Before the children, flanked by the lesser tables, the center of the hall was empty except for one chair, and on that chair the minstrel sat and pleated moonbeams.

> *I loved a maiden,*
> *   Maiden oh . . .*
> *I loved a maiden,*
> *   Long ago . . .*
> *I traveled land, I traveled sea,*
> *I traveled all, by her to be.*
> *Maiden, maiden, maiden oh . . .*
> *   Long ago . . .*

Mother Unonini was not there. Mother Unonini was under the care of the physicians, resting in a dark room on a light diet, and Inos could not help but think that there was a small good in that evil, and the thought made her feel guilty.

The fearsome Doctor Sagorn was not there, either—another small good. Even if he was an old friend of her father's, his glittery eagle gaze and beak nose still frightened her, and she was quite happy that he had pleaded travel weariness to excuse his absence.

Jalon's song ended and the hall exploded with applause—clapping and cheering and drumming of heels on the stones. The minstrel rose and bowed to the king and then to the rest of the company, and then he came back up to his seat at the high table.

"Your throat must be dry, minstrel?" her father said.

"A little, Sire. And the audience could use a rest, also."

"That I do not believe. Steward!"

Jalon gratefully accepted a new tankard and said something about fine northern beer before quaffing it. All around the hall conversations began to poke up like spring flowers through snow, as the spell he had painted faded away.

"The imperor has appointed a new marshal of the armies, minstrel?" demanded one of the pompous burghers.

Jalon smiled vaguely. "The old one died, didn't he?"

The burgher made an impatient noise. "But the new one? Is he warlike?" Inos could not recall that burgher's name. He looked like a rooster, with red wattles and hair that stuck up. He had perhaps drunk a little too much of the fine northern beer.

"I expect so," Jalon said. "They usually are, aren't they?"

"And the witch of the west is dead?" another asked.

The minstrel looked blank and then said, "Yes," uncertainly.

"This dwarf who's replaced her—what do you know of him?"

"Er . . . nothing? Yes, nothing."

One of the stately matrons frowned at him severely. "Then the Four now consist of three warlocks and only one witch, isn't that so? Only one of the wardens is a woman, Bright Water."

Jalon looked even more blank. "Her Omnipotence Umthrum? She's a woman, isn't she?"

There was a long, puzzled pause, and then a little, ferrety sailor said, "She died years ago. Before I was born."

The minstrel sighed. "I'm afraid politics is not a great interest of mine, master."

Jalon had come from Hub itself, capital of the Impire. The honored guests, eager for news and gossip, had been firing questions at him all evening, but he never seemed to have answers. He was a very sweet young man, Inos thought, but as insubstantial as a morning mist. She wondered how he ever found his way from castle to castle or town to town; he was probably always fro-ing when he should be to-ing, she thought, and chuckled to herself, with a glance in the direction of Rap.

"We have heard rumors of much dragon damage in the southern provinces," another burgher proclaimed, meaning it as a question to Jalon. "On Kith, especially."

"Oh?" the minstrel said. "I'm afraid I must have missed that."
The worthies of Krasnegar exchanged glances of exasperation.

"What sort of gowns are the ladies wearing in the Impire these
days, Master Jalon?" That was Aunt Kade, who must be worrying
about all those fabrics and how many of them she could purloin
for her own use and where she would find enough seamstresses
to sew them all in the few days before departure.

"Very high waists," Jalon said firmly. "Flowing out like trumpets at the floor, with fairly short trains. Puffed at the shoulders,
sleeves tight at the top, flaring at the wrist. Lace cuffs. Necklines
are high, with lace trim, also. Floral prints are very popular, in
cottons or silk."

The table reacted with stunned silence to this unexpected note
of authority. Inos noticed that her father was grinning.

"Master Jalon is a fine artist, also," the king remarked.
"Would there possibly be time for you to paint my daughter's
portrait before you leave, Jalon?"

Jalon studied Inos for a moment. "Had I a lifetime to spend I
could hardly do justice to such beauty, Sire."

Inos felt herself blush and everyone else laughed. They did not
have to laugh quite so hard, she thought.

The minstrel turned back to the king. "If I can lay my hands
on materials, Sire . . . they might not be readily available here.
But a drawing, certainly. It would be a labor of love."

"Could you sketch us some of these gowns you have just described, Master Jalon?" Aunt Kade inquired, blinking eagerly.

"Of course, Highness."

Aunt Kade beamed with evident relief and turned to Mistress
Meolorne to ask her opinions on seamstresses.

Inos looked longingly at the young folk beyond the tables. They
were chattering and laughing, Rap telling a story, Lin topping it.
What use was it to be a princess if you could not do as you
pleased? Why did she have to be trapped up here with all these
stuffy old folks? Quietly she eased her chair back.

Aunt Kade's head flicked round. "Inos?"

"I thought I might—"

"Let her," the king said softly. He did not say "It is the last
time," but she thought that he was thinking it.

Gratefully Inos rose, smiled a politeness around the guests,
and muttered something inaudible. Then she hurried across the
so-empty center of the hall to the group on the floor. The young
ones saw her coming and started to open a path for her, and they
cleared an opening all the way to Lin and Rap. Rap shoved at a

couple of dogs, and Lin heaved himself aside one-armed. Now why did they all assume she would want to sit just there?

But she did.

As she settled down, he turned to look at her and his big gray eyes grew even bigger at the sight of the pearls.

They smiled doubtfully at each other.

"How was the man-at-armsing?" she whispered.

He grinned sheepishly. "Boring!"

She smiled. *Good!* In that case . . . "I'm sorry I was nasty to you, Rap."

He turned a little pink, looked down at his knees, and said, "Then we can still be fiends?"

They sniggered in unison.

She put her hand on the floor, next to his.

His hand slipped over hers.

No one would notice.

He had big, strong hands, warm and calloused. Man's hands.

Yes, he was taller. It had not been the boots, and his worn old doublet was tight across the shoulders. A friendly smell of horses always hung around Rap.

Running about with stableboys, her father had said . . .

"Rap, I'm going away!"

She had not meant to mention that problem. He looked at her with surprise all over his plain pudding face, though it was a lot less pudding than it used to be.

"South," she said quickly. "To Kinvale. To learn how to be a lady. With Aunt Kade. On the next ship."

Inos bit her lip and stared at the distant high table. The hall had gone rather misty.

His hand tightened on hers. "How long?"

"A year." Inos took a deep breath and made a big effort to be regal. "You see, the duke is a sort of relative—Duke Angilki of Kinvale. Aunt Kade was married to his uncle. And my great-grandfather's sister was his . . . Oh, I forget. Inisso had three sons. One became king here after him, one went south and became duke of Kinvale, and one went to Nordland. Kalkor, the thane of Gark, is descended from him. But it's much more complicated . . ."

She stopped, because Rap would not be interested, and it was not very nice to talk of all those ancestors when he did not have any. Well, none that he knew of, she decided. He must have had just as many as she had, only not of noble blood. Her father said that the branches of her family tree were all knotted. There were not many noble families in the north country, so they tended to intermarry every few generations, as soon as it was decent.

Inisso had had three sons. Apparently that was important.

"When you are queen of Krasnegar, then I shall be your sergeant-at-arms," Rap said.

Oh, Rap!

"I would rather have you as master-of-horse, I think."

"Sergeant-at-arms!" he insisted.

"Master-of-horse!"

Pause. "Both!" they said together, and laughed together.

Apparently Jalon was not going to start singing again just yet.

For a few minutes nothing more was said, and Inos realized she was sitting smiling like a dummy at Rap, and he was smiling just as stupidly back at her. Why should she be smiling at a time like this?

Go away? To horrible Kinvale? What good was it to be a princess if you had to do things like that? And creepy old Sagorn had hinted that she might start a war if she ever fell in love with a man . . .

"I saw a God today."

She had not meant to mention that, either. In fact she had promised her father that she would not.

But Rap's solemn gray eyes were waiting for her to explain. So she did. And she told him about Doctor Sagorn and the silk and everything that had happened. She was not sure why she did, but she felt better afterward. After all, Rap could be trusted not to blabber to others, and no one was more levelheaded than Rap.

He listened carefully and then ignored the God. "Who's this Doctor Sagorn? Is he up there?"

"No," she said. "He was tired by his journey. Not a party man."

"Are you sure he isn't a sorcerer?" He was being very serious.

"Oh, of course!" she said. The idea seemed so idiotic now— she had been a fool. "He's an old friend of my father's."

"Who has not seen him in many years?"

"Yes, but . . ." she said. This was not like Rap at all! "And even the God had said . . ." No, They had not said; it had been Mother Unonini who had said that Sagorn was not a sorcerer. She fell silent, worried by the look on Rap's face.

"Tell me again what he looks like."

"Tall, gray-haired. Big hooked nose. Deep clefts down here. Rather pale face. I expect he doesn't go out much—"

"What's wrong, Rap?" Lin had appeared to be toying with the

cast on his arm, but he had been listening nevertheless. Lin was purebred imp—short and dark and notably nosy. He had grown, also, Inos noted; but his voice was still treble. A late developer.

Rap was scowling. "Nobody like that came in today."

Inos's heart jumped a beat and then carried on as if nothing had happened.

"Don't be silly!" she said. "You must have missed him. You couldn't possibly have seen every single person who came through the gates."

Rap said nothing, just scowled at the floor.

"Tell her, Rap!" Lin said.

"Tell me what, Rap?"

Rap stayed silent.

Lin said hotly, "Thosolin was a pig to him, Inos. He put him on guard and made him stand there all day in the sun. In armor! Didn't even let him go for a pee. No lunch. He does that with beginners. Testing, he calls it, but he just likes to see them faint from too much standing."

She squeezed Rap's hand fiercely. "Is that true?"

He nodded. "But I didn't faint." He turned and looked hard at her. "And your Doctor Sagorn didn't come in the gate."

"Rap!" Inos squealed. That was absurd! "I expect he walked in beside a wagon. I went out that way."

"I saw you," Rap said, without smiling. "You walked right by me. But no wagons came in today."

"He was following me up the hill, he said. And it wasn't very long after that that I heard him talking to Father—less than an hour."

"He did not come in the gate," Rap said.

His big jaw looked as stubborn as the rock of Krasnegar itself.

Youth departs:
> There are gains for all our losses,
>> There are balms for all our pain,
> But when youth, the dream, departs,
> It takes something from our hearts,
>> And it never comes again.

Stoddart, And It Never Comes Again

❨ TWO ❩

Southward dreams

1

The wind is in the south, we shall have rain.

So Rap's mother would have said. Probably it had been true where she had come from, but it was not true in Krasnegar. The wind was from the south, off the land, so it was going to be another fine day. It was the north wind, from the sea, that brought rain, or snow more usually. His mother used to have many strange notions like that, Rap knew now, although he could not remember very much of her. He could hardly recall what she had looked like, but he could remember some of her strange notions.

One of those was to wash every morning. That was not always easy in Krasnegar. Sometimes in winter the ice was so thick that it had to be broken with an ax, but in summer it was pleasant to wash in the mornings, and at any time he liked the habit. It made him feel good, so he did it, although most of the other men laughed at him or called him crazy or said it was unhealthy. A few of them never seemed to wash at all, but he liked the tingle he got from water and the way it wiped the sleep off his skin. And he often thought of his mother as he did it.

That morning he had not even bothered to take a bucket of water indoors. He was standing bare-chested by the trough in the shadowy, dewy stableyard when old Hononin came marching out, pulling off his shirt. Rap felt uneasy. Being shirtless out in the fields was all right, but Krasnegarians were puritanical about dress, and he felt uncomfortable at being discovered in a state of seminudity. Seeing the old man like that was even worse, and

quite unprecedented. His skin hung loose on him and a patch of
gray hair in the middle of his chest looked as if it might have
fallen off the bald spot on his scalp. Rap wondered if he ought to
leave, but he merely moved respectfully to the far end of the
trough and said nothing.

The little old hostler seemed even more gnarled and grumpish
than usual and he did not speak, either, just thrust his whole head
into the trough. That explained matters.

He emerged spluttering and shivering, then started cupping
water with his hands and rinsing his armpits and shoulders.

"The big one's fixed," he growled without looking at Rap.
"Want you to take it out before the next tide."

Rap looked around to make sure there was no one behind him.
There wasn't. Well! The sunlight brightened. A wagon ride was
a much more enticing thought than more sentry duty, even if
Thosolin did not indulge himself in other petty testings. South to
the mainland, where there was more to keep a man occupied . . .
But Inos expected to go riding and she would not have many more
chances before she left. He felt a sudden, nasty pang and told
himself to grow up and be manly. There was some evil in every
good, as the priests said, and a man must obey orders.

He thought tides. It would need fast work to rig up four horses.
"Who's driving?"

"You."

"Me!"

"Deaf today?" Hononin splashed his face again.

Rap took a deep breath. Then another. He tried to speak calmly.
"Who's going to mother me?" Ollo, probably. He was around
and he had brought the big one in.

"No one."

Rap put his head in the water to give himself time to think. It
proved to be a stupid idea, like being kicked. It filled his ears and
ran up his nose and he came up feeling much worse than when
he went in. But then he had not been drinking last night. Maybe
it felt better than a hangover. He gasped and spat.

It had not helped his thinking much.

Why the change of plan? The second wagon also would be
fixed before evening.

One wagon by itself was unusual. If the driver ran into trouble
on the causeway on a rising tide, then he might need another
team—quickly! Or a good sorcerer, as the saying went. One man
alone was unusual, too. And a beginner? By himself? Rap had
held the reins often enough on the easy bits, but that was all. Why

him at all? Why not Jik or Ollo, who knew what they were doing? Why him by himself?

Perhaps Hononin had heard about the testing yesterday. He might be frightened that Rap had impressed Thosolin and would be taken away from the stables to be a man-at-arms. Or perhaps the hostler did not want one of his hands treated like that again.

Yet Rap had never been trusted with a wagon on his own before, or not far, at least. Certainly not for the whole trip. He shivered with tingles of excitement. He would be one of the drivers, then—perhaps only the junior driver, but more than a stableboy. He could eat at the drivers' table! Man-at-armsing could wait awhile—he was young yet.

"You can do it, can't you?"

"Yes," Rap said firmly, and tried to look matter-of-fact. He could handle it. "You'll see me down the hill, though?"

"Can you do it?"

"Yes."

"Well, then," Hononin said. "I trust you, even . . ." He began wiping his face with his shirt and walked away. The rest of the sentence remained unspoken or was lost in the shirt.

I trust you, even . . . Even what?

Snowball had loosened her right front shoe. Rap went and told Hononin; Hononin cursed and headed for the castle commons. Apparently the farrier was not there, because the man who arrived to deal with the matter was Rap's friend Kratharkran, the smith's apprentice, ostentatiously wiping crumbs from his mouth and pouting at being dragged from important business. Although his father was an imp, Krath was more jotunnish than most jotnar and had been sprouting like a snowdrift lately. Rap had spoken with him the previous evening, but in his leather workclothes he seemed to have grown more overnight.

Despite his height, he had an absurdly squeaky voice. He peered down at Rap with disbelieving blue eyes. "How long have they trusted you with a wagon?"

"As long as they've trusted you with a hammer!"

They grinned in mutual satisfaction, and Krath set to work. When he had fixed the shoe, he solemnly asked Rap's approval, calling him "driver."

Equally solemnly, Rap thanked him and said it was a nice piece of work, which it was. Krath agreed and wished him luck, then strode off to resume his meal.

All of which had been very businesslike and felt good, but by the time Rap had the team harnessed and ready, he knew he was going to be cutting the tide very close. He found the old man counting sacks in the feed room.

"I'm ready," he said, trying to look and sound relaxed.

"Go, then." Hononin did not even turn around.

"You don't want to look it over?" The old man never, ever, let a wagon go off down the hill without a personal inspection, not even if Ollo or Jik was driving. And surely he would want to look at Snowball's shoe?

He still did not turn, obviously mad about something. "Just go!" he barked. "Don't miss the tide!"

Rap shrugged and left. He had not even been given the inevitable warning to take care through the town. Most odd!

Hurrying back to the yard he met Fan on her way to feed the chickens. He asked her to tell Inos that he had to rush off.

Shivery with excitement, he climbed up to the bench. Before he could crack his whip, he heard a high-pitched shout behind him. Lin was running across the yard with a bag in his one good hand. He looked up hopefully at Rap. "Want some company?"

"Sure," Rap said. Lin was a terrible gossip, but bearable. No one could find anything useful for him to do since he broke his arm. "What's in the bag?"

Awkward with his cast, Lin clambered up to the bench. "Cheese, mostly, and a bit of leftover mutton. Rolls."

Rap's inside was too jumpy to want food yet, but he should have thought of it for later. "Enough for both of us?"

Lin nodded solemnly. "The old man said you'd had no time for breakfast."

Rap lowered his whip again. "What's into him today?" he demanded. "He's acting odd! Since when has he cared if I missed my breakfast? Why's he running me out of town like this?"

Lin had great ears for scandal. His dark eyes twinkled. "You were holding hands with Inos last night."

"So?" Rap asked uneasily. "What's that to do with him?"

"Nothing, Rap. Nothing."

"Out with it!"

Lin giggled. "Her daddy noticed."

I trust you, even if others don't.

Rap slammed the brake handle fiercely, cracked his whip much louder than he had meant to, and sent the wagon rumbling forward.

* * *

Between the castle gate and the harbor were fourteen hairpins. Going down was easier than coming up with a load, but it was still tricky. Rap had watched it done often enough, but he had never been allowed to handle brake and reins in the town. It was odd that Hononin had not known that.

The first two were easy, but he breathed a hearty sigh of relief when they had rounded the third, which was canted steeply. A wagon out of control could be almost as bad as a shipwreck. He was aware that Lin was watching him closely and hanging on very tight with his good hand. Fortunately it was still very early and there were almost no pedestrians around to mangle.

Four and five were not too bad. Six was a horror, with the wagon standing on its head above the team, wheels scratching on cobbles. Too close to the wall, the unloaded, too-light rig started to slither sideways. Rap discovered that he was soaked with sweat and needed two more hands than the Gods had given him.

The next one was the worst.

He *was* going to catch the tide. He was *not* going to make a mess of this. If he failed he would never forgive himself, and Hononin would never trust him again. And Inos would hear how he'd run over pedestrians or smashed up a wagon or even knocked in the side of a house and killed horses—it happened sometimes. *Trust yourself,* his mother had said. *If you don't, who will?*

He yelped, pulled the reins, tightened the brake, and the rig stopped. Silence. Lin looked at him curiously. "What's wrong?"

Rap wiped an arm across his streaming forehead. He was panting as if he'd run all the way up from sea to castle. "Listen!"

Lin listened and his eyes widened—clopping hooves and the rumble of iron on cobbles. Then it grew suddenly louder and another team appeared ahead of them, crawling round bend number seven, horses wide-eyed and steaming, hugging the buildings to have room to swing their load through the curve. Then came the wagon, with the driver shouting curses and a load of new peat dribbling water off the back. Nasty stuff, fresh peat. It was heavy and it could shift, but peat couldn't be stacked over the winter in that climate, so the first loads were always still wet.

"Boy, if we'd met that . . ." Lin said, and shivered. Sometimes it could take hours to straighten out a meeting on one of the bends, backing the load down the hill—jackknifing it, even.

The oncoming team straightened up and began to move faster. Iki was the driver. He grinned and then showed surprise when he saw only Rap and Lin. Struck dumb by the thrumming of wheels, he pointed back down the hill and held up one finger. Rap nodded and signaled zero and tried to look as if he did this all the time. Then Iki had gone and Rap reached for the brake again.

"Rap!" Lin said. "How did you know?"

Rap hesitated. How had he known? His own team had been making far too much noise for him to have heard. Could the horses have heard and sent him a signal with their ears, a signal that he had seen without knowing? Not likely at all. Could he have caught a reflection in a window? The sun was shining on the windows, so that was not very likely, either. But he had known. He had been quite certain that there was a wagon coming at that corner. That was rather an eerie feeling. How had he known?

"Just one of the things you youngsters have to learn," he said. "You go scout for me."

Lin made an obscene suggestion. He studied Rap with a very puzzled expression for a moment before jumping down and heading for the corner.

They were losing time. Lin was clumsy with only one good arm, and Rap had to stop dead each time he needed to come aboard, then stop again to let him off before the next hairpin. They finally met the second wagon between twelve and thirteen, and then it was a fast run down to the harbor.

There were few ships there that day. The sun blazed hard from quicksilver water, the gulls were bobbing and preening, and the air bore the tangy scent of fish and seaweed. A very slight breeze was ruffling the surface, but there were no waves. Anxiously Rap eyed the causeway ahead.

"Too late!" Lin sighed.

"Not much swell," Rap said stubbornly. "I'll risk it."

He stood up and thumped the reins on the horses' backs, urging them to a canter, wondering if Lin would demand to be let off. He would not be able to swim with that cast on his arm, but Lin probably did not know how to swim anyway. There was no point learning—a man died of cold in a few minutes in the Winter Ocean.

Then Rap remembered that he could not swim, either.

Lin did not speak. The wagon picked up speed, thundering along the top of the quay toward the long curve of the causeway that led to the distant shore. Most of it ran over land—low islands and rocks, dry land except in the big winter storms—but there were four low spots and the tide was already running over three of them. The wagon bounced and rolled and sent seabirds screaming; then there was water on both sides of the way and Big Damp was coming up ahead.

Rap took that one at full speed. It was straight and shallow and he did not sense any worry from the horses. Water shot out in silver sheets and salt spray splashed in his face and then they were safe on the other side, Duck Island. It had been deeper than he had expected, though.

Lin, still sitting and thus lower than Rap, had been soaked. He whistled and then laughed, a little nervously.

"I hope that new wheel stays on," he remarked.

Little Damp was still dry, except for a few spray pools, where wavelets were starting to splash over.

Now they were climbing over Big Island, and Rap slackened the pace so as not to heat the horses. But he stayed standing.

The rocks and shingle alongside the road gave way to the harsh, stubborn grasses that enjoyed the challenge of living so close to the sea, and for a moment the water was out of view. Then the wagon rolled roughly over the crest and started steeply down. Ahead lay the main stretch of causeway . . . except that most of it wasn't there.

Lin squealed, "Rap!" and straightened up.

Rap had not expected the gap to be quite so wide yet. Already the blue tide was pouring through, shiny and beautiful under the sunshine. He had never seen this, except from shore. The wind was strong now and cold, whipping the horses' manes, but the waves were very small. The raised roadway ran out into the sea ahead for a short way and then dipped under. Far away to the left, jutting out from Tallow Rocks, was the other end.

There were two bends in the road. Somewhere.

"Rap, you can't!"

"Get off, then!" Rap snapped, without slowing the wagon. He was not going to sit for six or seven hours on Big Island and be laughed at for the rest of his days. In truth, he was already too late to stop, for the roadbed was raised and there was no room to turn; this part would be underwater in an hour or so. Backing up would be tricky. Then hooves started splashing and he saw eight ears begin to flicker with alarm. He could calm horses by singing to them—not that he had any sort of a voice, but horses were not music critics. He started singing the first thing that came into his head.

I traveled land, I traveled sea . . .

"Rap!" Lin howled. "You'll go off the road! Stop, for the Gods' sake!"

"Shut up!" Rap said, and went back to singing. The horses' ears rose again as they listened to him. They kept splashing their big hooves and the wagon continued to roll steadily forward. A couple of swimming gulls watched intently, bobbing up and down as the waves flowed under them.

Maiden, maiden, maiden, oh . . .

Far off to his left, two fishing boats were setting sail from the quay, and Rap wondered what they thought of this strange horse-drawn vessel plying their harbor. There were a couple of big rocks coming up on his right, green with weed and purple with mussels, being lapped by the small waves, and he knew about how far those were from the road. A fraction more to the left . . .

There was just enough wind to make the water ruffled and impossible to see through, but he could tell where the edges were by the way the waves surged over them. It was safer than it looked, he told himself.

Lin was starting to whimper.

I gave her love, I gave her smiles,
I wooed with all my manly wiles . . .

The rocks floated past on the silvery water, and the swell was beginning to trouble the horses, coming well up their legs now, over the wagon axles. They were finding the wagon hard to pull. They were towing it.

The water was deeper. The waves no longer showed the edge very clearly.

"Turn, Rap!" Lin sobbed. "We're at the bend, Rap! We must be! We'll go off!" He rose to his feet, awkwardly holding the seatback with his one good arm. They were going to get wet boots in a minute. "Rap! Turn!"

Rap was not sure. Distances were deceptive when they were all covered with water and there were no landmarks at hand. He was thinking of the road itself, beneath the water, two stone walls filled in level with shingle and rocks, greeny blue, probably, with the strands of weed waving in the current. There would be shadows of ripples moving over, like cloud shadows moved over the summer hills. Fish? He had not expected so many fish, little ones . . .

"Maiden, maiden . . ."

"Shut up, Lin!

". . . maiden, oh."

Now he could imagine that watery blue roadway making its turn. He pulled on the reins and the wagon curved slowly round and apparently he had guessed right, because they continued their slow progress.

Lin had started to pray to some God Rap had never heard of. A new one, maybe.

One of the fishing boats was heading in their direction.

The wagon had almost stopped bumping. The tide was stronger here, in the middle, leaving a wake as it flowed by the horses, and they were getting very nervous now, no matter how hard he sang.

"Maiden, maiden . . .

"SNOWBALL!

". . . maiden . . ."

Too far to the right!

He eased the lead pair to the left and they carried on. But if the wagon began to float, then it would surely drag the horses off the road.

The second bend, a big, wide curve . . . the wagon seemed to lift, skew left, then settle, then lift. He blinked sweat from his eyes, squinting against the sun's glare, visualizing that underwater causeway, easing the horses around the bend.

Staying away from the edges.

Then Tallow Rocks were straight ahead and the current was behind them and the road was starting to rise. He flicked the reins for more speed and licked salty lips. He'd done it!

His hands were shaking slightly and his neck felt sore. He arched his back to ease it and then sat down.

"Sorry, Lin," he remarked, "what were you saying?"

Lin's eyes were big as oysters. "How did you do that?"

Come to think of it, how *had* he done that? Rap began to feel very shaky. It was almost as if he'd been able to see the road under the water. He'd known where it was, what it looked like, almost.

He had not seen it, but he'd felt as if he knew what it would look like if he could . . . or as if he could remember having seen it like that. Which he never had; no man ever had.

Just as, earlier, he'd known there was another wagon around the seventh bend?

He did not say anything, just shrugged.

"Another thing we youngsters have to learn, I suppose?"

Rap grinned at him. "Practice by yourself, though."

Lin used some very special obscenities. Where had he learned those?

"Lin?" Rap said. "Lin, please don't go and make a big story out of this?"

Lin just stared at him.

"Lin! You'll get me in trouble."

"I suppose you weren't getting me in trouble?" Lin yelled. He must have been more scared than Rap had realized.

"It was nothing much, Lin. I was standing up. I could see where the water was flowing over the edges."

"Oh . . . sure!"

But Lin reluctantly promised not to make a big story out of it.

They left the water and followed the lumpy track across Tallow Rocks, wheels spraying silver drops in the air. The last dip was deep, but very short. The wagon might float there, but it would not matter for there was no current and the road was not raised above the shingle. He had done it!

The king had ordered him off Krasnegar before the tide.

Gods save the king.

"You shave now?" Lin asked suddenly.

"Of course." Rap had shaved the previous night for the fourth time and included his chin for the first time. He would have to get a razor of his own soon. Lin had a faint dark haze on his upper lip. And he still had a very odd look in his eye. "Why?"

Lin shrugged and turned away, but after a moment, he said, "Funny thing, growing up. Isn't it?"

Yes it was, Rap agreed, and concentrated on the next water barrier. But once they were safely through that, he relaxed and began to enjoy himself, enjoy the feeling that now he was one of the drivers—if the old man would ever trust him again after that mad stunt he had just pulled.

"Yes," he said. "One moment you're feeling all manly and the next you find you're behaving like a kid again. It's like being two people." A fellow's body started making all these odd changes without as much as asking permission . . . what right did his face have to start growing hair without asking him?

Like being two people . . . and you knew only one of those people. Growing up was becoming a stranger to yourself again, just when you thought you'd got to know yourself. And part of growing up was wondering what sort of person you were going to be. How tall? How broad? Trustworthy? A strong man or a weakling? And what were you going to do with that man? Master-of-horse? Man-at-arms?

"Girls!" Lin muttered to himself.

Girls.

Inos.

Now they were rolling along the edge of the shingle, passing the lonely cluster of shore cottages with their racks of fish and nets and a ramshackle corral and a couple of haystacks starting to sprout. There were stacks of driftwood that the old women gathered and heaps of peat moss. Bonfires of kelp were sending up blue smoke. There were girls there and they waved. The men waved back. The long bent grass waved, also.

"We could eat here," Lin said thoughtfully.

"Later."

Beyond the shiny blue harbor lay Krasnegar, a towering triangle with a castle as a topknot. Yes, it did look like a piece of cheese. Perhaps Rap was hungry after all, but he'd said *later*, so later it would have to be. A yellow triangle. Where had the sorcerer found black stone for his castle?

Inos was in that castle.

He thought of horse rides and clam digging and surf fishing; of Inos running over the dunes, long legs, gold hair streaming in the wind, and her shrieks and giggles when he caught her; of Inos scrambling up the cliffs in the sunshine, daring him to come after her; of hawking and archery. He thought of her face, not bony like a jotunn's or round like an imp's. Just right. He thought of singsongs and winter firesides with singing and joking and his arm around her as they sought pictures in the embers.

It hurt, but it was for the best. There could never be anything between a princess and a stableboy, nor even a wagon driver. He supposed that it had crept up on them. He really had not noticed it until the previous day. They had been a bunch of kids together, a dozen or more of them. It had only been near the end of the last winter that he and Inos had started to drift together, and together start drifting to the edge of the bunch. And then he had gone off to the mainland when spring came.

She had kissed him good-bye, but even then he had not thought very much about it—not until they were apart. Then he had realized how he missed her smile and the comfortableness of having her near—and realized that she didn't kiss other men good-bye.

And lately he had started to dream about her. But she would go off to Kinvale and find some handsome noble to come back and be king after Holindarn died.

And he would have to find some other girl to kiss.

Trouble was, there weren't other girls like Inos.

"Can you remember much of your mother, Rap?"

Rap looked in surprise at Lin, who was still a little paler than usual. "Why?"

"Some of the women say she was a seer."

Rap frowned, trying to remember if his mother had ever admitted anything like that or done anything like that.

"So?" he said.

"Growing up," Lin said. "I just wondered . . . You've been doing some strange things today, Rap. You've never been able to do things like that before, have you?"

"Like what? I didn't do anything!"

Lin was unconvinced. "Could it be something that comes with growing up, like shaving?"

Rap would not talk about such things with chatterbox Lin. "Does that cast bother you?"

Lin looked down at his arm. "Yes, some. Why?"

"Because," Rap said, "if you start hinting that my mother needed to shave, then you're going to have two of them."

2

Summer, said the hardworking folk of Krasnegar, was the two weeks they were given to prepare for the other fifty. There was no small truth in that.

True, summer usually lasted longer than two weeks, but it came late and left soon, and it was marred by endless toil. Without the profit of their summer labors, the people would not survive the merciless winter that was sure to follow. A few hardy crops were sown and most years those could be harvested before the first snows, to augment the grain that must be imported by ship. The other years were destined to bring famine and sickness before summer came again. Peat must be cut and dried and carried to the town in load after load, to blunt the deadly teeth of frost during the long nights. Hay, also, standing high upon the wagons, crossed

the causeway at every tide so that the king's horses could eat until
spring came again and the cattle might give milk for the children
the next year. Fish must be caught and smoked, livestock slaughtered and their beef salted; seal meat or whale meat laid by, also,
if the boats were blessed with fortune. Vegetables and berries,
rushes and driftwood and furs . . . the scanty fruits of the hard
land were carefully gathered and jealously hoarded away.

Here and there in the bare hills stood forlorn hamlets and
clumps of cottages, where life was even harder than it was in the
town. But for most of the year there was nothing for men to do
on the land except survive, and survival was easier in the city—
or death less lonely—and so the cottagers also huddled in with
the townsfolk during the long winters, like badgers in their earth.
When the snows streamed off the hills in spring, they emerged
once more to their toil, and voices were heard again under the
sky.

Without careful management their efforts would never have
sufficed, and the leadership came from the king, or more directly
from his factor, a tall and rawboned jotunn named Foronod, who
was everywhere at all times and reputedly wore out three horses
a day. His water-blue eyes saw everything, and he commanded
everyone in sharp, laconic phrases like small knives, never wast-
ing a word or a moment, never sparing a soul, least of all himself.
In high summer he seemed to sleep even less than the sun. His
gangling figure could appear at any time anywhere in the kingdom, long legs hanging limp at the sides of his pony, silver hair
flashing a warning before him as he came into view. His memory
was as capacious as the palace storerooms. He knew to the inch
how much hay had been gathered, how much peat; he knew the
state of the herds and the times of the tides and he could call down
the wrath of the Gods or the Powers on anyone caught slacking
or sleeping except for reasons of total exhaustion. He knew the
strengths and abilities and weaknesses of every man and woman,
girl and boy in his whole great workforce.

Foronod noted that a wagon had been repaired and returned.
He doubtless noted as well that a certain stableboy had been pro-
moted to driver, and that fact, also, would have been stored away
until it might be needed. But the factor had many drivers and that
boy had talents that others did not.

By nightfall, Rap was back with the herds.

3

"Turn around, my dear," Aunt Kade said. "Charming! Yes, very nice! Definitely charming."

Inos did not feel charming, she felt wretched. There was a nasty hard feeling at the back of her throat and a dull coldness all over her. Her arms and legs were made of stone. Last night she had slept in her own bed for the last time. An hour ago she had eaten her last meal in the palace—not that she had been able to eat anything. Every time she did anything at all now it was for the last time.

And her slimy mood was not helped by the charmingness of her dress, either. She was wearing her precious golden dragon silk and she hated it. Somehow she blamed it for starting all this. Now it had been made up into a gown, and she thought it looked ludicrous, not charming. She could not believe that ladies in the Impire wore anything so outlandish. The minstrel must have been fantasizing when he sketched such absurdities as lace dangling over her hands and shoulders like small pillows. Trumpets indeed!

And if the dress was bad, the hat was unthinkable—a smaller trumpet, a high golden cone all frilly with more lace. She felt like a freak in it, a clown. Every small boy in Krasnegar was going to laugh himself hysterical at the sight of her as she rode down to the dock. The sailors would fall off the ship laughing. Probably the ladies in the Impire would kill themselves. Inos was sure they would all be wearing bonnets like any sane woman wore.

The only consolation was that Aunt Kade looked worse. Her conical hat stuck up like a chimney pot and her dumpy form could never be made to resemble a trumpet. A drum, maybe, or even a lute, but no trumpet. She had appropriated the apple-blossom silk, which was all wrong for her shape, although Inos had to admit that the colors matched her white hair and pink cheeks. Aunt Kade, moreover, was excited, bubbling with happiness, chattering like a flock of birds in joyful anticipation.

"Charming!" Aunt Kade repeated. "Of course we shall have to acquire many more gowns when we are established at Kinvale, but at least we shall not seem too rustic when we arrive. And the good citizens of Krasnegar shall see how ladies should dress these days. I do hope the coachman remembers to go slowly. Hold your head up, dear. You look like a unicorn when you bend forward. Oh, Inos, you will love Kinvale!" She clasped her pudgy hands. "I so look forward to showing it all to you—the dancing and the balls, the banquets and the *elegant* conversation! I was not much older than you when I first arrived, and I danced every night for months. The music! Fine cooking! Gentle countryside . . . you have no idea how green and prosperous the landscape is, compared to these harsh hills. And the handsome young men!'' She simpered and then sighed.

Inos had heard all that about a million times in the last week.

Now was the time of spring tides, she thought bitterly. There would have been good clam digging this morning.

''And Duke Angilki!'' Aunt Kade was in full gush now. ''He was a very striking young man in his . . . well, I mean, he is a most *civilized* person. His artistic taste is quite impeccable.''

He is also thirty-six years old and has two daughters. He has buried two wives already. Although Inos had never met her distant cousin, she was quite certain that he was utterly detestable. She was determined to hate him.

''He will be so happy to see us!'' Kade peered into the mirror and patted her blue-tinted hair where it emerged under the silver trumpet on her head.

''I always thought that one should not go visiting without an invitation,'' Inos said bleakly; but she had tried that argument before and it had not worked. It would hardly work now, not with a ship waiting.

''Don't be absurd!'' Kade said, but without heat. ''We shall be very welcome. We have a standing invitation, and there simply has not been time to write and wait for a reply. Winter is coming. You will love the sea voyage in summer, my dear, but it would not be possible later. Ah! The sea! I do so enjoy sailing!''

''Is Master Jalon ready?'' Jalon was an infuriatingly vague person, but he would at least make the voyage bearable.

Kade turned to her niece in surprise. ''Oh, did he not tell you? He has decided to go overland.''

''*Jalon* has?''

''Yes, dear.''

''He's crazy!'' Inos tried to imagine Jalon wandering through all those weeks of dangerous forest, and her mind went limp. There were goblins in the forest. Jalon?

''Oh, quite possibly.'' Kade shrugged. ''But your father seems to think he can manage; he gave him a horse. He left this morning. I know he went looking for you to say good-bye.''

''I expect he was distracted by a seagull, or something.''

''Yes, dear . . .'' Kade peered around at the trunks and baggage. ''Which ones shall we be using on the voyage?'' she inquired of Ula, her maid. Inos had not been allowed a maid. One would suffice for both of them, Aunt Kade said, because there would not be room for more on the ship; and they could hire girls with better training when they arrived at Kinvale.

Ula was short and dark, dull and almost sulky. She was showing no excitement at all, but then she probably did not understand where she was headed, or what a month or longer on a boat must be like. Nor, probably, did Inos herself, she realized. On the charts it seemed simple—west to the Claw Capes, south into Westerwater, and then east again to Pamdo Gulf—but that also seemed an unnecessarily prolonged and roundabout torture when the land route was so much shorter, and so much more interesting! Aunt Kade had sailed back and forth between Krasnegar and Kinvale several times before, during, and after, her marriage. Her enthusiasm about the prospect of doing it again was ominous. Anything Aunt Kade enjoyed would have to be a ghastly bore.

Why could they not have gone by land? If a nitwit like Jalon could manage it, then anyone could. That argument did not work, either. Aunt Kade did not like horses, nor coaches.

Boxes and bales and trunks . . . How could they possibly have amassed so much luggage? It smelled of soap and lavender.

Ula indicated two large trunks and Aunt Kade began to cross-examine her closely on their contents. Inos did not bother to listen. She gave herself a last angry inspection in the mirror and stuck out her tongue at her ludicrous reflection, then stalked to the door. She would take a final walk through the castle and say a private good-bye to some of her friends.

The past frantic week had been so dominated by dressmakers and seamstresses that she had hardly spoken to anyone else. Since that shattering day when the God had appeared, she had been lost in a blizzard of silks and satins, of lace and lingerie. She had not ridden Lightning once, not once! Rap had vanished the next morning. The sinister Doctor Sagorn had growled a brief farewell a few days after that and disappeared as mysteriously as he had come. And now Jalon had gone riding off into the hills. By Winterfest he would probably still be going round in circles somewhere, she thought—if he had not been tortured to death by a band of ferocious goblins.

Before Inos reached the door, however, it opened to admit Mother Unonini, stark in her black chaplain's robe, smiling with responsibilities and clutching a roll of papers. She stopped and regarded Inos with surprise, and then made a curtsy. On her absurdly short legs it was a clumsy move, but she had never done that before. Suddenly Inos did not feel quite so hostile to Mother Unonini. She was another familiar face not to be seen again for a whole interminable year.

Inos returned the curtsy.

"You look very charming, my dear," the chaplain said. "Turn around!"

Inos decided she must look like a weathervane, the way everyone kept wanting her to turn around. She turned around.

"It does look nice," Mother Unonini said warmly.

Inos felt temptation and succumbed. "It's only an old table-cloth."

Unonini frowned, then suddenly laughed and put her arms around Inos and hugged her . . . garlic today, not fish. "We shall miss you, my dear!" She turned hurriedly toward Aunt Kade and curtsied again.

"I brought the text of the prayer you will be reading, your Highness. I thought perhaps you would like to look it over beforehand; practice a little."

"Oh, dear!" At once Kade was flustered. "I do hate having to read prayers! I hope you wrote it big? The light is so poor in the chapel."

"I think so." The chaplain fussed with her papers. "Here's yours. You will be invoking the God of Travelers. Corporal Oopari will address the God of Storms. The ship's captain will be doing the God of Sailors, of course, and he will have his own text. His Majesty will invoke the God of Peace . . . his own choice," she added disapprovingly. "It does seem curious."

"Diplomacy, Mother," Aunt Kade said. "He is concerned with relationships between Krasnegar and the Impire and so on." She held her script at arm's length and blinked at it.

"Can the corporal read?" Inos asked. Oopari was a pleasant young man. He and his men would doubtless do a good job of protecting her on the voyage, but she could not imagine him reading.

"No," said Mother Unonini. "But he has been rehearsed. You, Inosolan, will speak to the God of Virginity, and—"

"No!"

Inos had surprised herself as much as the others. There was a shocked silence and the two ladies both colored.

"Inos!" Aunt Kade breathed. "Surely—"

"Oh, of course not!" said Inos, aghast. "That's not what I meant!" She was certain she had gone pinker than both of them now. She looked to the chaplain. "I want to speak to the God who appeared to us that day. They are obviously looking after me. Well, are interested . . .''

Mother Unonini compressed her lips. "Yes, I agree that it would be appropriate, but we don't know who They were. I should have asked, of course . . .''

There was an awkward pause.

"Well," Inos said brashly, "then we shall have to think of a name. They told me to try harder, so the God of Good Intentions, perhaps?''

Mother Unonini looked doubtful. "I'm not sure that there is one. I should have to look at the list. I mean, They all believe in good intentions—the good Gods, of course.''

"Religion is so difficult!" Aunt Kade remarked, studying her paper again. "Why can't Inos just ask for 'the God I saw here in the chapel'? They would know, wouldn't They? Is this word 'devote' or 'devout'?''

" 'Denote,' " Mother Unonini said. "Yes, that is a good idea. And she can ask for help in trying harder.''

"Trying what harder?" a voice asked, and there was the king in the doorway, looking very grand in a long scarlet robe trimmed with ermine. It brought with it a scent of the cedar chest in which it snoozed away the centuries. Inos smiled at him and turned around before he could ask her to.

"Very nice! Charming!" He was carrying his crown under his arm. He did not look very well. He had been suffering from indigestion a lot lately, and the whites of his eyes had a nasty yellow tinge to them. "Trying what harder?" he repeated.

Mother Unonini explained and he nodded gravely.

Aunt Kade was studying her brother with care. "Kondoral will be saying the prayer for the palace and those who live in it?''

"Of course!" The king chuckled quietly. "We couldn't teach him a new prayer at his age, and we can't stop him saying it.''

"And I," Mother Unonini proclaimed proudly, "will invoke the God of Wedlock to find a good husband for the princess.''

She flinched under a royal frown.

"I think perhaps that would not be in the best of taste, Mother. It sounds rather predatory. After all, the purpose of her visit to our ducal cousin is merely to experience courtly life and complete her education. Husbands can wait.''

Unonini looked flustered and Inos felt a sudden wash of relief. Both her father and Aunt Kade has insisted she was not being sent off to find a husband, merely to learn deportment, but she still secretly dreaded that matchmaking was behind it all. This sounded like a very firm denial, though, being made to the chaplain, and hence indirectly to the Gods. Perhaps her father was reassuring her. She must find time for another private talk before they sailed.

"Oh!" Mother Unonini was at a loss now. "Then which God should I speak to?"

"You could take the God of Virginity," Aunt Kade suggested.

King Holindarn of Krasnegar caught his daughter's eye momentarily, blinked a couple of times, then turned hastily away. Inos stared back blankly. Certainly that remark of Kade's could be taken in a very catty way . . . but surely he had not thought that Kade had meant it like that? Anyone else . . .

But not Kade.

The service in the dank, dark chapel was horrible. Silk was not warm enough. Inos shivered the whole time. No Gods appeared.

The drive down to the harbor was worse. She tried to smile and wave to the politely cheering crowds while rain splashed into the open carriage. Her stupid, stupid hat wanted to blow off all the time.

All this pomp had been Aunt Kade's idea. She had talked the king into it.

The farewell on the dock was the worst of all, saying formal good-byes to the notables of the town, being polite, smiling when she wanted to weep. None of her own friends was there. They were working in the castle, or out on the hills: Lin and Ido and Kel . . .

And a young man with gray eyes and a big jaw. A young man stupid enough to drive a wagon through the sea itself when he thought it was his duty.

She blinked. The rain must be getting in her eyes, even although Ula was standing behind her holding a leather umbrella.

Aunt Kade was being impossible, chatting with everyone, taking ages.

The captain badly needed a bath, but she was glad when he interrupted all those interminable polite farewells to announce that they were going to miss the tide if they did not go soon.

His ship was even dirtier than he was. And it was so tiny! Inos tried to hold her gown off the grubby deck and tried to hold her breath in that revolting—

"What is that stink?" she demanded in horror. A month of this?

"Bilge!" Aunt Kade positively chuckled. "Try not to get your gown dirty, dear."

"Dirty?" Inos protested. "We'll all be pig litter in five minutes."

"That's why we brought old clothes for the voyage, dear."

Then she was being helped—none too gently—down a ladder and into a black and vile hold. The cabin . . . *These* were her quarters? A closet! She pulled off the hat and she still could barely stand upright. "This is my cabin?" she wailed at her aunt. "I have to live for weeks in this?"

"Our cabin, dear. And we have two trunks coming, remember. Don't worry, you'll get used to it."

Then her father was there, also, and those could not be raindrops in her eyes now and she must not upset him by weeping.

"Safe voyage, my darling." His voice was gruff.

She tried to smile. "This is exciting."

He nodded. "It will seem strange, but Kade will take good care of you. I hope old Krasnegar does not seem too horribly small and bleak when you return."

She swallowed a lump in her throat and it was still there. She had things she wanted to ask him, things she should have asked long since and had not wanted to, and now there was no time.

"Father?" Then she blurted it out. "You truly don't want me to marry Angilki, do you?"

They were so cramped in that odious little cabin that he hardly had to move in order to put his arms around her and hug her tight. "No, of course not! I've told you—it might cause all kinds of trouble with Nordland if you did."

Relief! The Gods were not as cruel as she had feared.

"But keep your eyes open," he said.

"For what?" she asked, and the ermine collar was tickling her nose.

He laughed softly. "For some handsome young man of good family. Preferably a younger son, and certainly one with some brains and tact. One who pleases you. One who would be willing to live in this wild, far-off country at your side and help you keep Krasnegar out of the clutches of Nordland and Impire both."

She looked up and the laugh was not in his eyes. Even in the bad light she could see the yellow. He looked ill!

"Your Majesty!" the captain said urgently from outside the door.

"Tides do not wait for kings, my darling." Then he was gone.

She was horribly aware of Aunt Kade standing there and she wanted to be alone.

"We can go back up on deck and wave, if you want," Aunt Kade said quietly.

"There was so much I wanted to say!" Inos was very much afraid she was about to weep. "And I couldn't say it because there was no time. All those formalities!"

"That's why we have them, dear." Kade patted Inos's arm. "They keep us behaving like royalty."

4

Southward lay the hills. On the hills were the herds, and therefore the herders.

Herding was lonely work and usually dull. The cattle and the horses were the first to return to the land in the spring, as soon as the winter hills began to molt into brown. Rack-boned and staggering, they were driven across the causeway and then by gentle stages up to the higher slopes to join as many of the sheep as had survived. There they prospered mightily. They grew fat and sleek and produced young—and also began to develop independence of mind. In particular, they took to hankering after the hayfields and crops. Much of the herdsmen's time was spent in keeping the livestock away from the farming. Cattle especially were stubborn creatures that could not see why they must graze the scanty grass of the uplands when the valley bottoms were more lush. Undiscouraged, ever hopeful and bovinely stupid, they would spend all day circling around, looking for a new approach. A few stout fences would have made life simpler for the herders, but in Krasnegar the cost of lumber made fences unthinkable. So there were no fences and the dreary contest continued, day after day, year in and year out.

Not long after his return, Rap was ambling the high hills upon a gray gelding named Bluebottle while three large, tangle-haired dogs bounded along at his side. He was wearing beige leather trousers that he had purchased in the spring. Their many patched patches bespoke a long history of previous owners, but they were very comfortable, and he regretted that his ankles were already growing out of them. He carried a shirt tucked in his belt on one side and a lunch poke on the other. Earlier there had been rain to give the world a clean, fresh smell, but now the sun smiled from a cloudless sky, the wind played lazily in the grasses, and a curlew wailed its mournful cry.

Dull! Almost he could have hoped for a wolf or two coming after a lamb or a calf or a long-legged foal, but wolves normally found easier pickings in the summer among the coneys and mice. And even wolves were not very exciting—the dogs took care of them, upon request.

That day Rap was minding the horses. They were not quite so idiotic as the cattle, but their leader was a stallion named Firedragon who had a driving ambition to keep his herd as large as possible. He objected mightily to having its members conscripted and driven off to take their turns at wagon duty. He was willing to forget about the hay crops in the name of freedom, dreaming of some promised land to the south, beyond the reach of men, to which he was determined to lead his people. These tendencies, also, it was Rap's job to discourage, with the enthusiastic but muddled assistance of his dogs.

The morning had been spent, therefore, in maneuvers, with Firedragon seeking a breakout to the south and Rap persistently cutting him off. At noon the game was postponed for some serious grazing and rolling, and Rap was then able to start thinking about lunch. His viewpoint looked down upon the highway, and it was then he observed a solitary traveler in obvious trouble. Having confirmed that Firedragon had temporarily suspended his planned migration—being presently more interested in one of the mares— Rap pointed Bluebottle down the hill and went off to assist. On the way he donned his shirt to be respectable for human company.

The highway was a barely visible track through the hills, here following a winding valley marked at long intervals by the graves of some who had tried to follow the trail in winter, but otherwise barren of any other sign of mankind. Plodding upon it was the traveler. Some way ahead of him, a saddled horse methodically cropped the grass. Every few minutes it would wander a few steps and return to eating, but those few steps were deceptively effective. The gap between quarry and pursuer was growing no narrower. It certainly never would, unless the horse was unlucky enough to catch its reins in a bush. There were very few bushes.

The wayfarer noted Rap's approach and stopped to wait for him, undoubtedly with relief. He flinched as the dogs bounded up, but once they had sniffed him thoroughly and decided that he was not a wolf in minstrel's clothing, they wandered off to inspect the scents upon the road.

Jalon was garbed in the same brown cloak and oversize doublet he had worn when Rap challenged him at the palace gate, and the same baggy hose.

"You are a welcome sight, young man!"

Rap returned the smile, slid from Bluebottle's back, and eased his aching legs. "It is a long walk to Pondague, sir."

"You think perhaps I should ride the horse?"

"It would be quicker." Obviously Rap had not been recognized, which was not surprising, for men-at-arms did not wander the hills. He unhooked his grub bag from his belt. "I was about to eat, sir, if you would care to join me? Company with lunch would be a rare luxury."

Jalon glanced at his mount, which was pretending not to be watching but had noticed Bluebottle. "I was going to do the same about an hour ago," he confessed, "but I forgot that a horse is not a harp, which stays where you put it." Then his smile turned to alarm as he saw Bluebottle also wandering off in search of lusher nourishment. "Have you not just made the same mistake?"

Rap shook his head. "He'll come if I call."

Now Jalon had noticed more and was staring in disbelief. "No saddle? No bridle? *No reins?*"

His surprise was understandable. Rap squirmed slightly. "It was a wager, sir. Some of the other men bet me that I could not ride herd all day like that. Usually I use saddle and bit, sir. Except for very short journeys."

The minstrel studied him for a few moments in astonished silence. "You can control a horse without?"

"Most of them." Rap felt more embarrassed than flattered. It was no great trick, for the horses had known him all their lives.

Jalon frowned. "Then can you call mine over? I have some royal provisions that I shall be happy to share."

Rap nodded. "That one I can. Sunbeam! Come here!"

Sunbeam raised her head and sent him a look of studied insolence.

"Sunbeam!"

She twisted her ears a few times, bent for a few more mouthfuls to show that she was pleasing herself, and then began to drift toward the men, nibbling as she came.

"They don't like to be rushed," Rap explained, but he did not have to call again. In a few moments Sunbeam arrived and nuzzled his hand. He loosened the saddle girths and tied the reins back out of harm's way. Then he detached the saddlebag and laid it down. He patted Sunbeam's rump and she wandered off to join Bluebottle.

"Incredible!" Jalon said.

"Sir, the way you sing is incredible. You must allow me a knack for horses."

Rap thought he had made rather a cute little speech there—for a stableboy—but it had an astonishing effect on Jalon. He started. His mouth opened and closed a few times. He almost seemed to lose color.

"Impossible!" he muttered to himself. "But . . . you are the one the princess went to!"

Rap did not answer that, but his face must have reacted, for the minstrel at once said, "I beg pardon, lad. I mean no harm." He knelt to fumble with the saddlebag.

His supplies were certainly more appetizing than Rap's. One spot being as good as another, the two of them sat down where they were. Jalon laid out a fine lunch of cold pheasant and fresh rolls, wine and cheese and big green pickles, but obviously he had encountered some problem and his eyes kept coming back to Rap's face.

"Your name is Rap, right?" he asked suddenly. "And you were the guard, also!"

"Yes, sir. I usually work in the stables, not on the gate. You were correct when you said that I must be new to it. You were the first stranger I ever challenged." He had also been the last. Thosolin had bounced Rap straight back to his post and then bawled him out thoroughly, telling him to stand there and look pretty and challenge nothing short of a gang of armed pirates in future.

"I'm not surprised you work in the stables," Jalon remarked, licking fingers, "with that kind of ability. Tell me about yourself."

Rap shrugged. "There is nothing to tell, sir. My parents are dead. I work for the king. I hope to stay in his service and be a man-at-arms one day."

Jalon shook his head. "I can tell from your face that there is more to it than that. I do not mean to be personal, but your nose does not come from Krasnegar."

However it was meant, that remark seemed personal to Rap.

"You have brown hair," the minstrel added thoughtfully. "The Kransegarians are either lighter or darker than you. Even if they are of mixed parentage, they are one or the other. Gray eyes? So your parents came from far away. From Sysanasso, I would guess. You're a faun."

"My mother, sir. My father was a jotunn."

"Tell me!" Jalon chewed a pheasant leg and fixed his strangely dreamy blue eyes on Rap, although there was certainly interest in those eyes at the moment.

Rap did not see that it concerned the man, but Jalon was a friend of the king and was therefore due respect from a servant of the king.

"My father was a raider, sir, one of a crew that roamed far to the south. Slavers. They found good trade selling their captives. My mother was one, but my father took a fancy to her and kept her. Later he settled in Krasnegar and became a net maker."

Jalon nodded thoughtfully. "Was he captain of the ship?"

Rap shook his head. "Just a crewman, sir."

"And what happened to him?"

This was none of any minstrel's business! "He broke his neck." Rap did not hide his bitterness. Maybe it would shame the man out of his curiosity.

It did not. "How?"

"He fell off the dock one night. Perhaps he was trying to swim, but the harbor was frozen solid—he was drunk. I am not of noble birth, sir!"

Jalon ignored the sarcasm. "It wasn't him, then."

He sat in silence for a moment, pondering. Rap wondered what that last remark had meant.

"And your mother, this slave who was not sold with the others . . . was she the common property of the whole crew, or just of your father?"

"Sir!"

Jalon smiled apologetically and then stretched out to lean on one elbow while he ate. "Put up with me for a moment, friend Rap. I am not good at this sort of thing. I know others who would do it better. But I sense something here . . . I have traveled widely and I have heard tales and seen sights that you have not. I have been to Sysanasso. It is hot and jungly and unhealthy. Fauns have wide, rather flat noses, and brown skins—browner than yours, mostly—and they have very curly brown hair. So your hair is a compromise." He grinned. "Or an argument?"

Rap smiled as politely as he could manage and said nothing.

Far away, Firedragon whinnied. Sunbeam replied, and Rap swung around and shouted at her. She seemed to sigh regretfully and went back to grazing.

Jalon was amused. "Fauns have the reputation of being very good with animals."

"That explains me, then."

The minstrel nodded. "All the keepers in the imperor's zoological gardens are fauns. So are many hostlers."

Rap had talked about fauns with sailors, but he had never heard
that before. "What else can you tell me about them, sir?"

Jalon wiped the neck of the bottle and passed it. "They are sup-
posedly peaceful, but dangerous when roused. Wouldn't be human
otherwise, would they?" He smiled. "People like to label people.
Jotnar are always said to be big and warlike, but look at me!"

"Yes, sir." No one could have looked less warlike than this
slight, flaxen-haired minstrel.

He cleared his throat awkwardly. "That's understandable, too.
I don't usually mention it in this part of the world, but there's elf
blood in my family. When I'm near Ilrane, of course, I apologize
for my jotunn part. I can't pass as an elf, though."

Rap had never met an elf. He'd heard they had unusual eyes.

"So there's nothing wrong with a little outcross!" Jalon said
in an unusually firm tone.

"No, sir." Rap sipped sparingly at the wine. He didn't care
for wine. If there was nothing wrong with being a halfbreed, then
why was the minstrel going on and on about it? Perhaps he thought
he was putting Rap at ease by mentioning his own elvish descent.

"Fauns?" Jalon muttered. "Oh, yes . . . they have very hairy
legs." He glanced at Rap's protruding ankles and then grinned at
his angry flush. He began musing again, almost to himself.
"Krasnegar is a hard place to live, but no worse than Sysanosso,
I suspect. How old were you when your father died?"

"About five, sir."

"You don't need to 'sir' me all the time, Rap. I'm only a
minstrel. Punch me on the jaw if you want to. What happened to
your mother then?"

Rap scowled at the question. He twisted around to look at the
horses. Firedragon was grazing, and apparently play had not resumed yet. "The king took her into his household, and she was
found to be a fine lace maker. I suppose she had been making the
nets my father sold. She died of fever about five years later."

Jalon rolled back on his side and stared at the sky. "No brothers
or sisters?"

Rap shook his head, then said, "No."

The minstrel pondered for a few minutes. "What sort of a
person was your mother?"

"Loving!"

"I'm sure she was, Rap. You won't tell me any more?"

"Sir, there is nothing to tell!" Rap was very close to losing his temper, and that awareness would only make him lose it faster. Jotnar had notorious tempers, and he was half jotunn, so he tried never to let himself get really mad about anything.

Jalon sighed. "You did not ask how I knew your name."

No, he hadn't. "How did you?"

"Why, yesterday it was being shouted all over the palace. There was a terrible row in the royal family. A week or so ago some idiot wagon driver apparently crossed the causeway at high tide—which is impossible, of course. It seems that the king had ordered him to leave the island and he had taken the orders a little too strictly for his own safety."

Rap's heart sank. He had hoped that his foolhardy escapade might have escaped notice, but of course Lin was a blabbermouth, and the crew of the fishing boat must have seen.

"It wasn't high tide!"

Jalon ignored the interruption. "The king blamed the hostler, who delayed the man by requiring him to take a wagon, instead of just putting him on a horse as the king had expected. The hostler probably meant no harm, but the result was that the man did expose himself to . . . certain dangers. The word 'miracle' was being tossed back and forth."

Rap groaned.

"It was only yesterday that Princess Inosolan got wind of the affair. She scolded her father royally. In fact, I have seldom heard such a tantrum."

"Oh, Gods!" Rap muttered. Why in the world would Inos have done such a thing? Then he said, *"Gods!"* much louder, and jumped to his feet.

Firedragon was moving his herd toward the top of the hill, heading west. It would be a long chase to cut him off now . . . unless he was still within earshot? The wind was behind Rap, so it was worth a try. He cupped his hands and bellowed. For a moment nothing seemed to happen, but he kept calling, choosing the horses that responded best. He was just about to give up, leap on Bluebottle, and give chase—knowing that the pursuit might last for days—when the herd faltered. Two mares split away and headed for Rap. Outraged, Firedragon rushed after them to restore discipline.

Now Rap switched his attention to the other side of the herd. Already they were almost too far off to recognize, but he thought he could identify some and he began calling them. By the time Firedragon had recovered the first pair, three more and a foal had departed.

For a little while the battle continued, the stallion roaring with fury as he pounded back and forth across the hillside, trying to bully his charges back on the right track, Rap calling them away again as soon as his tail was turned. Then the stallion swung to stare at this puny and audacious rival and even at that distance he could be seen to be dancing with rage, head down, teeth bared, tail arched. He bellowed a challenge and began a long, long charge.

Rap began to worry. He would rather face an angry bull than a mad stallion. At first he let the horse come, for the confused herd had ended its milling and begun to follow, but when Firedragon had covered about half the distance and was showing no signs of second thoughts, Rap decided that he had better try to do something. If he couldn't, then herdman and minstrel would have to beat a very fast retreat.

"Firedragon!" he roared. "Cut that out! Go back! Back!"

Would it work? The stallion was very responsive to Rap, usually. He held his breath. Then the attack faltered. Firedragon veered away, bouncing and cavorting in frustrated fury. In a few minutes he seemed to calm down, then went cantering back to his herd. And apparently he had given up his attempt to sneak away over the hill. The horses seethed around briefly, then slowly settled down to eating once more. Bluebottle and Sunbeam had been watching with interest. Deciding that the show was over, they, too, went back to cropping the summer grass.

Rap rubbed his neck, for his throat felt raw. He sat down again to find Jalon staring glassily, his lunch forgotten.

"Thirsty work," Rap said, uneasy at that wide blue gaze. "May I have another sip of that wine, sir?"

"Have the whole bottle!" Jalon continued to gape for a while, then added, "Why do you bother shouting? You didn't believe they could hear you at that distance, surely?"

Rap considered that question while he drank. Not understanding it, he decided to ignore it. "Thank you." He put down the bottle and resumed his lunch.

After a long silence the minstrel spoke, but in a whisper, although the hills were empty of people as far as eye could see. "Master Rap, would you consider sharing?"

"Sharing what, sir?"

Jalon looked surprised. "Your secret. What lets you do that . . . and cross the causeway when apparently no one else would even have tried. My singing is of the same essence."

Rap wondered if soft brains were a necessary qualification for minstreling. He could see no connection between singing and causeway crossing, and very little resemblance to horse calling. This Jalon was a fine bard, but any man who let his horse wander away from him unintentionally in this country had clearly lost a few nails somewhere. Perhaps it went even farther than that. He might be a total lunatic.

"I call the horses' names, sir. They all know me and they trust me. I admit I wasn't sure about calming the stallion . . . he does sort of like me, I think. The causeway story must have been exaggerated. The tide was coming in, but there was no danger."

"So you can call mares away from a stallion?" Jalon nodded ironically. "Of course. You can journey where others can not. Kings are reprimanded for their treatment of you? Princesses want you to hold their hands . . ." He suddenly seemed depressed. "Is there anything I could ever possibly offer that would persuade you to share with me? I have wider resources than are presently apparent."

"Sir?" Rap could make no sense of the conversation at all.

The minstrel shrugged. "Of course not! And why would you trust me? Would you be so kind as to call Sunbeam? I have far to go before dark."

Rap hoped the man would not try to ride his horse until then. He would lame her for certain. But that was not Rap's affair. He called Sunbeam over and adjusted her girths again and replaced the saddlebag. "I thank you for a fine lunch, minstrel," he said. "May the Gods go with you."

Jalon was still looking at him oddly. "Darad!" he said.

"Sir?"

"Darad," repeated the minstrel. "There is a man called Darad. Remember the name. He is very dangerous and he will learn of you."

"Thank you for the warning, sir," Rap said politely.

Not just nails—the man was missing a few shoes, as well.

5

All things include
Both the Evil and the Good.

Inos repeated that sacred text a hundred times, but she still could not find the good in seasickness. It had to be totally evil. She desperately wanted to die.

The cabin was cramped and loathsome. It was smelly and dirty and dark. It went up. It went down. It rolled and it pitched.

For two days she lay and suffered abominably. Aunt Kade was infuriatingly immune to seasickness, and that fact helped Inos no more than her aunt's twittering attempts to cheer her up.

In the beginning was nothing. She sought help in religion, there being no earthly help in sight except hopefully a shipwreck and fast drowning. *The Good parted from the Evil and the Evil parted from the Good.* Just as she had so promptly parted from the mouthful of soup she had been persuaded to try. *The world is created in Their eternal conflict.* Certainly there was an eternal conflict going on inside Inos.

On the third day she began to feel a little better.

At times.

But not for long.

The slightest change in the motion of the ship and she was back in total evil again.

But there must be some trace of the Good in seasickness, for the sacred words said so. Perhaps it was humility. Fat, twittery Aunt Kade was a far better sailor than she was. Meditate on that.

The God had said there were hard times in store, but she had never dreamed that times could be so hard as these. *Only we have free will, only humankind can choose the Good and shun the Evil.* What choice had she ever made that had landed her in this?

Only we, by finding the greater good, can increase the total good and decrease the total evil in the world.

Start by abolishing seasickness.

Slowly life began to seem a possible option again. Slowly Inos started contemplating her future in Kinvale. Her father had gone there once, as a young man. He had promised that she would enjoy herself—year-round riding there, he had said, and good parties. Even Jalon had spoken well of life in the Impire, although he did not know Kinvale itself. Perhaps, she thought in her better moments, perhaps it might be bearable. It was only for a year, after all.

On the fourth morning, she awoke feeling ravenous. Aunt Kade was not in her bunk. Throwing on thick wool sweater and slacks, Inos prepared to meet the world again. Now she could accept that there was indeed a small good in seasickness—it felt so marvelous when it stopped. Greatly comforted that her religion had not been discredited, she headed for the deck.

She was horrified. The world was a heaving grayness. There

was no sky, no land, only hilly green-gray water dying away into haze in all directions. The ship had shrunk. It seemed so pathetically tiny and cramped, a little wooden box under a cage of ropes and dirty canvas, riding up and down over those gray hills. The wind was icy and cruel and tasted of salt . . . not even a seagull.

Two sailors stood talking at the back of the ship, and there was no one else in sight. She felt a stupid wave of panic rising and suppressed it. The rest of them must be around somewhere, and Aunt Kade, also. She started toward the two sailors, discovering that walking on a rocking ship was not as easy as she had expected. The wind whipped her hair and made her eyes water, and she finally reeled up to them, grabbed the rail they were leaning on, and blinked tears away.

The tall one was holding the wheel and regarding her with interest displayed on those parts of a craggy, weatherbeaten face not totally concealed by silver-streaked whiskers. The other was extremely short, squat, and unbelievable in pants and a huge fur jacket . . . bareheaded, filmy white hair mussed beyond recognition by the wind, cheeks burning like bright red apples and blue eyes shiny with happiness.

"Inos, my dear! I am so glad to see you on your feet again."

Inos, looking around in horror at the featureless desert of water, was beyond speech.

"You will need a jacket, dear," her aunt said. "The wind is quite chilly."

Chilly? It was an ax.

Kade beamed encouragingly. "We are making excellent time—North Claw in four days, the master predicts. The air will be warmer when we reach Westerwater."

Inos' teeth began to chatter. "I think I need some breakfast." She hugged her arms around herself. "Perhaps they would have something down in the kitchen?"

"Galley, dear. Yes. Of course you must be starved. Let us go and see, then."

"No need for you to come," Inos said, "if you are enjoying yourself."

"Of course I must come."

"Of course?"

Aunt Kade assumed her most prim expression. "This is not Krasnegar any more, Inosolan. I am your chaperone and I must look after you."

A terrible suspicion washed over Inos's mind. "You mean that you don't let me out of your sight from now on?"

''That is correct, dear. Now let us see if we can find you some breakfast.''

The ship sailed on, but Inos' heart sank . . . all the way to the bottom of the Winter Ocean.

There were worse things in store than seasickness.

Southward dreams:

> The hills look over on the South,
> And Southward dreams the sea;
> And with the sea-breeze hand in hand,
> — Came innocence and she.

Francis Thompson, Daisy

❮ THREE ❯

Clear call

1

"Why doesn't something *happen*?" Inos demanded in an urgent whisper.

"Why should anything happen?" Aunt Kade replied.

Inos ground her teeth quietly, glaring hatred at her embroidery. They were sitting in the willow grove at Kinvale with many other ladies of quality, all sewing or crocheting or merely chatting in the heavy sunshine. It was afternoon in late summer and nothing was happening. Nothing, it seemed, *ever* happened at Kinvale. Nothing was supposed to—that was the whole idea.

"Besides," her aunt continued placidly, "something did happen last night. You lost a brooch."

That was a devastating and unwelcome truth, and an unusually pointed reproof from Aunt Kade. Inos was being as difficult as possible, but her pleasure at having punctured her aunt's maddeningly constant good humor was spoiled in this instance by the reminder of her own stupidity. Losing a dearly loved heirloom did not compare with painting one tooth black and smiling excessively at dinner.

Embroidery was too intricate for Aunt Kade's eyes. She was knitting some useless garment that would undoubtedly be given away to a servant as soon as it was finished. The process was important, the result was not. Inos was making a horrible mess of stitching a nosegay pattern on the corner of a linen kerchief and suffering acute agonies of frustration and boredom. She had

73

been at Kinvale for a month. She would be there for nine or ten more months yet and *nothing ever happened*.

Except a few things she had made happen, of course.

She could concede that Kinvale was beautiful, a very great estate set in rolling hills, lush and rich as she had never imagined a land could be. It lay northeast of Pamdo Gulf, near the great port of Shaldokan—of which she had seen nothing at all—but far enough from the sea that it had never been pillaged by jotunn raiders, even during the worst periods of disorder in the past when the Impire had been weak. She had seen little of the smaller manors and hamlets nearby, but enough to know that they were old and settled and dull. The nearby town of Kinford she had visited briefly, and it was also old, prosperous, and apparently dull. The huge, sprawling ducal estate was old, luxurious, and driving her crazy.

The willow grove, where she was presently enduring a particularly acute boredom, was picturesque to a fault, flanking a lake that was itself resplendent with water lilies and graceful swans, set about with sculptures and little marble pavilions. Beyond the lake lay the park, where myriad servants tidied up the droppings of small deer and carved the boxwood trees into fantastic and amusing shapes. For someone who had seen exactly six trees in her life, Inos had tired of trees surprisingly quickly—they did not *do* anything. She had been impressed by the green hills, the farms, and the vineyards, but she had glimpsed all those only at a distance. Young ladies of quality were not encouraged to go mucking around in farmyards, and she had been swiftly intercepted on her one attempt to go exploring in that direction.

She passed her mornings now in lessons—dancing, elocution, and lute playing. In the afternoons she would sit and sew and talk with Aunt Kade and other matrons. In the evenings there was dancing or listening to music and then bedtime. And that was all. She had been allowed to go riding a few times with other wellborn maidens, but their path had been restricted to a cinder circle through the park, the horses had been ancient hacks, and their riders no more interesting—well-educated virgins whose brains had been wrapped up in embroidery and tucked away in some safe drawer at birth. Inos was permitted to read books, provided she did not overdo it. She might stroll on the terrace, so long as she did not leave Aunt Kade's sight or talk to strange men. She could also sit and grind her teeth at needlework and wonder what would happen if one evening she were to tear off all her clothes and turn cartwheels across the ballroom floor.

Amid the splendor and wealth she was miserably homesick for barren, shabby old Krasnegar. Amid nobility and personages of the highest breeding, she longed for the company of Father and Lin and Ido. Even dull old Rap would do.

She was not supposed to be out of Aunt Kade's sight unless some other old . . . gentlewoman . . . had been designated her keeper for a short while. It was humiliating! Did they think she was some sort of wanton? That she could not be trusted? Of course she was trusted, Aunt Kade would explain patiently. It was appearances that mattered. Climbing out casements, sliding down banisters . . .

Materializing in dignified silence, a young footman offered a tray of sweetmeats to Aunt Kade, who declined, and then to Inos.

"Thanks, Urni." She pointed to one of the yummy little cakes. "That one! Did Alopa bake these?"

The tray wobbled dangerously. Scarlet flowed out of his high, tight collar, rising all the way to his powdered hair. "M-m-ma'am?"

"Just wondering." Inos flashed him a benign but triumphant smile. "I thought maybe it was her baking that you were after in the little pantry two nights ago?"

Urni almost dropped her chosen cake from his tongs. The tray swayed again in his other hand, and he swallowed hard. "No, ma'am. I mean . . . No, ma'am."

She chuckled quietly and said no more, letting him beat a speedy retreat. Off duty, he was rather fun, was young Urni—or so the chambermaids reported.

As Inos was about to pop the first morsel of cake in her mouth, Aunt Kade sighed heavily. "You really should not speak to the domestics like that, dear."

"Oh?" Inos laid down her fork in case she was tempted to throw it. "It upsets you that all these old crones will see me failing to live up to their mummified standards of nose-in-the-air snootiness? You would prefer me to behave like a marble statue? Exactly what harm is there in treating a man like a human being?"

Kade finished the row and turned the knitting. "None," she told it. "Treat him like a human being by all means."

"I don't believe I understand that remark."

"You were not treating him like a human being. You were treating him like a tethered bear."

"I . . ." Inos fell silent, mouth open.

"They can't fight back, my dear. They, at least, would certainly prefer marble statues.'' Kade's eyes had never strayed from her knitting, but now she added, ''And here comes the duke.''

Inos looked up. Duke Angilki had emerged onto the terrace with a companion. That, Inos decided bitterly, probably qualified as an excitement. She had expected that a man who had buried two wives might be a monster, but she was now certain that they had died of boredom. Angilki was quite the dullest man she had ever met. He was tall and portly, with a flabby red face and a pendulous lower lip—the face of an overgrown, slow-witted child. He was utterly dominated by his fearsome mother, the dowager duchess, and his only interest seemed to be interior decorating.

He was extending Kinvale in all directions, but the architecture was incidental. Neither the building activity nor the final purpose mattered. It was style that counted, and the process itself. So the duke spent his days with artists and artisans in blissful contemplation of plans, sketches, and swatches. His artistic taste was impeccable, his results impressive. Kinvale was beautiful. But what good was it, Inos would demand of her aunt when they were alone, if it doesn't *do* anything?

At least she no longer need worry that Duke Angilki would force her to marry him so that he might become king of Krasnegar. Krasnegar would appeal to Angilki much less even than Kinvale appealed to Inos, and the duke himself had no visible interest in women. Had she been a roll of chintz, now, or a sample of wallpaper, then she might have caught his eye and brought a flush to his cheek.

A conspiratorial twitter from the ladies announced that the duke and his friend were advancing toward them over the lawn . . . probably coming to ask his mother if he could take a bath, Inos decided, but a quick glance around showed that the dowager duchess was not present. And the companion was a man. That was unusual. Houseguests came and went by the dozen at Kinvale—friends and relatives to the farthest degree—and they were almost all female.

Where were all the men? Possibly some were off soldiering somewhere, and perhaps others had soldiered at some time in the past and failed to recover from the experience. The few men who did show up at the banquets and balls were almost all much too old to be of interest and all basically dull, as well. Their profession seemed to be the elegant doing of nothing, their only recreation the slaughtering of birds or animals. A few of them had admitted to having useful occupations like overseeing estates. One or two had even let slip the fact that they engaged in trade. There had been travelers pass through, and soldiers and Imperial officials and priests. But were there no young, interesting men in the Impire?

Lately Inos had begun to perceive Kinvale as a zoo, a game farm, where the womenfolk were confined while the men stayed away and ran the world. This insight depressed her greatly. Already the ship road to Krasnegar would be closing down for winter and she had all those dreary months to look forward to before it opened again.

Now Duke Angilki had reached the edge of the grove of ladies and was making introductions. He was beautifully dressed, of course, his bulging doublet gleaming white and his hose bright scarlet. His cloak was a rich bottle green with a narrow ermine trim—probably much too hot for this time of year, Inos thought, but the heavy material would disguise his stoutness better than a lighter fabric. He had an excellent tailor. He moved on to the next small cluster of ladies, and she caught her first good look at his companion.

Mmm! Not bad at all!

The stranger was a comparatively young man, a rarity. Inos had met almost no men of her own age at Kinvale. Apparently males still in their acne and Adam's apple metamorphosis were kept out of the sight of genteel company, and now she thought she might even settle for early twenties. This one would do for a start. He was as tall as the duke, dark and slim, and his deep-blue doublet and white hose outshone even the duke's tailoring. He was wearing no cloak, which was daring of him—it emphasized his youth. He moved with grace. Yes! A little older than she would normally have preferred, but . . . not . . . bad . . . at . . . all.

"Don't stare, dear," Aunt Kade muttered, holding her knitting at arm's length and screwing up her eyes. "They're coming as fast as they can."

"What! I mean, beg pardon?"

"It would appear that they're heading toward us," Aunt Kade told her needles. "But of course they must pay their respects to the others first."

"That's what they call a young man, isn't it? I think we used to have some of those around Krasnegar."

"Sarcasm is not ladylike," Aunt Kade said mildly. "Try not to drool over him too much. He was at the ball last night."

"I didn't see him!"

"He noticed you." Aunt Kade's smile registered satisfaction. Angrily Inos pretended to concentrate on her embroidery.

Mention of the previous night reminded her yet again of the trag-
edy—she had lost her mother's ruby brooch. She could not forgive
herself for being so careless. She was certain that it had still been
there when she retired to bed and that she had unpinned it and
laid it on her dressing table. Yet that was obviously impossible,
because there had been no brooch there in the morning. Of course
the door of their suite had been bolted—Aunt Kade always insisted
on that. They had even considered burglary as an explanation, but
had been forced to discard it. A team of circus cats could not have
reached their windows. Of all the heirlooms that her father had
given her, her mother's ruby brooch had been the most precious
to her, and now she had been so unthinkably careless and stupid
and ungrateful and—

The duke! She bounced up hurriedly from her chair.

"Sir Andor," Duke Angilki explained. "Princess Kadolan of
Krasnegar."

The young man bowed over Aunt Kade's hand. Yes, very nice
indeed! He was an imp, of course—and how Inos longed now for
the sight of a tall, blond jotunn just to break the monotony—but
he was not short and he was not swarthy. His hair was black, but
his skin showed a gleaming, healthy tan, a smooth complexion
with just a hint of blue chin to save the perfectly regular features
from any hint of femininity. Handsome! Then he straightened and
turned to her and she saw smiling dark eyes and perfect white
teeth. Handsome did not do justice.

"And Princess Inosolan," said her portly host, "may I present
to your Highness my friend Sir Andor? Sir Andor, this is Princess
Kadolan's niece."

"I shall always remember this day," Sir Andor said, "when
all my standards of beauty and grace had to be discarded as inadequate, when all other ladies faded in my sight, when my highest dreams and aspirations were suddenly made worthless by my
first glimpse of feminine perfection in the divine form of the Princess Inosolan."

He stooped to touch his lips to her hand. Inos was still trying
to think of some equally outrageous reply when their eyes met
again and she saw that he was laughing. She was so surprised that
she did not hear what she said, but apparently it was satisfactory.

"You have just arrived at Kinvale then, Sir Andor?" Aunt Kade
inquired.

"Two days ago, ma'am."

"I have been trying to persuade him to spend some time with
us," the duke huffed, "but he insists that he must rush off."

"A month at the most!" Andor said. "I have most urgent responsibilities to call me away, although I know already that my heart will never leave. Even the presence of such celestial beauty is insufficient . . ."

Inos resumed her seat as the flowery phrases were tossed around, the duke and Aunt Kade apparently serious, while she was quite certain this young Andor was treating it all as ludicrous nonsense and offering to share the joke with her. It was a wonderful surprise to discover that she was not the only sane person in the world. Then the duke made some excuses and moved off, pausing to dispense more greetings. A miasma of disapproval arose from the company in general—obviously the sensational young Andor had been brought out especially to meet Inos, and that was being regarded as sneaky favoritism.

Aunt Kade took the hint and asked him if he would care to sit. He did so, studying her with an expression of wonder.

"Of course that is your portrait in the gallery," he said. "I noticed it at once. It quite puts all the other so-called beauties to shame, and yet it does not do you justice."

Aunt Kade preened. "It was painted many years ago."

"But a silver setting enhances the finest gems, and nothing else has changed. Your coloring . . ."

Inos had heard some outrageous flattery sessions in the previous month, but nothing that could have touched the performance that followed. With quick, deft strokes, like a skilled fishwife filleting, Andor reduced Aunt Kade to simpering blushes. Compliments so excessive could not possibly be intended seriously, yet that did not stop them being effective in the hands of an expert.

Then he turned his attention to Inos. She wondered what heights of hypocrisy he would scale now, but the cynical twinkle was back in his eye again, and he surprised her once more. "But you, ma'am . . . on reconsideration, I find your appearance most displeasing."

Inos had been preparing a small smile of ladylike modesty; taken unaware, she stammered. Aunt Kade opened her mouth to protest, then closed it.

"To come so close to perfection," Andor said, putting his head on one side and pretending to study her, "and then fail to achieve it is a sin against all art. It offends one's sensibilities. A much lesser beauty that confined itself within its own limitations would not impart this aura of failure, of excessive ambition unrealized." He leaned back to consider her further. "What is required, I think

. . . yes . . . what is really needed . . . is a touch of fire. Then
we should see divinity!''

He held out a hand with Inos' brooch on the palm.

Speechless with astonishment, Inos examined the brooch. Aunt
Kade expressed pleasure and demanded an explanation.

''A most curious tale!'' Andor said solemnly. ''Just after dawn
this morning I was putting a hunter over a few jumps, over on the
far side of the park there, when I saw a bird fly overhead with
something shiny . . .''

Had he told it with a straight face, Inos thought, she would
certainly have believed him, but every time Aunt Kade's eyes left
his face he gleamed a secret grin at Inos and she found she was
sliding closer and closer to an attack of giggles.

''I believe you can even see the very tree in which the jackdaws
have their nest,'' he said, rising and peering over the lake. ''Yes,
there.'' He pointed and of course Inos had to rise to see where
he was pointing. ''No, farther to the left . . .'' He led her around
one of the willows.

In a few moments, still trying to see the tree with the jackdaws'
nest, Inos found that she was out of earshot of Aunt Kade.

Still pointing, Andor said, ''Doesn't this place make you want
to puke?''

''Oh, yes!'' Inos peered along his arm for the benefit of the
many disapproving watchers and said, ''Raving mad. Is there
really a jackdaw tree?''

''Gods, no! I found your brooch on the rug last night. The pin
was loose. I had it repaired. Do you like riding?'' He was looking
back and forth from her to the horizon and she was nodding as if
he were pointing out landmarks, leading her eye to the mythical
jackdaws. ''Fishing? Boating? Archery? Right!''

He led her back to her chair and gave Aunt Kade a disapproving
frown. ''Your niece tells me she has not yet seen the water caves!''

What water caves?

''Well, we have only recently arrived at Kinvale,'' Aunt Kade
protested.

''But this is the best time of year to see them, when the river
is low. Don't you agree?''

He skillfully cornered Aunt Kade into conceding that she had
visited the water caves in her youth. Thus she could hardly object
when Andor announced that he would organize a party of some
young ladies and gentlemen to view the water caves. He went on
to discuss the annual salmon run, when the rivers were red from
bank to bank with fish as large as sheep, to grape tramping in the

vineyards, to the giant sequoias, to treasure hunts, to royal tennis, to hayrides and waterfalls and boating expeditions with picnic lunches, to bathing in the natural hot springs, to falconry and fly fishing, to a dozen other entrancing possibilities. There was no suggestion that any of these ventures would involve less than a dozen people and he tossed out the names of very respectable companions, evidently being on terms of friendship with almost everyone at Kinvale and most of the surrounding countryside as well. It was a staggering presentation and it left Inos' head whirling.

"Of course my niece is kept very busy with her music lessons."

"But my time here is so short!" Andor lamented. "Surely a week or two's delay in her musical career would not prejudice her future irreparably? The water caves will take a couple of days' preparation, but tomorrow . . ."

Eventually some of the other ladies decided that he had been monopolized too long, and he was delicately removed to make conversation elsewhere. Inos sighed deeply and smiled down at her neglected embroidery.

Suddenly Kinvale no longer seemed quite so much of a prison. If that stunning young Andor man was going to deliver on a fraction of what he had promised in the way of entertainment, Kinvale was going to be *fun*. There had been no one in Krasnegar who could even approach him for charm. Or looks. There was an excitement about him that Inos had never met, or even known existed.

She realized that the silence was becoming too expressive. "What a . . . pleasant person."

"It is nice to see something well done," Aunt Kade agreed complacently.

Inos wondered what exactly that remark implied. "Perhaps something *is* going to happen at last!"

"Perhaps, dear." Aunt Kade held her knitting away from her again and squinted at it. "But it's my job to see that it doesn't."

2

The moon was a silver boat floating above the sunset as a sodden punt drifted down the river, bearing Inos and Andor . . . and some others.

"You did not scream, Highness." Andor's eyes twinkled like

the first stars wakening in the east. "All the other ladies screamed."

"Did you wish me to scream, sir?"

"Of course! We brutish men gain savage pleasure from hearing you ladies scream."

"I must ask my aunt to arrange for me to take screaming lessons."

"Do so! And what did you think of the water caves?"

"They are ugly and dull. They cannot be viewed without getting soaked to the skin."

"This is true, ma'am."

"Which is why my aunt declined to come."

"And several other aunts."

"Do you think we can go back there—often?"

He laughed, leaning on his pole, bright eyes and white teeth gleaming in the dusk. "I think the water caves only work once. But there are other possibilities."

The moon was a giant pumpkin, flooding the midnight world with golden light, as the revelers in the hay wain returned from the berry pickers' ball . . .

The moon was a thin grin in the east as the astonished occupants of Kinvale were awakened at dawn by the strains of a small private orchestra performing on the terrace below their windows, being conducted by Sir Andor in a serenade to honor the birthday of Princess Inosolan . . .

There was no moon as Andor led Inos out on the balcony. The heavy drapes closed behind them, muffling the tuneful sounds of the ballroom. Stars had been poured liberally across the deep black sky, but there was a taste of fall in the wind, and the air was cool on her flushed skin.

Very gently Andor slid his hands around her and turned her to face him. At once her heart began dancing far faster than all those prancing couples they had just left.

"Inos . . ."

He paused. She wondered if he would dare try to kiss her, and how she would react. It was rare indeed for the two of them to have a moment alone, but she sensed that this was for more than idle chat. How long until Aunt Kade tracked them down? Then she noticed the concern in his face.

"Andor?"

He seemed to be having trouble finding words, and that was rare indeed for him. Suddenly he broke away from her and pounded his fist on the balustrade. "I should never have come here!"

"What? But—"

"Inos . . . your Highness, I . . . I told you the first time we met! I said then that I could not stay long. A month, I said. I have been here five weeks."

How her heart stopped dancing. Indeed it seemed to stop altogether. "You are leaving?"

He spread his palms on the marble and stared out over the dark-shrouded trees. "I must! It tears me to ribbons, but I must leave. I have given my word."

Happiness cracked, shattered, crashed down in a million shards like breaking ice. And a brainless little princess could find nothing better to say than: "When?"

"Now! At once! My horse is to be ready at midnight. I have stolen every minute I could. I must be in Shaldokan by dawn."

Inos took several deep breaths and forced herself to consider the matter rationally. She was only a child, after all. Andor was a man of the world—charming, learned, cultivated, experienced . . .

"There is an elderly friend . . ." Andor paused.

"Please! The details do not concern me."

It had been inevitable. She should have known. She had known, but she had not admitted it to herself. While visiting friends, as the gentry of the Impire so often did, Andor had taken pity on a lonely youngster. He had amused himself by passing the time in her company. It had been light entertainment for him. He probably did not even realize that for her it had been life itself, that he had saved her sanity in the boredom of Kinvale, that he had shown her what life was really for, that if she lived to be a hundred—

"Yes, they do concern you. To this man I owe a great debt. He is frail and he needs make a long journey. I promised to escort him, and the time is come."

After all, Inos should be grateful that she had enjoyed five whole weeks of such a man's company. The fact that the rest of her life was going to be a barren desert . . .

Andor turned to her again. He took her in his arms again. "But I swear to you, my darling, that I will return! I vow by the Powers and by the Gods that only my solemn word already pledged would drag me from you now."

Her heart went mad. *Darling?*

"I have asked you for no commitment." His voice was taut, his manner intense. "And I ask none now. I beg you only to believe two things—that nothing in this world but honor itself would drag me from your side, and that nothing save death will keep me from returning as fast as I am able."

"Andor . . . Oh, Andor! There is danger?"

He laughed, as if to dismiss such childish fancies. He paused. Then he sighed. "Yes! There may be danger. I could deceive most women, but you would see through my lies if I denied it. And I owe you the truth. If this task were something—anything at all!—that I could delegate to others, my love, then I would never hesitate. But there is some risk."

Oh, Andor! Danger? And had he said LOVE?

"I will return! And when I do return, my most adored princess, then I shall kneel and beg you to accept my service—" He pulled her against him, and the whole world seemed to whirl away into nothing. There was only Andor, Andor's so-powerful arms clutching her tighter than she had ever been held, Andor's superb male body hard against her, as she had often dreamed that one day it might be, Andor looking down at her with starlight shining in his big dark eyes—eyes that should be full of joy, and instead were haunted by the agony of parting.

"My service," he repeated softly. "My life. I came to Kinvale to while away a few days until I must go to aid an old family friend. You lost a brooch; I returned it and lost my heart. Even that first day, I knew. You are like no other woman I have ever met. If you want a knight to slay your foes, then my arm is at your command, and my blood is yours to spill. If you want a stableboy, then I will be your stableboy. Kennelmaster, poet, boatman . . . I will be for you whatsoever you want, your Most Wonderful Highness. Forever. And if, once in a while, you might condescend to smile in my direction, then that would be all the recompense my soul would ever seek."

She could not answer. It was unbelievable. She had not dared to hope. She raised her lips to be kissed—

Light flamed across the balcony as Aunt Kade pushed aside the drape. "Inos, my dear, they need another couple for the quadrille."

3

Summer aged gracefully.

As the first blush of fall was tastefully tinting the leaves at Kinvale, the legions of winter marched in triumph into the hills of Krasnegar. Like a defeated army in retreat, the workers fell back on the shore cottages, there to regroup and make a last defiant stand. The hilltops were white, the skies dark, and even the salt tide pools showed ice in the mornings. Wild-winged geese, wiser than men, fled southward overhead, honking sad warnings.

Now the nights were as long as the days. The causeway could be crossed in darkness only if the moon was full and the clouds scanty, but one tide in two did not give enough work time to clear the backlog. Every year these last two weeks were critical. In some years the moon was helpful; in others it was not. The wagons splashed out onto the causeway as soon as the tide ebbed, and the last crossing was made in the teeth of the flow. Often on the island side they did not waste time climbing to the castle—urgent hands threw out their loads on the dock and sent them back for another. Men and horses worked and rested, the wagons themselves rolled unceasingly, and when the tide was high they brought their cargoes to the landward end of the causeway and went back at once for more. The piles were still growing larger instead of smaller.

To the ephemeral settlement by the shore cottages came the herdboy Rap, driving in the charges the herders had guarded jealously all summer so that they might die now. He arrived just after sunset. Flakes of snow drifted aimless in the air—a warning from the God of Winter, but not yet a serious assault.

Rap fastened the corral gate, threw his tack on the heap, and headed off through the gathering darkness in search of food. He was bone-weary and grubby inside his furs, and he had a gratifying stubble on his lip, but his most urgent problem was hunger.

The shingle beach was an inferno of controlled confusion. Here the excess cattle were being slaughtered and butchered, their flesh salted into casks, bones boiled, hides cleaned and bundled for later curing. Blood and entrails were being collected and made into sausage. It was only here and at this time that fresh meat was freely available to the common folk of Krasnegar, and his mouth watered at the thought of it.

The flickering flames of the driftwood fires danced sideways below the wind, throwing unearthly glows on the high stacks of hides and peat and hay. Curls of snowflakes swirled over the hard dark ground, seeking sheltered places in the shadows to make small drifts. The wind brought smoke—tainted first with delicious cooking odors and then with the unbearable stench of the abbatoir. It brought the sound of cattle bellowing in the corrals and the rush of waves on the shingle. Men and woman hurried by, swathed in the anonymity of fur, stooped and huddled against the cold like bulky misshapen bears.

As he picked his way between the grotesque mountains of produce, Rap wondered how many wagonloads they represented. He wondered also how many days were left before the road would close. But those were Foronod's problems, not his. The king's factor must be a literate man, so however Rap might serve the crown of Krasnegar in his coming manhood, it would not be in the post of factor. He found the grub line and joined on the end, noting that most of the men and women there looked just as listless and filthy as he did.

"Hi, Rap! You've grown!" the woman in front of him said.

Her name was Ufio, Verantor's wife, and she was pretty. Rap grinned and said he was sorry, he hadn't meant to, and how was the baby. It seemed weeks since he had even seen a woman, let alone had a chance to talk with one.

Men he knew arrived and exchanged greetings; old friends, people he had not seen in months. They told him he had grown.

The line grew shorter before him, longer behind. He shivered and he shifted from one aching leg to the other. He pondered what task he might be given next. He was very much in between now: too old for the best of the kids' jobs, not old enough to be trusted with men's. Whatever it was, he would do his best. That had been another of his mother's principles.

Then he was trudging off over the shingle bearing a mug of something hot and a platter heaped with steaming beef. Seeking shelter from the cold, he edged into one of the cottages. It was packed like a fish barrel. The single bench was crammed with people, and the floor also was covered with bodies, eating or talking or snoring. The air was as thick as whale oil, reeking of men and food, but at least he was out of the wind. One lamp guttered on a littered table in the center. He found a space, sank down on the ground, and prepared to gorge.

"You've grown!" a man behind him said.

Rap peered, shifting his head to let light fall on the face.

"Lin? You've got a new voice!"

"About time, too!" Lin spoke with deep satisfaction.

"How's the arm?" Rap asked, with his mouth full.

Lin looked down at his arm in surprise, as if he had already forgotten his summer accident. "Fine."

Rap gestured with his head toward the door. "The work?" he mumbled, still eating.

Lin shrugged. "They say it'll be all right if the weather holds." At sunset the sky to the north had been blacker than the castle walls, but neither of them mentioned that. A wagon rumbled by outside, making the dirt floor throb.

"What's the news?" Rap asked. "I've been stuck up in the hills like a boulder all summer."

"Not much," Lin squeaked. He scowled at Rap's chuckle and managed to find his lower register again. He listed a few births and marriages and deaths. "They say . . ." His voice sank to a husky whisper. "They say the king is not well."

Rap frowned and chewed at a rib and wondered about Inos, far away in Kinvale. She would not know, of course, so she would not be worried. But what happened if the king died when she was not here to succeed him? The thought of young Inos suddenly being elevated to queen was staggering. Still, being unwell did not necessarily lead to dying.

Then, feeling bearish, as if he would never need to eat again and could cheerfully sleep from now until spring, Rap added his platter and tankard to a nearby pile. He wiped his greasy mouth with the back of his hand. Lin had found room to stretch out and was already into the droopy-eyelid stage. Probably he ought to do the same, Rap thought. There would be work enough in the morning and all the others in the cottage had been here longer than he had, so they should be called first.

A tall man stooped through the door and stood for a moment. He pushed back his hood and silence fell at the sight of the silver hair. His face was gaunt and pale as driftwood, with blue shadows under the eyes and a white stubble that was almost a beard—the factor. From the way he stood, he might have been inspecting his workers, or perhaps he was letting the troops inspect him, their leader. He was their symbol of defiance against the coming onslaught, his obvious exhaustion both a challenge and a comfort.

All eyes not closed by sleep fastened on his.

"Any wagon drivers in here?" Foronod demanded.

Rap scrambled to his feet as a voice from across the room said, "Yes, sir."

It was Ollo, and he was the best. Rap was already sitting down again as Foronod nodded to Ollo, but he did acknowledge Rap with a faint smile that probably meant *next year*. The two men departed and the cottage sank back into weary apathy again.

"He said drivers, not sailors," Lin muttered sleepily.

"Was it you who started that garbage?"

"No, it was you." Lin rolled over and put his head on one arm.

Pity about Ollo . . . Rap very much wanted to drive a wagon again. Once was not enough. He could hardly sit at the drivers' table when he'd only run a team once, and never up the hill, only down.

The bodies around him had shifted and penned him in. He had no room to stretch out. He was too weary to go look for somewhere else. He leaned his arms on his knees and yawned. They were not going to start breaking in new drivers at this point in the year, not in the final sprint.

His head dropped forward and jerked him awake again. It was good to have more company—he had grown very tired of the same few herder faces. He wondered what Inos was doing. He told himself not to be foolish. He thought of the castle and the stable-hands' quarters and the men and boys and girls he would meet again. Only one would be missing.

His head fell over once more, waking him again. He would have to find somewhere to stretch out . . . unless he could lie on his side and stay curled up . . .

Someone shook his shoulder. "Rap? You're wanted."

He sat up, confused and muzzy, uncertain where he was, then scrambled to his feet and lumbered after his guide, stumbling over bodies to the door. The air outside hit him like a bucketful of ice water; he gasped and pulled up his hood. The world was filled with streaming snow, a yellow glare in the light from the cottage. He hurried into the darkness after a rapidly disappearing back. The snow settled in his eyes and on his eyelashes and began plastering his parka.

He was led to a group planted around one of the fires, which was shooting flashes of light between their legs. The circle opened to admit him and he looked around the humped, anonymous figures, most holding hands out toward the blaze. A cauldron bubbled there, and steamed. Shivering and blinking, Rap recognized the tall Foronod at the far side and waited to hear why he was needed.

"Rap?" The factor was staring at him. They all were. "Could you follow the trail in this? On a horse?"

Rap turned and looked out into the night—nothing! Nothing at all. The snow had turned the night black, not white. He'd seen guiding done in other years—men with lanterns leading a wagon—but tonight a lantern would show nothing but endless snow rushing past. The air was solid with it, streaming insanely southward. Without a lantern there was nothing to be seen at all. Nothing!

Scared now, he turned back to face Foronod. "On foot, maybe."

Foronod shook his head. "Too late. Tide's coming."

So that was it? Rap wanted to be a driver, or a man-at-arms. They wanted a sorcerer, a seer. A freak. A damnable *freak*! He'd pulled that fool stunt with the wagon, and now they thought he could work miracles. Once could be denied. Twice would be proof. And what they were asking him to do was much more than driving through water. In this weather a man would barely see the ground from horseback. His mother, they thought, had been a seer, so he must be. He opened his mouth to say "Why me?" and what he said was "Why?"

The factor's head jerked and the pale blur of his face inside his hood seemed to stiffen. "Answer the question!"

Rap hesitated. He couldn't answer the question. "I . . . why?"

"Boy!"

"I'm sorry, sir . . . I need to know. I don't know why. I mean I don't know why 'why' . . ." Rap stuttered into unhappy silence.

"We need a guide."

And again Rap's mouth demanded "Why?" before he could stop it. He did not know why *why* was important, but it felt as if it should be.

The menacing silence was broken when a snow-dappled man standing next the factor said, "Tell him! If you're going to trust him, then trust him!"

Rap did not know the voice and what little he could see of the face was unfamiliar. Foronod glanced at the intruder. "What do you know about it? Who the Evil are you, anyway?"

"I'm from the south," the voice said. It was a gentleman's voice. "A visitor. But I've met seers before. You must give him your trust or he can't help you."

Foronod shrugged grumpily and looked back at Rap. "All right. I'm scared that this is the big one. It may not be—it's very early. But we have three loads of beef we absolutely must get across."

Despite the bone-cracking chill of the wind, Rap's head was still so clogged with sleep and weariness that it seemed to be running on one foot. *The big one* was the storm that closed the causeway for the winter, and it would blow for days. Slabs of sea ice and snowdrifts caked by frozen spray plugged the road—men and animals could cross afterward, but not wagons. He knew what three loads of salted beef meant, or he could guess. It would buy much time in the spring if the town was starving. Any risk was worth taking if this was the big one.

If it was not, then losing a wagon would cripple the supply train. That might be almost as bad—they needed every one. He might even lose all three if he trapped them in the path of the tide, and that would be catastrophe for Krasnegar. Foronod must be frantic if he was willing to take the gamble and trust the town to a boy—to a seer.

Trust him? Rap started to shiver.

A harder gust struck and the men staggered and leaned into it. Snow hissed in the fire and steamed.

Rap turned again and looked at the night. A lantern would be little help in this, hard enough even for the drivers to follow, useless to see where a horse was going. They were asking him if he could ride across with his eyes shut. He tried to remember that strange feeling when he'd brought the wagon through the water. There *had* been something there, something unusual, unwholesome. He did not want to admit he was a freak, but there *had* been something. Foronod must be desperate.

Trust yourself! Rap squared his shoulders. "I'll try."

"You and two to flank you?"

He hesitated and then nodded.

"Jua," the factor said. "And . . . Binik. Go—"

"No," Rap said. That did not feel right. I want Lin. And . . ." He did not know why he wanted Lin, except that Lin had survived this sort of madness before, so he would not argue. And one other? He surprised himself as much as he surprised everyone else. He pointed at the stranger. "Him!"

Foronod growled and demanded, "Why him?"

The stranger said quietly, "Trust him!"

"You ever been across the causeway, master?"

"No." The stranger sounded insanely unruffled. "That may be why he wants me. My ideas won't interfere with his."

Rap wondered if he merely wanted someone who believed in seers. He did not think he believed—not in himself as a seer. But there *had* been something.

Foronod shrugged. "Go ahead. It's your neck, stranger. You've got an hour at the most, lad."

"Lin's sleeping where I was," Rap said to the man who had brought him. "Bring him to the horses." To Foronod: "Sir, I'll need lanterns." Then he nodded at the stranger. "Come and get a horse."

He blundered off into the dark without waiting for any replies. He had never given orders to grown men before. Trust yourself! If you don't, who will?

The stranger's hand settled on Rap's shoulder. The darkness was that thick.

The best thing Rap could do now was walk into an offal pit and break his leg. Then they would know, wouldn't they? This was a test: find the corral. If he could not find that, then he could not find the causeway. He tried to remember where all the piles of hay and peat were, but he had not come this way when he arrived. He put a hand up to shield his eyes from the snow, but he could still see nothing.

He stopped.

Obstacle?

"What's wrong?" the stranger asked at his ear.

Rap reached out his right hand and touched hay. He shivered and changed direction. "This way." It worked at arm's length, then. Or had he just felt the wind eddying around the stack?

He found the corral, but he could have been following the smell, or the noise. He leaned over the rail and he could barely make out the big shapes steaming and champing in the murk. "Mustard? Dancer! Walrus!"

"How about Swimmer and Diver?" the stranger said with a laugh.

"Sir, please don't talk to me." Why not? What was Rap doing? His head was starting to throb. Mustard edged through the other horses toward him. Walrus, he knew, was cowering over on the far side. But he did not know how he knew that.

By the time Lin and others arrived with lanterns, Rap had extracted the three unhappy horses. They were all old, all likely destined to follow the cattle into the abattoir with their stringy old meat reserved for emergency supplies, but they were calm and solid. Docility was what he needed, not fire.

Then everything happened very quickly and he found himself at the head of the procession, holding on his shoulder a stick with a lantern swinging on it. Lin and the stranger sat their mounts on either side of him, also holding lanterns. Another flickered and winked on the lead wagon close behind them. What the lights showed mostly was racing snow.

Foronod was looking up at him, his face an ivory mask of anxiety almost as white as the snow-crusted fur that framed it. "Ready. The Gods be with you, lad."

Rap did not answer, because he did not know what to say, nor trust himself to say it. He raised and lowered his light as a signal, then held it out in front. He urged Mustard forward. The horse was shivering, but more with fear than cold, so Rap stroked his neck and muttered consolation . . . How had he known that? He gritted his teeth in anger at this unwelcome power, these uncanny abilities that seemed to be sprouting in his mind, as uninvited as the hairs that grew now on his body.

His lantern showed little more than a cloud of streaking white and a tiny vague patch of ground around his horse. The snow was coating the shingle, even deadening the sound of the hooves and the rumble of the wagons. He had no qualms over this first stretch—he could hear the waves off to his right, so all he need do was keep the snow coming from that direction, also, caking ever deeper on that side of his horse and his parka. This way he was leading the wagons along the beach and there was no danger.

Eventually he must make a turn. No sooner had he started to think about that than he felt urgency—*now*! So soon? He wavered in his mind and the urgency grew. He turned Mustard slightly, edging Walrus and the stranger over until they were facing into the wind. The muffled wagon noise followed them. The shingle rose, then sank again, and the snow lay thicker. Another slight ridge, then blackness—water.

"You two wait here!" he said, yelling against the storm. Then he forced a reluctant and ill-named Mustard forward, into the water. There were no waves, so it was the lagoon, but had he blundered into the deep part? The sound of the wagons had stopped behind him and all he could hear was waves, somewhere. A few creepy minutes of splashing ended and he saw the vague lightness of snow again below his horse's feet. So far, so good. He began to breathe more easily. He had found the ford.

He turned around and through the black fog he could just barely detect the lights he had left behind. He waved his lantern up and down, and they began advancing to meet him. Mustard was a little happier standing with the wind on his tail, but he was shivering violently.

Now Rap must find the end of the causeway. He left the others to follow at the wagons' creaking pace and pushed forward alone into the blizzard. Snow covered his face and dribbled down his neck. His headache was getting worse. It was hard to keep Mustard moving. The lights were growing faint behind him . . . he must not lose his followers. More important, though, he must find that causeway before the wagons rumbled down to the water's edge in the wrong place. Turning them would be bad enough; backing them up if they got between rocks might be close to impossible. He strained his memory to recall the exact direction and adjusted it for the way he thought the wind was coming . . . and he was too far to the right. How did he know that? He hesitated, then trusted his instinct and not his memory.

In a few moments Mustard's hoof struck rock. That was it! He'd done it again.

He was a seer and his flesh crawled at the thought. He cringed. Why me?

Now things ought to be simple for a while, and he became aware that his body was knotted with the strain, running sweat inside his shirt.

Lin and the stranger reached their places on either side of him and they could follow the edges of the made road—the snow had not buried it yet. He kept position between them. The wagons followed the three bright blurs.

Seer: one who sees. But he did not *see*, he just knew. He gained knowledge without using his senses—hateful! Then he remembered the minstrel's strange belief that the horses had not been able to hear him that day. Could he speak without using his voice, at least to horses? He tried a silent word of comfort to Mustard and thought he felt it received. Imagination? Hateful! Detestable! Freak! He had not tried calling the mares away from Firedragon since that day with the minstrel and now he knew why—he had been afraid of what he might learn about himself.

They had crossed Tallow Rocks already. Waves were splashing against the side of the road, sending up salt spray. There was no snow on the ground anymore, and the lanterns' faint glow was an uncertain reflection. Black ice—the deadliest stuff to try to walk a horse on, or drive a wagon. It was Lin and the stranger who were bearing the load now. Rap half expected one or other of them to vanish without warning, plunging off the edge into darkness and quick, cold death.

Walrus started to panic and slither. *Stop that!* Rap thought, and Walrus stopped. Coincidence.

They crawled along, and the waves were throwing water over the road, running off in glinting black sheets. Better than ice. This

was the main causeway and the tide would be over it now. Not so
deep as last time, but much rougher. This was important . . .
think of famine.

"Lin!" he snapped. "Watch where you're going!" They were
coming into the turn.

"I can't see, Rap." It was a boy's sob. Lin's voice had changed
back under the strain.

"I can't, either," the stranger said calmly.

Rap muttered a silent prayer to any God who might be listening. He was all knotted up again now. This was it. "Close in a
bit and follow me, then."

He advanced alone, feeling by some means he did not understand that the others were near behind. He forced old Mustard
down the center of the wave-swept causeway. It must be the exact
center, else either Lin or the stranger would slide off. They must
be sweating with the strain of staying out to the sides, resisting
the temptation to creep in directly behind Rap himself, but the
wagon drivers had to know where the road was, how much was
safe.

The center! Stay in the center. He did not try to think what the
causeway would look like underwater this time. It would be utterly black down there. He groped somehow for its weight, its
mass, its hard solid edges in the cold water surging around it.

Stay in the center!

He heard and *felt* the first team beginning to panic and he sent
reassuring thoughts back to them; realized that he had been doing
the same to Mustard and Walrus and Dancer for some time. His
head was bursting, as if someone had pushed fingers down inside
and was trying to pull it apart. This was important! There might
be famine in the spring—babies dying, children starving. The
water was not deep. The waves were rolling up over the causeway
and pouring off again. It would be easy to see the edges if there
was light, but all he had to look at was flying snow, a bright cloud
around his lantern, and he could not even see the spray splashed
up by his horse's feet.

The waves grew deeper.

The second bend . . . He shouted a warning to his companions, knew that they were safely far from those deadly edges,
checked the wagon also behind him without looking round, kept
talking to the horses in his mind.

He opened his eyes and wondered how long he'd had them shut.
Shallower . . .

Then the waves were not flowing all the way across. He was

coming up on Big Island. Big Damp and Little Damp were still ahead, but the worst was over.

The rest was a blur.

He stood on the dock road, clutching reins and weeping. Lin and the stranger were beside him, he knew, in a mob of shivering, trembling horses and shouting people . . . and some idiot was holding up a lantern and Rap wished to all the Gods that they'd take the damn thing away. Men were running down from the town, coming to help, asking questions, disbelieving the answers. There were tears pouring down his face and he was shaking with sobs. Shameful, but he could not stop. He was shivering more violently than the horses and he could hear himself weeping— having some sort of stupid fit, but the drivers were coming to him and pumping his free hand and thumping his back and he wanted them to stop and go away. He would not listen to what they were saying.

Someone took Mustard's reins from him. An arm was laid over his shoulders and at last that damned lantern was taken away and there was darkness.

"Let's get the man to bed!" a voice said angrily. "He's beat, can't you see?"

Not a man, sir, just a weak, sniveling boy.

Then came blessed relief, as that so-comforting arm was holding him, leading him away from the crowd and the voices and the faces, taking him away. Vaguely he knew that it was the stranger, the man from the Impire, and that stranger had done a fair job himself that night.

"Thank you, sir," Rap mumbled.

"You don't need to call me 'sir,' " the voice said.

"I don't know your name."

"My name is Andor," said the stranger, "but after what I've seen tonight, Master Rap, I'd be very proud if you would just call me 'friend.' "

Clear call:

> I must down to the seas again, for the call of the running tide
> Is a wild call and a clear call that may not be denied.
> > Masefield, *Sea Fever*

◖ FOUR ◗

Thousand friends

1

The king's face was pinched and straw-tinted, his beard visibly grayer than it had been only a few months before. The wrists protruding from the sleeves of his heavy blue robe were as slender as a boy's. He was restless, unable to settle, shifting from window to hearth and back, clutching his right side and keeping his jaw clenched much of the time.

Rap sat very straight on the extreme edge of a thickly padded leather chair and felt more uncomfortable than he could have believed possible. He was the owner of the largest and most obvious pair of hands in the Powers' creation and he did not know what to do with them. He was wearing his best, which was in truth but his better, for he possessed only two doublets and they were both too small for him. His boots were clean, after he had worked a whole hour on them, but he was sure that his Majesty would smell horse. He had shaved and scrubbed and he had plastered his shaggy brown hair down with egg white, which was what he thought his mother had used on it sometimes; but he still probably stank of the dogs who had shared his tent for the last month. Thinking of the dogs gave him an unbearable desire to scratch.

The sky was blue beyond the windows. The wagons were rolling again and the storm had faded with the tide.

When the king had thanked him—for that was why he had been summoned—Rap had mentioned the sunshine. His efforts had all been in vain, unnecessary. His Majesty had said that it did not matter, that it was the attempt that counted. Krasnegar should be just as grateful to him as if he had indeed staved off a famine.

Now the king seemed to be having trouble finding words, or deciding whether certain words should be said. "Master Rap," he began, then paused again. "Is that your real name, or is it short for something?"

"It's my name, Sire," Rap said automatically, then remembered that this was his king he was addressing. Before he could say more, the king continued.

"I received letters on the last ship." He paused to look out the window. "Inosolan and her aunt arrived safely at Kinvale."

Rap did not know what to say and was afraid that his face would be turning red. "Thank you, Sire." Hononin had told him he should say *Sire* sometimes instead of *your Majesty* always. Next time would have to be *your Majesty*, because that was two *Sires* in a row.

"I thought you would like to know," the king muttered. He swung around and walked back to the fireplace.

The king's study was a very intimidating room, bigger than the dormitory that Rap had shared the previous night with six boys. It was fortified with lumpish leather furniture and books, haunted by shadows, made warm by the glowing peat in the fireplace and by wool rugs on the floor, a brown and gold room. There were tables littered with papers, piled or rolled or loosely scattered. Maps hung on the wall, mysteriously inscribed with script incomprehensible to Rap. A massive iron-bound chest in the corner contained many things, including the king's crown . . . angrily Rap told his mind to stop prying.

The fire impressed him most, though. To squander precious peat so early in the winter with the sun yet shining outside was a truly royal luxury. He found the room very warm—that must be why he was sweating—and yet the king kept returning to the fireplace as if he were chilled inside his voluminous robe, his deepblue robe with its gold piping. The aimless prowling of that big, bundled man hinted of a bear at bay, cornered, and the dogs closing.

"Friend Rap, I owe you an apology."

Rap gulped and burst out, "Oh, no, sir!" and forgot the *your Majesty*.

The king did not seem to notice. "No one had ever told me about your mother's skill, or I should surely have guessed after your first exploit on the causeway. Perhaps I should have trusted my daughter's judgment more, too.'' He looked ruefully at the Other Man.

The Other Man was not helping Rap's edginess at all. He was elderly and tall and white-haired. He had a large curved nose and very glittery, deep-set blue eyes, and he stood as motionless as the furniture alongside one of the tables, a long-fingered hand resting on it. He wore a long robe like the king's, but dark brown, and he had done nothing but study Rap since he came in. If sorcerers ground herbs in mortars, then Rap was the next herb. This vulture-eyed sentinel must be the Doctor Sagorn that Inos had described—the one who had lied to her, or else was a sorcerer. And if he wasn't a sorcerer, he had still lied.

The Other Man smiled slightly in reply to the king and returned to staring at Rap. Rap looked away.

''Well, what reward can we offer?'' the king asked. ''What can we do for a young man who performs such a miraculous act for us?''

''Nothing is necessary, Si—your Majesty.''

The king smiled thinly. ''I insist on rewarding you.''

God of fools!

''Then I should like to be one of your Majesty's men-at-arms, Sire,'' Rap said hopefully.

The king frowned, glanced at the Other Man, and stroked his beard. ''You're a little young yet . . . and I'm not sure that that would be a very good idea anyway, Rap. You are going to find that some men resent your abilities, you know. By forcing you to reveal them in public, Factor Foronod and I have done you a grave disservice. Sword practice is dangerous enough without grudges and jealousies creeping in . . . although you would then have the ability to defend yourself, I suppose. Is there someone you especially want to maim?''

''No, your Majesty!'' That was a horrible thought.

''Then why do you need to be a man-at-arms?'' The king seemed puzzled.

Rap stammered.

''Dragons, Sire?'' murmured the Other Man. ''For rescuing beautiful maidens from?''

''I should have thought of that!''

Rap suspected he was blushing. They were laughing at him.

The king turned serious again. ''Can you read?''

''No, your . . . Sire.''

''I think you should learn, Rap. Both for your own sake and

. . . and for your future queen, if you plan to remain in her service.''

Now Rap was certain that he had blushed, from hair roots to
belly button, and he could only nod.

''Well, that takes care of two hours a day.'' The king chuckled.
''I think I shall appoint you as assistant to Foronod—serve him
right! I shall tell him to teach you some of his cares and worries.
You will learn a great deal about the palace and the town if you
do nothing but follow him around—and I am sure that he will find
more than that for you to do.''

There was nothing to say then except ''Thank you, Sire.''

Then the royal eyes met Rap's and seemed to drill right through.
''I think you are an honest man, lad. A queen of Krasnegar . . .
even a sly old king . . . can always use an honest man's loyalty,
and especially so if that man has useful knowledge, also.''

Rap gulped and nodded. ''I shall be proud to serve, sir—Sire.''

But he wondered whether he was pleased or not. He felt that
he had hoped for something a little more *manly* than factoring.

''In another month or two, we shall see again.'' The king was
wandering toward the window once more. ''Now, I am sure that
your mother warned you carefully, and you are fairly safe here in
Krasnegar, but remember to guard your secret. It is common
knowledge now. There can be evildoers even in Krasnegar.''

''Sir—Sire—I have no secret.''

The king frowned at him and looked to the Other Man, who
shrugged. The king came back to the hearth and eased himself
stiffly into a big chair. ''Then how do you perform your wonders?''

''They . . . they just happen,'' Rap said.

''Your mother did not tell you a word?''

Rap shook his head. ''No, your Majesty.''

''How long have you been able to do these things?''

''That day I got my chance to drive a wagon,'' Rap explained.
''That day was the first time . . . er . . . Sire.''

The king looked again at the Other Man and said, ''Sagorn?''

The old man was smiling. He had an old man's smile, thinning
the lips without showing teeth. His lower jaw seemed to slide up
between the clefts that flanked his mouth, closing tight like a trap.
Not a comforting smile—sinister. ''When Foronod asked you if
you could find the trail, you asked why—or so I am told. Why
did you ask why?''

''I don't know, sir. It seemed important.''

Doctor Sagorn nodded in satisfaction. ''It was the importance that was important, I think. You don't like using your power, do you?''

"No, sir!"

Again the gruesome smile. "So you suppress it. You only do it, or think you *can* do it, when it matters a lot?''

Rap puzzled about that. He did not want to know that the king kept his crown in that big chest, at the bottom, under the fur rug, and he had just about convinced himself that there he was only guessing. The first time on the causeway he had desperately wanted to do a good job of driving the wagon—that had certainly been important to him. "Perhaps that is so, sir. Then you mean I have always had it?''

"Since it was given you, certainly," the king said. "And it must have been your mother who gave it to you.''

"But . . . like my nose, your Majesty? Or my brown hair?''

The king shook his head.

Rap was bewildered. "I thought maybe it was something I was growing into, like shaving.''

"Or holding hands with pretty girls?" The king smiled— almost grinned. "Oh, that was not fair! I am sorry, my young friend. Just a joke! Forgive me! I think what you are growing into is responsibility—serious matters, where such powers can be of use to you. I am told you have an uncanny knack with horses, also.''

"That I don't mind, Sire." Rap risked a smile of his own.

Sagorn made a sniffing noise. "He can call mares away from a stallion.''

The king looked up, startled. "You jest!''

The old man gave him a curiously cryptic glance. "So I was informed by a certain minstrel who, quite typically, had lost his horse in the hills. Master Rap saved him. Then, not wanting to interrupt his lunch, he broke up a herd by shouting.''

The king looked from Rap to Sagorn and back again several times. "Rap," he said, "I am almost more impressed by that than what you did last night! Has this minstrel returned, also, then? I should like to hear the story.''

He looked to Sagorn, who hesitated.

"No, Majesty.''

The king started angrily, then turned to Rap. "I understand that you had two helpers. One was a stableboy?''

"Ylinyli, Sire. He is known as Lin.''

"I must thank him, also, then. The other was a stranger?''

"A gentleman, Sire," said Rap. "He told me his name was Andor."

The king's jaw clamped shut and he nodded, as if he had suspected as much. He glared again at Sagorn. "Why has he come?"

The old man seemed almost as angry, but very careful. "I could not stop him, could I?"

The king looked furious now. "The minstrel?"

Sagorn nodded and the king turned to Rap. "I repeat what I told you before, lad. Guard that secret of yours—it may easily be worth more than your life!"

Rap wondered how he could guard something he did not have, but the king had not finished. "And in particular, watch out for that Andor man. He is as warm as sunshine and as slippery as ice. I shall have to lock up every maiden in the kingdom if he is around."

Rap was very confused now. Why could the king not simply order the man away? True, the ships had gone and a journey by land at this time of year would be dangerous in the extreme. But a king was a king, was he not?

This king sank back stiffly in his big chair. He grimaced, as if in pain, and pressed his fingers against the lump in his side. *What lump? Stop prying!*

"Sire?" the Sagorn man said.

"It's all right," the king muttered, although his forehead was shining wetly. "Tell Master Rap about the words. Warn him of the dangers. He does not seem to know, and who better to tell him than the learned Doctor Sagorn?"

There was more to that remark than there seemed to be. The old man flushed angrily.

"With pleasure, your Majesty!" He turned to Rap. "Have you never heard of the words of power?"

"No, sir."

Sagorn shrugged. "All magic, all power, comes from certain words. There are a great many of them; no one knows how many. But they are what gives sorcerers their abilities."

Rap's jaw fell open. "You are not saying I am a sorcerer, are you, sir?" Horrible thought!

"No." The old man smiled slightly and shook his head. "But you must know at least one word—and an unusually powerful one, because to be a seer normally requires more. It takes at least three to make a sorcerer. I think that the words may be growing weaker. Were I to set up in public as a sorcerer, I should want no less than four. Inisso, however, had but three.'' He glanced at the king.

"Never mind that!'' Evidently the spasm had passed, for the pain had left the king's face. He glowered angrily.

Sagorn bowed slightly, ironically. "As your Majesty wishes. One word, Master Rap, does several things, but mostly it enhances natural talents. You obviously have inherited a knack for animals from your faun ancestors, and the word has raised it to occult proportions. Your mother was reportedly a seer. We asked the seneschal about her. He says that she could foretell events—when a girl would marry, or the sex of babies. Can you do such things?''

Bewildered, Rap shook his head.

"Can you sing? Dance? What are you good at?''

"Horses, sir, maybe. Good with horses.''

"You did not know that the king would summon you today before you were actually told?''

"No, sir.''

"You wanted to be a man-at-arms. Have you ever had fencing lessons?''

"The sergeant tried me out, sir, with a wooden sword.''

"Were you good?''

Rap's face grew warm again. "He didn't seem to think so.''

Sagorn exchanged nods with the king. "Then we must assume that you know only one word, and the skill you displayed yesterday must be another natural talent in you, although what it is in other people I am not sure—a sense of direction, perhaps. Some people never get lost. Or just good guessing?'' He stroked his chin thoughtfully. "After all, foresight is just a sort of guessing.''

The king interrupted. "The jotnar have legends of men they call *farsighted*, able to pilot boats through shallows, or fight in the dark.''

"Ah!'' Sagorn looked pleased. "I had forgotten that! So it may be that he gained some talent for farsight from his father, and again the word has magnified it greatly.''

He paused, looking quizzically at Rap, who nodded, although all this sounded very confusing. Yet his mother had told him once that his father had been a good pilot—and he had walked home in the dark a hundred times, she had said, before at last he fell off the dock.

"So one word makes you a sort of genius in your own field. But even one word can do other things, as well. It makes its owner an effective sort of person. Successful. Lucky. Very hard to kill, they say." He glanced momentarily at the king.

Lucky? That settled it, Rap thought—he did not have a word.

"Tell him about two words," the king growled.

Sagorn raised an ironic, shaggy eyebrow, then again he bowed and turned to Rap. "Not all the books agree, you understand? Words of power are not discussed openly, and there is much that even I have not been able to discover, in a long lifetime of searching. But it seems that with two words you start to get somewhere. Knowing two of the words makes an adept. Not a true sorcerer, but someone who can do almost anything—anything human. If you knew two words, young man, then one lesson would be enough to turn you into a swordsman, as you desire. Or an artist, or a juggler. Normally the true occult powers like farsight start to come only with a second word. Do you understand?"

"Not very much, sir. Do you mean like spells? I didn't say any spells to call the horses or find the causeway."

The old man shook his head impatiently. "No, no! You do not *say* these words. You only have to know them. They are passed down from generation to generation as the most precious thing a family can own. They are usually told only on deathbeds." His eyes wandered back toward the king.

The king was gritting his teeth again. "So you see why we think you know one of the words of power, Rap?"

"The minstrel, Sire!" Rap said. "He asked me!"

The king managed a twisted smile. "Any man who can sing like Jalon is automatically suspected of knowing a word. Any supreme talent like . . . any genius . . ." He broke off, took a deep breath, then grunted at Sagorn, "Tell him of the dangers."

Sagorn kept his eyes on the king, but spoke to Rap. "The words resist telling—they are hard to say. You truly do not remember your mother telling you hers?"

"No, sir."

"Yours is undoubtedly stronger than most," the old man muttered, but his attention was still on the king. "Perhaps it is making you forget that you know it, although I have never heard . . ."

The king uttered a groan and writhed suddenly. His hand was pressed to his side and now sweat dribbled down his ashen face.

"More of the cordial, Majesty?"

Holindarn nodded without speaking. The old man turned and went to a corner table. He returned bearing a glass and a tall vial full of some smoky green liquid. Rap rose from his chair, feeling out of place. Sagorn caught his eye and nodded.

Rap bowed and backed toward the door.

He was outside before he realized that he had not been told of the dangers.

2

Next morning Rap found Foronod standing with a group of other men on the shingle in the sunshine. The snow had almost gone. He waited patiently on the outskirts until the others had all been assigned tasks, then stepped forward in his turn. His only greeting was a nod. Although he looked as if he had not slept since the night of the blizzard, the factor made no comment on that affair at all, merely rubbing his eyes and listening in silence as Rap explained the king's command.

Then the silver mane nodded. "Can you read?"

"No, sir. But I am to learn."

"It will have to wait, though. Ready to start helping me now?"

"Yes, sir."

"I'm told there's a whale beached on Tanglestone Point. I need to know if it's fresh enough to harvest. Take a good horse."

Tanglestone would be a long ride. Rap took Firedragon, returning that evening weary and content, having achieved what he set out to do. And even Firedragon, had he been gifted with speech, might have reported enjoying the outing. It had been years since any other man had attempted to ride the stallion. No one else ever succeeded in staying on him very long, but Rap he never minded.

Three weeks later, Rap and Foronod fought their way through a blizzard, following the last caravan to cross the causeway. The big one had come at last and Krasnegar was now closed for the winter . . . or, as the inhabitants put it, the world was cut off.

The two rode in weary silence through the town. Foronod halted at the foot of a long flight of steps. He slid stiffly from the saddle and handed his reins to Rap. "Tomorrow, then," he said, and headed off on foot—to family and warm bed, to a long rest that no one had earned more, and possibly even to a hot bath.

Rap took the horses to the castle stables, wondering where he would go afterward. Dim and warm and rankly smelly, the stables themselves were more home to him than anywhere else was now. Cobbled floor, rough plank walls, shabby untidiness . . . they all offered a welcome familiarity, but after so long out of doors he also felt oppressed by being confined. He felt as if those walls were leaning over him whenever he turned his back—and there was always a wall behind him. He rubbed down Foronod's mare and was still working on his own pony when old Hononin appeared out of the shadows as if one small patch of darkness had just decided to solidify. He looked grumpier and surlier than ever.

He grunted a sort of greeting.

"It's good to be back, sir," Rap said.

Another grunt. "Is it? Where are you living now?"

"I was wondering the same."

Neither said the obvious—that Rap was too old for the boys' dormitory. It might even be full, anyway. But a factor's assistant would presumably be paid more than a stableboy, and perhaps almost as much as a driver. Rap had not asked.

"I shall find lodgings in the town, sir."

The little man scowled and snatched the wisp from Rap's hand. "I'll finish this; you look beat. You know the garret next the drivers' office?"

Rap nodded, surprised.

"It's been cleaned out. There may even be a bedroll in it. A man could stay there until he found somewhere better."

"Thank you, sir. That was kind of you."

Honinin just grunted.

Krasnegar might be battened down for the winter, but the factor still had much to do, and much of that he could delegate to his new apprentice. Rap was partly diverted by his morning lessons in the arts of reading and writing and summing, squeezed unhappily into a desk at the back of a schoolroom filled with children who giggled and found him an amusing giant. He chewed his knuckles, ruffled his hair, and wrestled with the mysteries of knowledge and the vagaries of a quill pen just as stubbornly as he had battled Firedragon.

The royal appointments of Rap as assistant to Foronod might have been well intentioned, but it greatly widened an already extensive moat. Of necessity, as the accounts were closed on another season, the king's factor must investigate many matters that had been pushed aside in the summer rush. A wagon crash, unpaid taxes, unexplained injuries, and mysteriously vanished goods—all of these came under review. Every year brought its accountings, to attribute blame or malfeasance, and that year had no more and no less than others.

Yet where the respected factor could rush in, his juvenile helper must tread with care. Rap found himself asking questions whose answers were not readily at hand, testing memories suddenly at fault. He spent a whole week in quest of a certain valuable keg of imported peach brandy that had vanished between the dock and the palace cellar; and he gained no friends thereby.

When he finally made his glum and quite negative report, Foronod scowled and asked grumpily, "You can't just *see* it?"

"No, sir. I tried."

That was a lie. Rap had tried very hard *not* to see it in his wearying treks through town and castle. Always he tried very hard not to use his farsight, if that was what he had. Yet he had an inexplicable conviction that the missing—and now empty—keg was located under the staircase by the armory latrines.

He had already passed beyond the populous domain of childhood, but the well-settled realm of manhood still lay ahead. The borderlands are thinly inhabited and never easy going, being roamed by monsters that prey most readily upon the solitary traveler—and now Rap had no companions.

When he set about a search for lodgings, he discovered what old Hononin had already guessed—that rooms were in short supply. Rap smelled now of the uncanny. An odor of sorcery hung about him, and while no one was so unkind as to snub him for it openly, his friends would drift in other directions when given the chance. The brand was unobtrusive, but it was there. He was human and he suffered. Women suspected that he could see through their clothes and they shunned him even more than men did. And no one wanted a lodger who could spy through walls.

Of necessity, Rap's temporary residence in the garret above the stable became his permanent abode. He moved his scanty possessions in and squandered most of his savings on buying a bed and was miserably content. He ate in the castle commons, but he did not sit at the drivers' table.

His work for Foronod might lack the romance of being a man-at-arms but it was a challenge; it implied that he was trusted. The factor was a hard master—demanding, saturnine, and slow to praise—yet he was fair. Rap respected him, did his best, and strove to be worthy.

The blizzards came more frequently, the days dwindled. Wagons rolled no more, even within the town itself. Yet Krasnegar had been built for its climate and pedestrians could travel by covered alleys and staircases. A man could walk from castle to deserted harbor without more than a half-dozen brief dashes out of doors. Peat fires glowed. The business of life continued safely below the storms, and pleasures continued, also. There was food in plenty and drink and companionship; singing and dancing; talk and fellowship and romance—but not for Rap.

He was not completely without friends. He did have one, a sophisticated man of the Impire, for whom the supernatural held no terrors; a man without visible occupation to fill his hours and yet of apparently unlimited financial resources—well spoken, much traveled, sympathetic, and even proficient in the use of swords.

"Fencing?" he said. "Well, I'm no expert, my friend, and I would not venture to draw at the imperor's court, where any young squire may turn out to be a swordsman of prowess, but I am probably as competent as any of the wood-chopping rustics I have noted here in the castle guard. So if you want a lesson or two, lad, I shall be most happy to oblige."

Rap said, "Thank you very much, Andor."

Krasnegar had never before met anyone like Andor. He was young, yet as poised as a prince. A gentleman and apparently wealthy, he mingled freely with both the lowly and the high. He was as handsome as a young God, yet seemed unaware of the fact. One day he could be found wrapped in filthy furs in the common saloons, trading vulgar ribaldry with sailors; the next he would be seen in satin and silk, holding respectable matrons spellbound at an elegant soirée; or with Kondoral, laughing heartily at the old seneschal's interminable, threadbare monologues. The very candles seemed to burn more brightly near Andor.

It was rumored that the king disapproved of him, and certainly he was never seen in the king's company, not even at the weekly feast for the palace staff, over which the king presided. As the days shortened, however, his Majesty stopped appearing at those functions, and then Andor began to attend—sometimes sitting at the high table with Kondoral and Foronod and the other dignitaries, sometimes squashed in with the servants near the squeaking spits of the fireplace, his arm around a wench.

His success with women became an instant legend; it verged on the uncanny. Resentment was inevitable and he was an imp—some jotunn would have to educate the intruder. Very soon after his arrival, while Rap was still on the mainland following Foronod, one tried.

It happened in a bar near the docks, and the details were never very clearly established. The volunteer enforcer was an enormous and ill-reputed fisherman named Kranderbad, who tersely invited the stranger outside. Reportedly Andor first attempted to talk his way out of the challenge, then yielded with reluctance. The imps in the group sighed unhappily, the jotnar grinned and waited eagerly for Kranderbad's return. But it was Andor who returned, and very soon. It was said that he had no bruises on his knuckles or sweat on his brow, and apparently none of the blood on his boots was his. Kranderbad was not seen in public for many weeks thereafter, and the extent of his injuries impressed even that rough frontier company.

Another attempt occurred a few days later and now the challenger had a friend waiting outside to help. Both joined Kranderbad in the infirmary, and one of them never walked again.

That one had a brother who was a barber, and the same evening he was overheard vowing vengeance. Before morning he was found in an alley without his razor, his tongue, or his eyelids, and thereafter Andor was left in peace to woo whom he pleased.

He established lodgings at the home of a wealthy widow. Her friends censured but were too intrigued to ostracize. They whispered among themselves that she seemed to have shed ten years.

Soon he knew everyone and everyone knew him. With very few exceptions, men found him irresistible and were pleased to call him friend. What women called him was less easily established, but none seemed to bear grudges, as they would have done if they had felt jilted or cheated. He was discreet—no match or marriage failed because of Andor.

He showed Foronod a better system of bookkeeping. He gave Thosolin's men-at-arms tips on fencing and he advised Chancellor Yaltauri on current politics in the Impire. He could dance superbly and play the lute well by local standards. He had a passable singing voice and a bottomless store of stories, from the literary to the scatological.

Krasnegar fell at his feet.

Yet even Andor could not be in more than one place at a time, and he spread himself thinly. He rejected any efforts by his admirers to become followers, for the young men of the town would have flocked along behind him like baby ducklings had he given them the chance. He roamed Krasnegar from palace to docks, and none of the hundreds who called him friend could claim to know him well or see him often . . . with one exception.

Why a sophisticated man of the world, a wealthy gentleman, should be interested at all in a solitary, awkward adolescent—a minor flunky lacking grace, family, and education—was a major mystery. But for Rap, it seemed, Andor had unlimited time.

Thousand friends.
   He who has a thousand friends has not a friend to spare,
   And he who has one enemy will meet him everywhere.
                              Emerson, *Translation from Omar Chiam*

❊ FIVE ❊

Demon lover

1

In the whole of the Northwest Sector of Julgistro Province, there was no grander social event than the Kinvale Ball. There were many balls at Kinvale during the season, but *the* Kinvale Ball was the one held each year just two nights before Winterfest. It alone supported half the costume and jewelry trades of the region. Being added to the guest list had been known to induce bankruptcy among the lesser nobility. Being dropped from it was generally regarded as justifiable cause for suicide.

Thousands of candles sparkled amid the crystal droplets of the chandeliers. Hundreds of guests danced in a whirl of opalescent finery—silks and gemstones, satins and lace, color like shredded rainbows. The wine, the food, and the music were unmatched anywhere in the Impire. Amid the dark and cold of midwinter there was gaiety and happiness, laughter and light.

Ekka, the dowager duchess of Kinvale, was long since past indulging in dancing herself. She walked now with a cane and as little as possible, but the Winterfest ball was a Kinvale institution that she guarded and cherished. She had probably attended seventy of them herself—she could not remember how old she had been when she saw her first—and she would let nothing diminish the tradition. She could not improve on the pattern, for as far back as she could remember no expense or ostentation had been spared to make the ball as grand and enjoyable as possible, and she took care that it never dwindled by as much as a fly's eyelash. Every year she watched the youngsters swirl past in their quadrilles and gavottes, and she was remorseless in her intent that they would enjoy themselves as much as she had done in her faraway youth.

Ekka was a tall and bony woman and had never been a beauty, although she had always had presence. She still did. Her nose was too large, her teeth too prominent, and age had increased her resemblance to a horse until she half expected her reflection to neigh at her every time she looked in a mirror. Frail now and unsteady on her cane, white-haired and wrinkled and ugly, she ruled Kinvale tyrannically, knowing that she terrorized everyone and gaining secret amusement from that fact. She had no power except the power to send them away, so what did they fear? That, she supposed, was presence.

She sat as straight as her crumbling bones permitted in a high-back chair on a small dais at one end of the great ballroom. From this vantage she oversaw the splendor with both pleasure and the unwinking stare of a snake. Should she notice any maiden whose decolletage fell below her standards, or any young cockerel dipping too deep in the wine bowl, then would she thump the parquet with her gold-topped cane to summon a messenger from a small army of pages that stood near to hand. The offender would be requested to attend her Grace forthwith.

From time to time her friends and guests would pause in their progress to wish her merry Winterfest, or thank her for the hospitality, or merely to reminisce. Persons of especial interest she would permit to perch briefly on the chairs beside her to exchange a few fleeting words, but that was an honor sparingly granted.

Now the band was playing a reel. The ballroom flashed and surged with color as the dancers pranced and leaped through the intricate patterns. Ekka watched the pairings form and reform, all the permutations and combinations flickering together in her mind, for Kinvale was both a finishing school and a marriage bureau. Matchmaking was Ekka's lifelong skill and recreation. To Kinvale came the eligible young ladies of half the Impire, with mothers or aunts or grandmothers in attendance, and few indeed were those who did not find themselves betrothed to their elders' satisfaction when they departed. Rank and wealth and looks and breeding—the possibilities and requirements were innumerable. It took a rare touch to blend them all in satisfying coalescence, and a diplomacy and knack bordering on sorcery to see that the young persons involved believed that they had followed nothing but their own wishes when they united in the pairings Ekka had selected.

Now the couples she had paired in her youth were sending their children or even grandchildren. At times she felt like godmother to the Impire.

The frenetic whirling reached its climax in the final chord, then an instant of silence. The men bowed to their partners, the partners curtsied. And all over the hall they each took a deep breath, for the tempo had been fiery. The ballroom seemed to gasp, then the tableau disintegrated in smiles and laughter and conversation, men moving to lead ladies back to their seats. Close by Ekka, Legate Ooniola was escorting Princess Kadolan of Krasnegar through the crowd with the same single-minded dedication he would have applied to maneuvering his legion. Ekka lifted her cane and caught Kade's eye. The legate obediently right-turned and delivered the princess to Ekka's dais. He bowed. Kade thanked him. He departed.

Puffing mightily, she sank down beside the duchess. Fans were in vogue again this year and Kade took advantage of the fact vigorously.

"Ooof!" she said. "I allow my ambitions to exceed my abilities! I feared I was going to have an apoplexy halfway through that one."

"I am sure you would never do anything so gauche, my dear. It is going well, I think?"

"Marvelous!" Kade sighed contentedly. "Winterfest is a dry crust anywhere but Kinvale. It is wonderful to be back again." Her eyes were raking the hall.

"Over by the far buffet," Ekka said. "With the legionary, the tall one."

Kade nodded and relaxed. "A great experience for her. She will never forget Winterfest at Kinvale. No one ever does."

"Kind of you to say so." Ekka frowned at the sight of the Astilo girl talking with the weedy Enninafia youth. His family did not need her money, and it could use an infusion of brains that her bloodlines would not supply. "Your niece does you great credit, ma'am."

Kade simpered and they both chuckled. They had been—and indeed must still be—sisters-in-law. Their acquaintanceship dated back for almost half a century. They needed very few words to convey meanings to each other.

"She benefits more from the current fashion than I do," Kade said wistfully. Ekka was too kind to smile. Only short weeks before Winterfest the dramatic news had come from Hub—trumpets were out, bustles were back in. Dress plans had been changed at very short notice, but the last thing Kadolan needed was a bustle. She had done the best she could, staying with dark-blue satin and a single strand of pearls, borrowing Ekka's own pearl tiara, but even in such simplicity she was still dumpy, and the bustle mocked her.

"At the back she benefits perhaps," Ekka remarked. "She is a little young yet for the necklines." She disapproved of the present style in necklines. They took the men's minds off conversation.

"Well, in necklines I am qualified." Kade raised her fan to conceal her mouth. "My niece had the audacity to tell me that my figure was altogether two things of a good much."

Ekka's thin dry lips sketched a smile. "Of course you chided her for unladylike thoughts and unseemly vulgarity?"

The orchestra was striking up a gallopade, and the floor began to swirl again with eager couples.

"Of course! But Kinvale has been wonderful for her! Six months ago she would have said it in public."

"That was what I wanted to ask you, dear. How is our young hussar faring?"

Kade sighed again. "She suspects that he may have left his helmet out in the sun too long. With his head in it."

"It is not unlikely," Ekka agreed. "I fear that I am running out of candidates, Kade. If you are still intent on leaving in early summer, we are facing a shortage of time. Shall we review the requirements?"

The gallopade was in full romp, and Inosolan was being passed down a line of men, laughing and smiling. Her dancing had improved beyond all recognition. The ladies continued their conversation while watching the dancers.

"Character, I fear, comes first," Kade said sadly.

"That is a problem. Anything else is easy. And character is not merely rare, it is hard to detect soon enough. Although nothing brings it out like matrimony."

"Too late then, of course." Kade accepted a sparkling goblet from a footman's tray. "Holindarn insists that she make a free choice, as I told you." She paused. "Even if her happiness requires her to remain in the Impire, he said."

Ekka was startled and said, "Indeed?" noncommittally, while she mulled this interesting complication. She could think of several families that would be gratified to pick up a meaningless royal title, so long as their son did not have to go and dwell in the barren north for it. Her own, for example—and there were other interesting implications.

"That certainly widens the field, then. He would allow her to relinquish the throne, you mean?"

Her sister-in-law hesitated again. "It may not be hers to relinquish, dear."

Silence was the best lubricant for confidences . . .

Kade frowned, as if she had not meant to go so far. "In the Impire you have had several imperesses."

"Mostly very competent!"

"History is not my strong point." Kadolan was still watching as Inos drew closer in the intricacies of the dance. "But in Nordland there is no doubt—only men can rule. Krasnegar has no precedents in the matter."

"So who makes the decision?" Ekka asked, nodding to some passing ladies.

"He does," Kade said confidently. "He will name his heir."

Ekka waited for more, then prompted. "But can he make it stick after his death?"

Kade smiled unwillingly. "Time has not blunted you, dear. That will depend on a lot of things. Will the people accept her? Will Nordland? Will the Impire?"

Mmm . . . obviously something more topical was bothering her. Something had provoked this confidence, or it would have come out months ago.

"And his decision, and all the others' decisions, will depend on her choice of husband?"

Kade nodded absently, acknowledging friends whirling past. "Very much so, I think. Certainly Nordland's." More silence and then she said, "And the timing."

Ah! "Timing, dear?"

Inos came dancing by. She noticed her aunt and smiled radiantly, then was swept away into the pattern. She was almost the only woman in the room who could wear a green like that. It set off her eyes beautifully—and almost as much as her golden hair, it let Kade pick her out in the crowd.

"Holindarn can train a successor," Kade said, "whether Inos herself or her husband. Ruling a kingdom, even a single-bed-size kingdom like Krasnegar, does take a certain knack."

This time silence was not enough lubrication. "He is a relatively young man yet," Ekka suggested.

"Of course."

But there had been a hesitation. Travel between Krasnegar and Kinvale was not impossible in winter. Trappers and other rough men could do it. Such men would do it for money. If Kade had been concerned about her brother's health, then she would certainly have arranged for someone in the palace hierarchy to keep her informed—she was not nearly as scatterbrained as she pretended.

"You have had no word lately, have you? No news is good news."

"So they say," Kade agreed, with a tranquility that did not deceive the dowager duchess for a moment.

For if Holindarn did not want his sister to hear, then he was quite capable of learning whom she had recruited and then derecruiting them. Had any message arrived at Kinvale, Ekka would surely have heard of it. No news, then, was bad news, and that was what was rankling.

And if Inos did not succeed, who was next in line?

"So the hussar we send back to his horse," Ekka said, "or we may aim him elsewhere—the Astlio girl, perhaps . . . Have any of his predecessors dropped sparks on the tinder?"

"Yes indeed. I wanted to ask you about him. You built a blaze with your first attempt, dear, and left no fuel for the others."

Ekka was surprised. "That merchant youth? What was his name? The one from Jini Fanda?"

"Good Gods, no!" Kade spluttered in a very unusual display of emotion. "Even I couldn't stand him. No, the Andor boy."

"Andor? Oh, that one! Still?

Ekka frowned. "He wasn't one of mine, Kade. You gave me no warning, remember. It took a little time to call them in from the pasture. Angilki invited that one." At that moment she noticed her son, dancing with the Yyloringy woman, his face as blank as a well-polished table.

"Perhaps a fortunate chance, then," Kade remarked sanguinely.

"Perhaps."

This time it was Kadolan who detected the hesitation. She turned to her hostess with an inquiring glance.

"It is his house, after all," Ekka said. "I can hardly stop him from inviting his own friends to stay."

"Of course not, my dear."

But this would not be the first time Angilki had unwittingly thrown complications into his mother's plans. She had told him more than once that he could invite anyone he liked except men— or women. The joke had escaped him. Jokes usually did.

"Well, Sir Andor undoubtedly had character," Kade said, "or at least charm. If diplomacy is a requirement for ruling Krasnegar—and it certainly is—then he would qualify on that. What else do we know about him?'' Inos was coming around again.

A very good question! Ekka did not think her memory was failing her yet. She was rather proud of her memory. But on the spur of the moment, she could recall nothing at all about that Andor boy. She had engaged him in conversation several times, of course. She had begun a careful probing. Curiously, though, it seemed that the subject of Sir Andor's background had always slipped out of play. All she could remember was laughing very hard at some of his jests.

"Why don't we check the files in the morning?" she suggested. "He brought letters, of course . . . and my notes. Just look at that wretched Ithinoy girl! How could her grandmother ever dream of allowing her to wear *puce*, with her coloring?"

"Ekka?" Kadolan said sharply.

Ekka sighed. "You should have suggested him sooner. We could have invited him to the ball."

"He is probably not available. He told Inos that he was leaving on some romantic mission of honor and danger. He has not written. She does not write to him."

The two ladies exchanged puzzled glances.

"But why leave?" Ekka said. "If that's what he was? If that was what he wanted?"

"If that was what he wanted, then he succeeded. She has not looked seriously at anyone else."

"He did not . . ." Ekka paused. Even with a very old friend, there are some questions . . .

"No! I'm quite sure. One can always tell. But he certainly could have done, had he wanted. She was very innocent, remember. Now she is perhaps a little wiser, but he knew every trick in the box. I fancy I know most of them, but that young man could have sidestepped me with no trouble, had he wished."

From Kade that was an astonishing confession. In her years at Kinvale, even before their respective husbands had died, she had been Ekka's pupil and partner in matrimonial machinations. Anything the Princess Kadolan did not know about chaperoning and the wiles of swains should not be worth knowing.

Still, Ekka was relieved. Three juvenile domestics had been dismissed soon after Sir Andor's departure, and probably several others had been more fortunate in their follies.

"So what was he after, I wonder? The crown?"

"Then why leave?" It was very unlike Kade to let worry show on her face. "What business could possibly be more important?"

"Perhaps he went off to take a look at Krasnegar?"

That remark provoked loud, unladylike guffaws from both of them.

The gallopade had ended. Angilki went by, leading the Yyloringy woman, breathing much too heavily and still half asleep with boredom.

"Well," Kade said cheerfully. "There would seem to be no use worrying about the Andor man. Inos does not know where he is, and if she doesn't, then I assume that no one does. We'll just have to keep the parade going and hope that she takes to someone else."

"Or until he chooses to return?"

"Exactly."

"And if he brings a proposal?"

"Oh, Inos would accept with her next breath. He bewitched her. And I have my orders. Unless I have very—*very*—good reasons, she is to be allowed to make her own choice." She sighed wistfully. "I can't blame her. He certainly did sparkle. Grim old Krasnegar would be a merrier place with him around."

But . . .

Ekka nodded as the music began again for the gavotte. If Inosolan did not succeed, who would? How soon was Holindarn going to die? She had been thinking in terms of years, and now it sounded like perhaps months. There was a title involved. There was a kingdom. More than that, there was almost certainly a word, part of the Inisso inheritance.

Ekka decided to keep her own options open. She would summon Angilki and inform him that he need not propose to the Yyloringy woman this evening after all.

2

Two days before Winterfest, a fencing lesson ended when Andor's wooden sword thunked across Rap's armored abdomen hard enough to split the leather, spill the peat-moss padding, and force an agonized "Ooof!" out of the victim.

"That will do for today, I fancy." Andor's amusement was evident even in a voice muffled by a fencing mask.

"Not fair!" Rap protested, straightening up with difficulty. "You said—"

Andor pulled off his mask and laughed. "I said that the point was almost always better than the edge, yes. But I did not say that one should never use the edge, my friend. That's why swords have edges! And you left yourself wide open for that one. Let's go and have a drink.''

Ruefully Rap noticed that Andor's hair was barely ruffled after almost two hours' vigorous exercise.

They put away the protective garments, the masks, and foils; they washed themselves at the communal trough; they prepared to depart. There were no other fencers in the garrison's gym. Krasnegar was preparing for Winterfest.

"A beer at the Beached Whale would soften the tissues pleasantly," Andor suggested, expertly snuffing candles. He was carrying a large and unexplained bundle of furs, which Rap was trying not to worry about.

"I'll keep you company for a while." Rap thought glumly of the lonely attic to which he must return, the long hours until the evening meal, and the longer hours after that until he could expect to sleep. Foronod's affairs were shut down now for Winterfest, so Rap would have nothing to do for days. Yet he had no great longing to linger in the crowded, ill-lighted Beached Whale with its thick fug of beery odor and oil fumes and reek of unwashed bodies. The gaming would stop as soon as a seer entered; sometimes women would ostentatiously depart. For Andor's sake he would be tolerated—briefly—but he was not the most popular of customers. He never stayed for long.

"On second thought," said Andor, who always seemed to know what a man was thinking, "let's go straight to your place. I have something private to discuss."

They stepped out into one of the covered stairways of the palace and picked their way carefully down toward the light of a distant torch sizzling in its sconce.

"How'm I doing, Andor?" Rap asked. "In fencing?"

Andor frowned in the darkness . . . Rap thought he frowned. "Well, you're still growing like a sorcerer's sunflowers, and that throws a man's coordination off. You'll soon be over that, which will help. Otherwise—you're average. Thosolin would be happy enough to take you on now. The Tenth Legion would not."

After a moment of echoing footsteps he added, "It's a pity you only have farsight and not some foresight as well; they often go together. Foresight makes deadly swordsmen, unbeatable. Even so, you should have known that carpet-beater was coming just now. It was not exactly a subtle stroke."

Rap snarled. "Damn farsight! I still won't believe it! I don't *see* anything."

"It's a name, that's all. And a precious gift. Stop fighting it!"

They went through a door and crossed a courtyard between high snowbanks, spectral in the starlight. The sky was a black crystal bowl, clear and bitter and infinitely deep. Soon the moon would come to dull the stars, but the sun was a brief visitor to Krasnegar at Winterfest. The air was deadly as steel. It could kill a man in minutes.

Then came more ill-lighted stairs and corridors. Starlight glimmered but faintly on the windows, yet Rap led the way without hesitation, his companion following closely. The final stair was black as a closed grave, but Rap hurried up it to his room. He went to the flint and candle on the shelf. He struck a spark and light danced over the floor. "There!"

"Most people keep their candles by the door," Andor said dryly.

Rap swore under his breath. He went out again and hurried along to the drivers' office to borrow a couple of chairs. There was no light at all, but he put his hands on them without hesitation. He told himself that he was doing nothing out of the ordinary—he had put the chairs back there after Andor left the last time, and no one came near that office for six months at a stretch, so he had known exactly where they would be. But as he carried them to his room, he knew that Andor's comment was valid—he did wander around in the dark. He had nothing to trip over in his little attic, only his bed and one small box, but he could always put his hand on anything he wanted. The thought troubled him. He was slipping, starting to make use of an ability that he refused to recognize or accept.

By the time he arrived with the seats, Andor had extracted the wine bottle from his mysterious bundle and was standing under the candle on its high shelf, fiddling with the seal. The bundle lay on the bed, a cushion shape of obviously fine-quality white fur, bound with a ribbon. Rap looked away from it quickly and told himself that it was not what he feared it was.

It was, though.

Andor glanced around for goblets, shrugged, and held out the bottle. "You first! Merry Winterfest!" He grinned.

"Merry Winterfest," Rap echoed obediently. He did not care much for wine on principle, but he took the bottle and swallowed a mouthful. He did not like the taste much, even. He tried to return the bottle, but it was refused.

"You are not your father. You have a word! People who know words of power do not have nasty accidents like he did."

Andor did not usually discuss such personal matters, and Rap was surprised that he knew the story. He took a long swig and collapsed into coughing and gagging.

"A man of taste and discernment, I see?" Andor sat down and sipped small mouthfuls for a while in silence.

Neither man had removed his parka. The wine would freeze if they took very long to drink it, but that was not unusual in Krasnegar. Only the rich could afford peat. Rap's garret did not even possess a stove, although it did gain some warmth from the horses that lived below. Andor was probably comfortable, for his parka and fur pants were thick and down-lined. Rap's were neither, and had he been alone he would have crawled into bed.

For the thousandth time he wondered *why*? He looked at the coarse plank walls, the low, canted ceiling, the equally rough floor. Every nailhead in that ceiling was highlighted by a small cap of ice. The tiny window was a shine of starlight through frost, a square eye of cold silver. *Why* would a man who could afford such clothes, a man who could enter almost any chamber in the city—with or without a beautiful hostess waiting—*why* would such a man spend hours in a place like this? Rap had not forgotten the king's warning, yet Andor seemed like a true friend, improbable though that was. He had never suggested any wrongdoing, he did not pry. And he was the only friend Rap had. For a man who had once fancied himself as popular, that was a galling reflection.

Andor offered the bottle again. "Drink up! I want you good and drunk."

"Why?"

Andor's teeth flashed in his irresistible grin. "You'll find out! I need your help on something."

"You can have my help sober, for anything." Rap took another swig.

He meant that. Andor was lavish with his time. By day he would often accompany Rap on his errands for Foronod, expertly checking the addition on a tally, carrying burdens like a common porter, throwing in a rapier question or two when a memory stumbled. Many evenings he had spent in this bare box, patiently explaining the mysteries of the alphabet and the arcane ways of numbers. He had pretended to enjoy being introduced to Rap's other friends, the horses.

Why?

Andor had been everywhere. As Rap knew Krasnegar, Andor knew the Imperial capital of Hub, the city of five hills. He had described its avenues and palaces, its fountains and gardens, in words enchanting to a son of the barren north. Silver gates and golden domes, lords and fine ladies, crystal coaches, orchestras and zoological collections—he had paraded them all through this dingy attic under the protection of glittering Imperial cohorts with bands playing and bright banners waving.

And not only Hub. Andor had visited great cities uncounted. He had traveled the far south and seen devastation wrought by dragons. For so young a man, he had visited an incredible list of places. He had been to Faerie itself, bathing on its golden beaches, paying a silver penny for a ride on a hippogryff. He had met gnomes and dwarves and elves. He had haggled for tapestries in crowded bazaars and edged along walls in sinister alleyways; he had watched beautiful slave girls dance before their masters in opulent courts. He had sailed the Summer Sea in barques with silken sails curved by the scented winds. He had wept at the baleful song of merfolk lamenting a dying moon.

He had also sat long hours in this rough wooden attic and talked of cannibal islands and castles of glass, of unicorns, of elven trees that touched the clouds and of the jeweled cities nestling on their boughs, of enormous animals with noses long enough to wrap around a man and pick him up, of floating sea monsters so huge that men built houses on their backs and cultivated gardens there, of volcanoes in eruption and hot springs in which the locals boiled whole oxen for feastings and the guests afterward for entertainment. He had described the lairs of trolls and ancient ruins half digested by desert sands. Talking statues and mirror pools that showed the future were familiar to him, and he knew many tales of wonders greater yet.

Why?

Only once had Rap even dared to ask *why*? Why was Andor his friend? Why did Andor help him, keep him company, tell him of the wonders of the world, and even assist in his education?

What, he had inquired diffidently, was in it for Andor?

Andor had laughed. "For friendship! The others are only acquaintances. And because I admire courage more than anything in the world."

"Courage? Me?"

"Remember the first time we met?" Andor had asked in apparent seriousness. "I had just arrived with the caravan, and a blizzard had just arrived, also. I was looking forward to a comfortable bath and a hot bed. I discovered that the tide had closed the causeway and there was a crisis on. I didn't understand, but I made it my business to find out, because I'm nosy. It wasn't difficult to locate Foronod and see that he was the boss. And then he sent for a boy! I said to myself, 'This man is crazy!' But he asked you if you could guide the wagons and you didn't say 'Sure!'—which a fool might have done. You didn't whimper excuses. You looked over the problem and set that big jaw of yours and said, 'I'll try!' And then I said to myself, 'He means he'll try his damndest. And this Foronod hasn't sent for a boy; he's sent for a man!'"

"Oh!" Then Rap had hoped he was not blushing, for he had felt immensely pleased that Andor of all men should think that of him. "And then I picked you!"

"You did. And I nearly panicked, right there. But you weren't just risking your own neck. Any fool can do that. You were going to carry the whole town. That takes a backbone stiffer than most men's. So I decided if you had that kind of courage to lead, I would have the courage to follow you. So I did."

And although Rap could hardly dare to believe that explanation, he had never asked again. If he made Andor think more about the matter, then Andor might come to the correct conclusion. He might just say "You're right; there is nothing in it for me," and leave.

But Rap was thinking over the problem now, for Andor was being uncharacteristically silent, passing the bottle back and forth in silence, staring moodily at the floor. Usually he was irresistibly good company, leaving no time for Rap to brood. This day he seemed to have a problem. Was he thinking of all the festivities going on, the dozens of parties at which he would be welcome, so long as he did not arrive with Rap in tow?

Then Andor looked up and grinned. "Drunk enough yet?"

"For what?"

"I want a promise. I'm going to tell you a secret and I want your promise not to tell anyone. Ever."

"You have it. Drunk or sober."

"Don't be so rash! Suppose I told you I was planning to kill the king?" Andor's eyes twinkled, reflecting the candle-flame.

"You wouldn't."

"All right, here goes. I've never told anyone this, though." He held the bottle up to examine its contents. "You and I have something in common. We both have a word."

Rap's heart crawled out of a chrysalis and gently opened butterfly wings. "You have farsight, also?"

Andor guffawed. "If you knew how many collar studs I lose, you wouldn't ask! No, not farsight."

The wings were folded away again.

"Then what's your talent?"

Andor grinned more widely. "Girls!"

"Oh!" Rap knew that he must not show his distaste, or he would seem like a narrow-minded provincial. Andor was a so-phisticated citizen of the Impire. Rap knew of his reputation, but he had always thought it to be mostly jealous gossip, wild exag-geration like the stories of men being kicked to jelly in alleyway brawls. He would certainly not believe *that* of Andor, even if the girls part were true. "I'd be willing to trade," he said.

"Not likely!"

"But why are you telling me this? Why aren't you out exercis-ing your talent? All the girls are in holiday mood."

"You're probably not drunk enough yet, but I'll risk it. I'm leaving."

Rap's first thought was one of despair. Krasnegar seemed sud-denly unthinkable without Andor. "What? Why?"

The bottle was thrust back at him. "Take a *big* drink. Listen! I'm leaving, because I'm bored. I thought a winter in the north would be exciting, but it's dull as shelling peas."

"Who's going with you?"

Andor shrugged. "I've knocked about the world a lot. I thought I'd just take a horse and go."

"You're crazy! Mad! Mad! Mad! What about the green men?"

Andor shrugged, took the bottle back, and stretched out his legs. "I've been asking about them. I'm told that one man is usually safe. Goblins respect courage and they honor a solitary traveler. A group may get into trouble."

"Fingernails!" Rap shuddered. Goblins murdered travelers in horrible ways. It was said they would hand a man a pair of tongs and demand a fingernail as road toll. If he had the courage to pull out one of his own fingernails, they would let him go. If he didn't— they didn't.

"The only alternative is an armed escort, at least a dozen. Better two dozen. And I can't afford to hire that many."

"Andor, this is the northland. The cold is a killer. It's not like hiking across a desert or somewhere warm. You should take someone with some experience."

There was a pause while the candle flame danced in silence.

"I have a better idea," Andor said. "By the way, merry Win-terfest!" He pointed to the bundle on the bed.

"You shouldn't have!" Miserably Rap leaned elbows on knees and buried his face in his hands. From the wine or from embar-rassment, he felt sick.

"Will the boots fit? A man's feet are usually the first part of him to stop growing."

"They look all right." Rap did not even turn his head to look at the bundle—mukluks and fur trousers wrapped in a parka, fur from young polar bears, lined with the down of ducks . . . garments of a quality he could never hope to own in his lifetime. He did not have to open the damned parcel. "It's very, very kind of you, Andor. No one's given me a Winterfest present since my mother died. But what could I give you in exchange? Horse buns?"

"It is a bribe, of course," Andor admitted cheerfully. "I was hoping that you might agree to share. Yours seems to be stronger than mine, so a sharing would be a gift to me."

"Share what?" Rap looked up in both hope and puzzlement.

"You tell me your word and I'll tell you mine. Two words make an adept. On my trip, I'll be safe from cold and goblins both—if you'll do that for me."

Unhappily Rap shook his head. "I don't have a word. The king asked me; I told him the same. Do you think I would have lied to my king? I know no word of power. These horrible things just started happening to me by themselves."

"You must have a word! It's too late to deny it, Rakkie-boy! Yes, they're usually kept secret, but yours is common knowledge now."

Rap remembered how his lecture from Sagorn had been cut short. "The king told me that there were dangers in knowing a word. What dangers?"

"Gods, man!" Andor almost shouted. "They're valuable! Incredibly valuable! They're magic-proof themselves, so they can't be extracted by sorcery, but every sorcerer in the world always wants one more word, to become more powerful. One of these days someone's going to nail you to a post and start heating irons! That's another reason we should share—we'll be much safer as adepts, because we'll have abilities we don't have now."

"I don't want to be a sorcerer!" Rap cried. "I want to be a man-at-arms and serve Queen Inosolan. That's all I pray the Gods for!"

"Rap!" Andor said impatiently. "Two won't make you a sorcerer, but with two you can be a champion whatever-you-want, including a champion swordsman. You'll be able to beat anyone in the world, except another adept or a mage or sorcerer. Doesn't that idea appeal to you?"

"It sounds sort of sneaky." Rap surprised himself by grinning.

Andor chuckled and looked hopeful. "And in the forest I'll be in no danger at all. Well, not much."

The forest! Swordmanship forgotten, Rap came back to sad reality. "But I don't have a word to share."

Andor sighed and held out the bottle again. "All right! If you won't, then you won't."

Rap slid off his chair, onto his knees. "Andor, if I could, I would! I'd give you mine and not want yours, and I'd try to forget mine. But I don't have any magic words! I swear it!"

"You must have! Don't grovel—it's not manly. Tell me how your mother died and what she said to you the last time you saw her. The words are usually passed on a deathbed."

Rap climbed back on his chair. He felt dizzy with the wine and sick to his heart. He would oh-so-gladly tell Andor what he wanted to know if he could. Andor was a good friend, the only friend he had, and he felt soiled and petty at refusing him. "Jalon has one?" he asked. "He offered to share, too, and I didn't understand!"

"Of course he does. No one could sing like that otherwise."

Rap knew that Andor had met Jalon. "Why not share with him, then?"

Andor hesitated and then said, "We tried. We both know the same word, so nothing changed. Now, your mother?"

But Rap knew that there was no help there. As happened every few years, fever had swept into the town from a visiting ship. People had been dying every day. Anyone becoming ill in the palace was removed at once. It was his first year in the stables. He had spent a morning mucking out and gone home, expecting his mother to be there working at her lace, as she usually was, with his lunch ready and a smile and a hug and a little joke about her working man. It had been two days before anyone thought to tell him where she was, or why she had gone. Even then he had not been allowed to go and see her. She had died on the third day. So there had been no deathbed farewells, no secret words of power passed.

He told the story and Andor looked baffled.

"She came from Sysanasso," Rap said. "Perhaps their magic is different and they don't use words of power?"

"Yes they do. I've been there." Andor had been everywhere. He fell silent, looking sulky.

Despite himself, Rap reached out with his mind and saw those glorious soft furs on his bed. The thought of owning them was

like the thought of a hot summer's day and a picnic on the shore
with . . . with Inos or someone. He could not accept such a gift.

"Well!" Andor brightened again. "What I really need is a
good sorcerer, as the saying goes, but I shall find a companion,
some man who is good with horses, courageous, dependable . . ."

"I'm glad to hear that, Andor. To go by yourself would be very
foolish. I'm very sorry you're leaving, but I shall feel happier if I
know you took someone with you who knows the north. And I'm
very grateful for the gift, but I can't accept it."

"I hadn't finished! Here, last drop." Andor handed back the
bottle. As Rap was draining it he said, "Courageous, dependable,
preferably a seer—"

Rap choked.

He finally stopped coughing and gasping. "No! I'm not a trap-
per or a seal hunter! I'm a city boy!"

"You're a man, Rap. A good one."

Rap shook his head. He certainly was not man enough for that
madness—weeks of trekking through forest, with wolves and goblins . . .

"You're a man!" Andor insisted. "Being a man is not a matter
of whether hair grows on your chin, lad. It's inside your head.
Some males never make it at all. Being a man is rolling up your
sleeves and telling the world 'Now I'll play by the real rules—no
more wooden swords. If I succeed, then the credit belongs to me,
not my parents or teachers or employers, and I shall savor the
prizes without guilt, knowing I earned them. And if I fail, then
I'll pay the penalties without whimpering or blaming anyone else.'
That's what manhood is, and it's up to you to decide when it starts.
I think you made the decision that night on the beach, my friend."

Friend? But what was this friend asking him to risk? Rap was
very glad he had declined that gift. Brave was good, rash was
not.

"I am proud to be your friend, Andor," he said, struggling for
words with a strangely heavy tongue. "And if I thought my help
would be of value, then I would give it eagerly. But I think I would
just be a liability to you. Really!"

"The king is dying."

Right on cue, the candle guttered and went out, leaving faint
starlight and a long silence.

"You're sure?"

"Sagorn is. I've spoken to him. Do you want to hear it from
him, or will you trust me?"

"Of course I trust you! When?"

"Can't say when. Not today or tomorrow, but he'll never see grass again. That's what Sagorn says, and there are no wiser doctors than he."

The enormity of it felled Rap. All his life King Holindarn had ruled Krasnegar, a remote, benevolent, all-seeing father to his people, and all the more so to a boy with no father of his own. He had seemed as stable and permanent as the rock itself. The thought that one day he might suddenly not be there was impossible to grasp.

"Inos! Oh, poor Inos! when spring comes, she'll be waiting for the first ship to bring his letters and instead it will bring that news."

"Who knows what news it will bring?"

"What do you mean?"

In the darkness, only his farsight told him that Andor shrugged. "When a king dies, his successor had better be on the spot and ready."

"You mean someone may try to steal the throne?" But obviously that was what Andor meant—stupid question. Try to behave like a grown man, dummy! "Who would do that?"

"Anyone who thought he'd get away with it. Sergeant Thosolin has the armed men. Foronod may think he'd make a better monarch than a slip of a girl, and many would agree. Furthermore, the news is sure to reach Nordland before it gets to Kinvale, and the temptation to the thanes will be fresh seal to orcas. If Inos is not right here, then she has very little chance of ever becoming queen. That's my guess, anyway."

The injustice of it burned like lye. "Then why doesn't the king send for her?"

Andor sighed and adjusted himself to a more comfortable position. "Sagorn says that he refuses to admit he's that sick. He can't keep food down, he's in constant pain—but he's not going to admit anything. Secondly, he refuses to risk men's lives. Which is stupid, since half the men in town would volunteer. But he has forbidden any expeditions."

Poor Inos!

"Is that the real reason you're leaving, Andor? To tell her?"

Andor's teeth showed faintly in the gloom. "It's nothing to do with me, laddie."

More silence, then he said quietly, "But we could travel together until we got over the mountains. Once we're in the Impire, it's easy, and I would see you on the right road for Kinvale. We could hire a guide, if you want one, but you'd have no problem there.''

Rap's hands were shaking, and he clasped them together on his lap.

A long pause . . .

"Wooden swords, Rap? Or the real thing now?"

"I have no authority! Who would believe me?"

Andor did not even bother to answer. Inos, of course.

"Appoint myself? Disobey the king's command?"

"Where is your loyalty, Rap? To the king or to her?"

Darkness and silence.

"If you must choose—and now you must—then where is your loyalty? Do you not think that Inos would want to be at his side in his last days?"

Rap did not need to answer that question.

It was a craziness. The odds were appalling. But Inos *would* want to be at her father's side, and Inos was his friend—or would be, were she not a princess. Andor was right, as usual. In such an emergency, Rap must prove his courage, prove his manhood to himself, and show Inos his lo . . . loyalty.

He shivered. He was not sure which scared him more, the weather or the goblins. He had seen goblins hanging around the harbor. They were short, very broad people with gray-brown skin and jet-black hair. They called themselves the green men, and in certain lights their skin did have a greenish tinge in the brown, like old tarnished brass. In summer the men wandered around wearing an indecent minimum, each one usually followed by three or four women covered from head to toe. But all the stories agreed that they practiced torture.

It was a hair-raising thought—setting off with Andor on a journey through that cold, a journey that would take weeks. The air itself could kill.

"When?"

"Now." Andor was smiling again now.

"Now?"

He pointed to the window, which was glowing more brightly silver. "The moon is rising. Everyone is so busy getting ready for Winterfest that we won't be missed."

"But . . . we need supplies!"

"Name them. I've got my list, let's hear yours."

"Four horses. Bedding. Food. Fodder—lots of oats. Weapons. A pot to melt snow . . ." He dried up and Andor chuckled.

"I thought of a few more things, but it isn't really very many. No wooden swords?"

Rap gulped, smiled, and said, "No wooden swords."

Andor reached out a hand to shake. "Good man! If we get caught by bears in the harbor or by a blizzard in the hills, we'll die, but that we have to chance. Otherwise we just keep going—the hills, then the moors, then the forests, then the mountains. Once we're over them, then it's plum cake. Three weeks in summer . . . say five now. Then a week for Inos to get ready. Angilki will lend her some men, I think, or she can hire some. Five weeks back. Three months, or four at the outside. Sagorn thinks he may just last that long. Remember, he has a word of power, and that will help him."

Sagorn had said the words made their owners hard to kill, and he had glanced at the king when he said it.

"The king has a word, too?"

Andor nodded. "Inisso had three, it is said, and he divided his power—one word to each of his sons. I can't believe he would have done anything so stupid, but that is the legend. Kalkor of Gark probably knows one of them, even yet. He's a superb killer, a thane's thane. Duke Angilki must have one, 'cos he's an utter idiot, but a demon with wallpaper—so I've heard—and the kings of Krasnegar have always had one. That's how they have retained their independence for so long. But if Inos doesn't get back here before her father dies, then it will die with him. The throne is not all she will be cheated out of, Rap."

"But how could we collect all that stuff and get away unseen?"

"I told you—Winterfest. No one will question you, anyway. They'll assume you're doing something for Foronod. And you can walk around in the dark! Where are the bedrolls kept, the thick ones?"

"I don't know. In the storeroom by the smithy, I suppose."

"Look for them!"

Rap scowled, and knew that his scowl would show in the silvery tendrils of moonlight spreading into the little room.

"Rap! I wouldn't risk this madness with anyone else but you, and I won't if you're going to be a mule-headed pig. That farsight of yours will be our trump card. Nothing can sneak up on you, if you'll use it. But use it you must! And you need practice. Now, are the bedrolls there?"

Rap thought about the storeroom and said, "In the corner beside the axes."

"Axes! Good! I forgot those. You get the bags and—"

"The stable gate is locked. The keys are on Hononin's belt."

"Then I'll get those."

"You?" The hostler was one of the very few people in Krasnegar who did not like Andor. Hononin detested him, apparently.
The hostler was a grumpy old demon.

"Yes, me!" Andor laughed. "Where can I find him, do you
suppose?"

3

For the next two hours, Rap felt as if he were fighting a blizzard. The new clothes alone would have been enough to put him
in a daze, and the thought of trekking off into the wastelands of
the taiga, the prospect of an adventure with a hero like Andor,
the chance of seeing Inos again . . . Emotions swirled through
him like a spring tide. Moreover he now must force himself to
use his uncanny sensing ability instead of suppressing it, and soon
his head was throbbing with the effort. Yet farsight was a wonderful assistance for a common thief.

The realization that he was stealing upset him even more than
the thoughts of danger ahead. He tried to convince himself that
everything he was taking would be returned eventually, except the
food. Andor had said that he would handle the food, and he had
promised he would leave payment. Sweating in his opulent new
furs, Rap scurried around the palace storerooms, collecting things
and carrying them to the stables, using no lights, yet rarely having
to hesitate or fumble.

The bedding was where he had known it would be, and so were
axes and oats and spears and shovels . . . he cached his loot in
an empty stall and then set to work on horses.

Firedragon was a temptation, but he was stud for the royal herd,
so the temptation would have to be resisted. Young animals would
be the best, but even some of those were beginning to show the
effects of their harsh winter confinement. In the cold, uncaring
moonlight he saddled Joyboy and Crazy; he loaded Peppers and
Dancer with the bags of fodder and equipment.

Then he was ready and he slumped down on a bag of chaff to
catch his breath, wondering what he might have forgotten. The
stable was dark, warm, and smelly with horses, filled with their
little snufflings and shiftings, homely and familiar . . . and as
Rap sat there, the implications of what he had done suddenly
struck him like snow falling off a roof. The storerooms had opened
to him because he was Foronod's helper—Foronod's trusted

helper. He had been entrusted with the keys, and he had betrayed that trust! He was disobeying his king. Who was he to summon Inos to a perilous trek back through the winter forest, when her father would not? Had Andor bewitched him? He began to shake and stream with sweat. Traitor! Thief!

He was crazy! Perhaps there was just time to correct his error before Andor arrived—then no one would ever know. Frantic with guilt, with fingers that seemed clumsy as toes, Rap began unloading the ponies.

He had hardly started when a door creaked. He jumped, but he knew it was Andor before he could see him.

Andor thankfully slid a huge pack of supplies off his back. "Good man! Almost ready, I see. You're a wonder, Rap, even among northerners—and you know what people say about them."

"No? What do they say about us?"

"Oh," Andor said vaguely, "you know. Self-reliant, tough, dependable. That sort of thing. Now to business!" Grinning, he held up Hononin's keys and jingled them.

How had he managed that? Rap's heart pumped cold terror as he remembered the tales of the fisherman Kranderbad and the others. "What did you do to him? Tell me!"

"Not a thing, my lad. He's still drinking Winterfest punch at the King's Head."

"He gave you the keys?"

"No. He dropped them on the floor right here, but he doesn't know that yet. Now, what are we missing?"

Ten minutes later they unlocked the stable gate and walked out into the bailey and the deadly cold.

"Damn!" Andor said. The expedition had run into trouble already. Although the outer gates were never locked, only barred, a giant snowdrift lay across them. The postern was open, and a path through it well tramped, but the packhorses would not be able to pass that way with their burdens.

"We'll have to unload and load up again outside," Rap said, feeling the bite of the cold already.

"I suppose so," Andor muttered. "Is there anyone out there to see?"

"I . . . I don't know!"

"Use your farsight."

"I can't!" Rap felt a sudden panic. Was his mysterious power going to fail him now, when he had just agreed to use it? He could sense nothing—which told him how much he had already become accustomed to using his farsight without realizing. A tremor of guilt teased at his conscience again. Were the Gods about to with-draw their gift to him?

Then Andor chuckled. "Try this, then. Go outside and see what happens."

Puzzled, Rap handed him the lead rein and stepped through the postern. A moment later he returned. "You're right! The gate stops it—whatever it is."

"Should have known! The castle is magic-proof."

"Magic? I'm not a sorcerer!"

"No, lad, but your farsight is something more than mundane. Why do you suppose old Inisso built a castle, anyway? There are no armies here! Sorcerers fear only other sorcerers, so the castle wall is magic-proof. Magic'll work inside or outside, but not through the walls . . . I've heard of that. I'd forgotten. Well, come on! We'll freeze to death if we don't start moving!"

With Andor following, Rap led their string down through the alleys of Krasnegar and the Gods seemed to be cheering them on. The few people they met were so far advanced in festive prepa-rations that they did not wonder where Rap might be going with horses at that time of year. Most did not even recognize him in his new clothes, and the rest were content to call a cheerful greet-ing as he went by. The town gates were unlocked. Andor swung up the bar, Rap followed him out to the docks—and stopped to check for bears.

Nothing moved in the black stillness. Neither eyes nor farsight detected danger. Spring and fall were when white bears roamed the coast. Midwinter should be safe—but not necessarily.

"Can't see anything," Rap muttered nervously.

"Right!" Andor led the way to a boat ramp, and the insane escapade had begun.

Windless and still, the night was yet cold beyond belief. Steam from the horses rose like the smoke of bonfires. Sealed cozily inside his new furs, Rap could feel the deathly touch only on the small corners of his face that were still exposed, but the insides of his nostrils crackled. Snow crunched noisily below hoof and boot.

The half moon had banished the aurora and most of the stars. Now its ghostly light fell from a clear black sky to glitter on the ice-covered bay. The islands of the causeway were drifted over and tangled with piled floes, but the bay ice itself would be safe enough—if they could ever get to it, for its edges were a crumpled horror of tilted blocks and jagged monoliths, sharp ice and soft

snow mixed in random confusion. Drifts and shadows concealed
deep holes, deep enough in some cases to reach down to the water
itself, with only a treacherous thin cover of new ice. For the first
few minutes Rap floundered, convinced he would never find a
way through such a trap, tripping and constantly sinking through
surfaces that looked hard and yet were not. The horses behind
him were doing no better and he could sense their terror.

"Take your time," said Andor's voice from the back, calmly.
"The farsight will help you."

Rap's right foot sank deep into soft snow. He stumbled against
a crystal wall, extracted that foot and lost the other, then both,
and stopped of necessity, buried up to his thighs. He was gasping
with nervousness and exertion, blowing clouds of steam that glistened faint rainbow colors in the moonlight. He thought of the
endless leagues before him. At this rate they would starve to death
before they even reached the mainland, far less the forests.

"Wait!" Andor called as Rap struggled to free himself. "Close
your eyes!"

Rap closed his eyes. He knew that there was a giant canted
slab on his right, and a heap of massive blocks to his left, but of
course that smooth stretch ahead was all snowdrift and the ice
below sloped steeply down. His eyes had not told him that. Over
there, however, the snow was thinner . . .

It seemed a long time, but it could hardly have been more than
ten minutes before he had found a route through the labyrinth,
out on to the smoother surfaces in the center of the bay, where
the floes had not been so contorted by the tide. Then it seemed
safe to mount the horses. He had mastered the technique. He did
not need to close his eyes now, he could blend the two types of
sight in his mind and reach out ahead. When they came to the
jumble on the opposite shore, he led the string through without
having to backtrack once.

"Magnificent! Rap, my lad, you're incredible! This is going
to be a joyride."

Praise from Andor was a hot drink, sweet and warm all through
Rap.

And his magic worked on land, as well. He soon developed a
sense for the depth and packing of the snow—where the horses
could go and where they could not. In truth there was not much
snow on the ground. Krasnegar was a dry place and the snow
seemed impressive only because the wind made every flake do
the work of ten. Open areas were mostly swept clear, and drifts

formed only in the lee of obstacles. His headache faded as his
confidence grew, or perhaps that was an effect of the clear and
frigid air. Their route was less direct than would have been possible in summer, but they began to advance steadily into the hills,
four horses in line sending up thick clouds of steam in the moonlight, the jingle of harness blending with the crackle of the snow
crust, their shadows tracking beside.

As the sun ruled Krasnegar's sky in summer, so the moon
prevailed in winter. A full moon hardly set at all, riding high
around the sky, ducking but briefly below the northern horizon to
hide from the transient sun. But now the moon was waning and
it would fail them in time. Yet even at midwinter there would be
some daylight, and a brash new confidence was telling Rap that
he perhaps did not need light at all.

They took their first break in the same little valley where he
had met Jalon the minstrel, many months before, although now
the countryside was strangely changed by the snow and the spectral light. This far from the shore bears were unlikely, because
bears ate seals in preference to people.

Rap dug out a canteen from under a grain sack on Dancer,
whose body heat had kept it unfrozen.

"Careful with this," he warned as he passed it to Andor. "It
will freeze to your lips if you let it." He felt an unworthy twinge
of pride in his superior knowledge, the jotunn guiding the imp.

They chewed pemmican and spilled some oats on the snow for
the ponies. Rap muttered over their gashed ankles, he scraped the
packed snow out of their shoes and carefully picked the icicles
from their nostrils. He was almost laughing aloud with excitement, exhilarated by adventure and a sense of escape. Krasnegar
had been a jail for him—he had broken out into freedom. He made
a promise to himself: this journey would be the start of his manhood. If the air had not been so cold, he would have been tempted
to sing.

They made camp in a peat cutting under the glorious canopy
of stars. If there was some way to pitch a tent when the ground
was iron, then Rap did not know it. They finally used their tent
as a giant sleeping bag, putting the bedrolls inside it and then
wriggling into them.

"This," Rap said firmly, "is fun!"

"Great Gods!" Andor muttered. "He's mad." After a minute
he added, "But it's different, I'll grant you."

After another minute Rap whispered, "Andor? Have you ever had an adventure like this?"

"I'm not sure. I'll tell you afterward; this one may be different."

"How?"

"Because the others, I survived."

About two hours before noon, a faint glow appeared in the south and gradually spread into a vague twilight, then a dim and foggy daylight. For a few minutes an edge of the sun showed. Soon it was gone and the day faded as slowly as it had come.

The moorlands were difficult, the rough ground heavily laced with drifts, the best trail winding and twisting like a tangled cord. But now Rap's head did not ache at all, and he could choose the firmest route without even having to think.

Once that day they saw wolves far off, or at least Rap did, but they slunk away into blurry distance without any signs that they might be contemplating attack.

If the weather held . . . and the weather did. On the third day, while Krasnegar would be feasting and celebrating Winterfest, the moors dipped away and the first stunted trees stood as sentries for the great taiga ahead. Here ended the realm of the king of Krasnegar. Ahead lay a land that neither he nor the imperor could claim with conviction. Yet it was not no-man's land. Trees were shelter from even the worst that a blizzard could do, but they were shelter for other men, also, and those could be more deadly than any blizzard.

Seven days into the forest, they were still alive.

For two rank beginners, Rap thought, they were doing well. True, Andor was an experienced traveler, but he was a man of the south. Rap was a native, but a city dweller. Only trappers, seal hunters, and prospectors left Krasnegar in winter. All that he had known of life in the wastelands had been gleaned from conversations with men such as those, and there was much that must be learned the hard way.

But Rap and Andor learned. They learned not to build fires under branches laden with snow; they learned to take their boots into their bedrolls with them at night; they learned to stay in the densest forest, where the undergrowth and snow cover were least. In that primeval gloom there were game trails and mysterious paths along which Rap led the horses unerringly with the aid of his supernatural vision.

So far they had seen no signs of the dreaded goblins. Even animal tracks were scarce and neither of the men could read what stories they might have had to tell. Only once was there obviously wolf spoor, and for two hours thereafter Rap's ghostly farseeing was stretched to its limit as he nervously scanned the forest.

Andor grumbled that he would never eat pemmican or pancakes again, but Rap seemed to thrive on the monotonous diet. The horses were doing less well, and he hated to drive the poor creatures so hard. Their ribs showed like sapling groves. They staggered often. They spent the hours of rest pawing at the snow in search of the meager forest grass below.

And the human food supplies were dwindling fast. The self-taught pioneers would have to learn hunting soon or face starvation, but they agreed that they should press on southward as far as they could, as fast as they could, as long as the weather allowed. Some days they endured a bitter wind and light snow, but the trees gave shelter and no real killer storm had come seeking them.

Rap had seen trees before. There were a few twisted specimens in the castle gardens, and he had accompanied a search party southward two summers earlier, pursuing Firedragon and his herd. Yet he had never conceived that there could be as many trees in the world as he saw now in a single day; mostly spruce, black in their winter coats, silent and unfriendly. He had expected the taiga to be endless and featureless and unchanging, but it did change. It rolled up and down, it broke sometimes into open clearings, old firebreaks, which were tangled and hard going, and it had rivers and game trails and frozen marshes peppered with tiny, stunted spruce. He had never seen rivers before and he tried vainly to imagine how they would look with water in them instead of solid ice.

Some people never get lost, Sagorn had said, and Rap's sense of direction was unfailing. In the darkest dark or the whitest ice fog, he could always face to the south and he could always find his way back to the wagon trail whose general course they were following. The trail itself, however, was often plugged with drifts, and for men and horses, the trees made easier going.

On the seventh day they were still alive.

4   •

"Rap! Let's camp!" Andor's voice was a croak. There was no moonlight now, and the endless blindman's bluff was emotionally exhausting for him, as well as for the horses. Rap had become so expert that even in daylight he sometimes walked with his eyes closed, if the low sun shone in them.

Now the sun had just set, and Rap would have been willing to go on for longer. But he was secretly becoming concerned by Andor's weakness—imps did not fare well in winter. Rap had jotunn blood in him and was enduring much better.

"Good idea," he said. "I was just about to suggest it."

They found a campsite in a small clearing and set to work building a fire. Soon the light from the flames danced over snow and the encircling woods, and Andor had his eyes back. He rummaged for the food, while Rap set to work cutting more firewood and spruce boughs to build a lean-to. They were becoming efficient and they had long since discarded the tent as useless baggage.

Rap had moved into the trees, some yards from the flickering firelight. His attention must have wandered, for it was a sense of alarm in the ponies that alerted him first, and his farsight confirmed the danger a moment later. He plunged back through the snow to the camp and said: "Andor! Visitors!"

Andor looked up from where he was kneeling by the fire. His black impish stubble was caked with ice. His face was darkly filthy, and only a glint of firelight in his eyes showed from inside the shadow of his fur hood. "How many?"

Rap counted. "Twenty or so. They're moving around, making a circle." His hands were beginning to shake, and he was astonished to hear Andor utter a low chuckle.

"Then this may be your last chance."

"Last chance for what?" Rap did not want to raise his voice, and yet obviously the fire and the sound of his ax had already proclaimed their location like a carillon.

"Your last chance to share your word with me, of course. An adept would be in no danger, but I doubt that my talent will work well enough on these fellows. Spit it out, Rap! Quick!"

"I have no word!" Rap protested, horrified. Had Andor been thinking him a liar all this time?

Andor threw down the knife he had been using on the pemmican and put his mitted hands on his knees. "Last chance, Master Rap!"

"Andor . . ." Rap felt his world crumbling. His terror of the goblins faded before a heartbreaking sense of betrayal. "Is this all a trick? The king isn't dying?"

"Oh, he's dying. That doesn't matter much now, does it? You know what the goblins will do to us, don't you?"

They were closing in now, the circle shrinking. Yet eyes could not have detected them, and they made no sound. Only a seer could have known.

Rap wavered on the brink of panic.

"I have no word to tell! You tell me yours, then! If I do have one, then two will make me an adept, won't it? Then I can save us!"

Ander uttered a snort of derision. "Not likely!" He climbed to his feet. "Which way are they coming?"

Rap searched with his mind. The circle had stopped shrinking and there was a knot of men advancing. "That way."

"You're quite sure you won't tell me? It would be nicer than having bits pulled off."

"I can't! Tell me yours!"

Andor shook his head in exasperation. "That wouldn't work! You'd need time to learn to control it. I don't even need to become an adept, really—not for this. All I need your word for is to boost the talent I already have, more power. Then I'll win over the goblins, and we'll be made welcome. So you have to tell me yours, don't you see?"

Talent? Win? How could he have ignored the obvious for so long? "It's not just girls, is it?" Rap said bitterly. "It's all people. Men, too. You tricked me." Andor had done to Rap what Rap had done to Firedragon's mares. Thief! Traitor!

Andor shrugged heavy, furred shoulders. "The goblins are no trick, and I don't intend to stay around to entertain them. You're being foolish, Master Rap."

Then he turned to face the arrivals.

Three shadowy figures had emerged from the dark into the edge of the firelight, visible even to eyes.

If goblins valued courage, then they were not going to be impressed by Rap's quivering jaw, or the way he was keeping his knees pressed together. He resisted the temptation to sidle in behind Andor and hide.

The three came slowly closer, spears raised, inspecting their catch with care. They were short and very broad. They wore jerkins and trousers and boots, but made of buckskin instead of fur, gaudily decorated with fringes and beadwork. The fire's glimmer showed hard, unfriendly faces, dark-skinned and marked by complicated tattoo patterns around the eyes.

The one in the center seemed older than the others. He had the most ornate decorations on his clothes and on his face, and he spoke first, barking out a question that Rap could not understand, accompanied by a threatening movement of the spear.

Andor seemed to straighten up, tall and imposing. He rolled off a long answer in the same tongue, and his voice was harsher and much deeper than usual. Rap jumped with surprise when he heard it. It had never occurred to him that the goblins spoke another language.

Then he wondered how Andor knew it.

The spear points dipped slightly. The leader spoke another question, sounding surprised.

Andor replied and pointed to his face. Now Rap could catch a word or two. It was a strangely coarse dialect, but not a totally different tongue.

The chief snapped an order to his two companions and then advanced alone, holding his spear at waist height now. He peered up into Andor's hood.

Rap had just noticed that he could barely see over Andor's shoulder. Andor was much taller than he ought to be and certainly much broader. His parka strained over massive arms and shoulders. He looked wrong to Rap's eyes, and also to his farsight. There was a bigger man in there than Andor.

The chief had rattled off more questions, Andor replying. The chief showed irregular teeth in a broad grin. He reached out a mitt and turned Andor around. He wanted to see Andor's tattoos in the firelight, but in doing so he showed that face to Rap.

It was not Andor. It was a huge man, a man with the ugliest and most terrifying face Rap had ever seen—nose crushed over to one side, one corner of his mouth lifted by a scar, the corner of one eye pulled awry by another. Andor's dark, stubbly beard had vanished—this man looked newly shaved. He was not a goblin, but he had goblin tattoos around his eyes—pale jotunn's eyes, which now met Rap's and crinkled with contemptuous amusement. He grinned. His front teeth were missing, top and bottom, giving him a most hideous and sinister wolfish leer.

Rap backed away in dismay, almost into the campfire. "Where is Andor?"

"You won't be seeing him again, not likely."

Rap's heart was spinning, and he thought he might be going to faint. Andor had been there only minutes before. "Who are you?" he cried.!

"A friend of his," the big man said. "I'm Darad. You were warned about me."

5

The chief inspected Darad's tattoos by the trembling light of the campfire and apparently approved of them. He smiled and dropped his spear, attempted to embrace the giant, and received a bear hug in return. That ought to be a good sign for Darad, but who was going to hug Rap?

The chief's two companions were smiling also and coming forward for introductions and more embraces. The rest of the goblins floated in from the trees, silent as moonbeams, appearing suddenly in the firelight like ghosts. They were younger men, mostly, bearing spears or bows, and all wearing the same fringed and beaded buckskins.

What was going on? Obviously there was some sort of sorcery at work, yet Andor was most certainly not a sorcerer. Sorcerers need not endure the hardships of long days' trekking through the wastelands; they had abilities to avoid such dangers and discomfort. If Andor was a sorcerer and wanted that damnable magic word that he thought Rap possessed, he would surely have revealed his powers sooner.

And who was this Darad, against whom Jalon had warned him, this Darad who so conveniently bore goblins' tattoos and spoke their tongue? Rap trembled as he thought of Kranderbad and the others who had tried to fight Andor and had then been so callously maimed. The idea that the soft-spoken, kindly Andor might commit such atrocities, even in the heat of a fight, was just as unthinkable as the notion that he might be a sorcerer. Darad, however, looked capable of anything. Perhaps Darad was a demon who came to Andor's rescue when he was in trouble. If so, and if the goblins were going to be friendly, would Andor now reappear?

But the goblins were not being totally friendly. The four horses had been caught and led forward into the firelight, tugged unwillingly by their manes, too weak and dispirited to resist. Darad and the chief were in guttural argument with much pointing and waving of hands. As the voices rose, Rap began to catch a few of the words: *horse* and *four* and *saddle*. The old chief turned and looked at Rap, who quivered instantly and reminded himself sternly that goblins respected courage. The thought brought him little comfort.

The chief asked a question, Darad replied. Rap made out his own name, but little else. The argument seemed to go back to the horses, then to him again.

Darad stepped over, took Rap's arm in a grip that made his bones creak, and turned him away from the fire, toward the dark of the forest.

"I'll give you one more chance." His voice was low and harsh, blurred by the missing teeth.

"I don't know any words of power!" Hopefully Darad—and the goblins, too—would think it was the fearsome cold that was making Rap tremble so much. Why couldn't he stop?

"The chief must have a gift. I offered two horses. He wants all four. But he'll settle for something less."

"What?"

"You."

"You wouldn't!"

Darad grinned. His tongue and his eyeteeth were very prominent because of the gaps, and his grin was lupine and inhuman. His eyes were shiny and cold as the polar night. If Rap had been able to give him what he wanted, those eyes alone would have been persuasion enough.

"I don't know any—"

Darad pushed contemptuously. Rap toppled into a snowbank. By the time he had picked himself up, Darad and the chief were embracing again.

Experienced woodsmen would not have made their camp half a mile from a goblins' village. As soon as Rap was pointed in the right direction and jabbed forward by the point of a spear, he could sense it at the limit of his range. He had been careless; now he was going to pay dearly for his stupidity.

He staggered along, dimly aware of the guards around him, and of Darad and the goblin chief walking arm in arm at the front of the line. They were an incongruous pair, for the huge Darad made the other seem like a dwarf. The big man was hobbling, as if Andor's mukluks were hurting him.

Having registered that the horses and the equipment were being brought along, Rap concentrated on sensing out the clearing ahead, where four log structures stood in a square. He could soon tell that the closest was a stable containing three runtish ponies—small wonder that the chief had wanted all four of the Krasnegarian horses—but the farthest was much larger than the others and there were many people in there, mostly women. Of the two others, one seemed to be reserved for women and girls, and the smallest for boys. All three houses were sending up lazy columns of smoke into the crystal-cold night, but the big one was the communal house, and it was there that the procession headed. As it left the forest and crunched over the snowy clearing, a chorus of barking broke out in greeting.

Before Rap had any time to study all the details with his sensing, he had reached the largest hut and was hurriedly pushed inside. Blinded by a blaze of light, half choked by a fog of acrid smoke and fetid odors, he recoiled and was shoved forward bodily into a melee of undressing men. He tripped and rolled among greasy legs and smelly feet. He began to cough; his eyes streamed tears; he gasped in heat unbearable to him after a whole week of arctic cold.

All around him men were stripping off clothes; he rose and copied them out of necessity. The goblins stopped just short of total nudity, retaining only brief loincloths, the same indecent garments he had seen on goblins at Krasnegar. With head swimming and stomach all knotted up at the stench, quivering and sweating, he struggled to maintain control. *Courage!* he told himself. *Brave men do not vomit!*

He stripped to his shirt and shorts, and saw his furs tossed into a communal heap of buckskins by the door. Then an elderly, near-nude goblin shouted at him. Seeing that Rap did not understand, he ripped Rap's shirt off and hurled it furiously to the floor—apparently wearing a shirt indoors was an insult. He shoved Rap ahead of him, over to a corner, and gestured that he must sit down. Glad to obey, tormented by this shameful undress, Rap crouched down, hugged his knees, and made himself small.

The building was one giant room, longer than King Holindarn's great hall, made of enormous logs. The center held the place of honor, a low stone platform around a blazing hearth, where Darad was already stretching out on a pile of furs and looking comfortable.

The women were clustered around a much smaller fire at the far end of the hall, and farsight told Rap that they were preparing food. Neither hearth had a chimney; reluctant to depart through the hole in the roof, the smoke gathered overhead in a whitish cloud, billowing up and down like a sea swell.

Probably nowhere in the lodge was truly warm, except near the fires—Rap had been deceived when he first entered by the sudden

change and by having furs on. Where he was sitting now, down
low, the air was freezing, and polar drafts knifed in through chinks
in the logs to ice his back. He shivered constantly and was hard
put to keep his teeth from chattering. Perhaps the smell was not
quite so bad down there, but his eyes still smarted unbearably. It
was unfair to ask a man to pretend to have courage when he was
so cold, and the air so smoky.

The women were invisible, swathed in voluminous buckskin
robes reaching to the ground, their heads covered with wimples
of woven stuff, and only their hands and faces showing. The few
goblin women he had seen in Krasnegar had been shrouded like
that, even in summer.

The men, by contrast, were almost completely visible, their
dark-khaki skin shining greasily and displaying in the firelight the
greenish tinge of which the goblins boasted. They wore their heavy
black hair matted into a tail with fat and draped over one shoulder
to hang down their chests like a bellrope. All of the men seemed
short, although that was partly because Darad towered over them
like a swan among mallards, but they were wide and deep, their
limbs thick and heavy. Rap wondered how much of that meat was
fat and how much muscle; seeing the easy and limber way the
goblins walked around, he decided that it was mostly muscle.
Their eyes were wrongly shaped and set at an odd angle in their
heads, their limbs and bodies smooth, although most sprouted
scattered black bristles around their mouths—goblins had big
mouths, full of teeth that seemed too large and pointed.

Darad dwarfed them all. His pale-pink jotunnish body was
furred in yellow hair, but also heavily scarred and much tattooed.
Andor's flimsy underwear clung on him in shreds, provoking loud
hilarity until a suitably large loincloth could be found to replace
it. He had been given the thickest rug, next to the chief, and two
young maidens had been set to work rubbing grease into his pelt.
Looking like a white walrus basking among seals, drink in hand,
surrounded by admirers, he was obviously prepared to enjoy a
fine evening.

Knowing that he must seem as odd to the goblins as they did
to him, Rap was happy to remain as inconspicuous as possible.
But he did not only look wrong, he smelled wrong. His farsight
warned him, and he turned around hastily to meet the slitted eyes
of the largest dog he had ever seen. It might even be a full-grown
timber wolf—silver gray, and certainly weighing almost as much
as he did. Its lips were curled to display teeth like white daggers.
Its hackles were raised, it was already tensed to spring. None of

the goblins was paying any attention and the visitor was surely about to be savaged.

Quickly Rap turned on the charm that he used for dogs, like the charm that worked on horses. He smiled, he raised a hand . . .

"Here, Fleabag," he whispered. "Nice doggie?"

Fleabag postponed his attack to consider this unexpected development. As Rap's soothing thoughts sank in, his ruff began to settle. He edged forward with great suspicion and sniffed at the hand. His tail started to twitch.

Rap discovered that he was shaking. Having his throat ripped out by a wolf might be much pleasanter than whatever the goblins had in store for him, but it was still an event better avoided.

Other dogs arrived to inspect what Fleabag had found, sniffing and then licking. Apparently Rap had an interesting taste. The dogs stank foully, but not as badly as their owners did, and while Rap might have been able to send them away, they were company and they helped to shield him from the goblins' view. They lost interest eventually and settled down to sleep, spread out untidily on the floor around him. Even in Krasnegar, the palace dogs had tended to follow him about.

The men around the central hearth—the most senior sprawling on the platform itself, on furs, youngsters sitting on its edge or squatting on the floor—were all busily rubbing grease on themselves or on one another, combing and greasing their hair.

The goblin chief was a middle-aged man, potbellied and thin-shanked, but bearing himself like one who accepts no questions. His facial tattoos were richer and more complex than anyone else's, his rope of hair was streaked in silver, and he wore a necklace of many strands of bear claws, which clicked and clacked when he moved. He reclined beside Darad and the two of them monopolized the conversation.

Darad was a guest. No one offered Rap a drink, or even a fur. Was he guest or captive? He might even be a slave if Darad had given him to the chief. It was hardly flattering to be second choice to two horses, but perhaps that was a realistic evaluation.

Meanwhile he could only sit and shiver in cold and fear and lonely silence. He ought to say a prayer or two, but he wasn't much of a praying man and it seemed shameful to change now, when he was in trouble, after so seldom offering thanks for the good life he had enjoyed back in Krasnegar. The Gods might feel that his ingratitude was being well rewarded. If he'd done some serious praying sooner, he might have known that stealing the king's horses was very wrong behavior.

In the end he decided it would be all right to ask the God of Courage to send him strength to endure whatever was coming.

Darad was holding forth, waving his beaker with one hand and pointing to his various scars and tattoos with the other. The goblins listened intently, seeming impressed. Rap began to catch some of the language, especially Darad's words, and the name Wolf Tooth kept recurring. He concluded that this must be Darad's goblin name and he was talking of himself, telling of Wolf Tooth's triumphs and all the various tribes he belonged to worldwide, as evidenced by his tattoos. Sysanasso was mentioned.

So were murder and rape. Quite evidently Darad was a horror, as different from the gentle, sociable Andor as it was possible for man to be. Yet if a quarter of his tales were true he had traveled as widely as Andor had. He was also a braggart and probably stupid, but the goblins did not seem to mind that. After a while the women began to bring their menfolk dishes of food. Rap sat and watched them gorge. His mouth watered, hoping someone might think to throw it a bone.

The dogs snored and twitched in their dreams. Rap was weary, but fear and cold kept him alert. He wondered why women so greatly outnumbered the men. Scanning the other buildings with farsight, he saw that there the numbers were more even; girls in one, boys in the other. The difference was the adult men, therefore, and a reasonable guess would be that a war party was out raiding somewhere.

From time to time women would slip out the door and come back with more wood for the two monstrous fires. They at least wore robes, but men wandering out to relieve themselves did not bother to dress, although even the thought of going out unclothed into that unbelievable cold made Rap shudder. The buckskins that the goblins had worn earlier were much flimsier than his furs, so obviously goblins felt cold much less than faun-jotunn halfbreeds did, and the hearth was a place of honor, rather than of comfort.

The meal was finished. The drinking continued. After an hour or two, the chief looked across toward Rap and asked Darad something. Darad grinned and beckoned. Reluctant, feeling horribly embarrassed and vulnerable in his state of undress, Rap rose and advanced to the edge of the ring of junior goblins sprawled around the hearth.

His hosts inspected him with curiosity, with amusement, then with contemptuous comments that he could not catch. There was laughter. He knew he must look strange to them—the reverse of the way they looked to him. He would seem a very pale brown, very stringy, and too tall. His tussock of unruly brown hair would be entertaining, also. The minstrel Jalon had told him that fauns had hairy legs, and certainly Rap's legs had been been busily growing hairy recently. They obviously amused the goblins.

But evidently he had overlooked the feature that amused them most. The chief said something that provoked especially loud laughter. Darad's reply brought more.

He leered at Rap. "The chief offered to give me your nose, because mine is broken. I said mine was still prettier." He laughed again and took another drink.

The goblins all had wide, plump faces, but their noses were thin and very long. They also had big ears.

"When do I get to eat?" Rap asked.

Darad showed his tooth gap in another leer. "Why waste good food?"

"What's going to happen, then?" Even if courage was important, Rap just could not feel courageous—but now anger was coming to his aid. If they were going to kill him, he would rather they got started than just left him in suspense.

Again that wolfish grin. "Wait and see! I wouldn't want to spoil your surprise."

The chief turned and grunted an order. One of the youngest men sprang up and ran along the big room and out the door. As Rap watched with farsight, he hurried to the smallest building, the one where the boys and youths of the tribe were sitting or lying around a fireplace. There seemed to be one grown man there, perhaps a supervisor, and he now rose to follow the chief's messenger. Yet, while the messenger ran back, the newcomer took his time, idly kicking snow with his bare feet, brazenly strolling through that deadly arctic cold while clad in nothing but a strip of deer hide.

He sauntered into the hall and up to the fireplace, folded his arms, and looked expectantly at the chief. He was not a grown man, but not far off it—about Rap's age, almost as tall and twice the depth, a barrel-chested, powerful youth, as big as any goblin in the room. He already had more moustache than most, and the black rope of his hair hung almost to his waist. There were no tattoos on his wide, ugly face, but there was much arrogance.

The chief said something. The youth looked Rap over and then grinned hugely with his oversized teeth. He held a meaty arm against one of Rap's to allow a comparison. The audience exploded in appreciative laughter.

"This is Little Chicken," Darad explained helpfully. "High Raven's son. You'll be seeing more of him in future. More than you want, I fancy!" He laughed and then translated his joke for the benefit of the audience. They found it equally amusing.

High Raven must be the chief. That and his size explained this youngster's superior air.

"Do I have to fight him?" Rap demanded, uneasily studying Little Chicken's impressively thick limbs and chest.

"Just hold your end up!" Darad said, laughing again.

The chief snapped an order. Little Chicken nodded and grabbed Rap's wrist. The goblins respected courage; Rap felt pushed beyond all endurance by this mockery and ill treatment. He jerked his arm away and swung a fast punch with his other hand.

He hit nothing. He had no time to register the horrifying implications of that failure before Little Chicken doubled him over with a left hook in the belly and then flattened him to the floor with a thump on the back of his head. Dimly he heard the audience erupt in screams of mirth.

Little Chicken might be shorter, but obviously his greater weight was combined with much greater speed. He kicked at Rap to drive home the point and his father shouted what sounded like a warning. So Little Chicken casually knelt, tucked Rap under one arm, and rose to wander away while the spectators were still bellowing and hooting and rolling around on the platform.

Hands and feet trailing on the gritty snow, Rap was borne ignominiously over to the boys' building and dumped in a corner. The boys clustered around to inspect the dazed and still nauseated captive. They found him just as entertaining as their elders had done.

6

Princess Kadolan peered around the south drawing room, being careful not to appear to be peering—she did not think it seemly for a lady to screw up her eyes merely to see properly. In a moment she located the burgundy dress she sought, and the high-piled honey-blond hair. She set off at a measured pace, smiling and nodding to a few friends. The big room was almost empty, and also strangely drab. The snow floating down outside had muffled the morning sun and muted the normally joyful tones of Angilki's decor.

In searching out the brightest light for her sketch book, Inos had curled up on a love seat by the window. Her bright gown burned hot against the winter whiteness without and the potted plants within. Behind her, beside the casement, an oversize grandfather clock steadily chopped away at the seconds, contrasting the relentless march of time with youth and beauty. Portrait of an artist . . .

Kade knew well that in most women such a pose would be a deliberate stratagem, but in Inos it came from pure instinct. Imperceptibly Kinvale had melted away her awkward adolescence to reveal a stunningly beautiful young woman. She had gained poise and grace, and yet she still retained her bloom of innocence. That would vanish, of course, as soon as she herself became fully aware of the change, but—as Ekka had remarked only a few minutes ago—the smallest part of the problem now was motivating the prospective suitors.

Inos flipped over a page and frowned at it. Then she noticed Kadolan's approach, sat up straight, put her feet down . . .

"Don't get up, dear." Kade settled at her side. "Does this snow make you homesick?"

Inos flashed her a smile that could have demolished an Imperial legion. "This? I don't think a Krasnegarian would call this *snow*, Aunt. You couldn't lose a horse in this."

"You could barely lose a copper groat in it. No, unless it gets much deeper it should not spoil the skating party."

"I hope not," Inos said, gazing happily out at the winter-shrouded lawns and hedges. She had not known how to skate until a few weeks ago—skating was not a practical pastime in Krasnegar—but she had taken to it like a horse to oats. From her father she inherited a natural ability for such vigorous pursuits.

She glanced around to see who might be within earshot. Kadolan had already determined that no one was.

"You have come to scold me, Aunt. You have that this-will-hurt-me-more look about you."

"Oh, dear! Am I becoming so obvious in my old age?"

Inos chuckled and reached out to squeeze her hand. "Of course not! I am teasing. But I certainly ought to know when I have distressed you; I do it often enough, do I not?"

"No, dear . . ." Kade found herself being studied by the greenest eyes in the Impire, large and deep and unreadable.

"Well, I did!" Inos said, much amused. "I was quite horrid to you when we first arrived, my dear Aunt, and I am truly repentant. But I am seeing that expression much less often, so either

you have given up on me, or I am getting better. Which is it?''
When Inos chose to be charming, she was irresistible.

"You are doing wonderfully, my dear.''

A tiny gleam of pleasure was masked at once by a coquettish
smile. "But . . .''

"Well . . . That naval person has departed—''

"Captain Eggoli?'' Inos contrived to look shocked. "Should
he be traveling in his present state of health? In this snow?''

"He seemed quite eager to leave—and not at all eager to come
and make his farewells to you.''

Inos threw up her hands dramatically. "And I did so hope to
hear just once more how he keelhauled those poor mutineeers!
Surely it would have been proper for an Imperial officer to have
come to say good-bye?'' She could not quite keep the satisfied
twinkle out of her eye, although she was becoming much more
skilled at hiding her feelings now. Inosolan was much more skilled
at almost everything now.

And it really was very funny.

"What I cannot understand,'' Kadolan said, playing along, "is
how a strapping young sailor like that could have come down with
such a terrible cold when everyone else seems perfectly healthy.''

Still Inos kept a straight face. "I did hear rumors that he spent
a night in a potting shed.''

"That seems an unwise thing to do. The whole night?''

"A good part of it, I expect. He has very strong opinions.''

"Of himself, you mean? Oh, Inos! How could you?''

"Me? I wasn't there!'' With demure innocence, she turned to
gaze out at the big cottony flakes drifting past the windows. Eventually she looked back at Kadolan, and then they both laughed.
Their laughter was rather long and immoderate for high-born ladies.

Inos recovered first. She smoothed her sketch book with her
hand, took a deep breath, and said, "He really did deserve it! I
don't mind the ones who are looking for wives, Aunt. I mean,
I don't mind them looking. I mind some of them thinking I would
be interested . . . Oh, I'm not saying this very well.''

"Take your time, dear. I think we ought to have this out now.''

Inos looked startled. "Hair down? A woman-to-woman chat?''

"A lady-to-lady chat.'' The sort of chat they could not have
enjoyed even a few short weeks ago.

"All right! You and the dowager dragon—''

"Inos!'' Kadolan murmured reprovingly.

"Hair down, Aunt! You two have been parading your breeding stock—"

"*Inos!*"

She chuckled. "All right, but why do you think I had hysterics that time at the Kinford Horse Show?"

"I knew exactly why, dear, and so did everybody else."

"And I should have grown out of it by now? I'm sorry, Aunt. I just can't take it all seriously!" But her fists were clenched.

"You have to, my dear. You will be a queen one day. Your choice of husband is a matter of state. You know that."

Inosolan sighed and pouted. "Father promised I was not being sent here to be married off!"

"Your father wants you to choose, for love. Few kings would be so considerate. Obviously there is no one suitable in Krasnegar, so he hopes you will meet someone here. Here you have been introduced to some of the most eligible—"

"Dullest, fattest, oldest—"

"Don't be so conceited," Kadolan said primly. "People do visit Kinvale for other reasons than you."

Her niece colored slightly and said nothing.

"Also, Ekka has many other ladies visiting, also. She can hardly hand her gentleman friends a menu when they arrive, now can she?"

Kadolan did not add that all those other ladies were in despair, that Ekka's renowned matchmaking venture had not produced an engagement in months, that no living, breathing male guest had eyes for anyone but the fabulous princess.

Inos nodded repentantly. "I am trying, Aunt. I really am! I made some mistakes at first, but I think I'm doing all right now."

"You're doing splendidly, my dear. I'm very proud of you."

"Well, then! But there have been one or two, like the hearty Captain Eggoli . . ." The big green eyes grew round with wonder. "He really believed me! He really thought I was going to meet him in the potting shed, of all places, so he could—"

"I think I can guess what he thought."

Inos chuckled again, then sighed. "It isn't fair! It just isn't fair! Just because they're bigger and stronger than we are, they think they can run the world to suit themselves. And run us, too."

Kadolan could remember thinking things like that. "We are not totally without resources. Captain Eggoli is much bigger and much stronger than most, but he looked very miserable as he left. His nose was red, and his eyes were puffy as lambswool bedsocks."

Inos sniggered, then became suddenly wistful. "Oh, we can win a point or two, now and then. But it still isn't fair."

"No, it isn't. What are you going to do about it?"

"Oh! I've just made an epochal discovery, haven't I? Inosolan's Guide to the Universe! I suppose everyone sees it in her time! Did you experience the same shattering revelation at my age?"

"I was older than you, I think. But it is the way of the world, and we must just play the cards we are dealt."

"Or refuse to play at all?"

Kadolan sighed quite genuinely. "No, my dear. That is not an option—not for anyone, and especially not for you. And even if the rules are unfair, all we can hope is that everyone plays honestly."

Inos showed her teeth. "I'll keep them honest!"

Overconfidence would be her next danger, of course. Regretfully Kadolan decided that she would have to be frank, although she hated to hazard this precious bridge of trust and understanding they had so painfully built to each other. But now the stakes were high, time was very short, and the perils great. She reached out to the sketch book on Inos's lap and turned back the page that Inos had so casually flipped just before seeming to notice her aunt's approach.

The big clock *tick-tocked*, *tick-tocked*, thin-slicing eternity.

Kade said, "It's a very good likeness, my dear. I had not realized how talented you were."

Inos was scarlet, eyes glinting furiously. She did not speak.

"Tell me about him."

"I love him."

"Yes, I think you do. But tell me about him."

"What more is there to tell?" Inos was hurt now, and angry, and defensive. "What else matters?"

"Quite a lot, dear. You see, Sir Andor was a mistake."

Inos drew a deep breath, and Kade interrupted before emotion could provoke indiscretion.

"I mean that he was not invited here to meet you. He was not invited here to meet anyone. He was not invited here at all, Inos. He brought letters of introduction, of course. It was the duke who asked him to stay."

"Oh." Inos was far from stupid. She smiled triumphantly. "So it was chance? Not the dowager dragon? The Gods intervened!"

"Possibly. The trouble is . . . his letters were signed by some very odd people. His Grace has many curious friends for a man

of his rank—artists and builders. The nobility write introductions
for one another all the time, of course, but one of Sir Andor's
references came from an artist, and another from a scholar. Most
nobles would not accept such letters.''

''And the others?''

''From quite minor gentry. Ekka has been making inquiries.
They now admit that they hardly know him.''

A dangerous frown came over her niece's face. ''Are you suggesting that Sir Andor is a fraud? An imposter? Because—''

''I'm not suggesting any such thing, Inos. You spent five weeks
in each other's company. You must have talked about yourselves.
So you tell me about him.''

Inos turned away quickly to stare at the window. Her hands
moved restlessly. ''He had to leave upon a matter of honor. It
may be dangerous, he said. But he promised to return, and I
certainly trust—''

''That wasn't what I asked, dear.'' Kade spoke softly, treading
gently. ''Who is his father? Does his family have money? Land?
Titles?''

Looking suddenly much younger—looking rather like a cornered fawn—Inos said, ''Those things do not matter!''

''They do not matter very much, I agree. A good man is a
good man, and I believe that you father might even accept a com-
moner, if he was a man of honor and good qualities. But they
may matter if Sir Andor deliberately set out to win the heart of a
princess by pretending to be something other than what he is.''

''He did. Did win the heart of a princess.''

''Then it does matter. Inos, you must see that?''

Again Inos turned her head to study the snowy scene beyond
the casement, the drifting flakes. The big pendulum behind her
stroked more seconds off their lives.

''Yes,'' she said at last. ''I see. I do see, now. I don't know—
he told me nothing about his family.''

''You did not ask?''

''No. I didn't. I would now, I think . . . He is knowledgeable,
very well traveled. He has had very wide experience. And charm!
Oh, Aunt, you must admit he has charm!''

''Mountains of charm! Ranges of mountains of charm. Very
good company, I agree. Krasnegar would be a much brighter
place with Andor there.''

''Even the jotnar would like him! In a week he would have the
rock itself turning cartwheels.''

"Polar bears would bring him the catch of the day." That had been a childhood joke between Kade and Holi.

Inos missed it. "He is obviously a gentleman."

"Obviously he acted like a gentleman while he was here."

Inos blushed furiously. "Yes, he did!"

"I did not mean it that way, dear. He did not say when he would return?"

"No. But he will! I am certain."

"Then we must just wait, I suppose."

"And meanwhile keep the parade going?"

"Ekka says she has almost run out of candidates."

"Good!"

Kadolan bit her lip. Obviously this conversation had served its purpose and should now be drawn to a close, but she had one more necessary spoonful of wisdom to administer. It also would hurt, but better to hurt more now, while Inos was already upset, than to wound her again on another occasion. Still no word had come from Krasnegar, and there should have been something. It would not be fair to burden Inos with mere suspicions—and Kade kept reminding herself that they were only suspicions—but time might well be running out, and the child had perhaps forgotten the stakes in this game she was being forced to play.

"How do you judge, my dear?"

Inos frowned. "Judge what?"

"Whom. How do you judge the candidates? Against Sir Andor?"

"Against Father."

That could never be true. "Then you are comparing very young men in a difficult and unfamiliar setting against a mature king in his own kingdom. Is that fair?"

"Is it fair that I should have to judge at all?"

The situation was hopeless. Holindarn had insisted that his daughter be allowed to choose, and obviously she would have the Andor man or no one, and the Andor man was not available. Maybe in another year or so, when she had grown up more and had time to forget that first awesome flash of romance . . . all of which was exactly what Kade had told Ekka half an hour ago.

She sighed and rose. "Just be grateful that you have the chance to judge at all, dear."

"Is that a threat?" Inos was reaching for her anger.

"Of course not. I'm trying to give you a warning: Remember what your father said."

The anger was held back, momentarily. "About what?"

"About war. If the Impire and Nordland went to war over Krasnegar . . . whichever side won, do you think you would be allowed to choose a husband then?"

But Inos had not forgotten the stakes. The Kinvale lacquer cracked to show the frightened child hiding under the ladylike decorum. "Ah, yes! What a pity Thane Kalkor is married! What a pity you and Ekka can't invite him here, also, so you could parade me around in front of that one!"

Kade had no need to fake a shudder. "His manners would be the problem, dear, not his marriage. If he fancied you, then he'd just give his current wife to one of his churls and take you in her place. They do that all the time."

7

Faint daylight was seeping through the chimney hole in the roof when Rap was jerked away by a snowy boot being wiped on his face. The nightmare figure of Darad was looming over him, swathed again in furs, with his gap-toothed leer somewhere near the ceiling.

Rap had found a tattered rug to wrap himself in and had even gained a place fairly close to the fire by the simple method of throwing some of the smaller boys out of the way. The older ones had found this action amusing and had not objected. They had allowed him to drink from their communal bucket, but he had still not been fed. His belly cramps came from hunger as well as the aftereffects of Little Chicken's haymaker.

Woodsmoke from a single hearth, the rank stench of bodies and rancid grease, smelly rugs on a packed dirt floor—the boys' hut was a smaller version of the adults'. At the moment Rap was the only occupant. He had slept well and felt rather pleased at that.

"I came to say good-bye, Stupid."

Rap lay and scowled up at Darad for a moment, gathering his wits. "Good-bye." What else was there to say?

The big man glowered. "This is your last chance, Stupid."

He had said that the night before. "What's my choice, then?"

Darad took a moment to answer, while frowning with the pain of thinking. "Tell me your word and I'll get you out of here."

"Or what?"

"Or you get tested. Against Little Chicken."

"What sort of test?" Rap made a quick scan with his farsight and discovered that the missing boys were all over in the big building, eating.

Darad had struggled through to a decision, and now he dropped to one knee, poking at Rap with a mitted hand the size of a small shovel. "They like lots of wives, see?"

Rap did not see, but he stayed silent.

"So they get rid of the weaklings, see?" Darad sorted out another thought and continued. "It's their winter fun. When two boys are old enough, they test them. The winner gets his tattoos."

"And the other dies?"

"Right!" Darad smiled at Rap's brilliance.

"And I look like a pushover, so the chief's son gets me?"

Darad nodded vigorously. "And you haven't got a hope."

"I haven't got a word, either," Rap said. "Tell me yours and I'll get both of us out of here."

Darad jumped up furiously. "You think I'm crazy? Give you half my word? You're stupid." He drew his foot back, and Rap hastily curled up, waiting for the kick.

But the giant merely laughed and stalked away, slamming the door. Relieved, Rap rearranged his furs against the cold air. Then he watched Darad's departure.

Joyboy staggered when that huge carcass scrabbled up onto his back. He didn't want to go, and the giant kicked him hard enough to bring tears to Rap's eyes. Eventually Darad prevailed and rode off into the forest, leading Peppers.

He was heading south. Darad would have no interest in visiting Kinvale to warn Inos of her father's illness. There would seem to be no reason why Andor should do so, either, were he to reappear in Darad's place. But Inos must be told—which meant that Rap would have to escape and do it himself.

Stubborn, his mother had called him. Inos had, also, although usually she had preferred *pigheaded*. Well, if stubborn was what it was going to take, then stubborn he would be.

Rap sat up, wrapped himself in fur, and again scanned the big house. He had never felt hungrier, but somehow he was certain that he was not going to be fed. The boys must have crept out very quietly, deliberately not waking him—big joke! He was expected to run over and try to join them, so Little Chicken could have the satisfaction of making him beg, and then refusing.

Rap decided he could stand the pangs a little longer, and postpone his captors' satisfaction. If torture was what they had in mind, then they would not let him become too weak.

He began to puzzle again over the mystery of Andor and the

monstrous Darad. What was Darad? Man or demon? Would a demon be as lean-witted as that? The minstrel Jalon had mentioned Darad, and Andor knew Jalon. They had all wanted his word . . .

Then something Darad had said finally registered. Revelation fell over Rap like grain from a burst sack.

Give you half my word?

That was why Andor had refused to share! When you shared a word you divided its power. If that was not so, then the words would be passed around like jokes—everyone would know words. Pandemia would swarm with sorcerers. There had to be a reason why words were not freely shared, and that must be it—sharing reduced their power!

Andor had not mentioned *that*!

Nor had Jalon.

Nor had Sagorn.

The king had. "Remember to guard your secret," he had said, thinking that Rap would understand.

Now he understood! Inspiration after inspiration flashed through his mind. Words were usually passed on deathbeds. Sagorn had said so, and Andor, also.

Two people sharing a word each got half the power. But the words had been passed down for generations. Obviously they did not lose half their power at every telling, or they would long since have disappeared completely. So! So—if two people shared, they each got half the power, but when one of the two died, the other had all of it again?

Right! That was certain.

Died—or was murdered.

That was why it was dangerous to know a word.

And why it would be even more dangerous to share one.

If Rap had possessed a word to share and had told that word to Andor, then Andor or his Darad-demon would have killed Rap at once, to gain the other half, also.

That was something else that Andor had not explained.

Demon lover:

    A savage place! as holy and enchanted
    As e'er beneath a waning moon was haunted
    By woman wailing for her demon lover.

                        Coleridge, *Kubla Khan*

❆ SIX ❄

Forest weeping

1

Soon after Darad departed, the boys returned from their meal. Little Chicken beckoned Rap and led him out across the compound, barefoot and virtually naked. The air felt worse than ice water, freezing the tears that ran down Rap's cheeks. Within seconds he was shaking uncontrollably; his toes and ears were numb. Little Chicken was wearing no more than he was, but he grinned at Rap's discomfort and sauntered at a leisurely pace to show how little the cold bothered him. Their destination turned out to be a garbage tip at the back of the big house, where scraps were being dropped out through a flap. Fleabag and his pack were snuffling and growling as they scavenged among the remains. Anything worth eating was grabbed by the nearest dog, which then raced off to dine in private. Everything else was soon trampled and frozen to the ground.

Little Chicken made eating gestures and pointed.

Rap shook his head and turned away, but not before he had seen the gloating amusement—a man would eat anything when he was hungry enough. Tomorrow, or the day after, Rap would be at the garbage, disputing with the dogs for offal.

Back in the hut, Rap soon discovered the rules. He could go out any time he wanted, but he must not take any of the fur robes or the buckskins that lay heaped by the door. Bare feet and his shorts were all he was allowed. That restricted his movements like a chain on an ankle. Nor might he enter any of the other buildings.

The log house was home to thirty-four boys, ranging in age from toddlers up to Little Chicken, who was easily the oldest and largest, and certainly the ruler. Males had little to occupy them in the great forest in winter, for the women did all the work. The boys spent their time in sleeping, combing their long hair, and rubbing themselves with the well-matured bear grease that gave them their loathsome stench. Thinking it might have some value for keeping out the cold, Rap tried it himself, but the only advantage he could find was that it stopped his skin cracking. He felt no warmer for it and thereafter he stank as badly as the others.

They also played complicated games with sticks and a board; and they wrestled. Little Chicken loved wrestling, but there was no one there large enough to give him a reasonable match. Rap would have been the closest, but there seemed to be some reason why Little Chicken must not tackle him, for which Rap was duly grateful. Little Chicken, therefore, would organize teams of the others, usually Fledgling Down and Cheep-Cheep, the two next in age, but sometimes four or five of the smaller boys. Then he would take on the whole team. He always won, usually ending by bouncing his opponents off the walls.

Within a few hours, and merely by sitting and listening to the boys' chatter, Rap began to uncover the secrets of the language. It used comparatively few words, and only in simple ways. Many were exactly the same as the words he knew, and many others were almost the same with certain sounds switched in a predictable fashion—*th* to *t* and *f* to *p*, and a few others. Soon he was making sense of the talk.

Then he made the mistake of asking a question. Little Chicken barked out, ''Not answer!'' and jumped up. He scrambled across and arranged himself cross-legged in front of Rap. ''You speak now?'' he demanded intently.

''I speak slow.''

That was very satisfying news. ''Seven days I get my name!'' Little Chicken grinned, showing his oversize goblin teeth.

Rap looked blank.

''New name! Not Little Chicken—Death Bird.''

''Good name!'' Rap said politely. Not knowing the word for tattoos, he waved a finger around one eye, and a vigorous nod showed that his guess was correct.

Obviously this was all a cheat. Little Chicken was at least two years older than any of the other boys, and Rap had already noted some tattooed and married men who could be no older. So Little Chicken had been held back, the fruit kept on the tree until it was overripe, so that he would have an unfair chance in the testing, whatever that might be. Now this pushover stranger had arrived to make the contest even more unfair. Little Chicken was justifiably confident.

"Tell me about testing?" Rap asked.

Little Chicken looked surprised, and then an expression of great delight came over his big ugly face as he realized the extent of Rap's ignorance. "No!" He swung around and snapped orders to the others—no one must talk of the testing. Happily he turned back to his victim.

"After testing I have good ideas!"

"Yes?" Rap was certain that he was going to disagree.

"I light small fires on your chest!"

Rap did disagree.

"I pull off ears and make you eat them!"

"I pull feathers off chickens," Rap said firmly.

"Flat Nose!" Little Chicken sneered. "I push your toes up your nose."

Rap made a loud clucking noise and flapped his arms. That worked. Little Chicken almost gnashed his teeth with fury, while a few of the braver boys behind him snickered.

Frequently thereafter Little Chicken would come to sit and stare gloatingly at Rap and announce some new atrocity he had just thought of, but the clucking noise was a potent reply. It drove him almost to distraction, and often drove him away. Either some rule prevented him from using violence, or else he was saving that for later.

The grisly threats were unbelievable, Rap decided—just another strategy to unnerve the victim, as the garbage had been. He firmly resolved not to let it rattle him, but that was not an easy resolution to keep. By the time the village settled down to the sleep that night, his head was swimming with the weakness brought on by hunger.

But he had farsight. He had easily located the food store, in a room at the back of the single women's lodge, and there seemed to be no locks on any of the doors. Kept awake by his howling stomach, he lay in his fur robe among the sleeping boys and waited through the long hours until the whole tribe seemed to be asleep and all activity had ceased, even in the married quarters. Then he arose, dressed himself in the largest buckskins he could find in the heap by the door—they could only be Little Chicken's—and quietly staggered out into the dark.

There were no sentries in that climate. The dogs kept guard

and Fleabag himself was the first to notice him, but Fleabag seemed to be peculiarly susceptible to whatever it was Rap could do with animals. He came up sniffing and allowed his ears to be scratched. If Fleabag was not a purebred wolf, he was something close to it, but for his new friend he lay down and required that his chest be rubbed. Then he accompanied Rap past the big lodge where the men slept among their wives, over to the house of the single females.

Gratefully Rap slipped inside, blocking Fleabag's attempts to follow. He stood in the dark, until his violently shaking limbs were under control again. At the far end lay the young girls, old women were at the front. There were two hearths, but the fires had been banked and the room was dim. Quivering with hunger and nervousness, he began picking his way very slowly toward the big larder that made up the rear half of the building, stepping around or over the sleepers. Here was the tribe's holy of holies: the winter food and the unmarried girls. Nowhere could be more off-limits for a stranger, but certainly Rap had nothing to lose.

Holding his breath, mouthing a silent prayer against creaking hinges, he eased open the big door and swiftly grabbed up a lump of frozen fish. He closed the door again, turned—and his heart made a wild leap, as if trying to escape on its own and fly away to Krasnegar. A very tiny woman was standing right in front of him, peering up with difficulty because of her extreme stoop—a dim, hunched figure canopied in the voluminous robe and hood of a female goblin. Her face was dark and dim, unclear in the crawling glow of the embers, but he could see wrinkles, and she was obviously very old.

For what seemed a small eternity, neither spoke. He felt sweat trickle down his ribs like ice. Why did she not raise the alarm?

"Faun?" she said softly. Her voice was the dry crackle of a boot on frozen grass. "Why a faun here?"

Rap said nothing. He tried to lick his lips and tasted blood from their open frost sores.

"Far from the vales," the crone warbled in a tuneless but fortunately quiet croak, *"Where his ancestors manifest* . . . No, that's not right. Not manifest! *Magnify*?"

She showed a few sharp goblin teeth, gnawing her wrinkled bottom lip. "Why is he using power here, eh?"

Rap tried to speak, and his tongue stuck to the roof of his mouth. Apparently she had not thought to shout an alarm. He forced his quaking limbs to obey, sinking down on one knee to be less conspicuous if anyone else roused. Now their eyes were about level.

"I'm hungry," he whispered. "That's all."

She did not seem to hear. "*What goes creeping where my love lies sleeping?* Eh? Fauns near my sweeting? Power in the dark woods. Fauns!"

"Please don't wake the others."

"He uses mastery on the dogs, that's all." She was very, very, old, and probably mad.

Then his heart made another frantic bound—she was not there! His farsight was detecting nothing where his eyes saw her, and his eyes could also see the embers on the hearth shining through her robe.

An evil spirit? He tried to rise and his legs would not move. He rubbed his eyes, and the vision seemed to solidfy, blocking out the gleam of the hearth. He clenched his teeth to stop them chattering.

"Strange," she muttered. "Can't see him properly."

"I'm hungry," Rap repeated, barely hearing the words himself. "That's all. I mean no harm."

He moved a hand, to see if it would pass through the apparition, and his fingers touched buckskin—he whipped them away. The old hag had noticed. Her eyes seemed to narrow and focus more securely on him. "You! Faun! Why can't I foresee you?"

Rap shook his head, confused. "I'm hungry," he whispered again.

"Hungry? You?" She cackled in sudden mad merriment, and Rap cringed, expecting all the sleepers to leap up; but no one stirred.

The crone's laughter stopped abruptly. "My sweeting!" Her voice was quiet again, like wind on hay. "You must not hurt him!"

"Hurt who?"

"Death Bird. He is the promised one."

Rap could not remember the name. None of the boys was called that, he was sure, and he did not think he had overheard "Death Bird" in their conversation. He shook his head.

The little hag worked her mouth, as if chewing, then hummed for a moment, and finally began to croon again. "*When summer came to Uthol's valley* . . . Remember, faun—he is precious."

And she was gone.

Someone turned over by the near fire and mumbled for a moment in sleep.

Rap waited until his heart stopped beating like hailstones, then struggled shakily to his feet. Apparently none of the sleepers had heard the mad old woman, not even her snatches of song. That seemed very improbable! He began making his way back to the door, his whole body quivering violently in reaction. But he could almost convince himself that he had merely seen—and heard and touched—a hallucination brought on by starvation.

He slipped outside swiftly lest a cold draft awaken any sleepers, then hurried back through the black agony of the night, mentally forcing the dogs' attention away from his precious bundle. When he reached the boys' dormitory, he could feel pain in his mouth at the thought of food, but he laid the frozen lump near the embers and managed to restrain himself until it was almost half thawed, praying that the hiss and crackle would not awaken Little Chicken or any of the others. He scorched his fingers retrieving the disgusting, delicious mess of raw and charred fish, and crawled under his rug to gorge on it, and he ate every bit except a few bones, which he burned.

Then he slept.

Every night thereafter, he returned to the larder and stole food, for there was nowhere he could hide a supply from both dogs and men. He was not detected, and he did not see the cryptic delusion of the little old woman again. He did not go near the garbage tip, to Little Chicken's great disgust and mystification.

The other boys were forbidden to speak to Rap, even to tell him what the testing would involve. It could not be physical strength, because he was bigger than either Cheep-Cheep or Fledgling Down, yet he was obviously Little Chicken's preferred opponent. He supposed it must be some forest skill, like archery. The only thing he would not expect was fairness. Nor did he intend to stay around to find out.

He spent most his time planning his escape, but every idea he could think of was either impossible or was at once made so, almost as if the goblins could read his thoughts. Darad had taken Rap's mukluks. High Raven had confiscated Andor's and kept them in clear view beside his sleeping place, so footwear would have to wait for last. Rap had to make a long search with farsight before he located his parka and fur trousers, only to learn that they had been disassembled and stitched together as a rug, again for the chief's personal glory.

That news was terrifying, as if a captive in a dungeon had learned that the key to his cell had been melted down. It threw a

depression over him such as he had never known. His nightly
prowls had shown him that buckskins were much inferior to furs.
Within minutes his teeth would be chattering. He was no goblin,
able to survive in the forest without furs. He was imprisoned by
invisible bars of pure cold.

Dancer and Crazy had been placed in the stable with the goblins' stock, and he could see no problem in stealing them when
he was ready to make a break—until the fifth day, when two men
saddled them up and rode them away. They did not return. Rap,
therefore, would be forced to steal one of the stunted goblin ponies and would not have the advantage of a better mount in the
inevitable chase.

He had abandoned his early idea that half the men were away
on a raiding party. There were no other men. Darad had explained
what happened to half the adolescent males in the tribe, and Rap
had reluctantly come to believe that Little Chicken's grisly jokes
were not mere sadistic humor—they were real plans. The loser
would be dismembered by the winner.

Unfortunately, his escape was going to be certain suicide. With
the aid of his farsight he could likely steal the mukluks and a pony
of sorts, but not the clothes he needed. He would freeze to death
in buckskins, unless he was recaptured first. Nevertheless, freezing seemed like a more enjoyable death than the procedures Little
Chicken kept devising, so to the forest he must go.

He left it too late. A wicked wind sprang up at sunset on the
day he had planned for his departure, and he glumly decided to
wait for the next night, although that would be his last chance
before the testing. And either Little Chicken had been lying, or
had made a mistake, or else Rap had miscounted, but he awoke
to find the boys excitedly dressing themselves in their buckskins,
which he had not seen them do before. He could detect frantic
activity in the women's hut and the married quarters, and soon he
saw other goblins streaming in from all points of the compass,
bringing their womenfolk and their children along on horseback
to watch the fun. Obviously this was the day of the testing.

He still did not know what was expected of him, except to die
bravely.

And slowly, of course.

2

The wan polar day gleamed hesitantly through a white ice fog, a mere watery glow on the southern horizon, casting no shadows, and barely brighter than good moonlight. Wind was lifting wisps of snow and trailing them along the ground. The feasting had been going on in the main hut for several hours and the only persons not included were Rap, Little Chicken, and some of the most ancient women, who arrived at the boys' cabin with bags of equipment to prepare the contestants. They began by sitting them on stools and smearing them both with bear grease. They dressed Little Chicken's hair in the usual slimy rope, but Rap's tangled mop frustrated them. He did not recognize any of them as the woman he had seen in the night.

The crones toiled in silence, ignoring Rap's questions, but Little Chicken chattered in great spirits. He sat on his stool as the women worked on him, gloating at Rap and rehearsing all the vilest torments he could think of.

"You make good show, Flat Nose!" he begged. "You die long!"

All Rap could do was try his clucking noise, and today even that failed to ruffle Little Chicken. "Death Bird!" he insisted, and grinned happily.

Oh, Gods!

Rap reeled back on his stool, choking down a cry of despair. *He is precious?* Even if his hunger had made him hallucinate a vision of a goblin sorceress, how could it have put that name on its lips? Had the apparition been real, after all? Was he doomed to fight a champion guarded by sorcery?

Then he remembered that Little Chicken had mentioned his new name earlier, the first time they had spoken. Rap had forgotten it, that was all. So this was merely another instance of Rap's mind playing tricks on him. There had been no old woman. Obviously she had been nothing but a figment of his tormented brain.

And Rap had evidently concealed his momentary horror, because Little Chicken had not noticed it. "Clover Scent!" he added, and sighed with pleasure.

Any change of subject was welcome. "Clover Scent?" Rap asked shakily.

"Also today I marry Clover Scent! I give her bits of you for wedding present."

Rap did not ask which bits, and the prospect put his companion back on his grisly litany again. Rap scanned with farsight and detected a very young girl being groomed in the single women's hut.

But now the contestants were almost ready. The old hags produced thick fur mitts for them; then fur shoes of a type Rap had not seen before. They seemed impractical garments, cut low on the ankle, useless in snow, but they were enough to tell him what the testing would involve and why he, a nongoblin, was preferred to the smaller Cheep-Cheep and Fledgling Down.

Little Chicken watched him work it out and grinned.

The mitts and shoes would be worn to prevent fingers and toes falling off, and soon earmuffs appeared as well. But there would be no other garments except the usual loincloths.

A strong stud makes a strong foal—Rap had heard that at least once a day from old Honinin for years. Darad had said the goblins weeded out their weaklings, and obviously they bred their men to be resistant to cold.

"Very cold day, Flat Nose. Bad wind."

The feasting ended; the villagers and their guests came streaming out into the fading twilight and the bad wind. It was a very bad wind, swirling the snow around the compound and streaming the smoke from the chimneys. The cold was so intense that the snow creaked underfoot. Even the goblins did not like it, and the children had been wrapped in furs as well as their usual buckskins. The spectators huddled together, more in bunches than in an even circle, waiting to view the contest. They stamped their feet and grumbled, and their breath was whipped away in quick white clouds.

In the center of the circle lay a tree trunk, and the sight of it gave Rap the last clue he needed as he was led forward, swathed in a thick fur cape. Even with that, he was shivering. The wind stung his bare ankles with gritty snow and bit his face. It was hard to breathe in such cold; his eyes watered, his nose streamed, and the mucus froze on his stubble. He cringed at the knowledge that he was surely going to be stripped of the cape very shortly and he wondered whether the resulting torture of the wind could be very much less than what Little Chicken would do to him afterward.

Yes, it could. His best strategy was to hang on as long as possible and hope to freeze to death.

"Just hold your end up," Darad had said.

Little Chicken marched to one end of the tree trunk; Rap was

directed to the other—the thicker, heavier end, of course. Four
men advanced to lift the log, and Rap wondered whether he would
be able to support the load at all, even without the cold to worry
about. He looked down the horrible length of it—rough bark and
nasty stubs of branches sticking out at intervals. The men stooped
and heaved, and up it came, caked still with snow on its under-
side.

Then his cape was snatched away and the sudden impact of the
air on his skin was worse than being plunged into ice water. He
gasped with the pain of it and saw Little Chicken enjoying his
reaction. At once he was pushed forward, under the end of the
tree trunk, and the men lowered it. Sharp, hard bark bit into his
shoulder, the weight almost buckled his knees, and he scrabbled
for a grip with his fur mitts.

Little Chicken took hold of a convenient stub of branch. There
was no such handhold at Rap's end, so he had less leverage to
work with—High Raven had missed no bets at all. The goblin
gripped firmly and stepped back, pulling.

Rap had not been prepared to do anything but take the weight.
The sudden jerk almost pulled the log off his shoulder. He stumbled forward and started to fold under that monstrous load, then
straightened up with a huge effort, ripping skin from his shoulder
in the process. Little Chicken grinned happily and pushed; Rap
staggered backward, and again almost fell. The spectators cheered
and shouted ribald comments.

Obviously anything went in this game, but after those two play-
ful attempts Little Chicken gave up his efforts to dislodge Rap's
grip—he would spoil the fun if he succeeded. He spread his feet,
steadied the log with one hand, and put the other on his hip in a
show of bravado. Then he just stood and smiled, waiting for the
cold to do its work.

The spectators were silent now, hunching their shoulders
against the wind, stamping their feet in the snow, waiting also.
Small children fretted. Dogs sniffed curiously around the visitors'
ankles. Wraiths of snow circled across the compound and the
chimney smoke hurried away.

They would not have to wait long. Rap could feel the life draining out of him. It could only be a few minutes before his body
temperature fell to the point at which he would faint. Or else he
would simply drop the log, for his muscles were leaping in un-
controllable spasms, his legs trembling violently; he could hardly
stop his knees from buckling. His teeth were rattling, his skin
turning white. Soon he would be as pale as a jotunn. He tried a

quick heave on the log and it was immovable. Little Chicken did not even have to raise his spare hand to steady it, nor move his feet. His grin was growing wider and wider as he watched Rap weaken. Another couple of minutes ought to do it.

Rap recalled his vision of the old woman warning him not to harm Little Chicken, and thought that ought to be funny, somehow.

What use was a word of power here? What use stubbornness? What use was Rap going to be to Inos, who would be robbed of her throne because he had failed in his attempt to warn her? Why did his talent have to be farsight, instead of physical strength or stamina, or Andor's irresistible guile? Only farsight and a knack for horses . . .

Or dogs! Rap uttered a silent scream. He felt Fleabag's equally silent bristle of alarm from somewhere in the crowd.

Either the light was fading much faster than usual or Rap was on the point of fainting, for dark waves were surging across the compound.

Little Chicken had raised his free hand back to the log, so he was probably about to try another push, or a pull, and that would be the end—Rap was barely able to keep upright standing still. The slightest jerk would fell him.

Fleabag! Help!

Just for devilment, Little Chicken gave the trunk a quick twist. The bark scraped on Rap's shoulder. He was too numb to feel much pain, but also too numb to react properly, and the log almost rolled off. He recovered and sent a desperate appeal to Fleabag, a picture, directions . . .

The waves of blackness were coming faster, making rushing sounds like water on the shingle at Krasnegar. The compound rose and fell, flickering now. The end was very close. Little Chicken could tell. He began rocking the log to and fro gently, amusing both himself and the audience by watching how Rap tilted to and fro beneath it, his legs locked, his eyes barely open, his breath coming in short gasps. The swings began to grow larger, to and fro . . . Which way would Rap fall?

Fleabag!

A dog as large as a full-grown timber wolf came racing across the compound at full wolf speed, heading for Rap. As it passed Little Chicken it veered unexpectedly, careering into the backs of his knees. Dog and boy and log collapsed in a heap.

Rap staggered wildly, but he had managed to hold up his end of the tree for an instant longer than Little Chicken had. The other end had fallen first. Then he toppled into the fur robe that was thrown around him. Waiting hands snatched him up and rushed him to the lodge for treatment. Fleabag slunk away, looking confused. The spectators burst into noisy debate as they streamed off in search of warmth.

Little Chicken was left where he was, prostrate on the snow, beating one fist against the log in fury and weeping bitter tears that froze before they reached his chin.

3

Barely conscious, Rap was carried into the communal cabin, and there blacked out completely from the shock of sudden warmth. But the women were experienced in dealing with cases of severe exposure and they had their remedies ready. In a few minutes he became aware of their attentions, and of a large audience, also.

Not all the torture of the goblins' testing was reserved for the loser. Repeatedly he recovered consciousness and fainted again from the agonies as his limbs and body thawed, as he was compelled to move when he wanted to die, as hot fluids were forced down a tube into his stomach. He was massaged and rubbed and pummeled. Yet he hung on stubbornly to the thought that he was enduring this in public, and goblins admired courage. More important, he thought that Little Chicken would be watching. So he choked back the screams, to sweat and shudder through his ordeal in jaw-clenched silence.

The faintness passed in time, but he was left dazed and confused by shock and by the potions that had been forced into him. He was vaguely aware of voices asking what man-name he would take and he heard his own sniggering reply that Flat Nose was fine. He barely registered that they spent a long time working on his face.

Finally the mists inside his head began to clear and he found himself sitting on the men's platform around the central hearth in the big house. He was the only one on it, as if he were a king on his throne. The building was packed with residents and guests— men and boys in their usual shameless state of undress, women and girls swathed like tents—all standing or sitting six or eight deep around the walls, leaving a vacant space in the center of the room, between the two hearths. The great fire was blistering his back and the smoke billowed low overhead like a ceiling.

He squirmed as he realized that he was thus on display while wearing nothing but a loincloth. Then he saw that the empty floor in front of him was not quite empty. His long shadow jiggled and danced on it, while sitting cross-legged in the center and deliberately placed in that shadow was Little Chicken, face expressionless, stoically awaiting his fate. His long queue, of which he had been so proud, had been hacked off at the roots, and he was wearing nothing at all. In mixed company? The shock of that discovery was enough to jerk Rap out of his confused lethargy. He looked around.

That was the signal. High Raven came strutting forward, his bears'-tooth collar clicking, his rope of gray hair hanging down over his paunch. He also wore a ceremonial cap of black feathers with a high-curved raven's beak, sticking out above eyes that glittered in the firelight, full of hate and fury.

He raised his arms and bowed low. "Hail to Flat Nose of the Raven Totem!"

The audience echoed him. "Hail to Flat Nose of the Raven Totem!"

Rap had no idea what was expected of him, so he staggered to his feet. He was at once embraced by High Raven in a hug made slippery and smelly by their mutual coatings of bear grease.

"High Raven honors his son, Flat Nose!" High Raven embraced him again.

Two younger men came forward, looking no happier, and also embraced Rap—Dark Wing and Raven Claw. These were Little Chicken's brothers and now apparently Rap's, also, but the words and gestures of welcome stopped short of their eyes.

Then the new member of the family was presented with gifts— a ceremonial stone dagger and a complete set of buckskins, from boots to hood. Obviously these had been prepared in advance for Little Chicken. Equally obviously, some words were then expected from Rap, so he stammered that he was honored to be admitted to Raven Totem and the beadwork on the clothes was the finest he had ever seen. Then he ran out of ideas.

But apparently he was performing satisfactorily, for now the visiting chiefs were brought forward to be introduced—Death Hug of the Bear Totem, Many Needles of the Porcupines, and a couple of others. None of them was bothering to conceal his amusement at the way High Raven had outsmarted himself and lost a promising son. They were laughing at their host, and that humiliation was likely hurting him more than any regrets he had for Little Chicken.

Each chief said a few words, and Rap soon gathered that the

inexplicable assistance he received from Fleabag was being regarded as divine intervention, which explained why Little Chicken
was not howling for a rematch. Rap thought of the strange old
woman he had seen. *Chosen one . . . he is precious?* Her prophecies had not come true. Obviously she had been nothing but a
delusion.

The last of the honored visitors returned to his seat. So far, so
good! Rap was beginning to feel more like himself, his head was
clearing, and now he was apparently a goblin in good standing.
He wondered if he could obtain assistance for his journey south.

He could dream again of reaching Kinvale! And after he had
given Inos her warning, he might even manage to track down
Darad and gain revenge.

His pleasant speculations were shattered when the next stage
of the program turned out to be a wedding. He had forgotten
young Clover Scent, but now she was led forward, swathed from
crown to toes. She stood in expectant silence, eyes downcast, only
her rather dull and plain face visible in her wimple. Her name
was inappropriate. She looked much too young to be a bride, but
under the gown she had a very promising figure, soft and rounded,
yet youthfully firm. Rap had now accepted that he knew what
people looked like inside their clothes. He just couldn't help
knowing.

But he did not want a goblin wife.

How should he address High Raven? "Honored Father," he
stammered "I must soon go away. The way of my people is to
have but one wife . . ."

He was worried that this refusal might be interpreted as an
insult, but no—for the first time High Raven's burning resentment
seemed to cool a fraction. He bared yellow teeth in a predatory
and approving smile. Darad had explained, of course, that the
purpose of this murderous ceremony was to leave fewer men to
share the women.

"I will take her for you?"

Rap thought that Clover Scent might prefer one of Little Chick-
en's brothers, but he was not going to argue the matter. He nodded, and that was enough. In no time High Raven, as chief,
performed the ceremony, marrying Clover Scent to himself, as
bridegroom. The bride's expression did not change by a flicker,
so either she did not care or she was being very tactful. High
Raven had lost a son and gained a wife. He seemed to be pleased
by the exchange.

Rap had not eaten all day. A quick steak would be a very nice thought.

But now came the moment he had been unconsciously dreading. Clover Scent had been removed. He was left standing in his place of honor with High Raven—and Little Chicken was still sitting in the middle of that arena. He knew the agenda. He rose and came forward, head held high in spite of his nudity, the center of attention. He dropped to his knees in front of Rap.

"My life is worthless," he proclaimed, in what was obviously a ritual speech, "and must be short. Let my death be long." Then he stared up at Rap unwinkingly.

Rap studied him with astonishment. In Little Chicken's place he would be a quivering, gibbering, ashen-faced jelly. Did he really not care? Then he saw the tiny flags of fear: the tightness in the strong neck muscles, the tenseness around the eyes, a fine dew of sweat sparkling on the greased forehead. *Only the brave truly know fear*, Sergeant Thosolin liked to say, *for only they have mastered it*. Rap felt admiration then. Little Chicken was afraid, but he had mastered his fear.

"You know our customs?" High Raven inquired.

Even leaving aside warnings from delusive old women, Rap had no intention of damaging any part of the young goblin—but he could not resist taking a little revenge for the days of taunting. "Little Chicken has told me many good ideas."

High Raven seemed pleased. He nodded. "How do you work?"

Seeing Rap hesitate, the chief explained—some performers liked to hang the victims by the hands, which made the show easier for the audience to see. Others preferred to stake him out on the floor, where he was more accessible, or over trestles. The choice was Rap's, for this was to be his show.

Rap pursed his lips, as if considering the matter. Then he appealed to the victim. "Which do you think best?"

The irony did not escape Little Chicken; his eyes narrowed briefly. "On floor!" he said emphatically. "Last longer."

Now Rap's conscience rebelled. This teasing was a torture in itself. "I do not wish to do this thing."

Father and son reacted with shock.

"It is duty!" Little Chicken shouted, looking quite horrified. "I will tell you things to do! Many things, much pain!"

"Silence, trash!" High Raven turned to Rap. "Who will you have do this, then?" Perhaps he was hoping to be appointed substitute torturer as well as substitute bridegroom, to be avenged on this son who had so shamed him and his house.

Rap was sweating now, and not only from the heat of the roaring furnace behind him. He suspected that if he said the wrong thing he might yet find himself staked out and providing the entertainment. Much worse was the realization that Little Chicken's fate might be unavoidable, in which case the kindest course would be for Rap to undertake the job and give him a quick death in a clumsy amateur's mistake. Could he bring himself to do that?

"What happens," he asked, "if I do not say another to do this?"

Little Chicken howled and hurled himself forward to embrace Rap's feet. "No!" he shouted. "I will make good show! I will die very slow! Long pain! Much agony!"

Unbelievable! Rap stared down at him, speechless. What alternative could possibly be worse than what he was asking for?

High Raven had colored in fury and he glared up at Rap. "You bring shame upon the clan! You disappoint our guests!"

"It is not the way of my people!" Rap protested, glaring back. He had long ago discovered that sometimes the only way to handle old Honinin was to use that glare—*stubborn*. It did not work on High Raven, though.

"We are your people! The Raven Clan!"

"Also I have another people."

The chief was almost foaming with rage. "Insult! Renegade! You will leave this house. Go! Take trash with you!"

Rap thought of the arctic night waiting outside and the flimsy buckskins he had been given. He wondered if he would be allowed to take even those, or would just be driven out as he was.

"I am your guest! I wore good furs. You send a guest away, keep his furs?" He knew what had happened to those furs.

So did High Raven, but he did not know that Rap knew. He scowled and glanced around. "Furs will be found. You will go tomorrow." He looked down at the groveling Little Chicken, who was wailing and rubbing his face in the dirt. "And take trash."

The audience was muttering with disapproval and disappointment, but it sounded as if Rap would be allowed to depart safely, and also that he had just acquired a companion—a companion who would have every incentive to break his neck at the first opportunity.

But Little Chicken was harder to convince than his father. He rose to his knees and raised clasped hands in a last desperate appeal to Rap. "Flat Nose! Do not leave me in shame! I make good show! Never cry out! Long, long pain!"

His distress seemed so real and so intense that for a moment

Rap hesitated. He had certainly played foul in the testing, cheating Little Chicken out of what should have been an easy victory. Was it fair now to cheat him out of the lingering death he dearly wanted? Little Chicken, it seemed, would not be able to live with himself . . . but Rap had to live with himself, also, and he had been the winner. He shook his head.

The burly goblin threw back his head and wailed a long, long howl of lament. Then he clambered to his feet and slunk away, doubled over with shame, hiding his nakedness now with his hands.

From the look in High Raven's eye, Rap was no longer welcome in the place of honor. He was about to leave when he saw his gifts still lying on the platform. Thinking he might persuade Little Chicken to accept them, he gathered them up quickly, then walked away. The crowd parted to let him through, glaring contemptuously.

High Raven raised his arms to the company. "Raven Totem does not disappoint guests! More food! More beer! Cheep-Cheep, Fledgling Down—come forward."

Rap's knees quivered in a sudden surge of horror—he had just condemned one of the younger boys to take Little Chicken's place on the butcher block. He thought that Little Chicken deserved it more, but then he remembered that it was only his arrival and betrayal by Darad that had prevented either Cheep-Cheep or Fledgling Down being there anyway, so really nothing had changed. Not his fault.

He reached the back of the crowd and stopped, baffled. Some of the spectators were still turning to send angry glares in his direction. He had no friends in that place, but now he was probably not eligible to sleep in the boys' house, so he would have to stay. Then a hand fell on his shoulder like a falling tree. He was spun around to face Little Chicken.

He had found a loincloth, but his face was still filthy with the dirt from the floor, streaked by tears. It also wore an expression of urgency. "You come!" He moved toward the door.

Rap dug in his toes and tried to resist the pull. Go out into the night with Little Chicken? Instant suicide!

The young goblin seemed puzzled by Rap's reluctance, then he guessed the reason. He smiled bitterly. "Flat Nose frightened of trash?"

Rap squared his shoulders and went. Little Chicken did not saunter this time. He dashed through the unbearable dark cold.

Rap ran at his heels, bare feet rapidly going numb in the snow. They arrived at the boys' house and plunged in.

It was empty and dark, the fire shrunk to embers. Little Chicken scooped up an icy rug and draped it around the quivering Rap, who dropped his bundle of gifts to huddle the fur tight about him. His companion set to work at the hearth, blowing and poking and stirring life into it. Soon he had flames leaping again. Then he looked up to study Rap—who was shivering mightily inside his robe. Little Chicken squatted in nothing but a leather apron, yet apparently at ease in the freezing temperature.

"Not go tomorrow. Go now!"

"Why?" Rap's mind screamed at the thought.

"Dark Wing, Raven Claw. My brothers follow us."

They would want revenge? But a man who had so recently begged for death should not be suddenly eager to escape it. Rap was suspicious still.

"I need my furs," he said.

Little Chicken scowled. "Furs bad! Buckskins better. I show you."

"You stand the cold better than I do." That remark was not enormously tactful, and the goblin heaved a sigh of regret.

"Yes. But I look after you now."

"Why should I trust you?"

Little Chicken jumped up and stamped his bare foot furiously. "I look after you!" he shouted. Apparently Rap had discovered yet another way to humiliate him. He was dark-faced and breathing hard, and his big fists had clenched until the bones showed white. Rap kept a puzzled silence.

Little Chicken grunted. "I am your trash—slave. My duty to look after you. Where we go?"

"South. Across the mountains."

Little Chicken nodded as if that were two doors down the street and not weeks away. "I take you. We go now."

The fire was starting to flame up noisily and brightly, but Rap was still shivering. Then his fur robe was snatched away and Little Chicken began slapping big handfuls of grease on him, spreading it in a disgustingly thick layer.

"Here, I can do that," Rap protested, trying to take the bucket.

Little Chicken knocked his hand away and kept on working. In a few moments Rap discovered that the grease did seem to keep the cold out, when it was thick enough. Then he was being helped into the new buckskins, his protests completely ignored. They fitted surprisingly well, yet Little Chicken fussed and adjusted ties and straps on waist and ankles and wrists, taking a long time to dress his new master to his satisfaction. Then he said, "Sit!" and began greasing himself. Rap tried to help and got shouted at, but was grudgingly allowed to coat his slave's back for him. For trash, Little Chicken was remarkably lacking in respect. He donned his old buckskins, which had been lying in lonely neglect by the door. Then he said, "Stay! Back soon," and vanished out into the moonlight.

Rap's farsight traced him automatically, discovering then that the whole horde of goblins was pouring out from the big house. The boys were ready, and a bonfire had been lighted to brighten their coming contest. Little Chicken dodged around the far side of the stable, made a quick dash to the women's house, and headed for the food store.

Cheep-Cheep and Fledgling Down were led out in fur robes. Now Rap tried desperately not to watch, but apparently farsight could not be turned off at will—not, at least, when there was something of interest happening. He tried to distract himself by inspecting the horses in the stable, for the visitors had brought twenty or more of the scrawny ponies with them and he must be sure to select the best for his escape . . . but in spite of himself, he was a spectator. He knew how the youths staggered as they took the strain of the load, how they began to tremble when the cold ate into their exposed flesh. They did not push and pull as Little Chicken had done; they just stood and stared doggedly at each other and tried to endure. They lasted much longer than Rap had, but then Cheep-Cheep buckled without warning. Fledgling Down was wrapped up and rushed off into the lodge again. The spectators followed, two of them dragging the unconscious Cheep-Cheep.

Then Little Chicken returned. He carried a very small backpack, most of which seemed to be occupied by a wallet of bear grease. It also contained fire-making equipment, a couple of knives, a little food, and much cord, which might be for trapping or fishing. From somewhere he had obtained two short bows and two quivers of arrows. Rap was a sorry archer, but he decided he could carry his set as a spare for Little Chicken to use.

"Eat!" The goblin thrust a wad of hard wafers into Rap's hand. They tasted like hay mixed with honey, but he was starved and chewed them greedily, crouching by the hearth.

Little Chicken had not eaten that day, either; he sat by the door and munched loudly, apparently finding the vicinity of the fireplace too warm for comfort. He also talked continuously with his mouth full, in his usual laconic phrases. "Moon up. Go to Por-cupine Totem. No rush now. Cheep-Cheep make good show. If Fledgling Down, not last so long."

"How can you know that?" Rap asked, squirming. His far-sight told him that Fledgling Down was already sitting on the platform, being hailed by whatever his new name was. He had recovered much faster than Rap had done.

"Good blood!" Little Chicken explained: Cheep-Cheep's brother Sweet Nestling had lost to Raven Claw two winters before and had done very well, the best show in many years. "First dug out toenails," he said. "No scream. Said 'Thank you.' Then hammer toes flat, one by one, with rocks. Said 'Thank you.' Much applause. Then—"

Rap had lost his appetite. "I don't want to hear!" he squealed.

For an instant the old mockery gleamed in Little Chicken's eye. "Then sharp stick from fire . . ." If Rap disliked hearing such barbarities even when they did not concern him personally, then here was a way to get back at him. So Little Chicken proceeded to narrate all of Sweet Nestling's death agonies in meticulous detail. He spoke with great admiration, sounding sincerely re-gretful that he had not been allowed to try to better the perfor-mance, and watching Rap's nauseated reaction with bitter joy.

By the time the meal was over, Rap knew that Cheep-Cheep was already hanging in the middle of the lodge, waiting for his long ordeal to start. He must get out of range quickly.

"Let's go," he said, wondering if he would freeze to death before Cheep-Cheep died. "How many horses do we take?"

Little Chicken frowned. "No horses. Run."

"Run all the way? No horses?"

"Horses?" Little Chicken spat. "Horses for babies and old women. Men run!"

Before Rap could argue, a handful of bear grease was pushed in his face. Little Chicken spread it with care, on Rap's lips and eyelids and even on the insides of his nostrils. Then he adjusted Rap's hood, pulling down and lacing a mask that Rap had not known existed, covering his face completely except for eye and nose holes. He did the same for himself and turned for the door, conversation now being almost impossible.

He was serious, obviously—they were going to run to the mountains. He began a slow jog as soon as his moccasins touched the snow. Rap fell in behind him, not truly believing that the feat was possible. All the way? The cold would freeze their lungs in minutes.

They jogged out the gateway and started across the clearing.

Two men against the wastelands? Two boys . . . Rap felt horribly vulnerable, much more so than when he had set out from Krasnegar with Andor. Perhaps it was the absence of the horses, perhaps just that now he knew more. Only the two of them, master and slave? He had trusted Andor completely. How could he ever trust Little Chicken, who might well intend to imprison Rap in some convenient spot and then put his good ideas into practice?

One more companion would be a wise precaution, Rap decided.

Fleabag, sleeping happily in his snow hollow, jerked his head up as if he had heard a call. He rose and shook himself. He bowed low to ease his front legs. He pointed his nose at the sky to stretch his back legs. Then he set off into the forest in a wolf's long, easy lope.

4

Buckskins were indeed better than furs—for running. They weighed nothing, they seemed to let the sweat out without letting the cold air in, and feet could flex inside the soft moccasins and so stay warm. Encased in grease and leather, Rap jogged over the moonlit snow behind Little Chicken and gradually began to feel more confident. Fleabag soon joined them and then took up position ahead.

After covering a league or so, Little Chicken dropped to a walk. He snapped off the icicles below his nose so that he could open his mask, but when Rap raised his mitts to do the same, the goblin knocked his hands down.

Red and puffing, he studied Rap impassively for a moment, then asked, "Blisters? Rubbings?"

Rap mumbled something incoherent and shook his head.

Little Chicken nodded in grudging satisfaction. "You run good, town boy."

Rap grinned, but only to himself. He nodded.

"Go much faster, then?"

Rap nodded with less certainty, and the goblin chuckled as he closed his hood, but when he broke from the walk into a jog again, he kept the same pace as before.

Any resident of Krasnegar needed good legs. Rap had hoped

that his week on horseback might have left him in better shape than Little Chicken was. As the hours crept by, he discarded that idea. The night became a blur of snow and trees, of shadows and moonbeams, of pounding heart, of smoky breath out and icy breath in, of chest burned by the frigid air, of Fleabag loping along, always at a distance, of Little Chicken ever just ahead, usually jogging, rarely taking a walk break. At times they must run with hands held high to divert branches, at times they were slowed to a snail pace by cluttered deadfall. But mostly they just ran. There was no conversation and Rap would not have been capable of it anyway. He was soon unable to think or feel anything except a steady, grinding, suicidal resolve that the town boy was going to keep up with the goblin.

Just before moonset they came to Porcupine Totem, and when the dogs began to bark, Little Chicken stripped off the masks. He pushed Ràp ahead as they approached the doors. By that time Rap was too weary to wonder why, but he was accepted as Flat Nose of the Raven Totem without question. Most of the clan were absent, visiting Raven Totem for the entertainment, but there were a couple of young men left in charge, and many old folk, and some children too young to travel.

The village layout was very similar to the Ravens', perhaps a little larger. Rap staggered into a lodge that seemed quite identical and met insufferable heat and glare. His knees almost buckled on the spot. Yet the household had been asleep and was only just reviving the fire for the visitors, so perhaps the hall was really quite cool. Little Chicken's fingers expertly unfastened Rap's buckskins for him, and he stepped out of them with relief, sank down on the hearthstones, and greedily drank of whatever it was they gave him. His mind was as full of smoke as the ceiling. All he wanted was sleep, sleep, sleep . . .

Then Little Chicken, stripped to a loincloth as he was, pushed him down flat on the big fireplace and produced a bucket of the inevitable grease, contributed by the hosts. He inspected Rap's feet carefully, then set to work at giving his legs a vigorous massage, skillfully unknotting the tendons and easing the aches. It was heaven.

"Soft, town boy," he growled contemptuously.

Rap agreed, thinking that he could not have run another two steps. When the massage was over, he offered to do the same for Little Chicken, although he knew he would be very unskilled.

Little Chicken's eyes flashed in anger. "For trash?"

Probably he did not need a massage. He looked as fresh as when he had started out, hours before. After snatching up a dish of food that was waiting by the side of the fire, he stalked to the door. Rap's farsight showed him heading for the boys' building.

It was then that Rap realized why he had been pushed forward for the introductions, and why the skin around his eyes hurt—which he had not noticed before. It was only after he had gulped a quick meal and thanked his hosts and rolled up in a greasy, stinking fur to sleep that he wondered what Inos was going to say about that.

He had hardly closed his eyes, he thought, when Little Chicken was shaking his shoulder and starting another massage to loosen muscles knotted up in sleep. Then he sternly ordered Rap to go out to the pits right away. Two of the women rushed to prepare food for the guests even as Rap was being dressed again by his handler. Little Chicken obviously took his duties seriously, whether they be to die entertainingly or to serve a master. He would allow Rap to do nothing that he could do for him, not even lace a boot; he would accept no help for himself. In his own eyes he was trash, neither boy nor man, merely a possession that should try to be useful and must pamper this fragile nongoblin.

He led the way southward without another word. Had it not been for the first glimmers of dawn light, Rap would not have believed that his stay at Porcupine Totem had lasted more than a few minutes.

The following days passed in the same way. Each morning Little Chicken obtained directions. By moonlight he brought his owner safely to another village. Conversation was impossible in the masks, and when the journeys ended Rap was too exhausted to try. In any case, his companion refused to stay in the adults' building once he had given Rap his massage and seen him settled.

Rap talked a little with his hosts, but he had nothing to tell them, and their news was meaningless to him. His questions about Darad brought only angry silence—just by asking, he was breaking the rules for guests. He was never refused hospitality or courtesy, but the welcome was grudging, partly because he was not goblin-born, mostly because of Little Chicken. To own trash was a crime. Rap had offended by not giving his defeated opponent the death he deserved and wanted.

Gradually Rap's fitness improved, aided each evening by the most enormous meals he had ever eaten, much of them fresh meat that was a great luxury to him. Gradually Little Chicken raised the pace, but only slightly, for the villages were set an easy day's run apart, and greater speed would have brought no advantage. The daylight was becoming noticeably longer as the sun began its slow return to the northlands and the travelers worked their way south.

About the sixth morning, just as it was time to fasten the masks and leave the lodge, Little Chicken paused and regarded Rap with a glint in his eye.

"Salmon Totem," he said, "then Eagles, then Elk. Three days?"

"Right."

"Or sleep in snow, then Elk. Two days?"

Any perceptible hint of a challenge from Little Chicken was unbearable. "Let's do that, then."

The goblin's angular eyes widened. "And run faster?"

"Fast as you like!"

"Town boy!" Little Chicken laughed, and contemptuously pushed a handful of grease in Rap's face.

A few hours later, grimly aware of the tearing pain of the faster pace, Rap thought to wonder why his companion had not brought food if there was to be no lodge at the end of the day's trek.

The answer, obviously, was that a goblin could live off the land. They stopped when Little Chicken judged the light too poor for running—he did not know that Rap could see in the dark. He lighted a fire and then made two others. Three small fires were better than one big one, he said, and then he screamed in fury when Rap tried to help by gathering firewood. Needing a bucket to melt snow, the goblin used his backpack, dropping hot rocks in it. While the resulting water was necessary and welcome to Rap, it was the strangest-tasting brew he had ever swallowed.

"I find food!" Little Chicken announced. He pointed scornfully at Fleabag, whom he had completely ignored until that moment. "You keep that here?"

Rap agreed, and did so. He was glad of the company, sitting in the darkly haunted forest, watching the shadows of the densely enclosing conifers dance around his triangle of firelit snow, and trying not to wonder what he would do if Little Chicken failed to return. Fleabag just pawed out a hollow and went to sleep.

But Little Chicken did return, in an astonishingly short time. He came bearing two white rabbits, which he had caught beyond farsight range, so that Rap did not know how he had done it. He could hardly have been quicker had he run to a market for them.

He was an expert skinner and a skilled cook, too, damn him!

The campsite was in a hollow, half filled by a deep snowdrift, and Rap soon discovered that this was not by chance. As soon as he had eaten, Little Chicken set to work digging out a snow cave there, scooping like a dog, and again indignantly refusing assistance. When it was dug deep enough, he began gathering spruce branches, breaking them off trees made brittle by the fearsome cold. Again Rap tried to help and this time Little Chicken did not shout at him. Instead he demonstrated his vastly greater strength by snapping with apparent ease any bough that Rap had failed to break. Rap gave up in humiliation and returned shivering to the fires.

Finally the cave was lined to Little Chicken's satisfaction. He backed out and nodded to Rap.

"You first," he said. "I follow, close door."

"What about Fleabag? He would keep us warm."

Little Chicken's expression should have been invisible in the dark, but Rap knew that he was regarding Fleabag with hostility. "Won't come."

Rap hesitated and then said, "He will for me."

After a moment's pause, the goblin said, "Show!" very quietly.

Rap crawled into the cave and summoned the dog without a word. Fleabag awoke, trotted over, and peered into the hole to see what his friend wanted. Then he obediently crept in and lay down alongside Rap, panting foul carrion breath in his face, swishing boughs with his tail.

The cave was a narrow tunnel and it seemed impossible that a third body could find room, but Little Chicken entered by lying on his back and wriggling, using his feet to push snow against the entrance until it was closed to his satisfaction. That was strenuous work and he ended crushed against Rap, puffing as hard as Fleabag. Rap would certainly be warm enough during the night between those two, sheltered from the wind and insulated by snow.

There was no light and Little Chicken's face was too close to be seen properly if there were, but Rap knew the thoughtful expression it bore in the darkness. He waited for the question.

"How you do that?" said a whisper close to his ear.

"I don't know, Little Chicken. I talk in my head. It works on horses, too, but most of all on Fleabag."

The goblin stared blankly at nothing for a while and then asked, "You knock me down in testing?"

Here it came! "Yes. It was not the Gods. It was me."

Rap was not sure why he had provoked this revelation. He did not think he was boasting. Probably he was clearing his conscience. He sensed the big mouth opening as Little Chicken bared his fangs and for a moment Rap half expected to feel them sink in his throat.

It was a smile. Unaware that he was being observed, Little Chicken was grinning into the darkness. "Good! Town boy won." After a while he chuckled. "Good foe! Did not know. Know now."

He said no more. He was still lying there leering at the dark when Rap fell into an exhausted sleep.

Recognizing no rules, the goblin could not resent cheating. His satisfaction came from learning that he had been beaten by a mortal and not some superhuman freak event . . . or so Rap concluded.

Rap was wrong.

Three fleabags emerged the next morning, into a thick white ice fog. The forest vanished within yards, trees fading away into the pervasive grayness in all directions. Still, bitterly cold, and treacherous, ice fog made all ways seem the same.

"Nice cave," the goblin said sarcastically. "Stay long time."

"South is that way. I will lead."

"Go in circles."

Rap shook his head. "Not me. South to the river, then upriver to Elk Totem, right?"

His companion shrugged, probably thinking that the exercise would do no harm, and he could always backtrack, or make another cave. So that day it was Rap who led, trotting through a white world striped with gray tree trunks, a silent goblin at his heels. The river appeared where it was supposed to and they followed it upstream. Farsight told Rap where to cross the ice and cut through the forest again, and he brought Little Chicken right to the door.

He was wondering what reaction he would get to this second revelation of supernatural power—awe? Respect? But when the buckskins came off in the firelit lodge, Little Chicken merely smiled with more secret amusement and made no comment.

Rap went to the hearth and was introduced to the rest of his hosts, being given the usual oily embraces. Little Chicken appeared with the inevitable grease bucket.

"I don't need that any more," Rap said firmly. "My legs are strong now. No massage."

He turned his back. He had forgotten that Little Chicken took his duties seriously and was an expert wrestler. Without warning Rap was flat on his face, with the goblin kneeling on him.

The audience enjoyed that massage more than Rap did.

Lynx Totem . . . another Eagle Totem . . .

At Beaver Totem they were stormbound for four days while the worst weather of the winter howled like giant wolves around the cabins. So unbearable was the chill of the wind that even Little Chicken dressed in his buckskins to run from cabin to cabin, or to attend to calls of nature. The goblins strung lines between the buildings lest they become lost in the snow and freeze to death within yards of their own doors.

Rap spent most of the time in lonely brooding. He had been four weeks on his journey now. The king might be already dead and Inos had not been told of his illness.

Or had she?

He watched the goblins as they lived their boring winter lives, studiously ignoring him except when hospitality demanded that they must offer him food or drink. He endured Little Chicken's mocking contempt on the rare occasions when he appeared in the adults' building. He wished fervently that his talent for befriending animals would work on people, like Andor's.

Always his thoughts came back to Andor.

King Holindarn knew a word of power. So Andor had said.

If Andor had gone to such trouble to try to learn Rap's word, then he would also try to steal the king's.

Words were passed on deathbeds. If Inos could return to Krasnegar in time, her father would tell her the word that had been passed down from Inisso. More and more, Rap was becoming convinced that Darad would revert to Andor, and Andor would seek out Inos at Kinvale. He would use his occult charm upon her to win her trust, then accompany her back to Krasnegar. She must be told about her father, but she must also be warned against Andor.

He had gained a week while Rap was a prisoner at Raven Totem. He might be gaining time now if he were already over the mountains, beyond the storm's reach. As soon as the weather cleared, Rap would tell Little Chicken to increase the pace again. Somehow he must keep up.

The weather cleared at last. The journey resumed and became more than an endurance test. Now it was a contest. The runs became longer, the rests shorter. Little Chicken would offer the challenge, and Rap would stubbornly accept. He ran until blood flowed from his nostrils and life was an endless torment of pain and exhaustion.

It was madness. With his farsight, Rap was incredibly sure-footed, but if Little Chicken sprained an ankle, the two of them would die in the wilderness. They both knew that. Rap was not going to admit that he was in any way inferior to the goblin. But he was, as Little Chicken could demonstrate with no apparent effort. Rap's supernatural abilities he merely ignored, so that they did not count. Day by day he raised the wager. Day by day Rap would call his raise. He despised himself for it, but he could not stop. He had cheated the goblin out of the opportunity to torture him—so now he was torturing himself. The agonies might not be quite so severe, although at times that seemed debatable, but they went on longer—much, much longer, day after agonizing day.

The harder Rap tried, the more amusing the goblin seemed to find him . . . and the harder he tried.

Then one night, Rap thought he saw his chance. It had been the worst run yet—as they all seemed to be—and he reeled on his feet as he gathered firewood. The goblin allowed him to help with that task now, because his efforts were so obviously inferior.

Suddenly, through the blur of fatigue and pain, Rap sensed movement within his range. He straightened, searched, and decided that it was a small deer. Calling for silence, he sent Fleabag out to circle beyond the doe and then drive it. Puzzled but impassive, Little Chicken squatted down, watching without a word. Rap strung his bow, notched an arrow, and waited, trembling with exhaustion and mental effort, carefully tracking his quarry's approach. The deer burst through the trees where he knew it would, at easy range. He shot.

He missed.

Without seeming to hurry at all, Little Chicken rose, lifted the bow from Rap's hand, stooped to pick up an arrow, aimed, shot, and unerringly nailed down their supper just before it vanished into the trees. He handed the bow back with a smile that showed more enamel than any human mouth should contain.

Shrouded in silent misery, Rap watched the skinning and cooking. It had been fatigue making his hands shake, of course. Even as clumsy an archer as he was should not have missed that one. He had tried to look clever and he had made a fool of himself again. Every joint and muscle in his body was shaking. This last leg of the journey seemed to have lasted for days without a break. Had he thought to notice the moon's position when they started, he could have estimated the time, but he knew only that it had been many, many hours. He was so grossly exhausted that he was not sure he would be able to eat any of the venison anyway. He could barely keep his eyes open, his chest burned, his legs ached— and Little Chicken seemed as fresh as if he had just climbed out of bed. There had to be a limit to the amount of this torture that a man could take, and Rap was certain he had reached it now. Why not just admit that the contest was hopeless? Who cared? What did it matter?

Then Rap saw that the goblin was studying him from his crouch by the cooking fire, and his big ugly mouth was curled in disdainful amusement again. "Eat now, Flat Nose. Then sleep? Or run more?"

Rap glared back at the smirk.

Something inside him whimpered as he spoke.

"Run more, of course," he said.

5

A hiss of rain rushing over glass died away into petty dripping noises. Logs at the far end of the room spat and spluttered sleepily in the great hearth, and somewhere far off a door was tapping. Rain was a sign of spring, Inos thought happily, and she marveled once more that it should come so soon. For long months yet the iron heels of winter would stamp on poor old Krasnegar, but yesterday she had gathered snowdrops. *Flowers!* Trees had never impressed her much, but flowers did.

It was a drowsy do-nothing afternoon and she was curled into a big chair in the library with a book of wide erudition and archaic, inscrutable handwriting. Near the fire Aunt Kade nodded over a slim romance. Various other ladies and gentleman were also pretending to read—few of them seriously. Inos was serious, but about ready to admit defeat. She could ask to have a scrivener transcribe the key passages for her, of course, but she had an inexplicable certainty that she was not supposed to be troubling her pretty little head over this particular tome. The request would not be refused, she thought, but the results might be a long time in coming, and meanwhile the book itself would be unavailable.

Spring! Summer would arrive in its turn and her ship would be waiting. She sighed and twisted a lock of golden hair and stared at the rain-blurred windows. Krasnegar? To be really honest, she did not long so much for Krasnegar now. She missed her father of course, but who else? There was no one of her rank there, and no one of her age who would understand one word she might say about Kinvale.

Inos turned to gaze for a moment at Aunt Kade's drooping eyelids, wondering how she had stood it. Forty years or more she had lived in Kinvale, as wife and widow, and then she had thrown it all up and gone back to Krasnegar to mother a suddenly be- reaved niece. A mere niece—a niece who had not appreciated her until she had seen what the old dear had given up. To return to stark and barren Krasnegar for a niece, when Kinvale had offered so much?

And she? Of course she must go back. She could not doubt it. She would return in the summer, unwed and unbetrothed, appar- ently.

Five months since Andor had gone . . .

Aunt Kade and her Grace—or Disgrace?—the duchess had run out of candidates at last. The long parade of suitors that had begun with the glorious Andor had ended now with the unspeakable Proconsul Yggingi. Andor had been an accident and Yggingi was a disaster. Yggingi had not been invited to Kinvale for Inos' sake— Kade had assured her of that quite vehemently. After all, he was twice her age and already married. Unfortunately Yggingi himself did not seem to appreciate such considerations. He was the worst yet, the bottom of the barrel, and not even the official barrel. Any barrel. There were a few pleasant young men in residence at the moment—men who might be allowed to brighten a maiden's day, if not share her life—but not one of them dared come near Inos now. Yggingi's menacing glare had walled her off as his private preserve.

One of the reasons she had fled here, to the library, was to escape the creepy attentions of Proconsul Yggingi. A library was the last place *that* man was likely to visit.

How beautifully Andor had read poetry to her!

None of the others had ever compared to Andor. Of course she had never expected that a lightning strike of romantic passion would be waiting in the clouds. A princess must expect to settle for rank, character, and a purely conventional physical relationship. All she could hope for there was that the man not be totally disgusting. But even being practical, she had found nothing of a size to match her mesh—except Andor. If she discounted him, there was no second best.

And she must discount him. Five months . . .

She raised the book again and made another attempt. *A Brief History of the Late and Dearly Mourned Beneficient Sorcerer Inisso, His Heirs and Successors, with an Adumbration of Their Acts and Accomplishments.* Dull to the risk of lockjaw, but relevant. A strange man Inisso must have been. Why should he have built his tower on the far shores of the Winter Ocean? Stranger still, why should he have divided his heritage? For it seemed that he had bequeathed each of his three sons an equal share of his magical powers, and apparently that was a most odd thing for a sorcerer to do. There were broad hints here, she had discovered, that some of that magic had been passed down in her own family. She would ask Father about that when she returned. She smiled at the thought of her practical, matter-of-fact father secretly performing sorcerous rituals.

She had never even had a chance to visit that forgotten chamber of puissance at the top of the main tower.

It was curious that she should have found this tattered and dog-eared tome in the library at Kinvale. Very dog-eared—it had been much read over the centuries . . . By whom? Of course the Kinvale family was also descended from Inisso. She and the droopy-lipped Angilki were related through Inisso, as well as by countless later cross-linkages. So was the sinister Kalkor of Gark, gruesome man.

Kade had noticed her settling down with the monster volume and had asked what it was. Her first reaction had been approval—Witless Young Maiden Starts Taking Interest—but that had been followed by a strange uncertainty. Inos could not imagine her aunt ever reading such a nightmare of ennui, but knowing Kade, she might very well have a good idea of the gist of it—better than Inos would gain by her studies, likely. What she really needed was someone to discuss it with. But whom?

The library door swung open on well-oiled hinges to admit a footman, a gawky, baby-faced footman, looking around with large eyes, seeking someone.

So spring would be followed by summer and Inos would return to Krasnegar with Aunt Kade, and in a year or two they would come back to Kinvale and try again. She was young yet. Andor could not be the only bearable man in the world.

The rain slapped again, louder than usual, and Inos turned to stare at the windows without really seeing them. Why had the Gods been so cruel? Why produce the perfect candidate before she could understand how incredibly superior he was—and then whisk him away again? He had saved her sanity, of course. He had blazed through Kinvale like a vacationing God. In a few short weeks he had shown her how to live, had demonstrated what life should really be. But comparing Kinvale-with-Andor to Kinvale-without-Andor was almost like comparing Kinvale to Krasnegar. The shadows had returned when he left—not so deep, but emptier. He had sparkled with fun from dawn till exhaustion, a bottomless well of amusement, zest, entertainment, flattery, serious conversation, and—and *living*.

Disgusting he was not.

Five months! Now she knew better. Older and more mature now, she could see that the naive child she had been then could have held no real interest for a man of the world like Andor. But he had taken pity on her and entertained her, cheering her up. Then, when he had seen the juvenile infatuation he had unwittingly provoked, he had found a gentle way to end it. The dramatic post-haste flight into the darkness, the romantic tale of honor and danger—those had been so much kinder than just saying he had more important things to do now, thank you. He had known that she would grow up quickly, and then, when she was mature enough to survive on her own feet—as she now was—then she would see that it had all been a mirage. And all for the best.

The sound of a cough caught her attention and she looked up to see that the young footman was shifting from one foot to the other in front of Aunt Kade, while wrestling with the terrifying problem of awakening a sleeping princess without coughing hard enough to disturb the other assorted nobility slumped in the nearby chairs.

Probably the dressmakers had arrived with the gowns for the Springtide ball. Amused, Inos watched to see how the youth would solve his puzzle. In the romances, the correct way to tackle that particular assignment was with a kiss; but if he were to try that in the library at Kinvale, he would very soon find himself being scorched by the breath of the Dragon Herself.

Even at that age, she thought, Andor would have gone for the kiss and gotten away with it.

Then he glanced frantically around the room, and his eyes caught hers. She took pity on him and nodded.

As Andor had taken pity on her. Andor had shown her what

she should look for in a suitor—and perhaps done so deliberately, although he had thereby raised her standards so high that they might never be satisfied. The rock of Krasnegar was a tombstone. A man like Andor had all of Pandemia to play in and need not throw away his life in the barrenlands. A princess had duty and obligations. She must live out her days on the rock, but to ask anyone else to do so, just for her sake . . . For the millionth time, she pondered the ironic truth that a princess lacked some freedoms a common serf could take for granted.

The footman arrived before her and bowed. She thought this one was the Gavor her favorite *coiffeuse* spoke of, and if half those stories were true then he was quite a lad. But now he was showing nothing but polite inquiry on a boyishly pink face.

Inos resisted a temptation to suggest he try a kiss to awaken Kade. She had learned now that excessive familiarity merely unsettled domestics; their life was easier when their place was clearly defined for them. "You can give me the message, and I'll see that the princess gets it," she said.

Gavor, if that was his name, did not try to hide his relief. "That is most kind of you, ma'am! Her Grace requests that both you and your aunt attend her, should it be convenient."

Not the Springtide gowns! Inos slammed her book shut with a thump that awoke half the snoozing peers in the room and she flashed the stupid boy a glare that made him blush to the ears. He should have come straight to her, instead of doing all that dithering in front of Aunt Kade—sometimes they just did not seem to have the brains they were born with! But she rose calmly and said merely, "Thank you." She headed for Aunt Kade. Ekka did not enjoy being kept waiting, and Inos must certainly go around by her own room on the way and brush her hair.

The dowager duchess's boudoir—which Inos thought of as the Unholy of Unholies—was a tribute to her son's peerless taste in decor. It was at once large and light, imposing and intimate. White and gold and powder blue, it bore a heady scent of grandeur and a glitter of pomp, yet nothing obtruded. The walls were paneled in silk within white moldings, the furniture shone in white lacquer trimmed with gilt. Clouds of gauzy lace sheathed the big windows, although that detail always reminded Inos of spiders' webs. A cheerful crackling blaze in the marble fireplace drowned out the sound of rain, keeping the room uncomfortably warm, soothing old bones.

Following her aunt in through the door, Inos first saw Ekka

herself, straight and tyrannical on one of the high-backed chairs she favored, with her feet placed tight together on an embroidered footstool. Her chair was higher than any of the others, so that she could dominate, as from a throne. One dark-veined hand rested on her cane, exactly vertical at her side. She wore a high-necked, long-sleeved gown of shining ivory satin and her white hair was as flawless as carved and polished marble, incongruous above a dessicated face of weathered walnut.

Other chairs were arranged in a semicircle before her. Just rising from one was the portly duke, immaculate in aquamarine. He looked worried and puzzled, as if wrestling with some problem, and his drooping lower lip was even wetter than usual. He could not have been sucking his thumb, could he?

Already on his feet beside him was the obnoxious Proconsul Yggingi, a hard, curt man in his forties. Ugh! His hair was cropped so short that his square head seemed bald, and as usual he was decked out in bronze and leather, from cuirass to greaves. Dancing with Yggingi was like wrestling a water butt. As usual, too, he was clutching his helmet under one arm—perhaps he had a deep fear of earthquakes and did not trust the Kinvale ceilings. Other officers visiting Kinvale did not wear their uniforms all the time. His wife was rarely seen in public, a semiinvalid whose existence he ignored while relentlessly pursuing Inos. His only topics of conversation seemed to be his military career and his unparalleled success at massacring gnomes in a previous posting. He was so detestable that even Aunt Kade could rarely find a good word for him.

So what had provoked this summons? Inos wondered, as she curtsied to the spiteful old relic on her raised chair, to the ponderous duke, stiffly bowing; curtsying less deeply to the egregious Yggingi; and there was another man, standing by the window, looking out at the—

Andor!

The world stopped.

It was Andor, really Andor. She knew that godlike profile even as he began to turn. He was wearing the same blue doublet and white hose he had worn the first time they met, but now also a long cloak of cobalt velvet trimmed with ermine, sweeping down to silver-buckled shoes. He turned slowly, to look at her, ignoring her aunt and everyone else. His dark eyes fixed on her alone.

Man as man should be.

He was thinner, paler . . . a terrible ordeal? Disaster, or some superhuman suffering, bravely borne? And not over yet, perhaps, for there was vast trouble or sorrow in those unforgettable eyes—none of the bubbling gaiety whose memory she cherished so dearly.

He paced over to her, while she attempted a smile of welcome and carefully did *not* gawk like a moron. He took her hands and bowed over them. His eyes had already spoken volumes—regard, pleasure at seeing her . . . deep sorrow?

Sorrow?

And finally he said, "My Princess!"

"Sir Andor!" She could say nothing more. His princess! Oh, yes!

Finally Andor acknowledged Kade, swooping her a bow.

"Sir Andor!" She beamed. "How nice that you can rejoin us!"

And the old harridan on the high chair had not missed an iota of that reunion, not a crumb.

"Be seated, ladies!" she croaked in her thin, antique voice.

Unable to stop staring at Andor, Inos allowed him to lead her to a chair and then watched as he walked over to sit opposite her, gracefully swirling his cloak out of the way as he sat. Kade and the other men had found chairs somewhere.

What could possibly be so wrong?

"Sir Andor has brought news for you, Kadolan," Ekka said.

"For me, Sir Andor?" Kade was being cautious, her eyes flickering from Andor to Inos and to the others. For her, that was a strange failure of poise.

"Your Highness," Andor said, pulling his gaze from Inos, "I am the unhappy bearer of grievous tidings. Your royal brother is . . . is most gravely ill."

Inos heard herself gasp, but Aunt Kade recovered herself at once. Now she knew what was involved, she registered only polite surprise. "You have come from Krasnegar, Sir Andor?"

He bowed his head slightly. "I have. You will wonder why I did not tell you that it was my destination when I left here, and that omission I must explain to you at length. But I stayed there until almost Winterfest. When I departed, your brother was failing fast."

Father! Inos clasped her hands tightly and forgot that this was Andor speaking. Oh, Father!

Andor glanced at her and then back to Kade. "I have brought a letter from the learned Doctor Sagorn, but he disclosed its content to me. He does not expect his Majesty to recover from this affliction. A few months at the most." Taking a packet from the pocket of his cloak, he rose and moved over to deliver it.

Father! *Father!* Dying? No! no! no!

Aunt Kade took the letter and held it out at arm's length to scan the inscription. Then she laid it unread on her lap and folded her hands over it, while Andor swept back to his seat.

"You think then that we should be prepared to depart on the first ship of spring, Sir Andor?"

"If the venerable sage is correct, ma'am, that may not be soon enough."

The harsh tones of the graceless Yggingi broke in. "Are you suggesting that these gentle ladies attempt the journey overland?"

Andor gave him a long and inscrutable stare. "That must be their own decision, Excellency. I have known worse journeys."

Worse! Inos thought of all the horror stories she had heard and shuddered anew. This marvelous Andor could dismiss that terrible trek so easily?

"Such as?" Yggingi was scowling at this poised young upstart.

"The Plain of Bones. Dyre Channel? Anthropophagi frighten me much more than goblins do."

"You met goblins in the forest?"

"Twice." Andor spread his hands and smiled. "I prefer not to discuss their habits in the presence of ladies, but I still have all my fingernails, as you can see. Childish savages, but quite hospitable. My wrestling was rusty, but apparently acceptable—a few sprains was all . . ."

Marvelous man!

"If Princess Kadolan decided to venture this journey, Proconsul," the duchess asked in her threadbare voice, "could you provide an escort for her?"

The big soldier regarded her thoughtfully for a moment. "I have the troops, certainly. The worst of the cold is behind us, but it would still be a test of endurance, even for men. For ladies of quality, it would be a serious ordeal."

He stopped and waited.

"It would certainly be an adventure," Kade remarked cheerfully. "Inos and I must discuss it when we have read what the skilled Doctor Sagorn has written. We shall keep your generous offer in mind, Excellency."

Inos found her mouth hanging open and closed it quickly. That her aunt would even think of such a journey was unthinkable.

"I am most curious, Sir Andor," Ekka creaked, "as to why you set out from here for Krasnegar without informing my sister-in-law or her niece of your destination. They would have wanted to send letters." She bared saffron fangs in a smile that should have frozen his blood.

Andor acknowledged the point with a token of a nod. "It is not a matter of pride to me, your Grace." For a moment handsome young man stared up at ugly old woman in what seemed strangely like a contest of wills, but then he continued placidly. "I stupidly placed myself in a grievous conflict of honor. It concerned a promise made to an old friend, one to whom I owe much, a dear friend also of my father's—"

"I have forgotten your father's name and station, Sir Andor."

"Senator Endrami, ma'am."

Inos resisted a temptation to leap up and cheer. Let them chew on that! An Imperial senator? No lowly adventurer, Andor, but the son of a senator?

The duchess granted the score. "I did not forget, then. I had not been informed. A younger son, I assume?"

"His eighth." Andor's smile could have tamed a clutch of basilisks. "A much younger son of a much older father. I honor my father's memory, your Grace, but I prefer to be judged by whatever I make of my own life, rather than by his accomplishments."

Another point to Andor!

"However," he continued, "Doctor Sagorn is an old and dear friend, one who helped me much in my youth. He, in turn, was indebted to a friend of his, King Holindarn of Krasnegar, whom he visited last summer, at his invitation. He saw then that the king was likely dying."

Father! Inos gasped and looked at Kade, who avoided her eye. So she had known, or at least suspected!

Andor had paused for them to consider his words. He continued, speaking now to Inos. "Sagorn knew of potions that could ease your father's suffering, but the ingredients were not available at Krasnegar. So he returned to the Impire to collect them, and by then the shipping lanes were closing for the winter. He asked me, as a favor, if I would escort him back to Krasnegar, for the overland trail is a long and hard travel at his age."

Now Inos understood. She smiled her understanding and gratitude.

Andor, however, frowned. "It was then that I made my foolish error. He needed some time to gather his materials and he had mentioned to me that the king's daughter was coming to Kinvale. I presumed upon mutual friendships to call and meet her." He brought the pouting duke into the conversation with a glance. ''It was sheer nosiness . . . and I—I lost my heart.''

Inos felt herself blush scarlet and quickly looked down at her lap.

''You see my predicament,'' his voice said softly—and surely he was still speaking to her. ''I had been sworn to secrecy by Sagorn, for ailments of kings are matters of high import. So I could not discuss my mission.''

She raised her eyes to meet his. She smiled her forgiveness. She smiled that she had never doubted him.

He returned the smile, a little—thanking her for it—but his eyes remained grave.

''And so we went to Krasnegar. By Winterfest Sagorn had no doubt. The king commanded that the secret be kept, and the matter should properly have been no affair of mine. But now I knew Inosolan. I was his Majesty's guest, and his daughter's slave, but not his subject. Once again I found myself trapped in a conflict of honor, for I knew that Inos would want to know. So that was my penance for nosiness—that I must take her the doleful tidings. I bought a couple of horses, and here I am.''

Inos gasped in horror and disbelief. For her he had faced the frozen immensity of the forest—alone! So lightly! For her! Alone!

''A remarkable tale!'' the duchess said acidly. ''Kade, we should not detain you in your time of grief. Whatever we may do to aid you, you have only to ask, as you know.''

It was dismissal. The men rose as the ladies did. Andor was first at the door.

He kissed Inos's hand and bowed to her aunt. ''If you do decide to go, ma'am,'' he said, and it was not clear to which princess he spoke, ''then I would beg of you to let me accompany you. It would be the least I could do to repair my folly.''

What folly? Inos floated out behind her aunt and, despite the wounds caused by the news of her father, some part of her heart soared like a skylark into the heavens.

6

The dowager duchess of Kinvale watched the door close. Then she unleashed her bleakest stare. ''You are welcome here, Sir Andor. But tell me—I believe that the noble Senator Endrami died over thirty years ago?''

He did not even blink. ''Twenty-six years and three months,

ma'am. I was a posthumous baby, but not quite so posthumous as that.''

"So the Lady Imagina who married the Margrave of Minxinok must have been your cousin?''

"My oldest sister, your Grace. She died when I was very young. I never knew her.''

Endrami had been a distant—an extremely distant—relative, and the boy's information was correct. So either he was genuine or he had done his homework well, perhaps even well enough to spring those traps she had just tried to set. The Endrami lands were all down in South Pithmot; it would take weeks to confirm his story. "What chance that the girl can reach Krasnegar before her father dies?''

He shrugged. "It is in the hands of the Gods.''

"But we must all help the Gods to aid the Good, mustn't we? How do the king's subjects feel about a queen of such youth, and unmarried?''

"I never heard the matter discussed, your Grace. The king's danger was still a secret.''

"I see." Feeling unusually baffled, Ekka turned to her son, who was staring at the rug, pulling at his lip in that childish habit of his. "Angilki, you forget your duties. Sir Andor must be weary from his journey.''

The duke awoke with a start and sprang up obediently. The door opened and closed again.

Ekka was left alone with Proconsul Yggingi, who sat with his helmet on his lap, regarding her impassively.

"It can be done?'' she asked.

"Yes.''

She approved of his brusque manner. "A deal, then?''

"Name it.''

"Make me an offer.''

He shook his close-cropped head and his face was unreadable. "You initiated this. You invited me. You have something in mind.''

She would crack that marble façade. "Gambling debts, mostly.''

He smiled grimly. "Mine, or do you also have a problem?''

It was she who was shaken. Such insolence she had not met in half a lifetime. "Yours. You are rumored to have gone through your wife's fortune in two years.''

He shrugged imperturbably. "A year and a half. And I now owe forty-two thousand imperials more.''

Incredible! It was much worse than she had heard. "You are in serious trouble, Proconsul." He would lie in debtors' prison till the rats ate him.

"I am ruined."

"Desperate?"

The twist of his lips was barely a smile. "I have no scruples, if that is what you mean. None at all. Have you?"

She laughed, surprising herself. "None. To business, then. There would appear to be a disputed succession in Krasnegar."

"Or soon will be. Certainly the jotnar there will not readily accept rule by a woman."

"It is a long time since my last history lesson, Excellency. You must know much more about such things than I do."

He chuckled. "The Impire is a shark, and it eats minnows whenever it can catch them."

He had a surprisingly apt turn of phrase for a brute soldier. Ekka had not needed to recall her school days to know that any trouble in other realms was usually turned to the Impire's advantage—a disputed succession, a civil war, or even a minor border squabble, and the legions would march in on the pretext of guarding one side or the other. It didn't matter which, because both sides were inevitably swallowed up promptly. They might fight loose again in a generation or so, but by then the looting had been done. And she certainly did not need to lecture Ygginisi on this.

"If the girl cannot rule, then my son has the best claim."

The big man cocked an impudent eyebrow at her. "I understood that Thane Kalkor had a better."

Ekka thumped her cane angrily on the rug—she was wearing a hole there, she reminded herself. It must have become a habit. "He has a claim through his great-grandaunt. But if a woman cannot rule, then she cannot pass on the title! So his case is self-defeating. His argument would be meaningless!"

"Jotnar's arguments are usually pointed." Ygginisi crossed his legs and wriggled himself into a comfortable but not very military slouch. "Granted that your son has a claim, but your son is a subject of the imperor. The imperor cannot deny a woman's right to rule, because his own grandmother was imperess regnant. So your argument is equally self-defeating. Interesting!"

She had not expected him to see that—it had taken her several days to work it out after Kade had let slip the tiger. Both sides ought to admit that the other's claim was better. Of course neither ever would. "Mmm. But if the imperor decided to . . . to go to my niece's assistance, then he would naturally dispatch you, as your precinct of Pondague borders on Krasnegar.''

He flushed slightly, which surprised her. "Not necessarily, but let us assume so for the moment. What exactly are you proposing, your Grace?"

"Take the girl back. If her father is dead—and if he isn't I expect the shock of your arrival may well precipitate his demise—then proclaim her queen, and she will in turn name you as her viceroy. Send her back here to marry my son. It would please me to have my descendants be kings, even if the title is moot."

He nodded and rose to begin pacing the room. That was a rank discourtesy, and the thump of his boots on her expensive rugs was extremely annoying, but she kept her face schooled as she had done for generations.

"That's clever!" he said at last. "The imperor will have the ruler—whichever of them it is—here in his fist, and Krasnegar will remit taxes, to help defray the costs of the protection."

"Moreover your creditors will be hard-pressed to reach you there, and you can loot an extra forty-two thousand imperials to pay your debts."

He stopped by the fireplace and turned to regard her with a smile that was close to contemptuous. "Not without provoking famine, I'm sure. From what I hear, it is a bleak little spot."

"Scruples?"

He shrugged. "I might become liable for impeachment, or at least replacement."

"My family is not without influence in Hub, Proconsul."

He chuckled. "True. Your son will not go to Krasnegar?"

"He would sooner die."

"But why send the girl? Marry them now, while you have her in hand. She can sign my commission before I leave."

This, of course, was the tricky part. She had foreseen this. "Being postdated, it would be a dubious document at best. The people might not believe, unless they saw her, and witnessed her willing signature."

He chuckled again. "But what of the jotnar? Gnomes and goblins are good sport, but fighting jotnar would be red work. You think Kalkor would accept this convenient arrangement?"

She shrugged. "I doubt if he really cares. Looting and raping are his wont, and he could have taken Krasnegar anytime he wanted. You can buy off the thanes."

"Maybe. You want the princess returned with the word."

"What word?"

He laughed coarsely and sauntered back to his chair. "It is common knowledge that the kings of Krasnegar still hold one of Inisso's words. My luck at the tables might change if I had a word."

She twirled her gold-knobbed cane, studying it. "Then the girl stays here. I have Inosolan, and without her nobody gets the word . . . if there is one, of course."

"I agree, then," he said. "You give me Krasnegar to hold in fief from your son, and I send back one word-knowing princess. You pay the expenses."

"Outrageous!"

Ygyingi chuckled. "Necessary! In your felicitous turn of phrase, I have already looted Pondague for all I can take. My men have not been paid for months and are close to mutiny. So a thousand as seed money, plus the princess, and I shall take her to Krasnegar. You shall have her back, with the word if she gets it."

From the first, Ekka had known the weakness in her plan—she would have to trust this self-admitted scoundrel. But if he needed money so badly, she had a little power left. "Your wife, I think, stays here. The journey would be too hard for her."

His eyes narrowed. "I believe the danger from the goblins might require more men that I first thought. Two thousand imperials for expenses."

Skinflint! But Ekka had nothing to lose except two thousand imperials and a sister-in-law. Angilki could breed a son on the girl and the next duke of Kinvale would inherit two words. It was certainly worth the gamble.

"Agreed, then," she said.

Tucking his helmet under his arm, Ygyingi rose and saluted. "Agreed!"

"So now you must try to get the child to Krasnegar."

He chuckled. "Ma'am, I shall get your princess to Krasnegar if I have to kill every goblin in Pandemia and drag her all the way through the forest, weeping."

Forest weeping:

And Sir Lancelot awoke, and went and took his horse, and rode all that day and all that night in a forest, weeping.

Malory, *Le Morte D'Arthur*

❰ SEVEN ❱

Damsel met

1

Wolverine Totem had once been the most southerly of the goblin villages, set high in forested foothills, near to Pondague. Long ago it had been raided by a troop of imps, the inhabitants slaughtered and the buildings burned. One house, originally the boys' cabin, had survived the devastation, and it was used now on occasion by travelers.

Rap had found it with his farsight in thickly blowing snow as a storm moved in. Little Chicken had been unperturbed by the weather, for he was capable of burrowing into a snowbank and staying there for days, not emerging for any purpose whatsoever. Rap, preferring freedom and fire, had been very glad to reach the dilapidated ruin. Now the two of them sat by a crackling blaze to wait out the weather. Shadows leaped and jiggled over the log walls, wind screamed overhead, and whiffs of snow blew in through chinks to pile up in corners. Yet the cold was much less now, farther south and closer to spring. Near the hearth, the temperature was almost comfortable. Rap had unlaced his buckskins, while the goblin had stripped to the waist and sat impassively, staring into the fire, poking it once in a while with a long stick, probably mourning his lack of grease for rubbing himself, his favorite occupation. Fleabag was stretched out on the dirt farther away, paws twitching as he chased memories through a forest of dreams.

Farsight failed to show anything moving outside. Even Little Chicken could not hunt in such a blizzard. Even Fleabag could not, or Rap could have sent him out to do so. They had enough food for two days, and the first day was almost gone.

Rap had slept. Perhaps the goblin had. Now Rap realized that this empty, echoing ruin had brought him his first real opportunity to talk with Little Chicken. Through all their weeks of travel together he had always been masked and running, or else too exhausted.

"I want to tell you my story," he began. "Tell you why we're going south."

The burly young woodlander looked up, but with no interest showing in his slanted eyes. "Not important to trash."

"But I'll tell you anyway—don't you like stories?"

Little Chicken shrugged.

"Very well," Rap said doggedly. "That man who brought me—Wolf Tooth, he called himself. He was some sort of demon."

That brought no reaction. None of it did. Rap told of Inos, and the dying King Holindarn. He told of Andor and his power to bewitch people into trusting him. He told of their trek together from Krasnegar, and the inexplicable appearance of Darad.

At the end of it all Little Chicken was still gazing at him impassively, without comment or apparent interest. Seeing that the recital had ended, however, he asked. "Then this chief will give you this woman?"

"Certainly not! She is the chief's daughter. I am only a keeper of stores. She must marry another chief."

"Why?"

That question proved surprisingly difficult to answer. So, also, did the next—why, then, was Rap going to all this trouble?

Loyalty did not translate into the goblin dialect. Friendship did, but Little Chicken could not comprehend that a man might be friendly with a woman. Women were enjoyable and useful. Friends were necessarily other males.

Friends . . . Rap was surprised to discover that he wanted to be friends with Little Chicken.

The young goblin's monstrous cruelty was not his fault. It came from the culture of his people, and he had never been taught better. Apart from that, he was admirable in many ways—self-reliant, confident, effective, and a superb woodsman. His courage was unbreakable, his strange loyalty to Rap apparently absolute. In a word, he was *trustworthy*, and Rap recognized no higher accolade than that.

"You run good, town boy." Those first words on their journey had been haunting Rap ever since. They had never been repeated, and all Rap's efforts had failed to draw another syllable of praise. All his pains and efforts had gleaned nothing but amusement and contempt. He knew now that no matter how hard he might strive, he would never match Little Chicken in strength or endurance. That inferiority rankled deeply.

So he was the lesser man, but even so, surely effort deserved recognition? Rap had driven himself to his utmost limits and failed to receive acknowledgment for it. The harder he had tried, the more disdainful his companion's reaction. He had revealed his supernatural powers and they had been dismissed as party tricks, beneath a man's dignity. Only one thing about the town boy seemed to satisfy Little Chicken—that he had cheated in the testing. For some reason that knowledge pleased the goblin greatly. And of that, Rap was ashamed.

By the second day of the blizzard, Rap was growing frantic. If he thought about Inos or Andor—or anything—then his mind curdled with anxiety. Time was running out, and he should be running, also, not sitting still. The sinister Darad must have crossed the mountains long since.

Rather to his disgust, Rap had also discovered that he was in need of exercise. Weeks of running had so conditioned him that he felt stodgy without it, and incapable of relaxing.

Snow was still falling, but it was the heavy, wet, warm-weather snow of the south, not fine, dry arctic powder. When the storm passed, Rap knew, he and Little Chicken would be able to travel without their masks, but the drifts would make the terrain more difficult.

Travel where? They had left the last of the goblin settlements behind. There were imp homesteads in the area, perilous for goblins and to be shunned. Somewhere nearby lay Pondague, an impish outpost guarding the only pass through the ranges. Had Rap arrived at Pondague with Andor, it would have meant the start of friends and safety. They could have acquired more horses, bought food, and even hired companions, had they wanted them. South of the pass lay the Impire, with good roads and post inns and safety.

Now Pondague was danger and enemies. Rap had no money. He wore goblin clothes and goblin tattoos, so he might well be cut down on sight if he ran into a contingent of Imperial troops. Living off the land south of the mountains was going to be difficult, or impossible. He knew roughly what farms were and how

farmers felt about poaching. He did not know where Kinvale was.
He supposed that it was a place like Krasnegar, but he had no
idea how far from the mountains it was, nor how to find it.

His first trial would be to sneak through the pass unobserved.
Probably he would be safer south of the mountains, where goblins
were no threat and hence would not so readily provoke violent
reaction. He would have to find someone—a priest, perhaps—and
explain his problem. With luck he might obtain a guide who would
believe his story and deliver him to Kinvale on the promise of
reward from Inos. Then Rap could dress like a civilized man again
and regain his self-respect. Inos would find employment for him
until he could return to Krasnegar with her, by land or sea, as she
chose.

Unless Andor had already got to her, of course.

Then what?

Eventually Rap decided that he did not know the answer to *then
what*? He rose, took up a spruce bough, and swept clean an area
of floor near the fire. The goblin sat cross-legged and watched
without comment or question.

"Right!" Rap stripped off his jacket. "Come and give me
some wrestling lessons."

Little Chicken shook his head.

"You're my trash, you say? Then I order you to come and give
me a wrestling lesson!"

A firmer head shake. Trash, apparently, could decide what trash
was good for.

"Why not?"

"I hurt you." A faint smile played over the goblin's big mouth.

"A few bruises won't matter. I want to learn, and I need the
exercise."

Another refusal.

Beginning to shiver without his coat, Rap swallowed any trace
of pride he might have retained. "Please, Little Chicken? I'm
bored! It would be fun."

"Too much fun."

"What does that mean?"

Little Chicken's eyes glinted in the firelight. "I start to hurt
you, might not stop. Too much fun."

He was quite capable of dismembering a man with his bare
hands. Hastily Rap took up his jerkin and dressed again.

The third day . . . a faint light was glimmering through the
chinks in the walls and windows that had been plugged with

branches. Rap had not realized until he came to this ruined cabin that goblin buildings had windows at all. Apparently they were normally covered over in winter.

He sighed and glanced again at Little Chicken, inevitably sitting cross-legged, bare-chested, idly poking his long stick at the fire. His patience was inhuman. In the firelight his dusky skin shone greenly. His curiously slanted eyes were unreadable.

Try conversation again? Just maybe a little companionship?

"When we get to Kinvale—" Rap's voice sounded strange after so many hours of silence. "—then I shall release you."

"I am your trash."

"Not forever! You have done wonders for me. I could never have come this far without you, so I am very grateful. If I could reward you, I would." Perhaps Inos would give him money to reward Little Chicken. What would he buy with it, though?

"Reward?" The familiar faint smile of contempt appeared on the goblin's face. "You will not give me what I want."

"What's that?" Rap rather thought he could guess the answer.

"Go back to Raven Totem. Kill slowly, much pain."

Rap shuddered. "I kill you? And then your brothers would do the same to me?"

The goblin shook his head. "Not if you do good work, make good show. Kill slow—win honor."

"Never! I could not do that to anyone. And I am grateful to you. I like you. I want us to be friends."

"I am your trash." Little Chicken directed his attention once more to the sparkling logs.

"You won't be able to help me at Kinvale," Rap said firmly. "Nor back at Krasnegar."

"I shall look after you." Little Chicken seemed to think that the conversation was over. Arguing with him was like trying to bail out the Winter Ocean with a leaky bucket.

"I will give you your freedom!"

The goblin shook his head at the fire and said nothing.

"You mean that you are my trash forever?" What could Rap do with a slave in Krasnegar, a slave who refused to be freed?

Little Chicken looked up now and stared steadily at him for a while. He seemed to make a decision. "Not forever."

"Good! Until when?"

"Until the Gods release me. Not you."

This was progress! "And when will the Gods release you?"

"I shall know."

Suddenly Rap did not like the expression on that wide, green-brown face. "And how shall I know?"

"I take care of you until the Gods release me," Little Chicken repeated. He licked his lips. "Then I kill you."

"Oh, great! You mean that you are my faithful slave until one day you decide you're not, then you just kill me?"

The goblin's oversized teeth showed in a sudden friendly grin and Rap laughed in relief. He had been afraid that Little Chicken was serious. It was a surprise to learn that he did have a sense of humor after all.

"You won at testing, town boy. Good foe! I did not know then. I know now."

Rap's merriment died away. "Do I get any warning?"

Little Chicken shook his head, still smiling.

"When do I get this surprise? Soon? Or not for years?"

"I shall know when. Then I kill you. Very, very slow. Long, long pain. Good opponent, I give you good death. Light small fires on your chest. Push stick under kneecap and twist. Many days. Sand below eyelids and rub with finger . . ."

No, he was not joking.

Once started, he could not be stopped. From then until dusk, when his voice failed and he became hoarse, he sat by the fire, slobbering with anticipation, eyes shining bright with hatred. Trembling much of the time with the effort of confining his activities to conversation instead of putting his plan into action at once, the goblin described in infinite detail the revenge he had been devising.

2

They were on their way! Inos could hardly believe that it was not a dream. But it was real! She was really sitting in a real coach, facing Aunt Kade and Isha, her maid—and sitting next to Andor, too.

Seven days with Andor back in Kinvale! They had been seven days of heaven, and days of frenzied packing, as well—what to leave, what to set aside for shipping, what to try to squeeze into impossibly small packs. They had also been seven days of farewells, of hastily arranged parties, of dancing, and of continuous heavenly music that no one but she had been able to hear. Or had Andor detected a chord or two? She hoped so. The obnoxious Yggingi had vanished, gone ahead to Pondague to arrange for an escort, and his departure had been almost as great a blessing as

Andor's return . . . No, it hadn't. Having Andor back, knowing that he had cared enough to cross the bitter taiga in winter, for her—that was the greatest miracle of all.

They had not had a moment alone, not one, but even in the crowds she had been conscious of hardly anyone but him—his smile, his laugh, his imperturbable strength. It had been Andor who had made it all possible at so little notice, purchasing a coach and horses, hiring men to drive it, planning itinerary—organizing and arranging. Aunt Kade had been grateful to leave all those masculine tasks to him. There had hardly been time, even, to brood very much over her father's illness.

Andor was coming back to Krasnegar! Because they had never been alone together, he had not repeated the pledge he had given her before he left, but his eyes had spoken it many times. Andor was coming to Krasnegar . . . to stay? Always?

May it be so, Gods! I did remember love, as I was bidden!

Outside the windows, the fields and woods of Kinvale rolled by in watery sunshine under a smoke-blue sky. The end of winter meant the start of spring—soon, but not quite yet. Grass was green, and shy flowers smiled in the hedgerows. Ahead and behind the coach, Corporal Oopari and his troop thumped erratically along. Krasnegar's men-at-arms were not notable riders, but they could manage on the straight, smooth roads of the Impire. They could certainly keep up with the rocking, clattering carriage. A couple of the men were new recruits, replacing others who had formed romantic attachments and chosen to remain at Kinvale. Ula, the maid from Krasnegar, was long forgotten. Stupid Ula had disgraced herself within days of her arrival and been hastily married off to a gardener.

Andor rearranged the rug spread over their laps, as the bouncing of the coach threatened to dislodge it. Her hand found his again, out of sight.

All those farewells . . .

"I can't believe it!" Inos said for the hundredth time. "We are really on our way!"

"You may find it all too real before we arrive, ma'am." Andor smiled.

With that smile beside her, Inos could face anything.

"It will be a great adventure!" Aunt Kade said brightly. Her shiny-apple cheeks were flushed with excitement, but not a single hair protruded wrongly from under her cornflower-blue traveling bonnet. "I have always wanted to try the overland route."

Well, if she could believe that, who was Inos to contradict her?

Aunt Kade's indestructible good humor could be very irritating at times, but it would be easier to bear on the journey than sulks, and few persons of her age would have been willing to contemplate at all what she was undertaking so cheerfully.

Andor pointed out the final glimpse of Kinvale, as the carriage crested a hill. Then it was gone.

"Well, Sir Andor," Kade said, snuggling into her corner. "At last we have time to hear all the news."

Again Andor's smile warmed the whole carriage. "Of course, ma'am! Remember that it will be stale, though—I left at Winterfest. But, apart from your brother, everyone in the castle seemed to be well. Chancellor Yaltauri's lumbago was troubling him. Doctor Sagorn prescribed a linament with a powerful odor of cheese . . ."

In moments he had the three of them in stitches, even Isha, who was not supposed to show that she was listening, and who knew none of the people being discussed. He ran through the foibles of the whole palace hierarchy and moved on to the notables of the town. Apparently he was already acquainted with everyone in Krasnegar and that was a surprising thought, one that would need a little time to absorb. Yet under her laughter Inos wondered about Ido. And Lin. What news of the friends of her childhood? A transient cloud shadowed her happiness. They would be friends no longer. An abyss of rank would cut them off now from the princess they had once accepted as one of themselves. What use to tell Ido of the latest dance craze from Hub? What need to play the spinnet for Rap? Chatterbox Lin would not care about Kinvale scandal, nor share what local gossip he had with his queen. Yet she felt an irrational nostalgic longing to know how the old gang was faring. Who was married, who was courting? Those things would interest her more than details of Chancellor Yaltauri's lumbago.

But she could not ask. A gentleman like Andor would not have troubled himself over chambermaids or scullions. Or stableboys.

Inos and Kade picked their way carefully down the hazardous staircase, to find Andor waiting for them, morning-fresh and resplendent in tan suede riding habit. He swept as deep a bow as was possible in the cramped confines of the hostelry. Despite the early hour, the inn was packed with people, most of them soldiers, apparently—noisy, bustling, a noticeably rough and unwashed collection.

"Highnesses, you slept well?"

Kade chirruped something much more cheerful than Inos could manage. A rank stench of men and beer was not a welcome greeting so early in the morning. Andor started clearing a path, leading them through the melee to one of the tiny tables in a corner by a window.

The inn had been a great shock to Inos. Somehow she had come to imagine that the whole of the Impire was as comfortable and luxurious as Kinvale, a very stupid assumption. The tiny bed she had shared with Kade had obviously been stuffed by stonemasons; the leaky thatch had been dug out of a silo, and there had been things living in that thatch. Just after she had retired, a great clamor of voices and horses had arisen outside and continued for hours. That must have been all these soldiers arriving, and now they completely filled the lower room.

The sun had not yet risen. Barely enough light spilled through the tiny, grubby window to show Corporal Oopari and one of his men sitting at the table. They sprang up, yielding their stools to the princesses. She wondered if this had been more of Andor's foresight. Isha would have to eat on her feet, as many of the soldiers were doing.

"For breakfast, honored ladies," Andor said in the unctuous whine of a waiter, "we offer a selection of either porridge or porridge. However, you may choose whether to eat the lumps or leave them. Our hot tea is cold and unloved. The chocolate is passable."

Inos suppressed a lurching feeling inside her, a yearning for the fresh rolls and sweet preserves of Kinvale. Porridge? Ugh!

"I should love some porridge," Aunt Kade said brightly. "After all that rich food at Kinvale, it will be a pleasure to return to a simpler diet. You, my dear?"

"Just the chocolate, I think."

The man-at-arms was dispatched into the throng. Apparently the hostelry staff had been immobilized by this military invasion. The table was small, splintery, and filthy.

"Your Highness!" Corporal Oopari was addressing Kade, and his tone snapped Inos out of her engrossing self-pity. He was an earnest young man, Oopari, but too old to have been one of her childhood friends, and too stolid to be good company anyway—dull, but dependable as winter. His family had served hers for generations. He had the dark coloring of an imp, with enough jotunn in him to make him taller and bonier than most men in the Impire. Someone jostled him at that moment, and he almost fell over the table. He straightened up without turning around to seek retribution or apology. That alone showed that he was upset over something, and his face was deeply red.

"Yes, Corporal?"

"I take orders from you only, do I not, Highness? That was what the king told me."

Aunt Kade looked up at Andor, who was standing at the corporal's side, likewise squeezed against the table.

"Proconsul Yggingi has joined us, ma'am."

"Oh!" Aunt Kade seemed to read something from Andor's tone or expression. She glanced around, and suddenly her smile seemed strangely forced. "All these men are here to escort us, you mean?"

Andor nodded solemnly. "A whole cohort. You will be well guarded."

Yggingi himself? Inos felt a strong upsurge of distaste, and then saw that something more was bothering the others.

"We don't need guarding yet, do we?" she asked. This was only the second day of the journey, and they were still well within the Impire. She had caught a glimpse of the mountains from upstairs, but still a long way off. The real adventure would begin on the far side of the pass, Andor had said, and he estimated at least four more days to Pondague.

"Apparently you are going to have an escort, whether you need it or not." Andor returned his gaze to her aunt. "Corporal Oopari has been informed that he is now under the proconsul's orders."

Kade looked flustered, while the angry, stubborn expression on Oopari's homely face reminded Inos momentarily of someone, but she could not think of whom.

"What is your advice, Sir Andor?" Why was Kade so concerned?

"I fear that the proconsul is correct, Highness. Private armies are not permitted within the Impire. Once we are past Pondague, then things will be different, at least in theory; but I understand that the proconsul is planning to increase the escort then."

"More than one cohort?"

"Four."

Kade actually wrung her hands. Inos had never seen anyone do that before, certainly not Aunt Kade. The roses in her cheeks had been stricken by a sudden frost.

"I erred?" she murmured, as if to herself.

"I did, certainly," Andor said. "But there is no other road, and we could hardly have slipped away unseen."

Inos did not understand, and she was staying quiet. Surely a large escort would be good protection against the goblins and, therefore, welcome news? She noticed that Isha was standing very close to the corporal, closer even than the press of the crowd required. So that was in the wind, was it? Inos had been wondering why the girl had agreed to enter the service of ladies who lived in a far country.

Aunt Kade restored her smile and directed it up at Oopari. "I think you had better agree to what the proconsul wants, Corporal. We can hardly have a divided command, and a proconsul is one of the Impire's most senior officials."

The honest, stubborn face flushed very red. "Then my services are not truly necessary, your Highness?"

Kade glanced again at Andor, as if seeking support, or hearing a message. "We do not question your loyalty or courage, Corporal, but your small band can hardly compare with an entire cohort. As Sir Andor says, we are to be well guarded. Do any more of your men wish to remain at Kinvale?"

Through clenched teeth, Oopari said, "All of them, ma'am. But we thought you had need of us."

Now it was Aunt Kade who turned red. "I quite understand, and if you wish to be released, then now is certainly the time. Sir Andor? If you would accompany the corporal . . . He has our money. Four imperials for him and two for each of the others? And would you be so kind as to take the rest of it into your own care?"

Obviously wrenched in several directions at once, Oopari looked down at Isha, and she was staring up at him in dismay. Aunt Kade noticed and sighed.

A few minutes later, Inos found herself alone with her aunt, clutching a large and clumsy earthenware mug of watery lukewarm chocolate. Andor and Oopari and the man-at-arms had gone, and so had Isha. Inos would have to brush her own hair now, and Aunt Kade's, also. Who would lay out and repack clothes? Perhaps they could hire someone else at Pondague. Anonymous Imperial troops still hemmed in the table, making her feel claustrophobic.

"This chocolate is really very good, isn't it?" Kade said, her normal calm restored.

"Aunt? How many men in a cohort?"

"Quite a lot, dear. We shall certainly be safe from goblins with four cohorts to guard us. I have too much porridge—"

"But no Oopari! Why did you dismiss him like that?"

Kade blinked innocently. "Because he wanted me to. Are you sure you wouldn't like some of my porridge?"

"Whatever he wanted, I would feel safer with him close."

Then a ladylike foot tapped Inos's ankle, Kade flickered her eyes warningly, and her voice faded almost to a mumble. "It was for their own good, dear."

Inos became suddenly more aware of all the men around her. They all had their backs turned, and they all seemed to be intent on other things, but . . .

"We don't want any accidents." Then her aunt added in a more normal tone, "The porridge is not too terribly lumpy."

"How many men in a cohort?"

"Five hundred, I think, but it may be more. I'm not sure."

Now Inos understood. She felt very foolish. Four cohorts? On important occasions in Krasnegar, Sergeant Thosolin could muster eighteen men-at-arms.

3

Dusk on the fourth day . . . Rap's belly roared louder than the storm now, but that was partly because the wind was fading. There was not much new snow coming down.

He had been chewing on a scrap of leather all afternoon, and then his farsight had sensed movement in the distance—right at the limit of his range, a small herd of sheep or goats. He could not tell if they were wild or stray, but there was no herder with them. He had started to lace up his moccasins, making Little Chicken want to know why. There had been an argument, the goblin insisting he was a much better marksman, Rap that he was more likely to find the quarry in these conditions.

The final result had been a compromise. Little Chicken had gone to do the killing, and Rap had sent Fleabag to drive the prey toward him.

So Rap now sat in lonely humiliation, listening to the wind's mocking wail, watching the shadows leap, and licking his lips at the thought of meat. His role might not be very manly or even dignified, but it was hard work. The herd was still out at his limit and seemed reluctant to come closer. Even controlling Fleabag was difficult at that distance. Rap's head had started to ache as it had not ached since his first days with Andor—

Forget Andor! Concentrate!

"You! Boy!"

With a wail, Rap released his mental hold on Fleabag and the

herd. He spun around, then fell back on his elbows at the unbelievable apparition in the corner.

A huge white chair had appeared there—no, it was a throne,
with a dais below it and a silken canopy above. It was built of
interlocked curved rods that he recognized right away as walrus
ivory, all intricately carved and inlaid with gems and gold; it was
grander even than King Holindarn's chair of state, which he had
used only twice in Rap's memory, on very solemn occasions. It
glittered, as if it sat in a brighter place than this smoke-filled,
dingy hovel.

There was a woman on it. She was very tiny, slumped slack-
limbed in the corner of the cushioned seat, her legs sticking out
like a child's. Her scanty hair was white and straggling loose. She
was very old, scraggy, and stark naked.

He echoed her: "You!"

Hastily he turned his head away. She could not possibly be
real, but even so—no clothes! It was the same old woman he had
seen the first time he had raided the Ravens' larder. He had been
very hungry then, too. It must be a form of madness, a flaw in
his character. Real men did not go crazy just because they hadn't
eaten for a couple of days. Real men could starve for weeks before they went mad. He wasn't a hardened woodsman like Little
Chicken, he was a soft town boy, a mere stablehand—

"The faun again!" The ancient cackled in shrill amusement.

Rap closed his eyes to concentrate . . . Sure enough, his farsight detected nothing there except fragments of firewood and a
snowdrift. He was hallucinating again. Determined not to be distracted from his purpose, he reached out for Fleabag—

"Faun! You stop that! Don't you know better?"

"Huh?" Despite himself, Rap's farsight switched to the source
of that voice. This time it saw. This time there was someone there.
He twisted around again. The throne had gone. The little old
woman was standing much closer and, mercifully, she was now
dressed in goblin robes, as she had been the first time he saw her.
Now she seemed to be quite solid and real. He moaned.

"Farsight, too?" The old woman waggled a finger at him.
"That's all right—safe enough—but that mastery of yours! Don't
you know that sorcerers can feel power being used like that?"

Dumbly he shook his head.

She walked a few steps closer, peering around. "Well, we can.
Not that anyone but me's likely to be watching in these parts. It's
all right to look and listen, see, but *do* anything, make things

happen, and you start ripples. You're strong, lad. You ought to know that. Why, you've got goblin tattoos!''

A sorceress! Andor had warned him that sorcerers were always on the lookout for more words of power. He had betrayed himself to a sorceress! Rap felt the hair on the back of his head stir. He began dragging himself backward on his elbows, across the dirt floor.

The woman followed, cackling. "A faun with goblin markings? That's new." She grinned at him like a skull, revealing a perfect set of teeth. "Goblin faun! What . . ." She hissed angrily. "No foresight? You blocking my foresight? No, you're not capable. Who?''

"Who—who are you?''

"Me? You ought to know. Ought to guess, see? Who are *you*, more to the point?''

"I'm Rap . . . Flat Nose of Raven Totem.''

"Raven?'' She looked quickly around once more. *"Where is Death Bird? What've you done with him?''*

"N-nothing!'' Rap quailed before a blast of anger as palpable as heat from a farrier's brazier. "Little Chicken, you mean? He's out hunting—''

"Where? Show me!''

Show? Rap reached out to point with a shaking hand, toward where the goblin was wallowing in a thigh-deep drift, a long way off.

The old woman stared that way, then shrilled her senile laugh. "So he is! Well, all right. But you take care of him, you hear! Very precious, that one! See, you're not to harm him!''

He? Rap? Harm Little Chicken? The woman was as mad as a gunny sack of foxes!

Bracing up his courage, Rap felt for the herd, and it had vanished. Fleabag was heading home again. Supper had fled, therefore, and he remembered that he had been hungry the first time he had met this strange sorceress. Even as he watched, she began to shimmer and fade, and his farsight had already lost her. "I'm hungry!'' he said. "I mean, Death Bird is hungry!''

She seemed to solidify for a moment and study him, head on one side, leering. "Fauns!'' she sneered. Then she uttered a shrill, childish snigger and clapped her hands.

Simultaneously she vanished and a curly-horned, black-woolled sheep thudded to the floor just before Rap's toes. The impact shook the cabin, and a great cloud of dust and snow shot out from beneath the animal. With a scream of alarm, it scrabbled to its feet. There was no doubt at all that the sheep was real.

After her warning, Rap dared not try his mastery on the animal, and his limbs were still shaking so much that he took longer than he should have done to corner it. Cutting a sheep's throat with a stone knife was harder than he had expected. He splashed a lot of blood on himself and was butted a few times. But why a black sheep? Had that been easiest for the mad old sorceress to see in the snowy bush, or was she making fun of a faun with goblin tattoos? Rap was too hungry to care.

He was eating roast mutton when Little Chicken returned, empty-handed, exhausted, and furious. But for the first time, the goblin seemed to be impressed by Rap's occult powers.

4

With a louder crack than usual, the rear of the carriage dropped, twisting to the left. It came to a shuddering halt.

"Are you all right, your Highness?" Andor inquired solicitously. He and Inos were crushed pleasantly together, holding hands under the lap rug, but Aunt Kade was now suspended above them, grimly hanging onto a strap.

"Quite all right, thank you, except that perhaps my highness is now a little more noticeable than usual."

Andor laughed appreciatively. "I shall see what has happened this time," he said, unlinking his fingers from Inos' and preparing to disembark. There were loud shoutings and nervous horse noises outside. Water splattered on the roof, although the rain had been showing signs of turning to snow. Andor opened the door and stepped out gracefully, managing both rapier and cloak with apparent ease. Kade clambered across to sit next to her niece on the lower side of the canted vehicle. She took up a lot more room on the bench than Andor had.

The fast progress they had made at first had now ended. On the straight and smooth highways of the Impire, the carriage had thundered along almost as fast as a rider could have done, but now they were in the mountains. The weather had turned sulky and the road upward, soon degenerating into a track. Farmland and pasture had given way to forest, and the way had become difficult, with tree branches often reaching out to finger the carriage as it passed.

Since the loathsome Yggingi had appeared with his men, a deep dread had fallen over Inos. The thought of two thousand

Imperial soldiers invading Krasnegar was terrifying—especially these troops. She could recall being told in Kinvale that the local military were a despicable lot, not to be compared with the elite corps found near Hub, and that to be posted to a remote frontier station like Pondague was a humiliation, or even a punishment, inflicted only on the rabble and scum of the army. Proconsul Yggingi was rabble and scum, also, in Inos' opinion, but she had not said so.

In fact she had not dared discuss the matter at all, with either Andor or Aunt Kade, and they, too, were confining their talk to trivialities. Partly this common discretion came from fear of being overheard, for now the coachman and the footmen who clung to the carriage were all Yggingi's men, and their ears were close to the windows. Far more worrisome to Inos, though, was the horrifying certainty that she had been betrayed.

Somehow the Imperial government had learned of her father's bad health and had decided to seize Krasnegar before the thanes of Nordland did. Only Hub itself could have mobilized the army. That meant *time*—time for reports and orders to flow back and forth, time for consultations and decisions.

But how had the Imperial officials known? Andor must have passed through Pondague on his way south. He could have alerted the odious Yggingi to the opportunity. Yggingi might then have headed for Kinvale, while Andor reported to some more senior officer before continuing on to inform Inos.

In the clear light of day such fancies seemed quite absurd. One glance at Andor's honest face, one smile from those steady eyes, and all her doubts blew away like dust. But in the long hours of night, as she tossed in unfamiliar beds in dank, smelly hostelries, they became all too terrifyingly real. Inos had invented stories where Andor had been an Imperial spy all along. She had frightened herself half to death with doubts about his background, his parentage, his childhood. She knew so little about all of those, and they seemed so very important when she was alone . . . yet they seemed so trivial when she was with him that she never seemed to remember to bring them up in conversation, as she had so often promised herself she would. When he was with her, she could face the future with courage—she would face the whole Impire, if necessary, and the jotnar, as well! Away from him, she felt like a lost child.

There was only Andor . . . and Kade. But someone had betrayed Inos.

It had been her aunt who had made the decision to journey

north—a sudden and very improbable venture for a woman of her years. Kade had at least suspected that Holindarn's health was failing even before she left Krasnegar. She would certainly champion an Imperial claim over Nordland's. To believe that Princess Kadolan would betray her brother and niece was quite impossible . . . and yet somehow it seemed no more incredible than doubting Andor. One of the two must be a traitor and Inos did not know which.

She felt very small, and alone, and vulnerable. She felt like a hunted animal, fleeing home to its lair with a dangerous predator in close pursuit. She had nowhere else to go and yet her lair would be no safe refuge, for the monster would follow her in.

Obviously she was on her way to Krasnegar whether she wanted to go there or not. If she tried to balk now, then her honor escort of five hundred men would at once become an armed guard, and she a captive. Yggingi had all but told her as much. Nominally she was returning to her home under his protection, but in fact she was only his puppet. The odious man had not revealed his plans, but it was a fair guess that he would try to force her to sign over the kingdom to the emperor as soon as her father died. She could only hope that Father was still alive, and still well enough to advise her. She had no one else she could trust now.

So Inos sat in silent fear and misery, while making polite conversation about the scenery.

Andor reappeared at the carriage door. "I am afraid you will have to disembark, ladies. Another broken axle."

He handed Aunt Kade down, then Inos. The trail was a narrow wreckage of mud, roots, and rocks, curving off out of sight in both directions around a hillside. Rain dribbled down from a canopy of heavy branches that shut off all but a few glimpses of low gray sky, while enclosing walls of ferns and bracken pressed in tightly on both sides. This was the third axle to snap in the last two days. It meant a long delay.

Inos looked around hopefully for somewhere dry to sit, pulling up the hood of her traveling cloak.

"What enormous trees!" Aunt Kade exclaimed. "They cannot be sequoias, though?"

"Hemlocks, I think," Andor said. "Or perhaps cedars. You! Trooper! Hand me down that chest."

The shadows were very deep and menacing. Inos felt uneasy, shut in by this dark primeval jungle. Even the air was full of damp woodsy scent, as if it never went anywhere and was a special local air. The small area of road that she could see was full of soldiers dismounting or jingling around, horses stamping, splashing, fretting, and tugging their reins, men grumbling and discussing the problem in rough, angry tones. From farther up the hill came rougher shouts yet, as the advance guard was informed of the holdup. Equally invisible downhill, the rear was clattering into silence, also.

The dense woods concealed the mountains completely. Inos had not seen a single large hill, only trees and a steeply climbing, winding road. She took Aunt Kade's hand, and the two of them stepped carefully over mud and puddles to the verge, seeking shelter and getting out of the men's way. Andor followed, carrying a chest to serve as a bench. Halfhearted smears of snow flanked the trail, dirty and woebegone in the dingy gloom.

Proconsul Yggingi came cantering back down from the front to see what the delay was. He dismounted with a splash and handed his reins to a legionary, then bellowed for silence and started shooting orders. Inos was pleased to see that he looked very uncomfortable in his uniform, as if the rain were running off his helmet and down his neck. Andor was wearing a big floppy suede hat at a rakish angle, handsome and debonair as ever.

Aunt Kade shivered slightly.

"I can fetch a rug, Highness?" he asked helpfully.

"No, no!" Kade said. "Silly of me. I was looking at these dark woods and thinking of goblins."

He chuckled reassuringly. "Rugs will not protect you from goblins! But don't worry—there are none this side of the pass. Correct, Proconsul?"

Yggingi was clearly furious at this latest delay. "None this side of Pondague. And I have been cleaning them out beyond, also."

"Are they so dangerous, then?" Inos asked, thinking that a herd of hippogryffs could sneak up on her through that deep darkness.

"Not really. Just vermin."

Andor said quietly, "Goblins are actually a very peaceful people."

"Peaceful?" Yggingi echoed. "They are monsters."

"But not warlike."

"No, not warlike! They have other means of disposing of their surplus men." An expression of distaste appeared on his flat, square face.

"Whatever do you mean, Excellency?" Inos asked, surprised that anything could disgust so coarse a man as Yggingi.

He hesitated and then said, "Many races weed out their young men. Most do it by warfare. Goblins use nastier methods, but the principle is the same, I suppose."

She had never thought of warfare in that horrible way. "Why? To leave more women for the others?"

"Inos!" Kade protested.

"Sometimes that is the motive," Andor said. "Or extra land, or just to keep the place peaceful. We are not making very good time, I fear, Proconsul."

Yggingi growled an agreement. "We shall probably not see the top of the pass by nightfall. There is a guardhouse there, but now you will probably have to bivouac, ma'am."

"Perhaps my niece and I should ride, then?" Kade suggested calmly.

The men looked down at her in astonishment. "Could—would you?" Yggingi asked.

"I should love to! I find that carriage very bumpy. How about you, Inos, dear?"

"Of course!" Inos agreed, amused at the expression on Yggingi's face, and Andor's. They did not know of Aunt Kade's unlimited ability to astonish.

Kade rose, determined. "Then we shall ride. Our habits are in that green box, Proconsul. If you would be so kind as to have it lifted down, we can change in the carriage."

Yggingi actually smiled—a gruesome sight. "And we can leave this wreck where it is. We should reach Pondague tomorrow, and after that you can travel by sled."

Aunt Kade beamed up at him innocently. "Oh, I think we can ride in the forest if we have to. I am a little out of practice, I admit, but I used to be a very keen horsewoman."

It would do her figure no harm, Inos thought, and a horse could be no more tiring than that bone-shaking carriage.

Yggingi, about to speak, stopped suddenly and peered into the trees. "What was that?"

Andor frowned. "I thought I heard something, too."

Inos had heard nothing, but her skin tingled—all the horses had pricked their ears in that way, also. The proconsul bellowed for silence in the ranks. The shout ran out along the line in both directions, and then there was only a steady dripping, and restless splashings of hooves.

"There it is again," Yggingi said, and this time Inos had heard something, also.

"Goblins?" she asked nervously.

"They don't shout. They keep quiet and run. If I'd thought

there was the slightest chance of goblin sport, I'd have brought the dogs.''

A distant voice. ''Princess Inosolan!''

Inos jumped. Her heart continued jumping.

Faint though it was, they had all heard it this time—Inos, her aunt, Andor, Yggingi, and the dozens of mud-splattered legionaries.

''It's a long way off!'' Andor's face had gone very stern. He pushed back his cloak to free his sword hilt.

Yggingi clicked his sword up and down in its scabbard, once, then again. ''Maybe not so far. The trees deaden sound.''

''Princess Inosolan!'' No mistake this time . . .

They were all staring at the woods now. Aunt Kade stepped close to Inos and gripped her wrist, as if fearing she might run off into the forest to investigate. Nothing was less likely. Inos shivered. Yggingi's sword hissed as he drew.

''You had better go back to the coach, ladies!'' He shouted an order and swords flashed out, while other men pulled bowstrings from waterproof pouches. Work on the axle had stopped.

''No, wait!'' Inos said as her aunt began to move. That voice?

''Princess Inosolan!'' Closer yet.

Who? There was something familiar about that voice. ''Yes?'' she shouted.

''Inos!'' her aunt cried.

And the voice replied: ''It's Rap!''

Rap? Rap who? *Rap?*

''No!'' It couldn't possibly be.

''Back in the carriage!'' Andor shouted, and he also drew his sword. ''It must be some sort of demon, I think. You agree, Proconsul?''

Yggingi's eyes had narrowed to slits. ''I never met any forest demons. Old wives' tales!'' He cupped his hands to shout. ''Come out and show yourself!''

''Tell your men to lower their bows!'' The voice was much closer, although there was nothing in sight. ''I am alone and unarmed.''

''I think it must be a demon!'' Andor insisted. ''They can look like anyone—very dangerous to trust a demon.'' He appeared more upset than anyone. He sounded almost shrill, and that was surprising, somehow.

Yggingi seemed to think so. He eyed Andor curiously, then called to his men to lower their bows. ''Come out!'' he bellowed, more loudly than seemed necessary.

And a man stepped from behind a tree right in front of them. How he had come so close without her seeing, Inos could not guess, but there he was—a slim young man in soiled leather garments, holding out empty hands to show his lack of weapons. He was panting.

"Inos!" he said.

Rap!

He had grown—taller and wider. His clothes were incredibly filthy and his face impossibly grimy, especially around the eyes. It seemed greasy, with the rain running down it in droplets, and it looked much thinner than she remembered, making his jaw look bigger than ever, his nose wider. He had a youth's thin moustache and patchy beard. He was bareheaded, his brown hair matted in slimy tangles. Ugly! But it was Rap.

She began to tremble, stupidly.

"He's no goblin, certainly," Yggingi said to no one in particular. "That's close enough! Who are you?"

"The princess knows me."

"Do you?" the proconsul asked.

"Yes," she said. "He's one of my father's stablehands. Rap? What are you doing here? And *what's that on your face?*"

Then she caught a whiff of an unbearable stench. "What's that smell?" Her stomach churned.

"That's goblin stink!" Yggingi said grimly. "Stand back from the ladies, you!"

Rap did not move, except to put his hands on his hips. He had obviously been running and he spoke in short bursts. "Sorry about the perfume. No bathtubs in the forest. I came to warn you that your father is dying, Inos. But I see that you already know."

Had Rap also come all this way to warn her? She glanced up at Andor, who had his jaw clenched and was scowling. "Sir Andor told me."

"Oh, it's *Sir* Andor, is it?" Rap frowned fiercely. "I have another warning for you, then." He raised a hand and pointed. "Don't trust that man! He's a—"

"Rap!" she shouted. "What do you know of Sir Andor?"

"He sold me to the goblins, that's what I know about him."

Sold him to . . . Again Inos caught a whiff of that terrible smell.

Andor raised his sword and took a step. She laid a hand on his arm to detain him. "Andor, do you know Rap?"

"This is not whoever you think it is, my darling. It's a forest demon. They can take many shapes. Don't trust a word it says. They are very evil."

"Andor! Rap, how did you get here? Aunt Kade, it is Rap, isn't it?"

"I don't know, dear. I never met him."

"What are you?" Yggingi demanded. "You're not imp and you're not goblin."

"It's a demon!" Andor insisted. "Or a wraith!"

A *wraith*? Inos shuddered convulsively. Surely not?

"I'm a faun." Rap was still watching Inos. "A jotunn-faun mongrel, and goblin by adoption. But not by choice—that was his doing." And again he pointed at Andor.

Inos wondered why she could not just quietly faint, as ladies of quality were supposed to do in moments of stress. Rap had always been so dependable! Others might make up fantastic stories or play elaborate jokes, but Rap never had. And it certainly seemed to be Rap, an older version of the boy she had known—except for the moustache, and those barbaric tattoos.

"Rap," she said, forcing her voice down from the squeaks it wanted to use, "what are those marks round your eyes?"

Rap gaped for a moment, raising his hand to his face as if he had forgotten the tattoos were there. "These?"

Andor stepped back with a laugh. He sheathed his sword. "I did meet him!" he said. "I didn't recognize him in that goblin disguise. I met him in Krasnegar. Tell her Highness how a goblin earns his tattoos, lad."

"I didn't!" Rap shouted.

"Didn't what?" Inos asked.

"You tell her, Proconsul," Andor said.

"No, you tell her." Yggingi was scowling.

"He tortured a boy to death."

And Inos said, "No!" just as Rap repeated, "I didn't!"

"He must have done," Yggingi said. "It's their custom."

Then Andor put his arm around Inos, and she was very grateful for it. "And he's the one who sold me the horses."

"Sold you the horses?" she repeated idiotically.

He nodded, still staring at the apparition from the woods. "I asked some people where I could acquire horses, and I was directed to that boy. We met in a bar and he sold me two horses."

Rap! They must have been her father's horses. There were no others in Krasnegar. Of course Andor would not have known that. Rap, selling the royal horses? In bars?

"Liar!" Rap shouted. "He's lying, Inos! We left Krasnegar

together and he sold me to the goblins. He bought safe passage for himself by selling—''

"Rap! No! I won't listen to—''

"Inos, he's a sorcerer!''

She had rather liked Rap once, she remembered, when she was younger. Of course in those days she had known very little about men and almost nothing about gentlemen. Fortunately she knew better now, after Kinvale, and she could appreciate the way Andor was keeping his temper in spite of the insults being shouted by this filthy derelict. Rap had obviously reverted to some sort of savage state—his faun ancestry coming out, probably.

"If you were sold to the goblins, you're in remarkably good shape!'' Ygginggi said. "Spying for them, are you? Come forward here with your hands high.''

"No!'' Rap said. *"Inos, you know I wouldn't lie to you!"*

Oh, Rap! Her heart lurched. Then Inos looked up at Andor again. He smiled sadly and shook his head. She saw how foolishly juvenile her momentary doubts must seem to him—and how mature he was not to lose his temper at the insults or at her silly wavering. She must not listen to any more nonsense, and that stench was making her feel nauseated. Inos lifted her chin disdainfully and turned, letting Andor lead her away.

"Inos!'' Rap shrieked. "He's a mage, or a demon, or something—''

Ygginggi waved his men forward. "Bring him in! Tie him up.''

Then all the horses reared and screamed in inexplicable panic. Hooves flailed. Men were hauled off their feet, or dragged through the mud. It seemed to be Inos who was the source of terror—plunging mounts fled from her in both directions along the road and even off into the undergrowth. Enormous animals bowled over whole groups of soldiers. The officers' roars were drowned in oaths and whinnyings, splashings and thuds. Amid this instant chaos, she found herself, with Kade and Andor, isolated on the trail as the whole cohort fought to regain control of its frenzied livestock. The goblin apparition had vanished away into drippy shadow under the ancient trees.

Andor hurried Inos back to the coach. "Take cover in here!'' he shouted over the racket. "This may be an ambush.'' Then he thrust her inside and Aunt Kade, as well, while the troopers were struggling to restore order to their mounts. Inos was glad to obey.

With the carriage still canted at an absurd angle, she found herself being half crushed by Aunt Kade, and yet she did not mind. The human contact was very comforting.

"It was Rap," she whispered, fighting tears and a heart as panic-stricken as the horses.

"Yes, dear."

"But selling Father's horses? In bars?"

"If he really did steal two of the palace horses," Kade said, "then he would have been found out, wouldn't he?"

"Of course!" There were not so many horses in the stables that two could go missing undetected, and not so many hands that the thief could long remain unknown. Stupid Rap! "So he was found out and ran away!"

"And he must have taken refuge with the goblins," her aunt agreed. "I don't know why he followed you south, dear. Perhaps he hoped to spin you some fantastic story . . ."

"Perhaps. That must be it." Young men did tend to behave oddly at that age, she knew. That was when the bad apples showed up—she had heard plenty of stories at Kinvale and been given plenty warnings. Oh, Rap! "It wasn't a *wraith*, was it?"

When a soul came before the Gods for weighing, the Evil was canceled out by the Good, and the balance went to join the Good, and live evermore as part of the Good. But in bad souls the residue was evil, and the Evil might reject it, to leave it wandering as a wraith, haunting the night.

Kade started. "Oh, I think it—he—was alive."

"And Rap wasn't evil!" Yet if he'd descended to selling horses in bars, what else might he had done before he died? Inos shivered.

"I don't think it was a wraith," Kade said firmly. "I don't think wraiths would smell that bad!"

Inos managed to chuckle and nod. She was relieved to find that she agreed. It had been Rap. Rap alive.

She glanced around. The soldiers were recovering and restoring order, but there was no one close to the coach. Not even Andor . . . "Aunt, how did Yggingi know about Father? Why was he waiting at Kinvale when Andor arrived? This must have been planned!"

Kade flinched. "It was my fault, my dear."

"Yours?"

"Yes. I let slip to Ekka that I was worried about your father's health. Chancellor Yaltauri was supposed to send me bulletins. He didn't."

"Then Ekka's behind this?" Now Inos began to understand.

"I fear so."

"So when—if—Father dies . . ."

"The proconsul will proclaim the duke as king, I think. I have been very foolish, darling. I did not see—"

Inos pecked a kiss on her cheek. "But it was not Andor?"

"No! I don't think so."

"I trust Andor!" Inos said firmly. "Don't you?"

"I . . . " Just for an instant Kade hesitated, and then she smiled. "You're asking me to choose between him and that very smelly boy?"

Inos laughed and hugged her. Invisible birds burst into glorious inaudible symphonies of song—no one had betrayed her except the odious dowager duchess! Kade had been foolish, but not evil. Andor was innocent—Inos would doubt him no more. Seeing Rap again beside him had somehow shown her how vastly inferior any other man must be. Andor, oh, Andor!

5

A wolf, a goblin, and a faun who had farsight—there had never been any danger that the troopers would find them.

After an hour or so, the expedition moved off along the mountain trail. Inos and her aunt were riding, and the coach had been left where it was. Inos's mount was staying very close to Andor's, but Rap could not tell at that distance whether or not it was secured there by a tether. He could not have summoned it anyway, because he did not know which horse it was. Andor might not know that; but, in any case, Rap had already discarded that plan as being too dangerous for Inos. It would also bring the whole imp army after him, and obviously his fantastic story was not going to be believed.

In thick woods on the hill above the road, he used his farsight to watch them all go. He was soaking wet and miserable, hunched on the ground, savagely digging holes in the moss with a stick—jab . . . jab . . . Fleabag was sleeping, but he alone of the three of them heard the hooves through the muffling timber. He lifted his head to listen. Little Chicken was sitting on a fallen log, elbows on knees, waiting as patiently as the trees themselves.

Jab . . . jab . . .

Rain was dribbling down Rap's neck, and he perversely left his hood down and let it. Almost he wished that the meeting had not happened, that he had missed Inos and gone on to lose himself in the Impire. But unlikely things happened to those who knew words of power—so Andor had taught him. And there was only this one pass through the mountains.

Spurned! Jab!

Rejected, even by Inos!

Jab!

But Andor had a word of power and he would be believed over anyone else. Trust was his talent.

Jab! The stick broke.

Rap rose to his feet.

"Now we do what?" Little Chicken asked.

Rap sighed. "You still my trash, goblin?"

This show of caution seemed to amuse the burly young woodsman. He nodded.

Despairingly Rap thought of the hard weeks ahead.

"Now we run back," he said, "back to Krasnegar."

Damsel met:

> Fairer than feigned of old, or fabled since
> Of faery damsels met in forest wide
> By knights of Logres, or of Lyones,
> Lancelot, or Pelleas, or Pellenore.

Milton, *Paradise Regained*

❰ EIGHT ❱

Casement high

1

Even to Krasnegar, spring came eventually. The hills were white and uninhabited yet, and the causeway still poulticed with crumpled ice floes and drifts, but brave men had trodden a footpath across it already, and a few more weeks would see the horses and cattle staggering back to the mainland.

There was no moon. Pale auroras danced in the sky like giant ghosts as Rap and Little Chicken emerged from one of the shore cottages, yawning and shivering in the dregs of sleep. A man could barely see his feet in that uncertain glimmer.

Rap took a few deep breaths of the frigid air, welcoming the familiar salty tang of the sea and the distant crackling of the tide wrestling ice. Then he turned to his companion. He had made this offer at the end of the forest, but he would try once more.

"I release you, Little Chicken. You have paid any debt you owe me many times over. Go back to your people."

"I am your trash," said the stubborn whisper from the darkness. "I look after you."

"You can't help me here! I am in grave danger, but you cannot help, and you will be in danger, also. Go, with my gratitude."

"I look after you. Later I kill you."

So the Gods had still not given the signal. Rap shrugged unseen. "You may have to be quick, if you want to be the first. Come on, then."

He began to run. When they reached the causeway itself, though, he was forced down to a walk, steering entirely with his farsight, and at times Little Chicken had to hold his shoulder to stay with him in a heavy, dense dark like blankets. They were halfway across before Rap remembered bears. This was a bad time for them, but now he had so much trust in his farsight that he was certain none lurked in the vicinity.

It had been a bad winter. Below the ice there had been much damage to the stonework, although no one else could have known.

Somewhere behind them in the moors, the imp army was camped. Rap had stayed a couple of days ahead of it all the way, and the journey had been far, far worse than his trip south. While the cold had been less severe, the snow had been deeper and stickier, the winds stronger. Worse yet, Rap and Little Chicken had traveled as heralds of disaster, croaking ravens prophesying war. The imps had burned every goblin village within reach of the road. Had the warnings not flown ahead of them, they would undoubtedly have massacred the inhabitants, also. The people of the first village had died, all of them, from patriarch to newborn. Inos' journey back to her homeland had been marked by pillars of smoke, by women and children fleeing out into the wasteland, by precious foodstocks pillaged, by unprovoked and unnecessary rampage. The leader of the imps, the one with the fancy helmet, was certainly an utter madman. What he sought to gain, Rap could not guess, nor why Inos had allowed it. He could only assume that she had been powerless to stop the destruction.

The wagon road to Pondague had been sealed behind her, for in future the goblins would brook no travel on it. No force less than a full army could traverse the taiga now. No more would trains amble north in summer with supplies. Krasnegar would suffer and its way of life become harder even than before. Madness!

Only once had Rap and Little Chicken departed from the trail. They had made a wide detour around Raven Totem, sending the words of warning by goblin messengers, running double shifts to catch the army again on the far side.

And now he was home. Rap emerged from the travail of the causeway onto the dock road, dark and deserted, swept clean by the wind. He swung up the bar on the gate. Those gates would stop white bears, but not impish legionaries. Once inside he began to trot again, out of old habit, with Little Chicken and Fleabag at his heels. Dawn would come in an hour or so. Soon the town would be stirring. He headed for the nearest stairway.

What did the imp army want of Krasnegar? Did it come to put Inos on her throne and defend her against the jotnar, or did it come to loot? Would it treat the town as it had treated the goblin villages? Certainly it could not be stopped short of the castle itself, and there would not be enough food in the castle to withstand a siege. Indeed, a former factor's clerk could guess that there would not be even enough food in the city for an additional two thousand hungry men. The crops and the grain ships were months away yet, the wagon road impassable.

Rap scanned each corner and branching carefully. In Krasnegar the law said that horse thieves were to be hanged.

He had planned to bring the horses back. He had expected to return with a grateful Inos, heir presumptive or already queen. Most of all, he had been mesmerized by Andor.

Andor! Rap could not think of Andor without baring his teeth. What that sorcerer had done to Rap was bad enough, but he had also used his power on Inos, and that was unforgivable. She would have been as helpless to resist Andor as Fleabag was to refuse Rap himself.

An early riser emerged from a doorway two corners ahead. Rap took cover in a doorway and waited, puffing gently, hearing Little Chicken doing the same beside him, and Fleabag's noisy pant.

"You run good, forest boy," Rap whispered. Little Chicken grunted quietly, but angrily. Rap smiled into the darkness. Goblins were not accustomed to stairs.

The town man vanished into another door and Rap set off again, his companions following the tap of his moccasins on the cobbles and steps. He had spent many hours planning this return, thinking while running, wondering whom he would seek out, reviewing all those childhood friends who had turned aside when he had demonstrated occult powers. His final choice had surprised him greatly.

He was approaching the castle. He could, if he wanted, run right in through the gates, for no guard was ever posted there, except in summer when there were strangers in town. Krasnegar had sheltered too long behind the diplomatic skill of its king, a skill buttressed by a word of power.

If Holindarn was still alive to tell Inos that word, would it serve her in the same way? Rap had not thought to wonder what change the word would produce in Inos. What was her great talent? Not diplomacy! Gaiety? Zest? Beauty?

Perhaps beauty. He would never forget her as he had seen her in the forest, unexpectedly sprung from the child he remembered to glorious woman, a slender wood nymph in a malachite cloak, with hints of golden hair inside the hood, green eyes shining in her winter-pale face. He wept himself to sleep with that memory.

Inos with her beauty augmented by magic would be a goddess. She was close enough now.

And so he thought again of Andor, baring his teeth. He had plans for Andor that he had never thought he could have for any man. Almost, Rap could think of turning him over to Little Chicken.

They stopped in an alleyway by a door and waited for their hearts to slow and breathing to calm. Nothing like a few months' running to put a man in shape, even for running up Krasnegar.

Rap scanned, sensing the small apartment of two rooms and a kitchen. There was a communal toilet on the other side of the alley, behind Rap. The owner was up and dressed, kneeling by his fireplace. His wife and children had died years ago, in the same pestilence that had killed Rap's mother, and he had lived alone ever since. Rap had never been invited into this tiny home; he knew no one who ever had.

He tapped.

Hostler Hononin looked around in surprise and then heaved himself to his feet. His feet were bare and his shirt hung down unfastened over his pantaloons and hose. His face was weather-beaten, lumpy, and wizened, and his stoop thrust his head forward aggressively. The tangle of gray curls around his bald spot was still rumpled by sleep; he appeared even more surly than usual as he padded over to the door.

"Who's there?" His voice was loud enough to make Rap jump.

Rap tapped again, reluctant even to whisper his name.

The little man scowled, then opened the door a crack—it had not been locked—and light jumped in Rap's face, dazzling him.

"Oh, great Gods, boy!" Hononin recoiled. "By the Powers! Rap!" He was stunned. Then he pulled the door wide. "Quick! Come in before anyone sees you! And who the hell is this?"

Then they were all inside and the door closed. Hononin choked and put a hand over his mouth.

"Sorry, sir. It's bear grease. It keeps the cold out."

The old man looked him over, then the others. Fleabag sniffed suspiciously at him. Little Chicken was staring around the little room, his odd-shaped eyes stretched by alarm and clasutrophopia.

"Did you tell her?" the hostler mumbled, through his fingers.

"She's coming. Tomorrow."

As his eyes adjusted to the light, Rap glanced curiously around the room. He had been gone so long that furniture seemed very strange to him—the table and two wooden chairs in the middle, and a big, overstuffed chair near the fire, with its insides falling out. Crude sketches of horses hung on the bare plank walls. One candle in a bone candlestick threw a wavering light over a heap of old tack in one corner and a small bench with saddler tools. A threadbare rug . . . Cozy enough in its way, though.

The old man nodded. "Good."

"He's still alive?"

"So they say."

Rap breathed a deep sigh. That was what he had wanted most—that she be able to say good-bye.

Hononin retched again and backed away. "You stink like you've been bathing in the honey pit. I've got some soap somewhere I've been saving. Ever used soap?"

"Once or twice, sir."

"Use it good. Need hot water. Get those rags off." He headed for his kitchen and soon a loud clanking told that he was working the pump. Rap began unlacing and instantly Little Chicken had knocked his hands away and started doing it for him. Rap knew better than to resist; his last attempt had given him a sprained wrist.

Hononin returned with a bucket and stopped to stare at this valet service. "Who the hell is he?"

"He's a goblin, sir."

"I can see that, idiot! And what are all those marks on your face? You gone goblin, too? Burn those rags—they'll help heat the water, and maybe get the stink out of here. His, too. You undress him now or does he do it himself? You've grown, lad. You leave any spare clothes behind in that room of yours? No, they wouldn't fit you now anyway. I'll go and see what I can find."

"This is good of you, sir," Rap said, naked now and bundling up his buckskins.

"Damn sure it is! You'll hang certain if Foronod finds you. So you stay here and get cleaned up. Here's the soap. Use it all. Filthy putrid pair, you are. And a lousy wolf. You didn't bring them back, did you?"

He meant the horses. Rap shook his head.

"Pity. Might'a let you off with a flogging."

Hononin thrust feet into boots. He grabbed his doublet from a peg, banged the door, and was gone.

It was a long while before the old man returned, and faint gleams of daylight were leaking in around the curtains. People paraded up and down the alley, greeting one another in Rap's native tongue and making his heart ache with it.

A long while . . . but it took all that time to remove the grease, even with soap and sand and hot water. Little Chicken resisted and argued, complying only when Rap explained that the smell would be investigated, and then the townsfolk would find Rap and kill him.

For the first time since Winterfest, Rap found a mirror. His own face was a shock to him, the face of a stranger. He did not think it was a boy looking back at him as he wielded Hononin's razor against some quite impressive stubble; illogically, he was pleased by the stubble and yet disgusted to see how furry fauns' legs could be when they were not smeared with grease. They were not the legs he had departed on. These were hairier and much thicker, while his face was hairier and thinner.

Fleabag had discovered Hononin's breakfast and eaten all of it except the butter, which Little Chicken had rescued. He wanted to smear Rap with it.

Then the hostler thrust his gnarled face around the door to warn his guests that he had a lady with him; but the guests already knew that and had taken cover in the bedroom. So he tossed a bundle of clothes in at Rap and went back to the front room to wait until they appeared. That took time, also, as Little Chicken would neither let Rap dress himself nor listen to an explanation of how hose worked. Little Chicken was going to be a large liability in Krasnegar.

At last Rap was ready and could go in. He had already identified the visitor—Mother Unonini, the palace chaplain. Rap knew her, but they had never spoken. Under a trickle of morning daylight, she seemed as forbidding as midnight.

She was a tall, stern woman in her black gown, sitting as straight as was possible in the overstuffed chair by the fireplace, her hands folded in her lap. She returned a nod to Rap's clumsy bow and looked him over without revealing her conclusions.

"Eat first, talk later." The hostler pointed to the table. Rap had already scented the hot loaves and his mouth was watering. Bread! He sat down and began to gorge. In a few minutes Little Chicken came in and scowled horribly at the sight of a woman with her head bared. Mother Unonini flinched at a man with his shirt open—which was not the goblin's fault, for all the buttons had already popped off. Rap managed a two-dialect introduction with his mouth full.

Little Chicken did not approve of bread, but he was hungry, also. He helped himself to a meal and sat on the floor to eat it. The hostler chuckled and took the third chair.

"Perhaps you can eat and listen, though." The chaplain had a hard, masculine voice. "I shall bring you up to date first, Master Rap, and then . . ." She frowned. "I do not care for nicknames. What is that short for?"

"Just Rap," said Rap.

That was not strictly true, for his real name was a great, long incomprehensible chant that he never used. He supposed it was a Sysanasso name. "Never tell your real name to anyone," his mother had said when she had told it to him, "because a sorcerer may learn it and use it to do you harm." He had believed her then, of course, because he had been only ten or so at the time, and ten-year-olds believe most of what their mothers tell them; but now he knew much more about sorcerers, and he could see that that had been only another of his mother's strange superstitions, like a south wind bringing rain. His friends would have laughed at such a name, though, so he had never told it to anyone, even Inos.

The chaplain pursed her lips disapprovingly. "Very well—Master Rap. The king is alive, but every day seems like to be his last, poor man. Even the cordials that Doctor Sagorn left will barely ease his pain now. We who are close to him pray for his release. It seems astonishing that he has survived so long."

"He has a word," Rap mumbled.

She raised her eyebrows and paused. "Perhaps! What do you know of . . . But, of course, you must have one, also. Foolish of me." She fell silent, reconsidering. The old hostler grinned fiendishly—a rare and unpleasant sight—and helped himself to some of the bread before it all vanished.

Mother Unonini continued, seeming now to choose her words more carefully. At times Rap had trouble understanding her—like most Krasnegarians, he spoke a pidgin of impish and jotunnish. Inos could switch from that to pure impish and back again. So did the king and his senior officials, but they did not sound as prissy as the chaplain, who had a southerner's accent worse than Rap had ever heard, even from sailors.

"The city is badly divided—between imps and jotnar, of course. The imps believe that the princess went to Kinvale to marry her cousin the duke, who has a good claim to the throne. They expect him to return with her. But the imps themselves are divided; many would prefer that the city be annexed as a province of the Impire.

The jotnar are unhappy at either prospect. They talk of Thane Kalkor of Nordland, who has a claim at least equal to the duke's."

"Foronod is their leader," Hononin interjected. "Some want to put him on the throne himself, but he seems to be supporting Kalkor. He's written to him, they say."

The chaplain frowned, as if he were giving away too much.

"Rap ought to know," the old man snarled. "Foronod was howling for his heart over the horses. If he hears that Rap summoned the princess back, then he will be even worse."

She nodded. "Certainly we must smuggle Master Rap and his friend back out of the city tonight. As soon as possible."

Rap stopped eating. After coming so far he was expected to leave?

Hononin cackled suddenly and they all looked at him. "I should warn you, Mother. When you see that jaw set like that, you might as well save breath. Obviously Master Rap is not leaving."

"He must!"

Hononin shook his head. "Perhaps, but he won't. Even when he was this high, that jaw was the signal."

Rap grinned suddenly. He had been right to come to the cantankerous old hostler, and it was good to find a friend at last.

"We shall see!" Mother Unonini set her own jaw.

"And you?" Rap glanced from her to the hostler and back. "Where are your loyalties?"

He was being presumptuous; the chaplain frowned again. "My objective must always be the greatest good. Civil war would be a great evil—life is precarious enough here without that." She considered for a moment and added, "If I had the power to impose a settlement . . . Inosolan is not yet of age. A regency council would be a fair solution—Factor Foronod and Chancellor Yaltauri, perhaps."

Lukewarm at best, Rap thought. He turned to the hostler.

"I'll try to keep your neck its present length, lad," the old man said, "even if it was my horses you took. But I'm staying out of politics. Too dangerous at my age."

Was no one loyal to Inos, then?

"Can you speak between gulps now, young man?" the chaplain inquired.

"I think so, Mother. It's a long story. You knew the man called Andor?"

She nodded. "A fine gentleman."

"No! I thought so, also, and I trusted him when he suggested that the two of us go and tell Inos—"

"Stop right there! Only two of you went?"

Rap nodded, surprised. She glanced at the hostler.

"I told you there were only two bedrolls missing," he said. "And the tent was too small for three."

"Three?" Rap echoed.

"Doctor Sagorn," Unonini said. "He left, also. It did not matter, for he had trained the nurses in the use of the cordial, but he went with you, we thought."

Sagorn, also?

Of course!

And Darad.

Rap pushed the remains of his meal away and started to talk. He was interrupted no more. In the corner Little Chicken ate steadily, while watching the incomprehensible talk with suspicious eyes, but it was a long tale, and even the goblin's appetite was satisfied before Rap finished.

The hostler and the chaplain looked at each other.

Hononin nodded. "I believe him. He's a good lad—no, a good man. He always was."

She nodded reluctantly and studied her fingers for a moment. Then she rose and started to pace back and forth across the little room with her hands clasped behind her. It was a strangely unfeminine action, and she had an awkward, jerky gait on her surprisingly short legs. She no longer seemed tall, as she had in the chair. At last she seemed to reach a conclusion, returning to her seat.

"Very well!" she said. "The hostler supports you, Master Rap, and that carries weight. But I have been thinking, also, of what the Gods want. It is common knowledge that a God appeared to Inosolan and myself. They gave her orders, and now I suspect that those referred to you."

Rap tried to remember what Inos had told him of the God and Their words, but it was a long time ago and his memories were blurred. He was about to ask, but she gave him no chance.

"I shall accept your story," she said pompously. "Obviously there is sorcery about, and you are probably right—someone is after the royal word of power. Inosolan will be in grave danger if she learns it. She may not, you know. The king is rarely conscious now. Yet you think that Andor and this Darad are the same man?"

"And Sagorn! And Jalon the minstrel, also!" He explained how Sagorn had appeared in the palace the previous summer without entering the gate—and Sagorn had returned in the fall at about the same time Andor had arrived, on the night of the blizzard, when Rap's farsight had become general knowledge.

Jalon had spoken of Darad. Andor had known Jalon, and Sagorn.

Yet it was incredible, even to Rap. He had met Sagorn once. He had shared a meal with the minstrel. Neither had been Andor, and certainly neither had been Darad. To think of the dreamy, amiable Jalon and the savage Darad was to link water and fire—they were incompatible. There was more than shape-changing involved here. If Jalon could turn himself into Darad at will, as Andor seemed to be able to, then why had he not done so when he was alone with Rap in the hills? Darad would surely not hesitate to use any means at hand to extract a word if he had the opportunity. For that matter, why had Andor not done the same when he had Rap alone in his attic those many long evenings?

Suddenly Hononin snapped his fingers. "The keys! You say that Andor got them from me? But I never saw him all that day."

"What happened to them?" Rap asked.

The hostler scowled hideously at him and then at the chaplain. "I don't know. Found them on the stable floor; thought I'd dropped them. I'd been sure they'd been on my belt as usual. It wasn't Andor, certain! Nor that Sagorn man."

"So he may have other shapes?" Unonini said. "That is bad news. And yet he can't be a sorcerer. If he is, then he does things the hard way."

"And what about this army?" Rap asked. "I don't know why Inos is bringing troops, but they must be stopped."

The chaplain shook her head. "Inosolan may have no choice. And we don't, either. Sergeant Thosolin and his men can't fight two thousand."

"Let them in?" Hononin looked disgusted.

"We must," she said. "What alternative do we have? They could burn the town and starve out the castle. You and I cannot even warn anyone without saying how we know, for then Master Rap would be in jeopardy. Inosolan is with them. Why should they savage her realm?"

"Why savage the goblins?" Rap asked bitterly. "They do no harm except to themselves."

That remark raised eyebrows and produced an awkward silence.

Little Chicken let out an enormous belch and grinned.

Little Chicken—who would be Death Bird now, had Rap and

Andor not blundered into the Ravens' territory—how much of this conversation was he managing to follow?

"I have a question, Mother," Rap said reluctantly. "Tell me about the Four, please."

The chaplain started. "What about the Four?"

"Who they are, what they do."

Her eyes narrowed. She dropped her gaze to her fingers and kneaded them for a moment. "I really know no more about them than you do—than anyone else does. What were you taught in school about the Four?"

"Nothing. I haven't had much schooling, Mother."

She nodded, disapproving. "I see. Well, back in ancient times, the Dark Times, Pandemia was a very violent land. There was magic about, and much evil in it. Sorcerers set themselves up as kings and waged war among themselves. There are legends of great massacres, of pillage and destruction, of men fighting dragons, monsters appearing and destroying whole armies, sheets of fire blasting hapless cities, and there are stories, too, of armies being released from binding spells and falling on their own leaders. It was a wicked time. You must have heard such tales!"

Rap shook his head, although he knew a little.

"Is this relevant?" she asked, staring.

"I think so."

Now the chaplain shot a worried glance at the hostler, who shrugged.

"The Imperor Emine II set up the Council of Four almost three thousand years ago. He gathered together the four most powerful sorcerers in all Pandemia and charged them to guard the Impire against sorcery. Hub is the city of five hills, you know." She sighed. "The city of the Gods! The most beautiful place, the center of the Impire, on the shores of Cenmere. I spent three years there attending . . . But I suppose that doesn't matter now. Well, the imperor's palace is in the center, and each of the four warlocks has a palace, also: North, East, South, and West. The imperor himself must always be a mundane, to preserve the balance. No one may use sorcery against the imperor himself, or his court, or family."

Rap nodded and waited for more.

Unonini seemed reluctant to give it to him, but after a moment she licked her lips and continued. "The system has worked, with a few temporary breakdowns, to this very day. Balance is the key, you see, just as the balance between the Good and the Evil rules the world, so the balance between the warlocks rules the Impire.

"If an evil sorcerer arises, then the wardens of the Four combine against him. Sorcerers are human, too, Master Rap. They
are torn between evil and good, as we all are—more so, perhaps,
because their power to do good or evil is so much greater. And
if one of the Four falls into evil ways, then the other three can
combine against *him*. It is the only way to prevent the sort of
anarchy that prevailed in the Dark Times. Balance!''

Rap nodded. "But tell me of the present wardens."

"Why?"

"I think I met one."

Unonini gasped, then again looked to the hostler, who scowled.

"Which one, lad?"

"A very old goblin woman?"

The chaplain closed her eyes for a moment, and her lips moved.

"Tell us," Hononin said, looking grim even for him.

So Rap told of the two occasions on which he had seen the
apparition, and of how she seemed to have a special interest in
Little Chicken. He kept his eyes off the goblin; he spoke as fast
as he could, and in the best impish he knew.

There was a pause, then the chaplain shuddered. "Bright Water," she whispered, and the hostler nodded.

"It sounds like her," he said. "Rap, lad, I think you did meet
one. She's witch of the north, and legend says she's about three
hundred years old—sorcerers live a long time. She's been one of
the Four longer than any."

"And?" Rap said.

Again it was the hostler who spoke, and even he had dropped
his voice to a whisper. "They say she's totally mad."

Rap glanced uneasily at Little Chicken, and his odd-shaped
goblin eyes were very intent. He grinned his giant teeth at Rap.

"Flat Nose, you did not tell me this."

"No," Rap admitted. "I thought maybe it was me who was
mad. I'll tell you later. I promise."

The goblin nodded.

"Tell me of the other three, Mother," Rap said.

She was reluctant. "I do not care to discuss them. No one does.
There is only one witch at present. The other three are men,
warlocks. South is an elf, East an imp, and the newest is West, a
young dwarf. I don't know very much, Master Rap. You haven't
met any of those, have you?"

Rap shook his head, and she looked relieved.

The hostler laughed uneasily. "There is one other thing that everyone knows that we can tell him, though. As well as claiming a quarter of the compass, each of the four has a speciality.''

The chaplain choked back an exclamation, as if she had not thought of that.

"What sort of speciality?" Rap asked.

The old man smirked. "Little things like dragons."

Mother Unonini thumped her hand on the arm of her chair, expelling a cloud of dust and feathers. "We don't know this! It is a commonly held belief, maybe, but people don't go round questioning sorcerers, Master Hostler, and especially not warlocks. Who can say what they do or don't do?"

Hononin glared at her. "I know what I was told, and no one's ever told me different. Earth, water, fire, and air—so my grandpappy said."

The chaplain glared back, then turned to Rap. "Tradition says that even Emine's compact did not stop the troubles at first—that the Four turned out to be as bad as any other group of sorcerers and strove among themselves for dominance. Eventually—I am cutting a thick story thin—eventually the Four agreed to share out the powers of the world between themselves. They had already divided Pandemia itself into quarters, calling themselves North and East and so on, but then they each took charge of a mundane power, also."

"Dragons?" Rap said. "Are dragons mundane?"

"Borderline." The chaplain rose and started to pace again in her ungainly way. "The Impire is not Pandemia, Master Rap. It is the largest dominion, of course, and because it is central, it has always tended to be the greatest—and of course it has the Four to preserve it—but there are many other kingdoms and territories beyond the Impire's borders."

Like Krasnegar, for instance. Rap nodded.

"But nothing can hope to withstand the Imperial army if it extends its full might."

"Except by sorcery."

"Of course. So the imperor and the Four agreed that no one might use sorcery on the Imperial army—neither to harm it nor to aid it. Like the imperor himself, it must be sacrosanct. The only exception is the warlock of the east. He can. The army is his prerogative."

Rap nodded again, beginning to see why the others had been so worried when he brought the talk around to the Four. "You mean that the witch I saw—"

"You saw a sorceress," the chaplain said, "and it may have been Bright Water herself, but we don't know that!"

"Either way, she couldn't stop the troops on their way here?"

The chaplain paused by the fire and glanced briefly at the hostler before continuing her lecture. "That's what they say. Those soldiers are part of the Imperial army, and to meddle with them would bring down the fury of the warlock of the east—and the others would support him in that instance. So 'tis said. One thing I do know—there must be many great sorcerers and sorceresses around Pandemia, Master Rap, but there is certainly none who could withstand the Four acting together."

Rap toyed for a moment with crumbs on the table. Sour old Unonini was keeping something back.

"I gotta go," Hononin muttered. "Word gets round I'm sick, there'll be mobs of nosy old women bringing jugs of bad soup here, just so they can pry." But he stayed where he was, on his chair.

Rap looked up. "What are the other powers, then? Dragons?"

Unonini pursed her lips, then nodded. "Dragons rarely roam outside Dragon Reach, but they are said to be the prerogative of the warden of the south. When dragons waste, then the imperor must call on South to drive them back."

"Even if he set them loose himself in the first place!" the hostler said with a foul grin.

The chaplain winced nervously.

"Well, why not?" the old man snapped. "Two years ago a flight of dragons wasted some town on the Winnipango. That's halfway across Pandemia from Dragon Reach, and they didn't touch anywhere in between! You telling me they weren't sent there? You know that sorcerers meddle, so why wouldn't a warlock use his own special power when he wanted to?"

"I never met a sorce—"

"Piddle! I never met a God, but I believe in Gods. And I believe the tales. My grandpappy went to watch a hanging once, down in Pilrind; and when they hauled the man up, he just disappeared! Faded like mist, he did! Left the noose just dangling, empty. Some sorcerer had rescued him."

The chaplain sniffed. "I never said there weren't sorcerers, nor that they don't use sorcery. Of course they do—all the time. An old schoolmate of mine once saw a poor, demented woman throw herself off a high roof. She should have fallen into a crowded street, but someone in the crowd must have been a sorcerer, because she floated down gently; like a leaf, my friend said."

"What's North's pre-prerogative?" Rap asked.

She hesitated so long that the hostler answered for her, confirming what Rap had suspected. "The jotnar. Army's land, see? Dragons fire. The jotunn raiders are the sea—water, that is."

"It's not as true nowadays as it was in the Dark Times," the chaplain added, "but the jotnar are still the finest sailors of the world. And they don't always confine their activities to trading, either."

Rap's father had been a slaver, and a raider when convenient, no doubt.

"Anywhere within reach of the sea," Unonini said, "is within reach of the jotnar."

It was what Rap had expected. "So if the imp army comes to Krasnegar, and Thane Kalkor brings his jotnar, then . . . What then?"

Unonini sighed heavily. "Then may the Good be with us! I don't suppose the Four often intervene in petty quarrels; little wars and small atrocities go on all the time. As long as sorcery is not invoked, then the warlocks seem to ignore them. But if Imperial legionaries face off against jotunn raiders—well, then the warlocks may very well become involved—very well! Bright Water is a goblin, and you say that the imps have been slaughtering goblins. By spring they may be battling her jotnar, here in Krasnegar." She shuddered and made the holy sign of balance.

"I must go," the hostler muttered again.

"Yes!" The chaplain straightened her shoulders. "I, also. And you, Master Rap, and your . . . companions . . . must stay here for now, and out of sight. I wish this wynd were not so much traveled."

"What's West's speciality?" Rap asked doggedly. Were the warlocks such very bad news? They might even help, as Bright Water had helped him. They might keep jotunn and imp apart.

"Weather, they say. And you think Inosolan will be here tomorrow?" Mother Unonini mused. "She will go straight to her father. I shall see that the doctors reduce the dosage and try to revive him for the meeting . . . if he lasts that long. Then they will both be in danger."

"Both?"

She nodded somberly. " 'Tis said that to share a word reduces its power. If the word is keeping him alive, he may die because of the sharing. And Inosolan will be in danger because she knows it."

They all worried over that thought for a while, and then the chaplain said, "If you insist on remaining in the town, then we must find somewhere safer than this for you, Master Rap."

"He's welcome here, Mother." But the hostler was eyeing Fleabag with a dislike that was obviously mutual.

"You do not even have a lock on your door! But where else can we hide him in a tiny place like Krasnegar? With two thousand legionaries coming? They will be billeted anywhere there is a span to spare."

Hononin heaved himself to his feet. "Nowhere I can think of."

"I was told once of a place," Rap said, "if you can get us there. A place where no one ever goes."

2

A single candle flickered and shivered in the night, casting its uncertain light on the dying king. His face was wasted, yellow and skull-like, his hair sparse and gray, his beard white. Even in sleep he writhed restlessly under the covers.

The drapes had been drawn all around the high bed, except for one small gap near the pillow. Sitting beside that opening, the attending nurse patiently waited out the long hours until her relief would come at dawn. From her seat she could not see the door to the chamber, and no one entering from the stairway could see either patient or nurse—unless that person had farsight, of course.

Mother Unonini crossed the room to talk to her, and to inspect the invalid, her lantern making inky shadows dance until she vanished around the corner of the fourposter. The chaplain was an ideal accomplice for intruders, able to go anywhere, answerable only to the Gods. Two youths and a dog came in silently behind her and crept across to the deep shadows on the other side of the bed.

Worms of fire crawled over the peats in the big fireplace and the room was heavy with their pungent scent. Curtains on one window tapped monotonously to draw attention to an ill-fitting casement. The drugged king moaned querulously in his slumber.

Quietly Rap laid down his bundle and waited, sending a restraining signal to Fleabag, who was eager to investigate the unfamiliar scents of the sickroom. Little Chicken also bore a bundle, but he continued to hold his, looking around bleakly at the shadows.

From the far side of the draperies came a crackle of vellum and Mother Unonini's hard voice. ". . . a special invocation. It will probably take me an hour or so . . ." For a servant of the Good, she was a surprisingly slick liar. Tactfully dismissed—and probably relieved that she need not listen to an hour's hard praying—the nurse rose and departed. Rap traced her progress as she descended the stairs within the far wall.

He could find no signs that the prowlers had been detected. Even the great hall at the bottom of the tower was deserted. The palace slept on, unaware that intruders had penetrated all the way to the royal bedchamber, unaware, as well, of the army poised to invade on the morrow.

Reassured, he tried to check overhead, also, and was seized at once by a strong desire not to pry. Inos had spoken of a spell protecting the long-dead sorcerer's secrets. Sweat broke out on his face and his head started to throb, but he forced himself to look. There was another staircase in the wall—he established that at the cost of a thumping in his temples and sick twinges in his gut—but it ran up to . . .

Nothing! The flat wooden ceiling marked the roof of the world. He relaxed then, knowing that the effort was fruitless. He had noticed this same opaque blankness when he entered the castle half an hour ago. Indeed he had noticed it when he left with Andor at Winterfest, although his farsight then had not then been as acute as it was now. Now he could sense almost every move in the whole building—even some irregular activities in one of the maids' dormitories of which Housekeeper Aganimi would certainly disapprove if she knew—but his knowledge stopped at the walls. Inisso had thrown an occult barrier around his bastion, cut it off from all the world.

And the chamber of puissance, if it existed—and Rap now felt strongly inclined to disbelieve in it—was outside that shield.

Then the lights and shadows began to move again as Mother Unonini came waddling around the corner of the bed and headed toward the high dresser opposite the doorway. Rap moved to join her, and then they both halted, irresolute.

"It's the spell," Rap said. Moving furniture around when the king was dying—it seemed like a desecration. It felt wrong. There couldn't be anything interesting behind it anyway.

The chaplain nodded uneasily. "You do it!"

"Little Chicken?"

The goblin shook his head vigorously, his angular eyes glinting wide in the light of the lantern.

"Scared?" Rap asked, although his own ribs were dribbling sweat.

The gibe brought the still-reluctant goblin, and the two of them lifted the heavy dresser away from the wall. The moment Rap saw the door, the strange reluctance released him. He grabbed up his bundle again as the chaplain produced a ring of massive keys and began trying them. In a moment the click of the lock rang like clashing blades through the silence. When she pushed the door, it uttered a groan that seemed loud enough to waken the whole city.

She paused and raised her lantern to see Rap's face. "Anything?"

He scanned again, all the way down to the great hall. Two dogs had been snoring before the fireplaces. They lifted their heads as the departing nurse emerged from the stairwell. When nothing else happened, they went back to sleep.

"All right."

Mother Unonini nodded and led the way up the narrow steps, her lantern showing matted white cobwebs and dusty treads curving up into darkness. It was as much as Rap could do to keep Fleabag from bounding ahead of her, for at the same time he was disconcerted by the eerie blankness awaiting him at the top. He felt like a fish being hauled upward to the water's surface. Closer and closer came that sinister nothingness. He was so accustomed now to viewing the world with his occult talent that he felt he was being threatened with blindness; the conflict between his two senses dizzied him.

Then his head broke through. The uppermost chamber rose to a conical roof and of course it lacked an opposing door leading to a higher story, but otherwise it seemed identical to all the other great circular rooms of the tower. The fireplace was empty. The garderobe door was closed, but Rap could sense through that.

He could sense the city, also. It was the castle now that was barred to him, locked within its occult shield. Sheer height made his head spin, as he felt the streets and alleys, and the distant icepack piled on the rocks, far, far below. He staggered and almost tripped on the last few treads.

The door at the top stood open and the intruders walked through into Inisso's chamber, the sorcerer's place of power.

"Well!" breathed the chaplain, raising her lantern and then lowering it quickly, seeing that its rays on the windows might alert any watchers outside. She was a very nosy person, of course. She had first been shocked when Rap had suggested this place as a bolt hole, but then her own obvious curiosity and the unexpected opportunity to pry had overcome her scruples. She must be feeling disappointed—there was nothing to see except dusty footprints showing vaguely on bare boards, where the king and Sagorn had walked on their visit in the summer. The air was cold and still and musty, but totally lacking in mystery. Just an empty room.

Being unfurnished, it seemed large. Fleabag began slinking around this vast circular emptiness, nose to the floor, pausing from time to time to analyze some detail of scent.

Little Chicken threw down his bundle and went to peer out of the nearest casement. Mother Unonini sniffed disapprovingly at the billow of dust he had raised.

Rap was still overwhelmed by his giddy sense of height. Combined with farsight, it was intoxicating, exhilarating, almost terrifying. Far, far below, a mother nursed her baby in a dark basement room, with the rest of her family asleep around her; bakers' apprentices were already stoking their masters' fires; a lover tiptoed past a bedroom door on his way home . . .

Was this what it was like to be a sorcerer? Did warlocks perch like brooding eagles, high on their towers in Hub, watching all Pandemia laid out below them, naked and defenseless? The wardens, being the strongest sorcerers of all, must have a range enormously greater than Rap's—had Bright Water really sensed him all the way from Hub? Was she even now slumped naked on her ivory throne in her own chamber of puissance, scanning the north, waiting for those ripples she had mentioned, ready to strike down any evil use of magic? What would such power do to its owner? He shivered.

The chaplain noticed. "I warned you that you would freeze up here!" Satisfied that her prediction had come true, she pulled her cloak tight with her free hand. But Rap was wearing a fur parka over his doublet and he was not cold at all; in fact it was the first time he had been comfortable all day.

"It isn't that. Mother?"

"Mmm?"

"If the Four guard us all against misuse of magic—"

"I do not wish to talk about the Four! Certainly not here."

Which is what Rap had been about to ask: Why had she been so reluctant to discuss the warlocks? Why was everyone, always? He had rarely heard them mentioned, ever.

"Look there!" The chaplain raised her lantern a fraction and pointed to the southern casement. "It's different!"

Little Chicken, having failed to see anything much to the north, now moved around to peer out eastward. He found glass puzzling, because it did not melt when he breathed on it.

The southern casement was certainly larger than the others.

The dormer was higher and wider than the other three and held not only the main arched window, but also two smaller lights flanking it. Rap tried to remember if he had ever noticed that lack of symmetry from below, and concluded he had never really looked properly. The pattern of lead between the panes was more complex and less regular, and that was another minor difference, but the panes showed just as black against the night outside.

"I wonder why?" Puzzled, the chaplain walked over toward it.

The window began to glow.

She stopped with a hiss of surprise. The many tiny panes between the leads were of all shapes and all colors, decorated with pictures and symbols: stars and hands, eyes and flowers, and many others less comprehensible, all vaguely visible in a pale gleam as if the moon were out there. The colors were as faint and faded as a very old manuscript—sienna, malachite, ochre, and slate. Rap's eyes saw them, but farsight told him there was only a window there with nothing unusual about it. Yet when he tried to make sense of the visual images, he felt as if they were changing. Each one was constant while he stared at it and altered as soon as his attention strayed. An umber bird's head in the upper right corner was now much lower than it had been. A ram's horn inexplicably seemed to curl to both right and left at the same time, and an image of a tawny flame writhing, a rose-and-lilac wheel turning . . . He shivered again.

Mother Unonini backed away and the moonlight died beyond the glass.

Little Chicken grunted angrily. Abandoning the east casement, he began stalking round to the south, one hand on the dagger in his belt, his shoulders bent forward, looking very much like Fleabag investigating a porcupine.

"Stop!" both Rap and the chaplain said at the same moment.

But Little Chicken kept on, walking slowly on the balls of his feet. The casement began to glow again, and this time the light was different; it was warmer and restless—not the moon, but firelight? Firelight at the top of a tower, seven stories above a castle that itself stood a hundred spans or more above the sea?

"Stop!" Rap said again, more urgently. He laid down his own burden—it held cups and food and useful things that might make a noise if dropped—and he hurried forward.

The light changed again, dramatically. By the time he had reached Little Chicken and grabbed his shoulder, the window was a blazing, seething brilliance, too bright to look at—surges of ruby, emerald, and sapphire stabbing amid flashes of ice-white like the facets of a giant diamond. Now certainly the symbols were changing more rapidly, flickering in the corners of the eye. Even to study a single pane was impossible against that glare.

Rap pulled and the goblin yielded. They backed away and the brilliance faded again until they were standing once more in the glimmer of the lantern. Rap's eyes hurt and the insides of his eyelids were stained with blurs of many hues.

Stiffly the chaplain rose from her knees, where she had been praying. Her face was pale and drawn in the gloom. "Magic!" she declared unnecessarily. "A magic casement!"

"What does it do?" Rap asked, still keeping a firm grip on Little Chicken.

"I don't know! I'm a priestess, not a sorcerer. But I think you had better stay well away from it."

All Inisso's other secrets had gone, but that one was built into the walls and could not be removed. Was this why the mysterious Doctor Sagorn had come up here with the king, to a room Inos had never been told about?

"Oh, I agree. Keep away!" Rap added in goblin.

Little Chicken nodded. "Bad!" He turned his back on the offending window.

"You still want to stay here?" Mother Unonini asked.

Rap nodded. "It's the safest place. And I can use my farsight from here." He would have to sit on the stairs to do so, below floor level, but she did not need to know that.

"Yes, but what can you *do*?" She had asked that question a dozen times.

He gave her the same answer as before. "I don't know. But somehow I must warn Inos that Andor is not what he seems."

She came close and lifted the lantern to study his face. "For her sake, or yours?"

"Hers, of course!"

She continued to stare. "If the people want a king instead of a queen, then they are not likely to accept a factor's clerk, you know."

Rap clenched his fists. "I was not suggesting that they would!"

"Do you think you can overhear what he says to Inosolan?"

Fury flared up in Rap, and evidently his expression was answer enough. She lowered her lantern. "No. I apologize, Master Rap. That was unworthy." She pulled her cloak tighter. "I shall go, then. You had better come down and replace the dresser."

Rap nodded. "And we'll push the door closed behind it."

The chaplain nodded. "Of course—but remember that it creaks.
I shall return tomorrow night, if I can, and bring some oil." She
shivered. "I must be crazy! I hope that I am interpreting the God's
words correctly . . . and that They were a benevolent God, on
the side of the Good. Kneel and I will give you a blessing; I wish
I had someone to bless this night's work for me."

Casement high:

> A casement, high and triple-arch'd there was,
> All garlanded with carven imagaries
> Of fruits, and flowers, and bunches of knot-grass,
> And diamonded with panes of quaint device,
> Innumerable of stains and splended dyes,
> As are the tiger-moth's deep-damasked wings . . .
>
> Keats, *The Eve of Saint Agnes*

⟦ NINE ⟧

Faithful found

1

The worst moment of that whole terrible day was Inos's first glimpse of her father, the sight of the poor withered relic that was all remaining of the exuberant, vital man she remembered. Compared to that, nothing before or after was. as bad—none of the murder or horror or sorcery that followed, not even the news of his death, for that was a release.

Of the morning she was to retain only confused images, a few fitful glimpses and recollections. She had left Krasnegar in summer drizzle, sitting in a landau with her father and Aunt Kade, cheered more or less sincerely by amused but affectionate townsfolk. She returned on a blustery spring morn, in sunshine mingled with flurries of snow, riding with Andor on one side of her and the despicable Proconsul Yggingi on the other. Now the citizens huddled in their furs to watch, or peered around shutters, their faces reflecting shock and anger at an invading Imperial army desecrating their streets.

The palace staff and the officers of the realm had been hurriedly assembled in the great hall that now seemed like a shoddy barracks to Inos. They, also, glared in impotent fury. Their greetings were curt, their welcomes insincere. Familiar faces bore unfamiliar expressions—old Chancellor Yaltauri and the much older Seneschal Kondoral, Mother Unonini and Bishop Havyili, and the tall, stark figure of Factor Foronod, his livid face almost as pale as the silver helmet of his hair.

How small Krasnegar was, how bleak, how shabby after Kinvale! The palace was a barn. And when she was ushered politely up into the withdrawing room she looked around at the gilt and rosewood furniture that Aunt Kade had brought back—three years ago now—and it seemed pathetic, a bitter mockery of what comfort and elegance ought to be. Yet it had not changed and she hated herself because it was she who had changed.

The way she spoke to them, the way she moved, the way she returned their looks—she had gone, but she had not returned. She never would return. The place was the same place. She was another person.

Then the doctors, bowing and mumbling and making excuses. His Majesty was conscious and had been informed—

It was at that moment that Inos issued her first command.

"I shall see him alone!" she stated, and she silenced their protests with the best glare she could muster. Even Andor. Even the hated Yggingi. Even Aunt Kade.

Astonishingly, it worked. They all agreed and no one was more surprised than Inos herself.

She climbed the familiar curving stairs alone, noting with surprise that the treads were dished by centuries of footsteps, noting how narrow the way was, and how the very stonework of the walls was glazed by the caress of innumerable garments. Kinvale had all been so *new*. She came to the dressing room and remembered it as it had been in her childhood, with her own bed against the northwest wall, although now there was an ancient wardrobe standing there. Nurses and doctors came trooping out the far door and bobbed politely to her and hurried across the room and off down the stair behind. And when the last of them had gone, she pushed unwilling feet to the steps and began to climb once more.

The drapes of the bed had been pulled back, the room was bright with transitory sunshine, and at first she thought there had been some terrible mistake, some macabre joke, for the bed looked empty. Then she came near and . . . and smiled.

She sat by him for many hours, holding his hand, making conversation when he was capable of it, else just waiting until he awoke again or the spasm of pain had passed. His mind wandered much of the time. Often he mistook her for her mother.

Aunt Kade came at intervals, tiptoeing and doleful. She spoke to him, and sometimes he knew her. Then she would ask if Inos wanted anything, and slip quietly away again. Poor Aunt Kade! Weeks on horseback . . . she had ridden all through the wastelands, bravely insisting that this was the greatest adventure of her life, not to be missed. It had not done a damned thing for her figure. She was just as dumpy as ever, and today she looked old.

The lucid moments were at once the best and the worst.

"Well, Princess?" he asked in his whisper. "Did you find that handsome man?"

"I think so, Father. But we have made no promises."

"Be sure," he said, and squeezed her hand. Then he began to mumble about repairs to the bandshell, which had been torn down before she was born.

Her mother's portrait had been cleaned and moved to one side. Alongside it hung Jalon's pastel sketch. It made her look absurdly young, a mere child.

Her father asked about Kinvale and seemed to understand some of what she said. He talked of people long dead and troubles long since solved. When pain struck and she offered to call the doctors, he refused. "No more of that," he said.

Much later, after a long quietness, he suddenly opened his eyes very wide. She thought it was another pain, but it seemed more as if he had remembered something. "Do you want it?" he demanded, staring at her.

"Want what, Father?"

"The kingdom," he said. "Do you want to stay and be queen? Or would you rather live in a kinder land? Now you must choose. So soon!"

"I think I have a duty," she replied. "I should not be happy evading a duty." He would approve of that, although she could not quite suppress her own resentment. Why must she be so bound, when ordinary people were not? She had never asked to be a princess.

He gripped her hand tightly in pain. "You have grown up!"

She nodded and said she thought so.

"Then you will try?" he asked. "You can do it, I think." His eyes roamed restlessly around the room. "Are we alone?"

She assured him that they were alone.

"Come close, then," he said softly. She bent over him and he whispered some nonsensical thing in her ear. She jerked up in surprise, for she had thought he was clear-minded. He smiled up at her weakly, as if that had been an effort. "From Inisso."

"Yes, Father."

"Ask Sagorn," he muttered. "You can trust Sagorn. Maybe Thinal, sometimes, but not the others. None of the others."

She thought that statement a harsh verdict on all the faithful servants and officials who had served Holindarn all their lives—

if that was who he meant. And who was Thinal? He was rambling. But Sagorn? Andor had said that Sagorn had returned after she had left, but she had seen no sign of him.

Her father winced suddenly, but then he said, "Call the council."

"Later," she said. "Rest now."

He shook his head insistently on the pillow. "I must tell them."

Just then Aunt Kade made one of her visits, and Inos told her to call the council. Doubtfully she went off to do so. In a short while they all trooped in, the bishop and Yaltauri and half a dozen others. But by then the king was mumbling about grain ships and white horses; the council withdrew.

After that, he seemed to sink rapidly. The silences grew longer, broken only by the hiss of the peat in the fireplace and a periodic cry of wind through the leaky west window. She recalled how that plaintive wail had frightened her when she was a child, and how that casement had always defied repair. Once or twice she thought she heard a faint creak from the ceiling, but she dismissed it as imagination. On Aunt Kade's next visit, Inos asked her to send a doctor, and thereafter she allowed the man to stay.

You can do it, he had said. Sitting by the bed as the long day passed, as the moments of consciousness became shorter and rarer, she felt a strange determination emerging, like a rock uncovered by the ebbing tide.

For him, she would try.

She would show them! And that thought seemed to give her strength she had not suspected she had. She waited, she endured, and she shed no tears.

The shadows moved. The day faded. Flames were set in the sconces. Finally, after the sun had set, when there had been a long time with no movement from her father beyond the shallow rise and fall of his chest, the doctor came and laid a hand on her shoulder, and she knew it was time to go. So she kissed the wizened yellow face and walked away. She went slowly downstairs, crossed the dressing room, down another flight, and paused in the door of the withdrawing room to look, and consider.

2

The council was gathered there, and some others, all waiting around in lamplight, for the windows were quite dark now. No one had yet noticed Inos in the doorway. Queens had no time for personal grief—she must look to her inheritance. She had discussed the problem often enough with Kade on the journey, and with Andor. Would Krasnegar accept a queen? A juvenile queen? The imps likely would, they had decided, but the jotnar were doubtful. Now her father had given her his realm, but he had not told his council; that might not matter very much, anyway, for the next move would be made by the hateful Yggingi, whose army held the kingdom. What would his terms be? Would she be forced to swear allegiance to his Imperial Majesty Emshandar IV?

So they were sitting or standing there, waiting as they must have waited all day, talking quietly; and the center of the group was Andor, slim and graceful in dark green, tall for an imp. He was the key to the kingdom, she thought. If she was to marry Andor, the council would accept him as her consort. He was young and handsome and personable and competent. Even Foronod seemed to be engrossed, smiling now with the others at some tale that would likely have made them all laugh aloud in a happier time. If Andor was the key, then Foronod was the lock, for he was a jotunn and probably the most influential. If the factor would accept Andor as king, then likely they all would. Except perhaps Yggingi.

Andor would not have returned with her had he not cared.

Then she was noticed. They turned to await her in sympathetic silence. Mother Unonini was there, black-robed and bleak-faced as always. Aunt Kade in silver and pink had been sitting at the bottom of the stairs like a watchdog. Bless her!

She hugged Aunt Kade and was hugged by the chaplain, smelling of fish. She wondered how she could ever have been frightened by this dyspeptic little cleric with her resentful air of failure and bitter exile.

One by one the men bowed, and she nodded solemnly in return: Foronod, grim, lank in a dark-blue gown, winter pale, with his white-gold jotunnish hair glowing against the outer dark of a window; old Chancellor Yaltauri, a typical imp, short and swarthy, normally a jovial but bookish man; the much older Seneschal Kondoral, openly weeping; the vague and ineffectual Bishop Havyili; the others.

"It will not be long," she told them.

Mother Unonini turned and headed for the stairs.

"You must eat now, dear." Kade led her to a table that had been laid out with white linen and silver and fine china, like a small oasis of Kinvale in the barren arctic, but bearing cakes and pastries that looked cumbersome and lumpish. And there—wonder of wonders!—balanced on its warming flame, Aunt Kade's gigantic silver tea urn, like a forgotten ghost from Inos's child-hood. The day she had met Sagorn and knocked over that urn—absurd, irrelevant, vulgar thing!—Father had joked about her burning down the castle . . . That insidious, unexpected, irrele-vant fragment of memory made a quick dash around her defenses and grabbed her by the throat and almost defeated her, but she averted her eyes quickly from the wretched tea urn and started to say that no thank you she couldn't eat a thing. Except that her mouth was full of pastry. So she sat down and stuffed herself, drinking strong tea poured by Aunt Kade from that same mon-strous urn, which was now only a very ugly utensil.

Then she looked up to see that Mother Unonini had returned. Inos rose slowly and was given another fishy hug. "Insolan, my child—I mean, your Ma . . ." The gritty voice hesitated, and then began a knell about the weighing of souls, and how much the Good had exceded the Evil in Father and all the predictable platitudes. Inos shut it out.

It was over, and she would shed no tears today.

It was a release.

There was some good in every evil.

There was also a medic, shuffling and awkward. She asked him, "What now?"

He began to mumble about the lying in state. She remembered her mother's lying in state in the great hall and the chains of weeping citizens filing by. So she told the man to go ahead, and some part of her was standing back, watching this masterly self-control of hers with amazement. Then there were more hugs from Aunt Kade and Mother Unonini, and a stronger one from Andor, and bows and mutterings from the other men, while she was vaguely aware that people were trooping through the room, head-ing up to the royal bedchamber. In a little while they carried the body back down, she supposed, but she turned her face away and ignored these necessary unpleasantnesses. Soon the great bell of the castle began to toll, slow in the distance, muffled and dread.

But the attendants departed at last, and the door was closed, and she could not ignore the world forever. The night had longer to run yet. When she turned around to face the men again, she discovered a newcomer—the odious, square-headed Proconsul Yggingi.

The king was dead; the ravens were landing. As always he was in uniform, clutching his crested helmet under one arm and rest-ing his other hand on the hilt of his sword of office, an elaborate and gaudy thing of gilt. She feared him, she thought, but only him. Anything or anyone else she could manage.

"Factor?" she said, knowing that Foronod was the most competent of the council. "What now? The city must be informed."

Foronod bowed and said nothing.

Which was not very helpful.

"Well?" she demanded. "When shall I be proclaimed queen?"

The craggy face remained without expression, but she could sense the fury burning below its jotunnish pallor. "That decision is apparently not presently within the jurisdiction of your late father's council, miss." He was biting the words. "Imperial troops have taken control of the palace and the town. Sergeant Thosolin and his men have been disarmed and confined. I suggest you address your inquiries to Proconsul Yggingi."

He bowed again and stepped back against the wall.

Inos restrained a mad impulse to burst into tears or throw herself into Andor's arms. She had led the predator back to her lair and now she must turn and give battle to it, to the monster whose thugs controlled her homeland. She looked expectantly and coldly—she hoped coldly—at the proconsul.

He lowered his head in a hint of a bow. "Perhaps we could have a word in private, Highness?"

Andor and Aunt Kade both started to protest.

"Highness?" Inos said.

She saw a glint of amusement in the piggy eyes. "Beg pardon—your Majesty."

Well! That might be her first victory. "Certainly, Excellency," Inos said. "Come with me."

Holding her chin up, she marched over to the doorway that led upstairs, wishing she had a long gown to swish impressively, realizing that she was still in her soiled riding clothes. Probably her hair was a mess, but at least she had not been weeping. She stamped up the stairs into the dressing room, with its wardrobes and chests and one large couch. It was really only a junk storage. She would have it cleaned out in the summer. The candles were inadequate, leaving the big room dim and crowded with shadows—which might be a good thing if it would help conceal her expression, for surely Yggingi was a much more experienced negotiator than she was. But she had nothing to negotiate. He was going to dictate his orders.

She stopped beside the couch, spun around, and said, "Well?"

He was still clasping his stupid helmet and his armor flickered with dozens of little candle flames. He was a square, broad man, a hard man, a killer. He moved too close, deliberately threatening.

"Did you get it?"

The question seemed so meaningless that she felt her mouth move and nothing came out.

"The word!" he snapped.

"What word?"

He flushed angrily. "Did your father tell you the word of power? Inisso's word?"

She was about to say "No!" and then she recalled that among all the other gibberish her father had spoken about Inisso . . .

Yggingi saw her hesitation and bared his teeth in a smile. "Do you know what it means?" he asked quietly.

She shook her head.

He took another half step closer and had to bend his head to look down at her. His breath was sour, and told her that the palace wine cellar had now been liberated.

"You have three things of value, little girl. One is a very pretty body. We may negotiate on that later, but I can find those anywhere, almost as good. You also have a kingdom—sort-of-have a kingdom. I never thought I wanted that, and now I've seen it, I'm sure. It certainly isn't worth fighting over, but I'm told that the jotnar are on their way, so I may have to fight. But the third thing you have is that word. And that I want. That is what I came for."

Gibberish! She doubted that she could recall much of the nonsense her father had spoken, but if this horror thought that she had something he wanted . . .

"What's it worth?"

He laughed. "Your looks. Your virtue. Your life. It's worth more than all of those."

She pushed down terror. She had expected him to order her to sign away her inheritance, or possibly to announce her engagement to Angilki. She had never expected this nonsense about words. "Why? My life for a word?"

"Do you know who's paying my troops? Your precious aunt, or whatever she is to you, the duchess of Kinvale."

Ekka! So it had been that damned hag after all! Inos tried to replace fear with anger, but failed. She did not speak.

"Two thousand imperials she gave me to bring you here, plus whatever I can squeeze out of Krasnegar. All she wants is you, with that word—sent back to marry her idiot son."

"Never!"

He grinned. "I agree. I never liked that deal. Besides, it's not possible. I closed the road, didn't I?"

She just looked at him in silence, bewildered, fighting to keep herself under control. She was crushed back against the couch and could not retreat.

"No way out until the ships come," he said. "I closed the road, I roused the goblins. I wanted to keep certain friends of mine from coming after me, but it also means that no one can get out! We're trapped!"

"How much?" she said with sudden wild hope. "How much to ransom Krasnegar?"

He chuckled. "Just the word—the word to ransom it from the jotnar. I must have that word!"

"Why?" He must be totally mad, and certainly there was a very strange look in his eyes.

"Because I'm a soldier! I have a talent for stamping out vermin. With a word—" Then he seemed to realize how little she understood of this raving. He wheeled around, marched back to the door, and shot the bolt. Then he tossed his helmet down on a chair and stalked her, as she retreated, until finally he had her against the wall. He grabbed her shoulder and grinned at the sight of her terror. He licked his lips.

"You begin to believe I'm serious? Well, I'll make you an offer, little miss. Give me the word, and I'll see you're proclaimed queen. I'll defend your throne from Kalkor, and from your rebellious subjects, too, and I promise I won't hurt you. Marry that Andor man if you want—I don't care about that. But otherwise I shall start now by breaking your pretty little nose, and go on from there until no man will ever want to marry what's left of you. I think my offer is worth considering, don't you?"

It was an extraordinary offer. It was better than she could have ever dared hope. No one could question her rule if she had Yggingi's armed might at her back. But could she believe him? Could she trust him? And could she recall the gibberish her father had spoken, and could Yggingi tell the difference if she simply made up some more gibberish of her own?

"Well?" he shouted. His fingers dug deeper into her shoulder. She tried to break loose and was appalled at his strength.

"I—"

A sudden noise—from above?

Yggingi raised his head and regarded the shadowed ceiling. "What was that?"

She did not know either. It had sounded like furniture moving above them, in the bedchamber, and she had thought all the medics and undertakers had gone. Dark with suspicion, Ygging wheeled and marched over to the doorway to the staircase up, drawing his sword as he went.

Inos fled to the other door and began to wrestle with the bolt, and for a terrifying minute it seemed to be too stiff for her, then it moved. She hauled the door open and fell into Andor's arms.

Well, one of his arms. He was holding his sword in his other hand. "All right, my darling?"

"Yes," she said. "I think so."

He pulled the door shut and used both arms, holding his sword behind her. Much better! He tried to kiss her, but she was frightened that a kiss might snap the thin thread holding her together, so she declined the kiss. But it was wonderful to be held.

"He's a horror!" she mumbled into Andor's shoulder.

"The worst sort of dreg," he agreed. "You go on down to the others and leave the proconsul to me."

She pulled away, startled. "No! Andor! He's a soldier—"

Andor flashed his teeth in a confident grin. "I shall be in no danger. It will be a pleasure."

"Fight him?"

"I'm quite capable, my princess. I just prefer not to do it before witnesses, so you go down."

He had never told her that he was a duelist—wonderful man! And no one had ever offered to commit a murder for her before. Just for a moment, she teetered on the brink of hysteria, then she recovered. "No, Andor! He has two thousand men here. You mustn't!"

"This may be my only chance to get him alone, Inos."

"No! I forbid it!"

"If you wish." Looking disappointed, he sheathed his sword. "He's only the first, you know."

"What?"

"The first one after your word of power. It's common knowledge that the kings of Krasnegar inherited one of Inisso's words. Everyone will assume that you have it, whether you do or not."

She broke loose. "I don't understand." Why was the proconsul not already coming after her?

"It would take too long to explain." Even in the darkness of the narrow stairwell, concern glowed on that handsome face. "You mustn't tell the word to anyone!"

"No," she said.

"No one!" he insisted. "They're dangerous to know, but much more dangerous if you tell anyone."

"Yes," she said, not understanding. "I'll remember."

He studied her for a moment. "There's no real defense, Inos, but there is one thing you could do that would help a little. It might make Yggingi hesitate a bit, and it would certainly cut off one line of attack."

She was totally confused now. "What's that, Andor?"

"Marry me. There's a chaplain down there. She can marry us on the spot. Tonight. Now."

"Andor!" Again she was at a total loss for words. Too many things were happening too quickly. Finally she said, "Dear Andor, that's a wonderful thought, but I can't decide something like that right now. And it would put you in danger, also!"

"No!" he said excitedly. He took her hand and began to lead her down the narrow stairway, speaking rapidly as if he were working it all out. "The factor says that Kalkor's coming to claim the throne. He'll be here as soon as the ice goes. Kalkor's a terror. No matter what Yggingi thinks, he'll wad up those imps and throw them away. But then he'll want to marry you."

"I thought he was married already?" she protested, before remembering what Aunt Kade had once told her about Nordlanders.

And Andor now confirmed it. They were already at the bottom of the stairs, outside the door of the withdrawing room, where everyone must still be waiting to hear the proconsul's terms. "Thanes change wives like shirts. Probably more often. But he can't marry you if you're married to me."

"He could solve that problem!"

"Only if he can find me!" Andor laughed. "I'm a good man at disappearing. Don't you see, Inos? That's your escape! Marry me, and I'll stay out of sight—I promise you I can do that easily enough, but I haven't got time to explain now. We'll let the jotnar kill off the imps. Then we'll go back to the Impire together in the spring!"

Again she wondered why Yggingi was not coming down the stairs after her. "And lose my kingdom? No, darling, I have a duty."

He smiled, and she heard it more than saw it in the dimness. "Good for you!" he said admiringly. "Inos, I love you! And if the kingdom is what you want, then we'll have to save it for you— and marrying me is still your best strategy!"

He was right, she thought. And then he had gone down on one knee before her. "Queen Inosolon, will you marry me?"

Her first, insane, thought was that she was filthy and bedraggled and wearing riding clothes, shivering in an icy stairwell lighted by one spluttering candle. All those wonderful gowns she had worn at Kinvale, in ballrooms, on terraces under moonlight— none of them had provoked a proposal. And her father . . . Then she told her mind to stop evading the question. With Andor she could face all of them.

"Yes," she whispered.

He jumped up and this time he did kiss her. Oh, Andor! Why had she not called him in to meet Father? Andor, Andor! Strong, and reliable, and—

"Quick, then!" He glanced up the stairs, so he also must be wondering what was keeping the soldier. "Now, my darling? Right now?"

"Yes!" She pushed open the door and marched in, holding Andor's hand. All across the big circular chamber, the spectators started in surprise. Those who were sitting on those flimsy gold and rosewood chairs rose slowly to their feet.

"Your Highness, your Holiness, Mother Unonini, gentlemen," Andor said. "Queen Inosolan has consented to become my wife."

She tried to see everyone's reaction at once, but they were too spread out. The imps, she thought, all looked pleased. Certainly Chancellor Yaltauri beamed. Bishop Havyili was asleep. Foronod frowned, but then he often did that. He did not speak. Aunt Kade . . . Aunt Kade was not smiling as she should be.

Queen or not, Aunt Kade was her guardian now, until she came of age. Or did that not apply to queens? How could she be a minor and reign as a queen at the same time? Inos led Andor over to her aunt.

"Well? Aren't you going to congratulate us?"

Flustered, Aunt Kade glanced at Andor and then back to Inos. "You are quite sure, my dear? It just seems . . . so soon . . ."

"Quite sure!"

Her aunt managed a smile. "Well, then certainly I congratulate you." But she did not look *certainly*—she looked *perhapsly*.

They hugged.

Still no Yggingi? Maybe they could manage what Andor had suggested—marry at once, before the proconsul came storming down to stop them. "Chaplain?" Inos said. "Marry us!"

That provoked some reaction. Aunt Kade's rosy complexion

turned almost as pale as her silver gown, and Inos had never seen that before. Mother Unonini went as black as her robe. The men muttered.

"That seems even more, well, unseemly," Aunt Kade said. "Your father is barely . . . It is very soon. Surely you could wait a while, my dear."

Inos glanced at the closed door. "I am sorry that it must be this way, but Andor and I think it would be advisable. Very quickly! A matter of state. Chaplain?"

Mother Unonini did not move from where she was standing. She pouted, bleaker than ever. "Inosolan, do you recall what the God told you? *Remember love!* Are you remembering love?"

Inos looked up at Andor. He looked down at her. They smiled. "Oh, yes!" she said.

"I think you should wait a—"

Inos did not let the chaplain finish. *"No!"* she shouted. "Now! Before the proconsul comes back! Quickly!"

Mother Unonini flinched and sought support from Aunt Kade, who bit her lip and muttered, "It might be . . . a reasonable precaution."

The chaplain shook her head vigorously. The men were mostly still frowning at this improper and irreverent haste. Inos wondered if she should be asking her council's permission, but if they did not suggest it, then she certainly would not.

Of course! Inos did not need the horrid chaplain. Indeed, she had been making a serious error. Gripping Andor's wrist, she dragged him across to Bishop Havyili, who was nodding peacefully on a sofa. The bishop was notorious for sleeping anywhere—even on horseback, her father had said.

"Your Holiness!"

"Mmm?" His Holiness opened his eyes.

"Marry me!"

"What?" Bewildered, the bishop struggled to his feet—old and dumpy and pathetically unimpressive for a bishop.

"Marry us!" Inos shouted, stamping her foot. "A matter of state! It's urgent! Now! At once!"

Blinking, but obedient, the bishop mumbled, "Dearly beloved friends—"

"Oh, never mind all that!" Inos stormed. Yggingi *must* be on his way now. "Get to the important part!"

The audience muttered again. The bishop spluttered and for a moment seemed about to argue. Then he changed his mind. "Are there any here among you present who know cause why this man

and this woman should not be united in sacred matrimony?''
Mercifully he did not pause for answers. ''Then do you, er . . .''

''Andor.''

''Andor, take this . . .''

His voice trailed off. His gaze went past Inos. The door creaked,
and she swung around in terror.

Slowly it swung open.

In came . . .

Impossible!

That was the second worst shock of that terrible day.

He bowed stiffly in her direction, across the whole width of the
room. He swallowed, hesitated. ''Sorry about your father, Inos—
your Majesty,'' he said hoarsely. ''Very sorry.''

He was holding Yggingi's sword of office.

3

Foronod said, ''The horse thief!'' and it was certainly Rap.

He was no longer the filthy goblin of the forest. He was shaved
and clean. His tangle of brown hair might have been cut with a
saw, but it was as tidy as it could ever be. He wore an ancient,
ill-fitting brown doublet and very patched gray wool hose. Only
the sword he was holding and the ludicrous raccoon tattoos around
his eyes marked him as anything other than some commonplace
flunky in the quaintly rustic palace of Krasnegar. But he did have
a nervous, rather sick expression on his very plain face.

And he did have the proconsul's sword.

Inos felt supernatural fingers stroking her scalp—a wraith? Why
would Rap's ghost haunt her, of all people?

Everyone else in the room seemed to have been turned to stone.

''Where is Proconsul Yggingi?'' Foronod demanded.

Rap glanced down at the inexplicable sword. ''Was that his
name?'' He coughed, as if feeling nauseated. ''He's dead.''

No, he was no ghost. Inos gasped with relief. It was Rap.

A mutter of shock was followed by a flickering of eyes as everyone tried to work out what his news meant—two thousand
Imperial soldiers in town and their leader murdered?

''Rap!'' Inos said. ''You didn't!''

He shook his head angrily. ''But I helped!''

And another youth stepped through the door behind Rap, a
young goblin, shorter and heavyset, with dark khaki skin and
short black hair, big ears and a long nose. He wore boots, hose,

and pants, but from the waist up he was bare, and the company hissed in disgust at this vulgarity.

He grinned widely, showing long white teeth. He held up a stone dagger—proudly, like a child bragging. Hand and blade glistened with fresh blood.

"This is Little Chicken of Raven Totem," Rap said. "He just avenged that village your proconsul slaughtered."

"I thought goblins preferred their victims tied up," Andor remarked coldly.

Rap seemed to notice Andor for the first time, and his gaze slid down to where Andor and Inos were holding hands, and back again. "This one made an exception. And I don't blame him."

Foronod moved to the downstairs door.

"Stop!" Rap shouted, lifting his sword slightly.

Inos glanced around the room. Only Andor had a weapon. The imps had disarmed the city.

The factor did stop. He turned to glare at Rap, who blushed.

"Sir . . . Sir, I guided your wagons for you once, didn't I? And that messed up my life. I need your help now . . . sir?"

Foronod's blue eyes were chips of polar ice. "A horse thief? A murderer?"

"Sir!" Rap hesitated. "Sir, when you heard I was the one who'd stolen the horses . . . were you at all surprised?"

The ice-blue eyes stared hard at him for a long minute. "Maybe I was at that."

"Then grant me a chance to explain," Rap pleaded. "It must be done now. There is another horse thief—and another murderer." He pointed his sword at Andor. "Ask him what he did with Doctor Sagorn."

Stunned silence. Then Andor squeezed Inos's hand and led her over to the table and a sofa, near Aunt Kade. "I think you had better stay here a moment, ladies," he said coldly. "There may be some danger."

"Danger?" Inos repeated. From Rap?

Then her missing wits seemed to fall back into place. "Rap!" she said. "How did you get here from Pondague?"

Rap looked surprised at the question, then a wisp of a grin crossed his face. "I ran."

"Inos, my darling," Andor said, "I don't think this is truly the boy you used to know." He made a scoffing sound. "Ran? That's quite impossible, obviously. Chaplain, Holiness—I think we may have a demon here. It appeared to us in the mountains on our way here. I'm quite sure that no one could have passed us on the trail."

Inos was looking at Rap's legs. He had grown taller since last summer and his face was thin, but she could not recall ever seeing hose filled more authoritatively than his were now. Ran?

Everyone else seemed to be leaving the situation to Andor. He strode forward a few steps. "Now, you—boy or demon or whatever you are—put the sword on that table. You'll be given a fair trial. Isn't that so, Chancellor?"

There was a silence, while nothing happened. Rap seemed to set his jaw more tightly, but he did not speak. The goblin grinned, eyes flickering around the faces.

Foronod was scowling. "Out with it! What are you implying about Doctor Sagorn?"

Rap answered without taking his eyes off Andor. "Only two of us left here, sir. You know that by the gear we took—saddles and bedrolls. I was never up in this part of the palace, but Andor was. What did he do with Doctor Sagorn?"

The factor looked at Andor, who said simply, "I know nothing about Doctor Sagorn. I left alone, on two horses I had purchased in good faith. As I told you, I had no idea that they were stolen. I got them from this boy, or whatever he is."

Foronod considered and then said, "There will have to be a trial. The proconsul is apparently dead and the Imperial forces will demand that we hand over the perpetrators."

Again he turned toward the door, and again Rap said, "Stop!" He looked to Inos and said stiffly, "Sorry, Inos. I have to do this. Factor, you owe me a little more time. Bolt the door please, so he can't escape. That man is a sorcerer."

Inos had to shout over the sudden babble. "Rap, stop that! You insulted Sir Andor before and I won't have it! He's a fine gentleman and I am going to marry him."

Rap shook his head, looking miserable. "I am truly sorry, your Majesty, truly sorry, but I have to. I wish it could wait until longer after . . . Well, it has to be done now."

"What exactly has to be done?" Andor inquired softly.

Again Rap appealed to Foronod. "Sir, if I ever did anything for you, will you please bolt that door?"

The factor frowned, shrugged, and went over to the downstairs door, picking up a massive pewter candlestick on the way. He shot the bolt, turned, and stood with his back to the door, holding the candlestick like a club.

Inos caught a pained look from Andor and said, "Rap!" an-grily.

"Please, everyone stand back," Rap said, and there was a stampede away from Andor, leaving him in isolation. With stud-ied unconcern he unclipped his cloak and tossed it gracefully over a chair. He was showing how a gentleman should treat such rude-ness, and Inos felt proud of him.

"Inos—your Majesty, I mean." Rap blushed at his error. "When that Andor is in danger, he turns into something else. It's the only way I know to show him up. I'm sorry."

Inos gasped at such insanity and the audience muttered. She felt very sad. "Oh, Rap! What happened to the old Rap I used to know? He was a sane, solid boy, not given to mad suspicions and delusions. I depended on that Rap! I . . . I liked him."

Rap turned very pale. He licked white lips and said, "Sorry, Inos," so quietly she could hardly hear him.

The calmest person in the room was Andor.

"Are you planning to challenge me to a duel, young man?"

"Sort of," Rap said.

"Just you, or your goblin friend as well?"

Rap shook his head. "Not Little Chicken." He turned his head and snapped something in goblin dialect. Little Chicken shrugged and moved away. That put him closer to old Kondoral, who be-came alarmed and edged sideways, out of reach.

"Well, go ahead!" Andor said. "If you won't drop that sword I shall have to make you drop it, as I am the only one armed."

"You know you're a much better swordsman than I am."

Andor shrugged. "A reasonable assumption, but we shall see."

Rap looked disgusted. "But you already know. You gave me lessons. Didn't you tell her Majesty that?"

Inos knew that Andor had felt confident of beating Ygginngi, a professional soldier. "Darling," she muttered, "please try not to hurt him any more than you must."

Andor might not have heard that quiet appeal. His blade hissed out, flashing gold flame back at the sconces. "Last chance! Drop that weapon."

Rap shook his head. "This is what you told me once, Andor—do you remember? No more wooden swords, you said. And something about earning the prizes or taking the punishment. So we play for real—showdown! Those are the rules. Ready?"

"Yes!" Andor started forward. A huge gray dog slunk in through the door at Rap's side, a dog as big as a wolf. It fixed yellow eyes on Andor and bristled menacingly. Inos heard herself cry out. She tried to move forward and Aunt Kade grabbed her wrist. The palace dogs had always followed Rap around . . .

Andor froze. Then he raised his left hand to his right shoulder, covering his neck with his arm.

Rap pointed, but the monster was already creeping forward toward Andor, who now began to back away, holding his sword stiffly in front of him.

Then his hip met the table and he could retreat no farther. As if that were a signal, the dog streaked across the room and flew for his throat like a silver arrow. Andor's sword stroke was hopelessly late, but his left arm was still high enough to catch the fangs. Man and beast fell back across the table amid a chorus of screams. Table toppled; china and silver and sword rattled down; the combatants rolled over and crashed to the floor. Aunt Kade released Inos, took one step, and expertly snatched the burner from below the tea urn as the urn itself toppled. Inos jumped aside hurriedly to escape a great explosion of tea—most of which seemed to head for Bishop Havyili—noting with relief that the castle would not burn down this time, either, and then both she and Kade backed off from the roaring, tangled scrimmage rolling toward their feet. Mother Unonini seemed to be screaming the loudest. The combatants writhed and thrashed. The wolf was growling, clothes ripping. Then Rap shouted, "Fleabag!"

The dog broke loose and backed off, snarling and showing teeth.

The man on the floor was not Andor.

More screaming.

The romances told of unfortunate women who went mad with grief. Inos wondered now if this was how such insanity felt, for surely what she saw could not all be really happening?

He was huge. Andor's elegant green doublet and hose had split in places and been ripped in others, revealing skin and a pelt of yellow hair. His left arm was dribbling blood, his chest was ripped and bleeding, also, but he was already sitting up, seeming unaware of his injuries.

"This is Darad!" Rap said sadly.

He was much bigger than Andor, and at least twenty years older. A jotunn, not an imp. He glared around the room with the ugliest, most battered face imaginable. Inos shrank back until a chair blocked her. Everyone else seemed to be pressed against the wall, staring wide-eyed.

Then the giant snatched up the sword and bounced to his feet. Foronod turned to unbolt the downstairs door.

"Stop that!" the giant roared, and the factor froze.

Darad looked to Rap. "Call off your pet, or I kill it."

Rap snapped his fingers and the great dog withdrew unwillingly, teeth bare, yellow eyes fixed on its former opponent.

Rap said, "Fleabag!" very loudly. With obvious reluctance, the dog slunk to his side. "Inos, I'm sorry about this. I had to warn you."

She found her voice. "Who are you? Where is Andor?"

The mangled face looked at her—cruel blue eyes, cruel. "Come here, Princess."

"No!" She tried to edge around the chair, and the monster moved like a striking snake, taking two huge strides, catching her arm, twisting her round and crushing her against him, her face in his chest, all in one blur of motion.

He chuckled gutturally. "Now we have a little security! Any trouble and the girl dies."

His strength was unbelievable—that one huge arm bound her immovably against a chest like a cliff. The icy touch against the back of her neck must be his sword. *Andor! Andor!* There was none of the faint odor of rosewater that she had noticed on Andor. This man stank of sweat, and faintly of goblin.

Then she made the mistake of trying to struggle—to bite and kick. Instantly the ogre twisted her arm up her back and squeezed all the air out of her, as if to show how easily he could snap her if he wished. Her ribs would collapse, her spine crack, she could not cry out, there was blackness and a roaring in her head, agony. Then suddenly he eased off, and she could suck in blessed air and her brain no longer seemed about to burst.

"Don't try that again!" he muttered.

No—Inos gasped, feeling her heart yammering like a mad bird inside her head, and also hearing the slower, level thump of the man's. He did not seem very worried by his predicament.

"Now—the dog behind the door!" he demanded.

Stupid Rap! Rap had called up this Darad-monster in place of Andor, but what could he possibly do to get rid of it? The reverse transformation would not be so easy.

And Rap was evidently trying to reason. She could not see, but she heard his voice, harsh and stubborn. "What are you going to do, Darad? You can't escape from here. Let her go. Give up!"

She felt a low growl rising inside the man before any sound came out. "The dog!" Cold steel touched the back of her neck again.

The door clicked as Rap obeyed. She felt the giant relax slightly. "Now drop the sword!"

With her head so awkwardly twisted, all Inos could see was Aunt Kade's horrified face, screwed up in terror. What was Rap doing?

"Drop it!" roared the giant.

She heard a thump that might be a sword falling. What were all the men doing? But they must be all hopelessly frozen. Again she felt that cold touch of steel at the nape of her neck.

"Now make your friend throw down his dagger!"

There was a pause, and she supposed Rap was obeying that order, also. She heard the goblin argue, then stop.

"That's much better!" the giant said. He spoke poorly and was probably slow-witted, although he could move faster than anyone she had ever seen. Blood from his arm was soaking through her doublet—she could feel it, like hot soup. "Away from the door, all of you!"

"You can't escape!" That was Foronod.

"Can't I? Then the girl dies first."

"No, you can't!" Rap again. "Call Sagorn. He's better at thinking, isn't he?"

But the men must have cleared the doorway, because Darad began to edge around the room, half carrying, half dragging Inos, keeping his sword arm toward the men.

She saw Aunt Kade and Mother Unonini, side by side, eyes wide with horror, mouths open. Darad went right by them, no doubt assuming that women were harmless.

But Kade was still holding the burner from the tea urn, and as soon as Inos was safely shielded by the giant's body, she removed the cover, took two fast steps forward, and threw burning oil all over his back.

4

Darad's agonized scream exploded against Inos's eardrums. She was hurled aside and fell headlong to the rug, hearing the sword clatter on floorboards nearby. She caught a glimpse of Rap and the goblin leaping forward as Rap seized a chair and swung it two-handed, shattering it on the giant's head. Even then, Darad seemed to throw himself down, rather than fall. He rolled over on his back to extinguish the flaming cloth, and Little Chicken landed on him with both feet. He jackknifed, throwing off the goblin, and had already started to rise when Rap disassembled more of Aunt Kade's rosewood furniture over his head. Then Rap reached for a third chair, but it was not needed.

Kade and the chaplain hurried to help Inos. The goblin bounced to his feet, lunged across the room, grabbed up Andor's discarded cloak, and was already ripping it into strips as he raced back to the prostrate jotunn. With astonishing speed, as if they had been practicing as a team, he and Rap bound the man's hands and feet, and suddenly the emergency was over.

Inos allowed Mother Unonini to lead her to the sofa, but then she pushed the chaplain away, not wanting anyone very close at the moment, for she was trembling, and queens must not tremble. She sat down and folded her hands in her lap and tried to concentrate on being regal. She was covered in cold tea and Darad's blood, of course, which did not help.

The older men were gathered around Kade, congratulating her on her quick-wittedness. Kade was preening, enjoying it. Not one of those men had done a damned thing of any use that Inos had seen, except stamp out a smoldering rug. It had all been Kade and Rap and Little Chicken.

The monster lay on the floor, tightly bound and reeking of burned hair. His back must be very painful, and his arm and head were still oozing blood, but he was staying silent, just glaring up furiously at the goblin, who was sitting cross-legged on his chest, leering triumphantly at him and playfully drawing little patterns in front of his face with the bloodstained dagger.

Rap was standing guard there, too, with the proconsul's sword in his hand. He was worried and seemed to be watching the goblin as much as the jotunn.

And now what was going to happen? Surely she could not take any more shocks this night? And she did not have Andor to lean on any more. Oh, Andor! She felt a great emptiness in her life—first Father, and then Andor . . .

Foronod stepped out of the group, accosting Rap. "You said you had an excuse for your horse thievery?"

Rap flushed. "Yes, I do. Andor!"

"You were still at least an accomplice!"

"He used occult power on me!"

Foronod grunted, sounding skeptical. The gangling jotunn could look down on Rap and was doing so now. There were very few men in Krasnegar who could withstand the factor's authority when he was in that mood, but Rap thrust out his jaw and scowled around the circle of other men, who were all listening intently.

"And on you!" he shouted. "You were going to accept him as king!"

He had struck a nerve there, the factor flinched. "In any case you now must answer a murder charge—you cannot blame Andor for that." He paused, suspicious. "How did you get up there, anyway? Either you've got a lot more occult power than you ever admitted, or you had accomplices."

"Accomplices?" Rap could look extraordinarily stupid when he wanted to. He turned his idiot expression on Inos. "Your Majesty? Do I answer this man's questions?"

Foronod spun on his heel. He was already at the door before Inos had scrambled to her feet.

"Factor! We did not hear your request for permission to withdraw." Was that her, really her?

The tall man swung around and returned her glare. "Good night, miss!" He bowed perfunctorily.

"That is not sufficient!" But she was too shrill, and she had almost stamped her foot.

Foronod was not intimidated by juvenile females. "It will have to do for now, miss. I shall inform the soldiers that their leader is dead. I expect they will wish to take suitable action."

Rap! He had tried to help her, and Inos would have to defend him somehow. She took a deep breath and forced herself to speak calmly. "You will do no such thing!"

Foronod's bony face was well suited for registering disdain. He paused with the door already open. "Indeed? And what do I say when I am asked where the proconsul is?"

Now there was a very good question! Inos looked at Rap, who shrugged; at Mother Unonini, who frowned; even at the goblin, who scratched his disgustingly bare chest and grinned all over his ugly, bristled face.

Aunt Kade sighed resignedly. "Tell them he is in conference in the queen's bedroom and must not be disturbed."

That suggestion was greeted with shock and silent outrage.

"What is this tale of Thane Kalkor?" Inos inquired.

The factor smiled, thin-lipped. "He has been informed of the situation. We expect him as soon as the pack ice clears the shore. How many men he is bringing I am not sure, but I expect they will suffice. A ratio of one jotunn to four imps is usually ample."

She noted the scowls on the faces of the imps present, a few grins from the other jotnar. But the door was still open and she must buy time to think before they all started pouring down the stairs and everything got out of hand.

Not that things were very well *in* hand at the moment.

"Kalkor is coming at your invitation?"

"An invitation of which I was one signatory, miss. Jotnar will not accept rule by a woman."

Half the population of Krasnegar were jotnar.

"That may be the law in Nordland, but there is no such law here. Chancellor Yaltauri, how do you feel about this treason?"

"You needn't appeal to him," Foronod said. "Months ago he sent off a letter to the imperor, petitioning for a protectorate status."

Inos wavered on the edge of despair. What use now was Kinvale? What use dancing and elocution and scales on the spinnet? What use embroidery and sketching? Why had her father not taught her some statecraft while there was still time—given her fencing lessons, even, or explained politics and what made men act like beasts?

Somehow she managed to step back from the abyss. "Very well!" she said. "You may withdraw, but you will not mention the proconsul unless you are asked. In that case you may follow my aunt's recommendation, and I shall worry later about my reputation. All those of you willing to accept me as your rightful queen please remain behind. The rest of you may leave."

Then she stood there and watched her hopes dribble out the door, one by one, defiant or apologetic or shamefaced. The last one to go was Mother Unonini, who stood by the door and hesitated.

"I offer you a blessing, child."

"If you were a loyal friend you would not be leaving," Inos replied waspishly. "If you are leaving I don't want it."

The door thunked closed.

Inos stalked across in a most unregal fashion and slammed the bolt. Then she turned to survey the wreckage of the room, chairs awry or shattered, one rug bejeweled with smashed china and a sea of tea stain, another a charred mess stinking of burned oil, another bearing a prostrate giant in shredded green garments, glaring death wishes at her. The fire had gone out and many of the candles, also. The stench of burning hung in the shadows, and the place looked like the aftermath of a riotous party. She wondered what the time was—it felt like the small hours of tomorrow.

Kade and a goblin . . . and Rap.

"I seem to have inherited a very small kingdom," she said bitterly.

Still standing guard over the prisoner, looking absurd in his tattoos, Rap sent her a very faint, wry little smile. "Then I can be master-of-horse and sergeant-at-arms both?"

"Oh, Rap!" He thought he had been helpful, and certainly he had meant well, but he had cost her any chance she might have had of winning her kingdom. By exposing Andor he had made her seem a fool and had also made the members of the council feel duped. They all resented that and they were blaming her. Obviously in their eyes she was not fit to be a queen. Without their support she had nothing. Had Rap not intervened, she would have been married to Andor by now and in a better position to face down the terrible Kalkor.

Or perhaps she would have been Yggingi's prisoner.

Or wedded to that horrid Darad ogre, also? She shuddered.

So Rap had helped and apparently he was the only one loyal to her. At the same time as she wanted to scream at him, she also wanted to run and hug him.

And for a moment their eyes passed that message. But it would not be fair. They were not children anymore. *Don't smile too much at the servants,* her aunt had taught her. She managed to walk over to him calmly, and she took his hands in hers. Big, strong hands. Man's hands. "Thank you, Rap! I am sorry I ever doubted you. I was horrid to you in the forest—"

"It was Andor did that! He made me steal horses, too!"

"Well, I'm very grateful for all your help and your loyalty."

For a moment he just stood there, staring dumbly at her, and she actually saw the shiny gems of perspiration appear on his forehead. Then he blushed scarlet and looked down at his feet.

"My duty, Majesty."

So the danger was past. *Oh, poor Rap!*

"The first thing we have to do is to think how to get you out of here," she said. "You hid in the top chamber, I suppose? Rap, I do so want to hear how you worked all these miracles! But first we must get you to a safe place."

"There isn't one," he said somberly. "That bolt won't stop a couple of thousand imps, and they'll be coming soon. I'd better just turn us in, me and Little Chicken. If they put off the execution until the jotnar get here, then Kalkor may pardon us. Maybe."

Inos clenched her fists. "There has to be a better idea than that! Aunt Kade?"

"I don't know, dear." Her aunt was leaning back on the sofa, looking old and bedraggled and utterly weary. "I managed to ruin your reputation, but I think I agree with Master Rap—it won't hold for very long."

"Rap, who is Little Chicken? A friend?"

"He's my slave." Rap was turning pink again. "And he won't let me free him."

Slave? Torture? "How did you . . . Why not, for Gods' sake?"

Rap had never been much of a man for smiles, but once in a while he had been known to indulge a sort of shy grin, and momentarily that showed now. Strangely she discovered that it was the most welcome thing she had seen all day.

"Because he wants to kill me. It's quite a complicated story."

"It must be!" But it would have to wait. Inos looked down at the prisoner, Darad. Had she been going to marry this? She shuddered again. "And this horror is Andor?"

"I don't know. He changes into Andor, or Andor into him. And I think they're Sagorn and Jalon the minstrel, too."

"Sagorn?" she said. "That must be what Father meant! He said I could trust Sagorn, but not the others, except maybe Thinal. Who's Thinal?"

Rap looked surprised. "No idea. But we can try to call up Sagorn, if you think we can trust him. I'm frightened of this monster getting loose."

"How can you do that?"

"Let's find out." Rap dropped on one knee and said politely to Darad, "Please will you turn into Doctor Sagorn?"

The absurdity of the request made Inos want to giggle, and she must not start down that slippery slope. The giant's ruined face twisted in anger. He growled an obscenity and strained against his bonds and the goblin's weight. He was obviously in pain, sweat mingling with the blood on his forehead.

Rap smirked meanly at him. "I shall let Little Chicken try to persuade you, then. That would be fair, wouldn't it? After all, you introduced us."

Little Chicken, still sitting on the man's chest, started to grin again, obviously understanding at least some of the talk.

"You wouldn't!" Darad growled from the floor.

"I would!" Rap said.

Little Chicken was certainly following the conversation. With no further ado, he coldbloodedly poked a finger in Darad's eye.

He howled. "Tell him to get off, then!"

Rap motioned for the goblin to rise. He stood up, and the man on the floor was Sagorn.

Little Chicken hissed loudly and jumped back.

Rap said, "Gods! That's quite a trick, isn't it?"

Again Inos remembered the ladies in the romances who went

mad with grief; she wondered how many of them could have had this much fun first.

"Doctor Sagorn!" Aunt Kade beamed, and Inos half expected her to add, *How nice that you can join us.*

The old man smiled up at them bitterly. "If you trust me, then you won't mind if I remove these bonds?" Despite his undignified position, his sparse white hair was tidy, and he seemed calm and composed. He slipped his wrists free easily, for the tethers had been fitted to Darad's mightier limbs.

Rap cut his ankles free, also, and then helped him to rise. "Let's see if we can find something better for you to wear, sir."

Darad's huge body had ripped Andor's garments open, and the shreds were barely decent on Sagorn. They were also soaked in tea and blood. Rap turned to Little Chicken and spoke in goblin. The reply was brief.

"What did he say?" Inos asked.

Rap sighed. "He told me to get it myself. He has very exact ideas of a slave's duties."

So Rap ran upstairs and came down with a brown woolen robe. Fleabag, now released, indulged himself in a tour of the room, sniffing vigorously and cleaning up the remains of the food.

The lanky old man stepped into the stairwell for a moment and returned wearing the gown, his dignity restored. He bowed to Aunt Kade and then to Inos. She remembered how he had terrified her at their first meeting, but the glittery eyes and eagle nose held no threat for her now, although she had just witnessed a very obvious sorcery. She wondered if that was because she was older, or whether she was just numb from the daylong battering.

"My sympathies, ma'am," he said. "Your father was a good friend to me in years past, and I grieve his sad end. I did everything within my skill."

She nodded, not trusting herself to speak.

Sagorn made himself comfortable on a chair next to Kade's sofa and everyone else sat down, also, with Little Chicken cross-legged on the floor, scowling deeply as he struggled to follow the impish tongue.

"You will want an explanation, I suppose?" the old man asked.

"Please," Inos said. "That was an unconventional entrance."

He smiled his thin-lipped grimace at her for a moment. "You are no longer the young lady who panicked at the mention of yellow dragons. Kinvale has done wonders for you. Can Andor claim some of the credit, I wonder?"

He was seeking to dominate her. "The explanation, please?"

"Very well." He turned to Rap. "Your guess was remarkably close, young man. There are five of us—myself, Andor, Jalon, Darad, and Thinal, whom you have not met. Many, many years ago, we together gave cause for annoyance to a powerful sorcerer. He placed a spell on us, a curse. Only one of us can exist at a time. That is the whole of the matter."

"But you are different persons?" Rap had always frowned ferociously when thinking hard.

"Quite different. Andor and Thinal were brothers, the rest of us merely friends. We have never met since that terrible evening long ago. We share a single existence and we also share the same memories. How did you escape from the goblins, by the way?"

Rap did not answer that. "A very convenient curse! You appear and disappear at will—"

"No! A terrible curse!" Sagorn glared. "We have been seeking release from it for longer than you would believe. Take Darad, for example. Would you like to be burdened with that man's memories? Murder and rape? He is a mad dog, crueler than a goblin. And we do not come and go at will, only when called. None of the rest of us likes to call Darad, so it may be years before he exists again—but when he does appear, he will still have a burned back and a cracked head and a sore eye and a ripped arm. I hope none of you is within his reach at that moment."

"And of course he will not be bound?"

"Not unless whoever calls him is bound."

They all thought about that for a moment.

"Father said I could trust you," Inos said, "or sometimes Thinal. Who is Thinal?"

"Thinal? He was our leader." The old man stretched his bloodless lips in a smile. "Yes, he is trustworthy after a fashion, as long as you have nothing precious around—like a ruby brooch, for example."

"He stole my brooch?"

"He can climb a blank wall like a fly. He also lifted the hostler's keys off his belt for Andor. He will oblige in such matters, but he will also steal for sport. As well as being light-fingered, he has a peculiar taste in practical jokes, but he does have a personal rule that he will always call back the one who called him, and we trust him in that sense. I can call any of the others at any time, but I have no control over what that one may do then, or whom he will call next."

"I find this idea rather confusing, Doctor." Aunt Kade could always be relied on for a massive understatement when needed.

"Tell us how you came and went. My brother sent for you last summer?"

He spoke more respectfully to her, gazing blandly across the debris and ruin. "He did, ma'am, and it was Jalon who received the message. He decided to answer the call and caught a ship for Krasnegar. That was a remarkable success for Jalon—in the past he has been known to take the wrong boat because he thought it had a prettier name. But he managed to reach Krasnegar, went to the king, and called me."

"But I don't see how you knew about my dragon silk," Inos complained.

"Jalon saw it at the gate. I told you, we share memories." The old man waited a moment, as if she were a slow child, then addressed himself again to Kade. "As soon as I examined Holindarn, I saw that he was not likely to live long. I think he had already guessed that. I needed medicines, so Jalon had to go south again. I am old, you see, and the others are growing concerned about me, so they do the traveling. Jalon decided it would be more romantic to go overland."

"And that was where I got involved," Rap said, remembering the picnic in the hills.

Sagorn nodded. "You revealed occult powers to Jalon, and so to all of us. I told you that we have been trying to escape from our curse. We had two ways to try—either we could persuade another sorcerer to lift the spell, or we could seek to learn enough words of power to do it ourselves. I have spent my life in studies to that end, striving to know more of those elusive words." He smiled his thin, cynical smile. "I was the youngest, once. I was ten. Darad was twelve, I think."

"But . . ."

He shrugged. "But I was smart, and Darad was already big, so Thinal let us join his gang. We broke into houses—even then, he was a skilled cat burglar—until we happened to choose the house of a sorcerer. That was not a wise thing to do! I have not seen them since." He paused, seeming lost in memory for a moment. "Always one of us *is*, four *are not*. To live is to age, of course . . . I have spent so many years in libraries and archives that now I am by far the oldest. Darad almost never gets into trouble he can't handle, so he rarely has to call for help. He is starting to feel his years, too. Jalon is easily bored, so he soon calls someone else—usually Andor, for some reason. Thinal . . . Thinal never stays for long. He has hardly changed at all."

"But you have occult powers of your own," Inos said. "Did the sorcerer give you those?"

He laughed scornfully. "If you had ever met a sorcerer, you would not ask! No. I doubt that you wish to hear that tale."

"Please do go on, Doctor," Aunt Kade said brightly. "This is a most interesting narrative."

He flashed her a calculating glance. "Very well, your Highness. In Fal Dornin I found a woman of middle years who knew a word of power—a single word. I called Andor."

"And he charmed it out of her?" Inos asked acidly.

Sagorn smiled his sinister smile. "Seduced it out of her. Of course it affected each of us in turn. I became a better scholar, Jalon a finer singer, and Darad a more deadly fighter. The next time he existed, he went back to Fal Dornin, sought out the woman, and strangled her."

Inos shuddered. "No! Why?"

"God of Fools!" Rap jumped up and rushed to the door. He pulled the bolt and went racing off down the stairs. Fleabag loped in pursuit.

"Rap!" Inos yelled, too late.

Sagorn smiled grimly. "He has gone to bolt the lower doors, I imagine. Master Rap has farsight, you know."

"*Rap* does?" Dull old Rap? Solid, ordinary Rap?

He nodded. "To a remarkable degree. That was why Andor went out of his way to befriend him. He must know a word, although he denies it. Either it is a very powerful word, or else— I have been wondering if the words themselves may have different properties, and his happens to fit his native talents particularly well. He has an astounding control over animals and also an astounding farsight. Yet he does not seem to have any foreseeing ability, and certainly his mastery does not work on people, as Andor's does. So he must know only the one word. Interesting! He has probably seen the soldiers coming."

Inos had almost forgotten their plight. "That was why we wanted you!" she exclaimed. "How are we going to save Rap and Little Chicken from the imps? What is going to happen when Kalkor gets here? How—"

Sagorn raised a slender, blue-veined hand. "You forget, child, that I know your problems! Andor and Darad were here, so I know. Don't worry about the imps. Their leader is dead. Tribune Oshinkono is no great warrior. He will have absolutely no desire to tangle with the notorious Kalkor. He and his men will be off down the trail to Pondague long before the jotnar arrive."

"How . . ." But of course Sagorn knew all that because Andor had made friends with Ygginginge's deputy on the journey north. Andor made it his business to know everyone. What Andor had known, Sagorn knew. Confusing! "But what about Rap? And what about me having to marry Kalkor?"

"Kalkor I do not recommend!" For the first time the old man looked sympathetic. "Not as bad as Darad, but compared to Kalkor, Ygginginge would have made a model husband. He will claim the throne, then force you to marry him to confirm that claim."

"Then what?" she asked glumly.

He pulled a face, twisting the clefts that flanked his mouth. "Krasnegar would not contain Kalkor for long—roistering and pillage are his bent—but he could keep the title and leave a subordinate here to rule for him. He will beat your word out of you, I expect. Then take a son off you, more than likely. Yes, that would be about his program."

"And after that?"

Sagorn did not answer but she could guess the answer.

"And after that I shall be of no further use to him!"

The dog came bounding into the room. Inos rose and crossed to the stair, arriving just as Rap came running up, flushed and panting. He slammed the door and shot the bolt. "Should have gone sooner," he said between puffs. "Only three doors between us and them."

"Rap," she asked softly, "what's this about you having farsight, and magical powers?"

He flinched as if he were a small boy caught with both hands in the molasses, then nodded guiltily.

Puzzled by his reaction, Inos said, "Well, that's wonderful!" She smiled encouragingly to put him at ease. "Now I know why we never let you join in the hide-and-seek games! I've always wondered about your knack for horses—and dogs. I'm not surprised to hear that it's occult."

He gaped stupidly at her. "You don't mind?"

"Mind? Of course not! Why should I mind?" What was it to do with her, except that Rap would make a superb palace hostler when he was older? "I'm supposed to have some magic of my own now, although I don't know what sort of powers I'm expected to demonstrate. But magically we're both the same, apparently."

His big gray eyes blinked several times, then a scarlet tide flowed into his face, and he looked down at his boots. Of course shyness was quite understandable in a boy of his age, with no schooling or training.

She took a quick glance to make sure the others could not hear. "Rap, I didn't know that Sir—that Andor had made friends with you when he was here before."

"Well, he did! I didn't sell him horses in bars—"

"I'm sure you didn't." Even to think of Andor still hurt. "But did he ever speak . . . I mean, you must have talked . . . Did he ever mention Kinvale, or . . ." Deep breath. "Did he ever talk about me?"

Rap looked blank. "You mean he knew you before? He told me he didn't even know where Kinvale was, exactly! And he certainly never told me he'd met you already!" He seemed to be growing angrier and angrier as he spoke.

Relieved, Inos gave him another soothing smile. "Come, then, let's see what we can do about these imps." She led him back to the others. Despicable Andor! Why were men all such liars and cheats? So faithless!

She went over to Sagorn, who was making polite conversation with Kade.

"Well," she demanded. "What are we to do?"

Sagorn scratched his chin thoughtfully. "We have four ways out of this, I think."

"We do?" Inos found that unbelievable, but he seemed confident, so perhaps the celebrated sage was about to justify his reputation.

"The simplest would require a friendly sorcerer. You don't happen to have one handy, do you?" He chuckled ponderously, like some wise old grandfather teasing children.

Inos felt a surge of annoyance at the mockery. Rap sensed it, also, and rolled his eyes.

Sagorn saw that and scowled. "Secondly, then, we could hide in the topmost room and trust the aversion spell, but that seems to have worn thin now. So we only have two choices, wouldn't you say?"

"The Darad man killed the woman in Fal Dornin to strengthen his power?" Aunt Kade asked, and for a moment Inos was baffled.

Sagorn, though, had turned to Kade with surprise and perhaps respect. "Yes. To tell a word weakens it."

"Halves it?"

"Not necessarily halves it, apparently. It is a great mystery to me why there should be any weakening at all; if you tell your

favorite recipe to a friend, that does not spoil the next cake you
bake.'' He scowled. ''Even the most respected texts do not agree!
Perhaps the weakening would be a half if you were the only person
who knew the word. Would telling to a third person reduce its
power by a third? Then by a fourth when you told another? I don't
know, after a lifetime.''

Kade was still blinking at all that as the old man plunged ahead
with his lecture, waving a bony finger to make his points as if he
had been bottling up his knowledge inside himself for years and
welcomed an audience.

''So not necessarily a half. After all, the words have been
around a long time, so each may already be known by many
people, perhaps dozens. One more person may make no difference or a lot. And how could you compare magic, or weigh it? It
must be as hard to measure as beauty. Can you say that Jalon is
twice as fine a singer as another, or three times? That a poem is
twice as lyrical? But a shared word is weakened—until someone
who knows it dies. Then the others' power is strengthened again.
That is why they are so rarely shared, why they are usually passed
on deathbeds—as your father told you his?'' He peered from under shaggy white brows at Inos.

She hesitated and then nodded.

''You must guard it well! You have been displaying remarkable
endurance for your age, child. Andor noticed tonight and so did
Yggingi. You are of royal blood, and a very determined young
lady, but the words have that effect on people, a sort of armor. Of
course neither could be certain, but they both assumed that you
had been told the word.''

''Everyone seems to have known about it but me!''

''They are always kept secret. I found hints of the Krasnegar
word in a very old text. That was why I—actually it was Jalon
then, also—why we first came here and met your father. He was
still crown prince at the time. He and I became friends and did
some journeying together. Knowing that he would inherit a word,
I made sure that he met the others, so he would know them if
they came after him later. They all felt that I had betrayed them,
of course.'' He sighed deeply. ''It is not only the others' evil
memories that are a burden. They have mine, also, and I can keep
no secrets from them.''

Inos thought about that. Perhaps it was not so surprising that
this strange group of invisible men would strive to be released
from their curse.

"But this word of power that you—Andor—learned from the woman in Fal Dornin? It did not break the spell?"

Sagorn stared at the floor sadly, shaking his head. "No. One is not enough. Probably we need three or maybe even four. And, knowing a word, we dared not then approach a sorcerer, for sorcerers are always on the lookout for more power." He rose stiffly. "The imps will be fetching axes. I am slow on stairs, so perhaps we should begin?"

"Begin what?"

"Begin our climb," he said. "We must go to the chamber of puissance at the top of the tower."

"Why?"

He bared irregular old teeth in a triumphant grimace. "To consult the magic casement, of course."

Faithful found:
>   So spake the Seraph Abdiel, faithful found
>   Among the faithless, faithful only he:
>   Among innumerable false, unmoved,
>   Unshaken, unseduced, unterrified,
>   His loyalty he kept, his love, his zeal.
>   Milton, *Paradise Lost*

❰ TEN ❱

Insubstantial pageant

1

Rap could tell that Inos had not expected the suggestion, for she colored angrily. He was managing not to stare at her, for when he did, and their eyes met, he was sure he started blushing at once, and certainly he felt as if he were all hands and feet and worried if his hair was a mess—it always was, of course . . . So he was pretending not to look.

But he could not keep his farsight off her. She was wonderful!

What fools they were, all those stupid old men! Why had they not seen what a marvelous queen she would be? She was a queen to her fingertips, noble and regal even in those bedraggled old clothes. He had been amazed by her beauty in the forest and he was still in awe of that, but now he could sense her grace, her royal bearing, her *majesty*. Her father's death had not broken her spirit, nor the horrible fright and disappointment he, Rap, had been forced to inflict on her to unmask Andor.

Any lesser woman would have blamed him for that, would have cursed him and spurned him. But not Inos! She had royal courage. She was not afraid of his farsight, like all his other friends had been.

Kinvale had changed her. She was no longer the girl he had grown up with, the playmate of his childhood. He felt a little sad about that.

But he had always known that she would be his queen, not . . . not anything else. He had said he would serve her, and so he would, and be proud to. And right now he was proud of the way she was standing up to that stringy old doctor with his sneering manner and stupid jokes about sorcerers.

"My father wouldn't let you do that!" she said angrily.

"Ah, yes, the spy," Sagorn said unpleasantly. "You heard more than you admitted that day, then?"

Inos blushed harder and looked furious. Rap felt himself bristle, wishing he could stop this sinister old scholar from insulting his queen. Whatever the king had said about him being trustworthy, he had obviously betrayed Rap to Andor.

He began moving toward the door. "Your father, child, did not have an army of impish cutthroats coming up the tower after him at the time. Now, did you or did you not seek my counsel?"

Inos set her teeth, but obviously she was going to give in and let Sagorn go up the tower. There was a dead body upstairs, and she had suffered quite enough already without having to look at that. Rap moved quickly, to reach the doorway first, and Little Chicken scrambled up and followed.

The room one floor up was very gloomy, filled with gigantic shadows cast by a single small candle flame. Rap hurried across to where Yggingi lay, just inside the other stairwell. The goblin would always extend trash's duties to include anything that let him show off his strength, and as soon as Rap took hold of Yggingi's ankles. Little Chicken shoved him aside. "Out window?"

That gruesome thought had not even occurred to Rap. "Ugh! No. In that closet."

The goblin dragged the corpse across the room and tucked it away among the king's robes, while Rap dragged a rug over and covered the puddle of blood. He hoped Inos would not wonder why it was there, and that the blood would not soak through. By the time he had done, the other three had arrived.

Sagorn stood a moment, breathing hard. "But you must understand," he was saying, "that we have no common purpose except to be released from the curse, and therefore to seek out more of the words. Otherwise we all go our own ways.

"Jalon soon got lost in the forest, and he called Andor. Andor did not have my scruples toward your father, and hence his daughter." He made a small bow to Inos and then headed for the couch. "So Andor went to Kinvale to make your acquaintance. He even dreamed of becoming a king, I regret to say."

"When he told us that he brought you back to Krasnegar afterward," Inos asked, "then he was sort of telling the truth?"

The old man leaned back, chuckling breathlessly. "Yes, he was, for once. Here he had two words to chase: yours, when you got it; and Master Rap's. By the sort of improbable chance that the words produce, he arrived at Krasnegar just as Rap was revealed as a seer.''

Rap closed the down door and bolted it. Little Chicken started playing with the bolt, flicking it back and forth, showing childish curiosity and delight. Rap listened to Sagorn's story with half his head. The other half was sighting. The imps had already found axes and were breaking down the door into the robing room. He should be flattered that they were sending a hundred men after him, he supposed.

"Your father sank faster than I had expected," Sagorn continued. "So Andor decided to go south and fetch you. He was annoyed that he could not charm Master Rap's word out of him. Nor would he give it when threatened by the goblins. How did you escape, young man?''

Rap told them briefly. Fleabag thumped his tail on the floor at the sound of his name. Little Chicken scowled, so he must be picking up impish as fast as Rap had picked up goblin. It would be harder for him, though, for impish was a more complex dialect.

"Darad is a fool," Sagorn said. "I despise his murdering ways, but he is not even efficient in them. He should have asked the goblins to extract the word from you. They would have been happy to demonstrate their skills.''

Except that Rap knew no word of power to tell; he shivered. "The imps are almost through into the robing room, your Majesty.''

Sagorn sighed and rose from the couch. "Next floor, then.''

"You chased me down these stairs once, Doctor," Inos said. "I thought at the time that you were remarkably unwinded.''

"No. Thinal did the running for me. The curse does have its uses, I admit.''

Rap called to Little Chicken for help and began pushing one of the big cupboards over to the door. Then they fetched another. Those might gain a few minutes—for what, though? When he crossed to the stairs, Inos's voice came echoing eerily down from above.

". . . exactly does it do?''

"It is a last relic of Inisso's works.'' The old man's voice came in bursts, now, as if he were very short of breath. "Magic casements—like talking statues and preflecting pools—are a supreme test of a sorcerer. They will show the future . . . and give advice.

That is . . . the scene they show . . . is a hint . . . of the best
course to take . . . a view down the best path . . . as it were.''

"Why would my father not let you try it, then?"

Sagorn had reached the bedroom door and stopped again,
wheezing. "If he had, it might have warned him not to send you
to Kinvale, and then this trouble might have been averted.''

"How could it have done that? A window do that?"

"It might have shown you here at Winterfest, perhaps? I admit
that it is dangerous. It drove your great-grandfather mad.''

Rap did not like the sound of that, remembering the awesome
glow he had provoked in the casement when he went near it—and
remembering, also, the strange apparition who might have been
Bright Water, witch of the north. She had gabbled something
about *foresight*. She had accused Rap of blocking her foresight.
Could there be a connection there?

Inos hurried across the bedroom, the death chamber. "Let us
go straight up," she said, and her voice almost cracked.

Rap felt a mad impulse to run after her and take her in his arms
to comfort. He wanted that so badly that he trembled. He kept
remembering how she had kissed him good-bye, almost a whole
year ago now. But queens did not kiss factors' clerks—or horse
thieves.

All the rest of Krasnegar had spurned him, and she had not.
He had never doubted that she would remain his friend, once she
was free of Andor's witchery. It was very difficult to remember
that she was his queen. If she were wearing a royal robe and a
crown it might be possible, but despite her royal bearing in that
shabby leather riding outfit, with her gold hair flying loose halfway down her back, she was still too much the companion of his
childhood—on horses, clambering over cliffs . . .

Sagorn was still catching his breath.

"You know I have only been up there once in my life?" Princess Kadolan said. She was puffing, also, but perhaps that was
only from politeness. "My grandfather died in a fire, I thought.''

The bedroom was brighter, with more candles still burning in
the sconces. Sagorn went to study the two portraits over the mantel. "Yes, but he was mad before that.''

"Oh, dear! You think he saw his death through the casement
and the sight drove him insane?"

The old man shrugged. "That is what your brother thought,
and your father before him. It is an interesting paradox. The
prophecy drove him mad, but had he not been mad, then he would

not have been locked up, so he could have escaped the flames. Curious, isn't it?''

Deciding again that he did not like this sinister, cold-blooded old man, Rap began heaving a dresser toward the door, and the goblin came to help.

The imps were into the robing room now, crossing to the stairs that led up to the antechamber. Once Rap reached the uppermost room, he would be unable to watch what they were doing. He hoped Inos was right to trust Sagorn, but it was not his place to advise her, and he had no advice to offer anyway. The situation looked hopeless. Once the proconsul's body was discovered, the culprits would be lucky if they were just thrown in the dungeon and not beheaded out of hand.

With the goblin at his heels, he followed the others, climbing the last flight unwillingly, sensing the blankness above him. When his head broke through that invisible barrier, he felt like a worm coming out of the ground. Again he was seized by a giddy excitement, an exhilaration stemming from the combination of great height and occult farsight, producing a divine—a detestable—ability to spy on everyone in Krasnegar outside the castle.

Sagorn was leaning one hand against the wall and breathing hard. Inos held a candle, standing with her aunt close to the doorway, staring across the empty chamber at the magic casement. It was dark and seemed no different from the other windows, except for its greater size. One of the others was rattling in the wind. Princess Kadolan shivered and hugged herself in the cold. Fleabag was wagging his tail, sniffing at the bedding and the rest of the two fugitives' camping equipment, lying in untidy disorder.

Little Chicken jostled past Rap, saying, "See!" He strode toward the south window. As before, it reacted to his approach by starting to glow, shimmering with a reddish-yellow light, and the multitude of many-colored symbols became visible in its panes. He stopped a few paces away from it, studying the imperceptible shifting.

"Curious!" Sagorn said. "Firelight?"

"And watch what happens when I go near, sir." Rap called Little Chicken back, and the casement became dark. Then Rap moved slowly forward, and the pulsating, hard white glare came again, the feverish changing of the bright-colored emblems. He turned around and saw the others illuminated by it, flecks of rainbow appearing and disappearing on their faces. They all looked worried, even the old man.

"I am no sorcerer," Sagorn said uneasily. "I have read of

these, but never seen one demonstrated." He paused. "There is another way of escape for us, you know."

Rap could guess what was coming, but Inos asked eagerly, "What's that?"

"I have a word of power. So do you now, ma'am, and so does Master Rap. Three words will make a mage, a sorcerer—a minor sorcerer, but even a mage would be strong enough to handle a band of stupid imps, I fancy. We can share."

Rap saw Inos bite her lip. "Even Andor told me not to."

"He expected to get it out of you, though. When you were alone together."

"Are you suggesting that that was the only reason he proposed to me?" she shouted furiously.

"I *know* that was the only reason," he snapped back. "I have his memories. Andor uses people like spoons or forks—women for pleasure, men for profit. He is the ultimate cynic."

"And I do not know any word," Rap said. "So I cannot share."

Sagorn studied him, raising a hand to shield his eyes from the glare of the casement at his back. "Jalon did not believe you when you told him that. Nor did I. Nor did Andor. Nor Darad. Now your life is again in danger, and this may be the only way to put Inosolan on her throne. Yet you still maintain that you do not know a word?"

"I do."

With a sigh the old man said, "Then I think perhaps I do believe you, this time."

"I will tell Rap mine if you will!" Inos said.

Rap gulped in horror. "But these are Imperial legionaries!" he protested. "Aren't they reserved to one of the warlocks?"

Sagorn gave him a long, hard stare. "It is true that the Imperial army is East's prerogative. Andor thought you were ignorant of such matters. Did you actually manage to deceive Andor, young man?"

"Andor began my education!" Rap said hotly.

"Painless learning may be worthless learning. Anyway, you are correct. To use occult force against these imps might well call down the wrath of the warlock of the east—supported, likely, by the whole Council of Four."

Rap felt as if he had scored a point, although he did not know what the game was. "Tell me, then. Had I shared my word with Jalon, or with Andor, would they have called Darad to kill me?"

Sagorn shrugged, uninterested. "Perhaps. I don't recall that either of them had decided. But Darad would have been called sooner or later, when one of us was in trouble. Then he would have come after you, to get more power; he is a simple soul. There would be more sorcerers around if sharing were easier, you see. It needs a great trust.''

"And you could cheat? Tell a wrong word?"

The old man smiled thinly. "I expect people usually do."

"And," Rap concluded, feeling triumphant, "the Darad problem still exists if we share now, doesn't it?"

Sagorn pouted, emphasizing the clefts that flanked his deep upper lip. "I suppose it does. Well, Queen Inosolan, shall we try Inisso's magic casement instead?"

The strain of an unbearable day was showing on her face, but Inos raised her head proudly and said, "If you wish, Doctor."

Nobody moved. Fleabag was panting, and the wind moaning around the turret. Very faint thumping sounds came drifting up from the imps' axes.

"Well, this is exciting!" Princess Kadolan said. "I have always wanted to see some real magic. Who goes first? You, Doctor Sagorn?"

He glanced at her disbelievingly and then nodded. "I suppose so. Come back here, Master Rap."

Rap walked over to them, and the icy chamber was rapidly plunged into darkness, Inos's candle barely visible. Then Sagorn moved slowly toward the casement. Again light shone on the dusty, footprinted floor and this time it seemed to be normal sunlight—white, but not the fearsome glare that Rap had provoked.

Sagorn went close and studied the emblems on the tiny panes. As before, Rap felt that they were changing, but could see no transformation actually happen. A red spiral near the lower left corner was farther to the right than he had thought, the gold and green seashell higher, a group of silver bells on azure petals . . .

Then the gaunt old man seemed to find courage. He reached up and grasped the fastening in the center, grunted quietly as if it were stiff, and pulled the two flaps toward him. As he stepped back, the casement swung open.

2

A gust of hot, dry wind swirled through the chamber, raising the dust in acrid, eye-stinging clouds. The sunlight, also, stung Rap's eyes and he squinted for a moment, registering only that the bright sand outside was little lower than the floor within, as if the tower had sunk into the ground. Then, as he adjusted to the sunshine, he saw that he was looking across a level space, a sandy and rocky ground, toward a rugged, sun-blasted cliff of black rock, littered at its base with boulders. The only vegetation consisted of a few spiky clumps of some plant he had never seen before; the heat coming in on the breeze was intense.

It was real, and not real. His senses insisted that he was standing in a room about one story above the ground, looking out an open window. Even the smell of the air was real, and the waves of heat shimmering off the sand. But his farsight detected nothing outside the casement at all. So accustomed was he now to using his occult talent that its failure unbalanced him and made him feel dizzy.

In the distance, three men were picking their way along the base of the cliff, between the rocks. He wondered why they did not move out into the open and walk on the flat ground. They wore robes with the hoods raised to shield them from the sun's glare, so he could not see their faces. The one in front was the tallest and his walk seemed familiar.

"That's you in the brown, Doctor, isn't it?" Princess Kadolan said.

Sagorn stepped back a pace and spoke without turning. "Yes, I think it may be. I wonder who the others are."

There was no sound except a faint rustling as the wind stirred dried twigs in the withered bushes below the casement.

Then the men all stopped and peered up at the sky. They seemed to study something, the middle one pointed. They began moving again, and as the first man moved around an especially large boulder—the size of a small cottage—he turned toward the casement, and the viewers. Certainly it was Sagorn, strands of white hair falling over his gaunt, angular face, but he was too far off for his voice to be audible.

The second man followed. He wore a greenish robe and hood, and his face was too pale to be anything but jotunnish, although he was shorter than most jotnar. All Rap could be sure of was that he sported a voluminous silver moustache.

Which was hardly helpful, because many sailors did. Then the third followed, but he was keeping his head lowered. All three disappeared momentarily behind high-piled debris.

"That was Rap!" Inos exclaimed. "The one in black?"

"No. Not Flat Nose!" Little Chicken growled angrily.

Rap could not tell, not knowing what he looked like from the outside, but he felt very uneasy.

"I find this extremely unhelpful!" Sagorn sniffed. "There is no way to tell where this is. That may be Master Rap with me, but I'm not sure. Does anyone recognize the second man? Where? When? What are we doing?"

Then a huge blackness swept over the two men and was gone—a giant shadow. They dropped hurriedly, cowering behind boulders and staring up at the sky. Faint shouts drifted in the wind.

Sagorn gave a strangled cry and stumbled back from the casement. The scene rippled, fragmented, turned gray, and was gone. Icy wind swirled snowflakes into the chamber. The old man tottered forward again to grip the leaves of the casement and force them closed against the Krasnegar night, fastening the clasp.

He swung around, almost invisible, for the candle had blown out long since and there was only a faint glow from the eastern window. "Did any of you recognize that shape?" His voice quavered.

"No," said the others, almost as one, but Inos' aunt said, "Yes, I think so. Wasn't it a dragon?"

"I think it was. Nothing else could be so big. I have been shown my death!"

"Then you had better stay away from dragon country, sir." Rap was feeling more and more unhappy. The magic had made his scalp creep, but perhaps that had been because to his farsight the scene had been invisible, a mysterious nothing. Of course his farsight had not detected Bright Water the first time he met her, either.

"And that was Rap with you!" Inos said.

"Not!" Little Chicken snapped.

Princess Kadolan and Sagorn tended to think that Inos was right. Rap himself was uncertain. But it could have been, and none of them had known the second man, except that they all agreed he was likely a sailor. That was not a very profound conclusion, because jotnar often were, and Dragon Reach was somewhere in the southern parts of the Impire, near the Summer Seas, a very long way from Nordland.

"Well, there are no dragons here now," Rap said, and cursed himself for babbling like a nervous child. But there were imps, and the steady thud of axes was coming closer.

"Who wants to try next, then?" Sagorn asked, shepherding them back against the far wall. "That was not very helpful."

"I shall try, if you like, sir." But Rap did not really want to know what was causing the unearthly radiance that he created beyond the casement. Apparently the others did not care to know, either.

"I should prefer that you stayed away from it, young man!" Sagorn now sounded more like his usual acerbic self. There were murmurs of assent from the women.

"Then I shall try!" Inos said, not sounding enthused. "I need guidance more than anyone."

Her footsteps headed for the casement and in a moment she was silhouetted against it as it began to glow. It was going to be daylight again, Rap concluded, but not so bright as in Sagorn's scene—a gray day. The iridescence of the symbols was less intense, the tints softer. Inos reached up to the clasp and pulled the leaves open.

Then she jumped back, a fist to her mouth to stifle a scream. There was a man standing just outside, his back to the viewers. Without conscious thought, Rap rushed forward. Suddenly—unexpectedly, unforgivably—Inos was in his arms. And they both ignored that fact, staring out of the magic casement.

The man was a jotunn, no doubt of that. He wore a fur around his loins, but the upper half of his body was bare, and only jotnar were that pale shade. His back and shoulders were slick with rain. They were also heavy with muscle and his arms were scarred, his legs invisible below the sill. His thick hair hung like silver plate to his shoulders, hardly stirring in the wind. It was not, as Rap had first thought, Darad. This man was younger, smooth rather than hairy. He had fewer scars and no visible tattoos. It was not Darad, but a man almost as tall. And he was starting to turn.

Rap noticed that Inos was clutching him, also, and her grip grew tighter as the man in the vision turned. Would he be able to see them as they could see him? Rap was just about to release Inos and reach for the flaps—

"It's Kalkor!" Sagorn's voice came from close behind them. "The Thane of Gark. And that's the Nordland Moot!"

The man had stopped moving, but he seemed oblivious of the watchers beside him, who were now seeing his gaunt jotunn face in profile. Looking at it, Rap could understand the man's reputation, and Inos began to tremble in his arms. In a way it was almost a handsome face, but Kalkor's appearance suited his reputation. Rap would have expected an older man, but he had never seen a face that so clearly expressed cruelty and implacable determination. It would take a brave man to risk the anger of Thane Kalkor.

There was some sort of ceremony in progress. He seemed to be waiting. Then another man stepped in from the side, an elderly man wearing a red woolen robe, sodden wet from the rain, and a ceremonial helmet decorated with horns. He carried a huge ax and he raised it now, holding it vertically in front of him, using both arms, unable to prevent its great weight from wobbling in his grasp. He gasped some hurried words in a tongue unfamiliar to Rap.

Kalkor reached out one hand stiffly and grasped the monstrous, two-edged battle-ax. It must weigh a ton, Rap thought, seeing how the thick shoulders flexed as Kalkor took the strain at arm's length, leaning back for balance.

The Nordland Moot? Now, peering into the misty background beyond the foreground figures, Rap made out what Sagorn had seen sooner—a wide flat area of turf, a bare green moorland under a weeping gray sky. Clumped in an irregular circle around the battleground was a huge audience, vague and indistinct in the mist and rain. It was a bleak and ominous scene, barbaric and deadly.

And yet . . . the watchers were all foggy and indistinct. There was something ghostly and unreal about that background, quite unlike the hard sharpness of Kalkor and his companion, or of the desert in the first showing. Was that just an effect of the rain, or not?

Rap's attention switched back to the action by the casement. Kalkor raised the ax to his lips, then laid it over his shoulder, moving with military precision. He adjusted his grip and swung sharply around, turning his back to the viewers once more. The shining blue-white blade seemed to be almost within the chamber.

The sounds downstairs had stopped momentarily, then picked up again, much louder. The imps must now be tackling the door to the royal bedchamber.

Kalkor was marching forward over the turf toward the center of the circle, the ax on his shoulder, wearing nothing but the animal hide wrapped around his loins, bare-legged and bare-footed.

The man in the red robe had withdrawn. It seemed safe to speak. "What's the Nordland Moot?" Rap asked.

"It's held every year at midsummer on Nintor," Sagorn said quietly. "The thanes settle their disputes by ritual combat."

"I bet that Kalkor never lost an argument."

"But this is Inos's prophecy! Don't you see, boy? Kalkor will seize her kingdom, and she will take her complaint against him to the moot!"

"I hope I am allowed a champion to fight for me," Inos said. "I don't think I could even lift that ax. That would be quite a handicap."

No one laughed. Muffled voices in the distance were the only sound, too far off for the words to be distinguished, but obviously coming from a large crowd.

"Champions are allowed under certain conditions. Darad has earned good money there. Needless to say, the rest of us do not look back on the memories very happily."

And the scene began to shimmer and fade, just as Kalkor's opponent became visible, emerging from the mist, advancing toward him from the far side of the circle. Came the darkness; snow whirled in again. Sagorn stepped forward to close the casement.

Inos clutched Rap fiercely. "That was you again!" she said, peering up at him. "Wasn't it?"

This time Rap thought he had been the one in the vision. The goblin and Sagorn agreed. Princess Kadolan pleaded old eyes and would not say. But whoever it had been, he had been much sharper and less blurred than the other figures in the background—was the casement defective, or did that distinction have some significance? Rap wondered how much danger there was in meddling with such occult power as this. It felt wrong.

"That's crazy!" he said. "Me fight Kalkor with an ax? You'd better find a better champion than that."

He realized that he still had one arm around Inos, and he released her quickly.

"This is very strange," Sagorn muttered. Even in the darkness, Rap knew of the puzzled expression on the scrawny face. "The Place of Ravens is marked by a circle of standing stones. I don't recall seeing those—did any of you?"

Heads were shaken.

"And it rarely rains like that on Nintor. And, Master Rap, why should you turn up in two other people's prophecies? Why do you agitate the casement so much when you approach it?"

Again Rap thought of the old goblin woman. *Why can't I foresee you?* "Perhaps I haven't got any future to foresee," he said bitterly. "But I do seem to be a popular player in these events. Which comes first, the dragon or Kalkor?"

"Whichever it is, you survive," Sagorn said, and there could be no argument about that. "And the legionaries, as well, tonight," he added, less certainly.

"Are you sure this contrivance is not just playing jokes?" Princess Kadolan asked hotly. "It still has not told us how to evade the imps. Listen!"

Rap did not need to listen. If the imps had broken into the bedroom, there was only one more bolted door left. He headed for the stair, meaning to find out—

"Me next!" Little Chicken marched over to the casement, making the eerie firelight flicker again beyond the panes.

"No!" Rap stopped and swung around. He had a premonition of what was going to be revealed, but his protest was too late. The flaps swung open once more, and the chamber was filled with a sound of applause and acrid, eye-watering gusts of wood smoke.

As Rap had feared, he was looking into a crowded goblin lodge, seeing over spectators' heads. Fire blazed and crackled in the middle of the stone platform, throwing light on the audience gathered around the walls: near-nude men and boys, shrouded women and girls. They were all jabbering with excitement and laughing. The naked victim was staked out on the floor, and the tormentor standing over him holding a flaming brand was Little Chicken.

Rap swung away, burying his face in his hands and feeling his stomach heave with nausea and terror. Inos screamed. So did her aunt, and Sagorn muttered something guttural under his breath.

Then strong hands grabbed Rap. "It is you!" Little Chicken was wild with excitement. "Come! You see!" He began dragging Rap bodily back to the casement and resistance made no difference. "Hear applause! You do well for that! You making good show! And I doing good job! See your hands? See ribs?"

"No! No!" Rap howled, struggling to keep his face turned, his eyes closed. "Shut the window!"

"Good show!" Little Chicken insisted, squealing with joy. "It is Raven Totem! There my brothers! Watch what I do now!"

Rap forced his eyes open momentarily and then shut them tight again quickly. The victim did look like him, and not very much older than the face he had glimpsed in Hononin's kitchen mirror.

And yet, there had been something wrong! He sneaked another quick glance and again had to shut his eyes hastily to prevent a fit of nausea. It was his face, but somehow blurred—fuzzy? Little Chicken sniggered wildly at some new horror and the goblin spectators burst into applause again.

Then, mercifully, the light faded against Rap's eyelids, the excited babble of the crowd died away, and he felt the icy touch of the polar night and the cool caress of snow on his face. He relaxed and opened his eyes.

A thump on the back from Little Chicken almost laid him on the floor. "I told true!" he sniggered. "I kill you! We make good show."

"Neither dragon nor Kalkor?" Sargon said acidly. "You are indeed a hard young man to kill. Perhaps that is all the message we are going to get—you will survive the imps, so why worry?"

"More likely it's telling us that I'm as good as dead already!" Rap cried, and was ashamed at the shrillness of his voice. "Or that the imps may give me a better death than anything else in my future."

"In either case it would just show the imps killing you, I think," the old man remarked calmly.

Inos put an arm around Rap and led him away from the window.

He might survive jotunn or dragon, Rap thought, but he would not want to survive goblin. The victim in that last scene had already been horribly mutilated.

"Was it me?" he whispered, trying to control his trembling. "I thought it looked strange—blurred, somehow." *Say it was not me!* Small wonder that Inos' great-grandfather had gone mad.

Sagorn hesitated. "Yes," he muttered. "I noticed that. I thought it was just the smoke stinging my eyes, but your friend here seemed sharp enough . . . So we have seen you three times. The first two glimpses were ambiguous and the third time was suspiciously unreal. I wish I knew more about these things! It is all so insubstantial! What we need is a sorcerer to explain them."

Crash! The door shuddered. The imps had arrived. Only one bolt now lay between Rap and their vengeance.

Inos hugged him more tightly. "But you will be my champion," she said.

That was a nice thought, but for the rest of his life he would know that his eventual fate was to return to Raven Totem and the loving care of Little Chicken—while not looking very much older than he did now.

He wondered what would happen if he killed Little Chicken first. He had put down the sword somewhere, but now he wished he had it handy. Would it be possible to make a liar out of the casement? Was that why Bright Water had warned him not to harm the goblin? Had she foreseen Little Chicken being hurt by Rap?

Again the ax crashed against the door. Not long now.

"We might as well let them in!" Rap said wearily. "I think I agree with the casement that a quick hanging might be all for the best."

"No!" Inos shouted. "Doctor Sagorn, a sorcerer could beat a dragon, couldn't he? And Kalkor? That's what it means! That is the message—we must share our words of power with Rap! He can't share with us, but if we make him a sorcerer—a mage—then he will save you from the dragon one day, and beat Kalkor as my champion! Don't you see? That is the only way he can survive the dangers we have seen in store for him, and he must survive two of them—I mean at *least* two, Rap, of course. And that fuzziness you saw—he was using magic against the goblins, too!"

Rap groaned. Not a sorcerer! Farsight was bad enough. The imps would be better than that.

"Darad—" Sagorn said, and paused. "I am too old to risk weakening my power, child. My health . . . You must share yours with me, also."

"Yes!" Inos said. "You and I share, and then share with Rap. We'll each have two, and he'll have three."

Rap groaned.

"Why not?" She stamped her foot with rage and dug her fingernails into Rap's arm.

He was finding it very hard to think straight with Inos holding him like this. "Inos," he said hoarsely, "I don't want to be a sorcerer, even a mage. Sagorn is saying you must tell him first. Then he becomes an adept, right? He might call Darad to kill you to become a stronger adept! I don't think you should trust him, not that much."

The old man flushed angrily. Inos released Rap with a sob. "The God promised me a happy ending. Carried off captive by imps? Breeding sons for Kalkor? And you're going to be thrown in the dungeons at the least, you dummy! I think that stupid casement is too old! It wasn't working right!"

The door shuddered and splintered. It had lasted longer than the others, so perhaps it held some residual magic. Rap could farsee the burly imp wielding the ax, the heads and shoulders of others behind him, lower on the stairs, seeming cut off at floor level.

"Listen!" Inos said firmly. "I will tell Doctor Sagorn my word, and then he will tell both of them to Rap. You won't be in danger then, Doctor, will you? I will trust you, as Father said I should."

The old man shrugged. "Your plan makes sense, Majesty. I can think of none better. We have indeed been instructed to share our words with Master Rap. You will just have to reconcile yourself to becoming a mage, young man! Obviously that is what the casement was telling us to do.''

Rap groaned again.

Crash! Splinters flew. That blow had come right through the planks.

Inos clasped his hand. ''Rap? Please?''

Please? He was making his queen beg? What sort of loyalty was that, to refuse the very first command she gave him? Rap squared his shoulders.

''Of course, your Majesty!'' Then he sensed the spasm of hurt that crossed her face. That wasn't right, either! ''I'll be proud to be your court magician, Inos—if I can be master-of-horse sometimes?''

He tried to smile and discovered that he had forgotten how to.

Inos took his hand. ''Thank you, Rap.''

''And you know that if I knew a word of power, I would tell it to you gladly?''

Sorcerer? Prying into people's minds as well as their clothes and houses? Manipulating people, like Andor? Killing them off when they got in the way, like Darad? *Hateful! Hateful!*

''Perhaps we should pray?'' princess Kadolan said quietly. ''When the God appeared to Inos—''

Inos started to say something, then glanced at the door as a whole plank shattered, hurling more splinters across the floor. Rap sensed the big imp outside lowering his ax, and the others surging up close behind him with swords drawn.

But he had *seen* the splinters, seen them with his eyes. The door was brightly lighted. So was the floor, with five shadows stretched out across it.

No! *Six* shadows!

Fleabag yawned and lay down. He had a shadow, also—seven!

Simultaneously they all swung around to see. Light was streaming in the still-open casement from a strange, many-colored mist that glowed outside. The extra shadow came from a woman standing before it, inside the chamber.

Disaster! Idiot! With his stupid pig-headed refusal to obey his monarch, Rap had delayed too long. He had been warned that sorcerers could sense occult power being used, and here was a sorceress come to investigate.

The magic casement had given the answer, the solution to all their problems, and he had mulishly thrown it all away.

Now anything could happen.

3

"Well, well, well!" said the newcomer. "What have we here?"

Rap grabbed Inos' hand and spun around, heading for the door—and his boots froze to the floor. He windmilled his free arm wildly to regain his balance. He tried to pull his feet out of his boots, but they would no come loose either—he was rooted. The others had all reacted in the same way and they were all similarly immobilized, cemented to their own shadows. Meanwhile, a brawny arm reached through the hole in the door and fumbled for the bolt.

Rap twisted around awkwardly to watch the woman plodding forward to inspect her captives. *A sorceress!* Dumpy and wide, she walked with a heavy-footed gait. She was swathed all over in some soft fabric of pure white, even more hidden than a goblin woman, for a veil concealed all of her face below her eyes. She was much too large to be Bright Water, witch of the north.

The rest of the Four were men, warlocks, so this was someone new, someone unexpected.

"A magic casement left open?" she said. "No bug screen? Someone has been very careless!" She was speaking impish, but with a strange, harsh accent.

Then she seemed to notice the legionary's hand, still struggling with the bolt at a difficult angle. She made a small gesture, and the imp froze. So did all those behind him, so far as Rap's farsight would reach—completely petrified. Struggling to comprehend the sheer size of this latest disaster, he registered vaguely that the newcomer had just used magic on Imperial troops. Was that good or bad for Inos? Would the warlocks now descend in fury on Krasnegar?

Yells of alarm came drifting up the stairwell as the soldiers farther down discovered what had happened to their leaders.

The woman stopped in front of Inos's aunt, hands on hips and feet spread, in a stance more like an angry fishwife than whatever Rap would have expected of a sorceress.

"Let's start with you, dearie," she said. "Who're you?"

The princess's pearly gown was bedraggled and tea-stained, her white hair mussed, but she drew herself up as tall as she could—which wasn't very—and said haughtily, "I am Princess Kadolan of Krasnegar. And you?"

The sorceress's eyebrows vanished up into her headcloth, and Rap sensed amusement. "Well! I'm Rasha aq'Inim, Sultana of Arakkaran."

"Oh!" The princess thawed at once and smiled. "How nice that you can join us, your Majesty!"

A sultana was a *Majesty*?

The self-styled queen laughed coarsely. "My pleasure entirely. Do excuse me just dropping in like this, without formal invitation and all."

"I only wish we could offer you proper hospitality."

"Oh, I quite understand! You'll excuse me a moment?"

She pulled off her head covering to reveal hair of a dark-red hue, its magnificent gleaming waves cunningly held by combs of silver and mother-of-pearl. Her gown was of much lighter, sheerer material than Rap had realized, and it sparkled with many jewels.

How had he failed to notice those earlier?

This astonishing sultana glanced coyly around the great circular chamber, dirty and cold and lighted only by an opalescent glow from the magic casement, and then she dropped her veil. She was much younger than Rap had realized, and of no race that he had ever met. Her skin, like her glorious hair, was a deep ruddy shade, her nose high-prowed and arrogant. She was not conventionally beautiful, perhaps, and past her first youth, but a magnificent, statuesque woman, with an air of power, and mystery, and, yes!—beauty! Certainly beauty—a stunning woman!

Princess Kadolan said, "Oh!" again, faintly, and then rallied. "I am sorry to say that you find us in rather a state of confusion, your Majesty."

Sultana Rasha glanced at the petrified arm protruding through the door. "I noticed. The lower orders can be tiresome at times, can they not?"

"Indeed they can. May I present my niece, Pri—Queen Inosolan?"

The sorceress glanced across at Inos and seemed to disapprove. Rap, at her side, tried to maintain a stern, warning expression, as if he were truly a protector, but he was struggling against a craven yearning to smile at the beguiling young Rasha.

"We are honored, your Majesty," Inos said frostily.

Queen Rasha's dark eyes narrowed. "So you should be. I do not recall a Queen Inosolan? Krasnegar? Goblin country?"

Princess Kadolan said, "My niece has just lost her father, King Holindarn. Today? I suppose it's tomorrow now—just yesterday."

The sorceress sneered at Inos. "And you inherited a magic casement, so the first thing you wanted to do was to play with it?"

"I was desperate!" Inos shouted. "Imperial troops have seized my kingdom, the people are on the brink of civil war, and Kalkor is going to invade as soon as the ice goes!''

Sultana Rasha's exquisite eyebrows rose again. ''Kalkor?''

''The Thane of Gark.''

''Oh, yes, I have heard of him.'' Now she was certainly intrigued. ''And what is the imperor's interest in a flyspeck fiefdom like Krasnegar? That doesn't sound like Emshandar. His new marshal, perhaps? He seeks to provoke the jotnar?''

''I don't think the imperor even knows his troops are here. The proconsul in Pondague made a deal—''

Inos stopped abruptly. Rap wondered why; he was having great trouble keeping his mind on the conversation. The sorceress was taking up far too much of his attention—the diamonds twinkling below her gorgeous earlobes, the smooth perfection of her arm. Funny how at first he'd mistakenly thought her arms were draped in sleeves! The effort of not using his farsight on her was making his head throb, and yet he hardly needed it, for her hot, ruddy-hued skin seemed to glow through the gauzy stuff of her draperies.

Rasha strolled toward him, but her attention was on Inos. ''A deal? Don't lie to me, girl. I can read your mind if I wish, or cast a truth spell on you. I prefer not to—it takes all the fun out of things. What sort of deal?''

For a moment Inos and Rasha stood eye to eye in silent challenge. They were about the same height, the same age—but how had Rap ever believed that Inos was beautiful? How plain and dull she seemed, compared to the other girl's radiance! How weary and bedraggled! Her grip on Rap's hand grew very tight, then she dropped her gaze.

''I have a distant cousin—or great-great-aunt, or some such relation—the dowager duchess of Kinvale. She wants to marry me to her son. He has a claim to my throne, if a woman cannot inherit.''

''So!'' The sultana beamed. ''And can a woman inherit?''

''I think so!'' Inos said angrily. ''My father said so! By the laws of the Impire I could.''

''But Kalkor disagrees, so the imps want to block the jotnar? Well, well!'' Young queen Rasha's smile was delectable, yet sinister enough to stir the hair on the back of Rap's neck. ''Politics is a tiresome men's game, but sometimes we poor, feeble women are forced to play a hand or two, just to protect our interests.''

''You will help me?'' Inos exclaimed.

''We'll see,'' the sorceress said darkly. ''I shall need to know a little more. She glanced around the room, and her eyes settled on Sagorn, standing stiffly at the end of the line. "Men can be so obnoxious at times . . ."

She frowned as if puzzled and sauntered over toward him. Rap had never seen a woman move with such grace. Even without his farsight he could detect the glory of her long legs moving within the filmy robe, and he caught glimpses of tiny silver sandals. Oh, those hips! Of course this was sorcery at work. No woman should be able to raise his heart pound like this just by walking across a floor. She had not looked like this when—but he couldn't recall what she had looked like when she first appeared. It was how she looked now that mattered. Oh, wonder of womanhood! Oh, vision of all man's desire! Sorcery curdling his brains—dangerous! He knew it, knew he was helpless against it. She was turning him into a helpless slave, a human jelly. All other thoughts had fled his mind.

Inos wrenched her hand loose from his sweaty grip and he barely noticed.

Sagorn straightened up and licked his lips. "Would you turn down the intensity a little, ma'am?" he mumbled. "It's very hard on the arteries at my age."

"But what a wonderful way to die!" She laughed and reached up to stroke his cheek with a teasing finger. Rap felt fires of insane jealousy leap through him like lightning bolts.

Sagorn moaned—and was the much-too-handsome Andor.

Queen Rasha sprang back, raising a hand as if to strike. For a bewildering fraction of a second, Rap imagined a glimpse of a heavy, middle-aged woman in a shabby brown wrap, with unkempt gray hair and bare feet, with wrinkles and sagging cheeks. Then the delusion was gone, and the glorious Queen Rasha was there again, radiant in gossamer and pearl, studying Andor in languid amusement.

With hair in disarray, in a gown too large for him, Andor was clutching his left arm, whose sleeve was already darkening with blood, yet he contrived to bow gracefully nonetheless. "Oh, yes!" he said. "Exquisite! Majesty, how may I serve you?"

Queen Rasha nodded to acknowledge the bow, regarding him with some curiosity. "A sequential spell? Fascinating! And well done, too—a very sharp transition. Can it truly be a matched set? Let's see, the old one would have been the scholar—"

"And I your devoted slave."

"Of course a lover," she said curtly, seemingly more to herself than to Andor. Before he could say more she cut him off with a snap of her fingers.

And he had gone. In his place was Darad, huge and ugly, his

head still dribbling blood from Rap's chair-work. He howled, clasping a hand to the eye that Little Chicken had injured. Andor's blood—and now Darad's own—had now soaked through the left sleeve of the robe, and his sudden move produced a ripping noise from an overstretched shoulder.

"The fighter!" The sorceress pulled a face and snapped her fingers again.

The gown seemed to fall inward, around the slight form of the flaxen-haired Jalon. His dreamy blue eyes widened at the sight of Rasha. "The artist, ma'am," he said, bowing. "Your beauty shall evermore be on my lips and my song raised in your—"

"Some other day." Sultana Rasha snapped fingers a third time, and the brown robe collapsed yet again. All that was visible of the latest occupant was a narrow, dark face peering out from under a tangle of lank black hair—a small and very ordinary imp-ish youth, his mouth and eyes now stretched wide in terror. With a wail, he tried to fall on his knees before the sorceress, but his feet were as immovable as Rap's, and he succeeded only in drop-ping to a squat. He raised clasped hands in supplication. The sound of chattering teeth filled the chamber.

"Well!" The sultana appeared to be less antagonistic than she had been toward his predecessors. "Scholar, lover, soldier, art-ist—and you must be the financier of the group?"

The youth wailed, big eyes peering up at her from a nest of heaped robe. "I mean no harm, your M-M-Majesty!"

"But you're a bazaar fingersmith if I ever saw one!"

He whimpered. "Just crusts, lady—a few crusts, when I was hungry."

This was the fifth member of the gang? Thinal, the thief whom Sagorn had called their leader, and Andor's brother. A less mem-orable face Rap had never seen. It was pocked, moreover, with oozing acne pustules and marred by unsightly tufts of hair. No one would willingly look even once at Thinal; he would disappear instantly into any crowd in any city of the Impire. Yet the king had told Inos she could trust him!

The sorceress nodded approvingly. "Very fine work. Who did it?"

"Or-Or-Orarinsagu, may it please your Omnipotence."

"A long time ago, then?"

"Over a c-c-century, Majesty." For a moment the teeth chat-tered again, and then the little thief managed to blurt out a plea: "M-M-Majesty? We c-c-crave release . . ."

"I should not dream of breaking up such a masterpiece."

The imp wailed and cowered down ever farther into the crumpled brown robe, so that only his hair was visible.

"Besides," the sorceress said, "having a whole handful of men available when required, but only one at a time to put up with—that seems like an excellent arrangement."

Leaving the lad apparently sobbing into his knees, she came strolling back along the line. She paused in front of Little Chicken and regarded him with dislike. "You must be a goblin. Your name?"

With his odd-shaped eyes stretched wider than Rap had ever seen them, Little Chicken merely moaned and reached out toward the sorceress. She drifted backward until he was leaning forward at an absurd angle, only the fixation spell on his feet preventing him from crashing to the floor. He continued to moan.

She studied him for a moment, then shrugged. "Not bad below the neck, but the face would have to go."

She left him there, completely off balance, and wandered past Princess Kadolan without a word, to stop once more before Rap and Inos. "Extraordinary retainers you chose, child," she muttered.

Why would she call Inos a child when she was no older herself? Her eyes were the same deep red-brown shade as her hair, and they were burning Rap's soul to ashes. The curve of her breasts below the filmy gauze of her robe was driving him mad, and her nearness made the blood pound in his chest until he felt it was about to burst.

"And a faun? What's your name, lad?"

He opened his mouth. "Raaaaa . . ." His name disappeared in a choking noise, as he felt himself strangle in sudden revelation. His name was not Rap. That was only a nickname, a short form of—*of his word of power*. He had never told anyone his real name, not even the king. It was a great long thing, *Raparakagozi*—and another twenty syllables—and he had not heard it since his mother had first told it to him, a few days before she became sick, warning him not to repeat it because if an evil sorcerer learned your name he could do you harm and of course she must have seen with her foresight that she was going to die and the fact that he could even remember such gibberish after all these years meant that it was his word of power and now he desperately wanted to tell it to this entrancing seductive beauty standing before him and yet some part of him was screaming at him not to—the words were hard to say, Sagorn had told him—and his tongue tripped between the two set of commands and . . .

"What is a faun doing so far north?" Queen Rasha inquired

before he had resolved his conflict and brought his mouth under
control. She curled a lip that men would have died to kiss just
once. "But he's only a halfbreed, isn't he? That's a jotunn jaw,
and he's too tall. But those tattoos! Why do savages think that
mutilation can possibly improve their appearance?"

"Huh?"

Tattoos?

"This is Master Rap, a stableboy!" Inos said, in a strangely
sharp tone. Rap did not look at her.

Queen Rasha sighed. "I do hope his duties are not too complex
for him." She seemed to lose interest in Rap. His world crashed
down into terrible black despair. It wasn't his fault he was a mongrel, and he'd have managed to tell her his name if she'd just given
him another minute or two. He so desperately wanted to please
her, just to earn one tiny smile . . .

"Krasnegar," the sorceress murmured, regarding Inos again.
"Inisso? A word or two of power, perhaps?"

"I don't know what you mean!" Inos shouted.

"Don't be tiresome!" Rasha sighed. "Granted the words
themselves are invisible, but I don't need the occult to tell me
when a slip of a girl is lying. And you do have an interesting
problem." She glanced thoughtfully at the door, still decorated
with a burly arm. "I don't think now is the time to solve it."

"What do you mean?" Inos cried. Rap's conscience stirred
vaguely. Something must be bothering Inos, and he should not
be staring so fixedly at Sultana Rasha.

"I mean," the sorceress said, rather absently, as if lost in
thought, "that when you opened that magic casement, it creaked
so loud that I heard it down in Zark. A casement shouldn't do
that. What could have charged it up with power like that?"

No one spoke, and she shrugged. "Just a malfunction, I expect. Old—it obviously hasn't been used in years, right? You were
lucky that most of Pandemia was still asleep. Including the sorcerers. Including, more important, the wardens! But to linger
longer would not be wise. Go now."

She pointed to the window. Inos turned. She began to walk
stiffly toward it, and then twisted around and held out her hand,
even as her feet were still moving.

"Rap!" she cried. "Help!"

With a shuddering start, he turned to look. As soon as his gaze
left Rasha, he broke free of his dreams. "I'm coming!" He tried to
move, but his feet remained as solidly fastened as before. He could
do nothing, and Inos continued to walk unwillingly to the casement.

Again she screamed. "Rap!"

"I'm coming!" he yelled, but he wasn't. Off balance, he toppled backwards and crashed to the floor, his feet still immovable. Elbows and head smashed into the boards. Heavens full of stars blazed before him.

"What is the meaning of this?" her aunt shouted. "Release her at once!"

But already Inos, still moving in small jerks like a puppet, had reached the casement and started to clamber over the sill. Peering through eyes blurred with tears of pain, Rap saw that the many-colored haze beyond it was a drapery of sparkling beads, flickering in a gentle breeze. The sun must be shining behind it, although the other three windows showed only a predawn glow. The whole chamber, he realized, was full of warm air, scented with flowers.

Inos staggered on the far side of the wall, cried, "Rap!" once more, and then vanished through the shimmering rainbow drape.

Failure! He had failed Inos!

"Queen Rasha!" Princess Kadolan said hotly. "This is highly improper! Return my niece at once, or else permit me to accompany her."

Rasha regarded her with some amusement. "You would not prefer to remain and lecture the imps on deportment? Very well—go."

Kadolan's roly-poly form hurried willingly across the chamber. She struggled for a moment with the climb, almost fell over the sill, stumbled through the drape in a tinkle of jewels, and was gone.

The sorceress glanced around the others. "Boys will be boys," she said. "Time for ladies to retire and leave you all to your male fun. Tell them to be sure and clean up the blood afterward!" She uttered an astonishingly raucous laugh.

Still half stunned, Rap was also bewildered—the sultana's draperies were not nearly as flimsy as he had thought, and her hair was covered again, and he could not recall her replacing her veil. She seemed much older than he had been thinking, and broad, not slender.

She took a couple of steps and paused to study the sleeping Fleabag, who leaped up and bounded over to her, his tail wagging vigorously. Again Rap felt the bite of jealousy.

"Splendid creature!" Queen Rasha said, with what sounded like real admiration. "You will make a fine pair with Claws." She glanced down at the prostrate Rap. "Yours, faun?"

Rap nodded, unable to trust himself to speak.

Fleabag turned, lolloped across the chamber, and bounded over the sill of the casement after Inos. Rasha waddled across the room and paused again at the window to look back suspiciously.

"Why should a queen call for a stableboy?"

Rap's mouth was suddenly very dry. Because he had a word of power, perhaps? He must not even think about words of power around a sorceress. That was what had been worrying Inos all along, he saw now, and he had been so bewitched by this—this *old woman*?

"Huh?"

Rasha shrugged. "No accounting for tastes, is there?" She moved again, seemed to float *through* the sill, and vanished. The misty brightness went, also, and a swirl of polar wind rushed into the chamber, bearing cold and snowflakes and dark.

Rap scrambled giddily to his feet, trying to rub head and elbows at the same time. Little Chicken roared in fury. King Holindarn's brown robe seemed to rise up of its own accord, so inconspicuous was the impish youth inside it. The troops beyond the door came back to life with a loud howl.

4

For the moment, the legionaries were having an argument, and the threatening arm had been removed. Rap turned away in time to see Thinal, holding up his gown with both hands, heading for the still-open casement. With his head still pounding, Rap lurched over to block him.

"Where are you going?"

So high was the collar around Thinal's ears that his nondescript, spotty face seemed to stare out of it, pale in the dawn gloom, as if the robe were swallowing him.

"I want to see if I could climb down, Rap."

Sagorn had said that Thinal was a human fly. Rap and Little Chicken weren't.

"Call Sagorn!" Rap shouted. "He got us into this mess. Maybe he can get us out yet!"

The young imp shook his head vigorously. "No. He's too frail now. We can't risk him."

Rap grabbed the thief's puny shoulders and shook him till his teeth rattled. *"Call Sagorn!"*

Thinal staggered back and almost tripped over his robe. "Don't do that!" he screamed.

"Do what?"

"Don't bully me! I frighten easy, Rap."

"So?" Rap advanced on him again.

"I might call Darad!" Thinal wailed, sounding almost in tears. "It's too easy! I might not be able to help myself!"

Rap took a deep breath. "Sorry," he grunted. Then, "Oh, demons!"

He whirled around to the door. The imps had massed outside again; again the arm came through the jagged hole. But the bolt was too far from the hole to reach with just a hand, and the timbers were very thick. The big imp had stopped and thrust his whole arm in, right to the shoulder. Before Rap could say a word, Little Chicken went sprinting across the room, leaped, and struck that so-tempting, protruding elbow with both feet. He bounced off and landed on his feet like a cat, while the imp's scream seemed to shake the whole tower.

Great! There went any hope of merciful treatment.

The legionaries helped their disabled comrade extract his shattered and mangled limb, all roaring furiously. Another giant grabbed up the ax, and the door shivered under his blows.

"Now what are we going to do?" Rap's head ached. He had betrayed Inos, but it did not look as if he would have long to mourn his inadequacy. "We could still share words," he suggested.

Thinal was edging toward the window again. "Not enough. Two only makes an adept. Maybe we could climb up on the roof and wait until they've gone?"

"They'll shut the casement!"

"We might break a pane or two first." Thinal shuffled a little farther—the human fly.

"We'll be seen from below; it's almost daylight." Rap sighed, feeling weariness settle over his fears like thick snow. "I think this is the end! I shouldn't have been so stubborn and argued so long. The magic told me to become a mage, and I wouldn't."

He had disobeyed his monarch's first order; or at least talked back. If he had done his duty promptly, he would have become a mage and served her by driving away the imps, forcing the townsfolk to accept her—how much could a mage do, anyway? Well, it didn't matter anyway, not now.

He forced a smile at the terror-stricken little thief. "Go on, then, if you think you can save yourself. Little Chicken and I will surrender to the soldiers, even if it means the last weighing."

The goblin had been listening. "No!" he shouted.

The door shuddered, and a whole spar fell out.

"Yes!" Rap said. "Unless you've got any ideas?"

A gust of hot, muggy wind swirled into the chamber. Surf roared.

Death Bird! Here!

All three spun around. There was no one in sight to explain the voice, but the casement now looked out on strange frondy trees silhouetted against a grayish predawn sky. Rap smelled sea and damp vegetation. Another wave broke noisily, somewhere nearby.

Stunned and wary, all three hesitated.

"Who said?" Little Chicken growled.

"Palms!" Thinal screamed. "Those trees, Rap! They're palms!"

The door shuddered again, the top hinge almost torn loose from the frame.

Death Bird! Hurry!

There was still no one visible to explain the dry old voice, but Rap knew it. "It's Bright Water!" Would she save the faun as well as the goblin she had called precious?

Thinal grabbed Rap's arm. "That Rasha—she was a djinn. From Zark. Where there's djinns, there's palms!"

"Right!"

All three moved at once. Little Chicken went fastest, clearing the sill in one huge bound. Then he seemed to realize his error, for he yelled from outside, "Flat Nose! Come!"

"I'm coming!" Rap called, and toppled over after him, tumbling onto hot, dry sand. Hampered by his robe, Thinal came last and tipped out almost on top of Rap.

The door fell bodily to the floor. The legionaries poured into the chamber.

They heard a faint, fading echo of a voice crying, "I'm coming."

They caught a faint wisp of warm, tropic air, and then an icy blast from the Krasnegar night swirled snow at them.

One window was open. There was some discarded bedding on the floor. Otherwise, the chamber was empty.

Insubstantial pageant:

These our actors . . .

. . . like the baseless fabric of this vision,

The cloud-capp'd towers, the gorgeous palaces,
The solemn temples, the great globe itself,
Yea, all which it inherit, shall dissolve
And, like this insubstantial pageant faded,
Leave not a rack behind.

Shakespeare, *The Tempest*

❰ ABOUT THE AUTHOR ❱

Dave Duncan was born in Scotland in 1933 and educated at Dundee High School and the University of St. Andrews. He moved to Canada in 1955 and has lived in Calgary ever since. He is married and has three grown-up children.

After a thirty-year career as a petroleum geologist, he discovered that it was much easier (and more fun) to invent his own worlds than try to make sense of the real one.